# UTTERLY

PAULINE MANDERS

This second edition (paperback) published in 2019 by
Ottobeast Publishing
ottobeastpublishing@gmail.com

First edition published 2013



Cover design Rebecca Moss Guyver.

ISBN 978-1-912861-03-3

A CIP catalogue record for this title is available from the British Library.

*Also by Pauline Manders*
Utterly Explosive (2012)
Utterly Rafted (2013)
Utterly Reclaimed (2014)
Utterly Knotted (2015)
Utterly Crushed (2016)
Utterly Dusted (2017)
Utterly Roasted (2018)

To Paul, Fiona, Alastair, Karen, Andrew, Katie and Mathew.

PAULINE MANDERS

Pauline Manders was born in London and trained as a doctor at University College Hospital, London. Having gained her surgical qualifications, she moved with her husband and young family to East Anglia, where she worked in the NHS as an ENT Consultant Surgeon for over 25 years. She used her maiden name throughout her medical career and retired from medicine in 2010.

Retirement has given her time to write crime fiction, become an active member of a local carpentry group, and share her husband's interest in classic cars. She lives deep in the Suffolk countryside.

ACKNOWLEDGMENTS

My thanks to: Beth Wood for her positive advice, encouragement and support; Pat McHugh, my mentor and hard-working editor with a keen sense of humour, characters and atmosphere; Rebecca Moss Guyver for her boundless enthusiasm and inspired cover artwork and design; Martin Nettleton, local gunsmith for his knowledgeable advice; the Write Now! Bury writers' group for their support; and my husband and family, on both sides of the English Channel & the Atlantic, for their love and support.

# CHAPTER 1

Nick stooped to scrutinise the carpet of bees moving like slowly flowing lava over the brood frame. Despite his height of six three he had a morbid fear of being stung. He was also aware his protective overalls were riding a little high and exposing his ankles. What was that he just felt? Something crawling up under his trouser leg? He started to sweat. This was rapidly turning into a nightmare.

And then it all ended.

There was a loud, sharp *phutt* and something flew into the side of the hive, embedding itself in the wood close to Jim Mann's leg.

'What the hell was that? The queen?' Nick asked in surprise.

Jim didn't move and for a moment Nick wondered if he'd been injured.

'Are you OK, Mr Mann?'

'Yes, yes I'm fine. That's....' He bent to look at the splintered wood. 'That's a pellet. Most likely a ·22 calibre pellet from an air rifle.'

'How can you tell?'

'It's happened before.' He pointed to an almost identical hole with splintered wood in the discarded roof of the beehive they were inspecting.

'But why?' Nick asked. He tried to keep his voice steady as he turned to look in the direction the pellet had come from. He was standing at the end of a large garden that backed onto agricultural land, and apart from some fruit trees and a low hedge, there was nothing to block his view over rolling fields of wheat stubble. There really was no one around. Jim Mann lived in Bildeston, a small village nestling in a shallow Suffolk valley. His garden should have been a haven of peace and quiet. Instead, it seemed to have become a site for target practice, least ways it was if you were dressed as a beekeeper.

'I'm sorry but what did you say your name was? You're new at Willows & Son, aren't you?' Jim spoke quietly as he replaced the brood frame and then the hive's roof, all his movements slow and deliberate.

'Sorry, Mr Mann, I thought I'd explained. I'm Nick – Nick Cowley. I'm the new apprentice at Willows. Henry, one of the carpenters, was meant to come out with me this afternoon, but he called in sick. I thought the foreman, Mr Walsh, phoned and you said it was OK for me to come on my own. But,' Nick needed to know, 'but why did this just happen? Who's shooting at us? Why?'

'Hmm… oh yes, that's right, he did phone this morning. Come on, let's go back to the house. I think we're about finished here.' He bent down and picked up the smoker. Plumes of cool smoke filled the warm afternoon air.

Nick couldn't believe the man still hadn't answered the question. He stood his ground. 'But why did someone just shoot at us, Mr Mann?'

'Not at us, Nick. It is Nick, isn't it?'

He nodded.

'Squirrels. Probably aiming at squirrels and missed.'

Nick cast around. The garden didn't look as if it should have a squirrel problem. There were no oaks, conifers or large trees and hardly any shrubs. He didn't buy the squirrel explanation and was about to say more, but Mr Mann had started to move. Nick tried to quicken the pace as they walked back up the garden. The way he saw it, the pair of them presented an even larger target than before, both still dressed in white protective overalls and strolling side by side carrying the smoker. If someone wanted to shoot at them again, now would be a good time. He took off his beekeeping hat and veil to reveal his short dark brown hair, already flattened and sweaty as it topped his pleasant round face. The tightly woven material might be designed to block a bee sting, but Nick doubted it could offer any protection against an airgun pellet. At least by removing it there would be less for the marksman to aim at.

'I hope you understand now why I wanted you to see an active hive?' Jim asked, full of zest and pausing as he spoke.

'It was active all right,' Nick answered, nodding and remembering the pellet. He couldn't help wondering if it might have been easier just to look at an old disused one or some construction drawings instead, but then he was forgetting Jim was an enthusiast and an old friend of the boss. He wanted to develop his own hive design and create a new prototype. The whole project seemed crazy. 'Can we get back to the house now, Mr Mann?' He rubbed his moist forehead with the back of his hand and looked directly at Jim. Was it the heat or was there something slightly wild about Jim's eyes still partially hidden behind the protective mesh? He'd seemed calmer before the shot.

'You see, I'm usually alone with my bees. Most beekeepers are. It's a quiet spot in the garden….'

'Isolated, yes.' Nick almost shivered despite the heat.

'And….' Jim let the word hang in the air. They walked on in silence for a few moments before he continued, 'To my way of thinking it'll be easier to get the design right by building it in wood first. Then when you've made all the adjustments, I'll look for a firm that can manufacture parts of it in some kind of plastic. For a start - a lightweight, insulated, waterproof roof.'

'An exciting project, Mr Mann.' Nick tried to sound enthused, but really he just wanted to get away. The shot had rattled him. 'I've got your drawings and I'll take them back to show Henry at Willows. He'll probably want to come out here to look at the hive for himself, when he's back.' Nick tried to suppress the grin threatening to spread across his face as he imagined Henry in a beekeeper's hat and veil. 'Now I really must be going, Mr Mann.'

Nick said goodbye, almost falling over in his rush to strip off the beekeeping outfit. He was hot. It was a pleasure to shed the protective clothes and get into the Willows & Son van, with its firm orthopaedic seats, dubious suspension and a top speed of 60 mph downhill. He wound down the windows and tried to create a breeze as he drove out of the Bildeston valley. It was at moments like these he knew he'd made the right decision. He loved Suffolk and he loved working with his hands. He still couldn't understand what had possessed him two years earlier when he ticked the UCAS application box and committed himself to an Environmental Studies degree in Exeter. It had been a mistake. Right at the beginning he should have done what he'd always wanted to do and sign up for the local carpentry and joinery course in Stowmarket. And now here he was, achieving that ambition.

Acre upon acre of recently harvested wheat fields surrounded him; there wasn't even a building visible on the horizon. You can't beat Suffolk, he thought as he traversed the deserted rural oasis. In fifteen minutes he should be back at the firm's workshop in Needham Market.

He was lost in thought and it took some moments before he realised the underpowered van was seriously losing speed. Within a few seconds the engine died and in silence he free-wheeled forwards. Nick pressed the ignition button, hoping it was only a stall. The battery responded but the engine didn't catch. There was nothing for it but to steer the lifeless van to one side of the narrow lane where it finally came to a halt.

'Shit! Now what am I supposed to do?'

Nick looked unbelievingly at the instrument panel. The temperature gauge didn't suggest a problem but there was no arguing with the fuel gauge. 'How can it be empty? I've hardly driven more than twenty miles,' he wailed, appealing to the countryside.

Nick was well aware that John Willows had an arrangement with one of the local petrol stations and the regular carpenters were expected to keep the vans topped up, signing for the diesel which was duly charged to the firm. 'Who bloody drove this last? Just wait till I get back,' Nick hissed. But that was the whole point, how was he going to get back? It was almost unheard of to send apprentices on jobs by themselves, and like a naive fool, he'd been excited by the prospect, even a little flattered. The bastards had played a trick on him.

'Oh great! No bloody signal either.' Anger turned to despair as he looked at his mobile, intending to phone for help. The pockets of poor reception were the most irritating thing about living in rural Suffolk; it didn't happen in towns like Ipswich.

'I'm going to have to bloody walk!'

Nick couldn't decide which was the quickest direction to find help. Should he head back or just carry on? He hadn't passed any petrol stations on the way, and he couldn't recall how long ago he'd seen a farm house. 'Bugger,' he yelled at the inert engine, 'bugger!'

The last time something like this had happened, Nick had been about fourteen years old. He was with a group of his mates, the singer in their fledgling band. They were mucking about, ostensibly walking in Thetford Forest during the summer holidays. They managed, while pretending to be rock legends, to get lost during the course of the afternoon. They knew they should look for telegraph poles or listen for traffic, but there weren't any poles or pylons in the forest and the trees muffled any sound. In the end they resorted to tossing a coin, a suggestion by the raw drummer; heads they continued forward and tails they turned off to one side. Then there would be further coin flipping for subsidiary choices. Someone had read a book in which the main character made all his decisions based on a roll of dice, and they were young enough, and certainly daft enough, to think it might add an extra element of fun to the afternoon. Like jamming. It had been cool at that age to throw common sense to the wind. They tossed the coin and one hour later arrived back where they'd started, having walked in a large loopy circle.

Nick was now aged twenty-one and arguably a little wiser. He wasn't lost; he had simply run out of fuel and needed to make a decision. Jackson Browne's *Running on Empty* ran through his mind, and although he hadn't thought of it for years, the words reminded him of the Thetford Forest walk. He reached for a coin from the depths of his pocket. The difference now was that he could only find a 2p coin, whereas when he was fourteen, his mother had sent him off with a handful of pound coins. He supposed she imagined there would be kiosks selling ice cream in the forest, but then she was the one with stars in her eyes and the Jackson Browne albums.

'Heads I head on, tails I trail back.' He flicked the coin into the air and – heads it was.

He slipped the coin back into his pocket, locked the van and started walking. He held his mobile phone all the while, checking to see if the signal indicator showed any reception. As he walked he stepped over the remains of a dead pheasant at the side of the gravelly tarmac. Road kill. Tyres had flattened the bird, grinding dirt and grit into what had once been magnificent plumage. Magpies would soon find it and strip the carcass clean. He shivered despite the afternoon heat. He didn't want to admit it but the dead bird had unsettled him. He was in the middle of nowhere, alone, without a phone signal and less than half an hour ago he'd been shot at. There was no choice but to keep walking.

Half a mile on he saw a notice: Rookery Farm. There was a clump of maybe a dozen tall horse chestnut trees and oaks, their lush foliage casting shade across a farm track. It wound off to one side down a gentle slope. With his spirits rising, he stepped onto the rutted surface and followed it into a large concreted courtyard. Two huge steel framed barns with metal cladding faced him and there was a large storage tank, just to one side, almost out of view. The place seemed deserted on first glance, but as Nick walked further, he realised he was being watched. A guy, probably much the same age as him and wearing old khaki-coloured over-alls, stood near the storage tank. He had a head of close cropped, ginger hair and he'd left a couple of days' stubble on his face. Nick guessed it probably hid some of his freckles.

'Are you looking for diesel?' he asked as Nick approached.

'How'd you know?' Nick was surprised. He wasn't even carrying a fuel can.

'Well most people are here for diesel. Where's your car?'

'I was driving the firm's van when it ran out. It's about half a mile back along the road, as if you were driving towards Bildeston.'

Nick watched as the guy looked at him closely. After what seemed like an age, he finally nodded. 'Got any money on you?'

Nick remembered the 2p coin. 'Not much, I don't need cash with me when I'm out on a job.'

'Oh yeah?'

'No, I'm only the apprentice.'

This time Nick's answer was greeted with a frown.

'How did you know we kept diesel here?'

'I didn't.' Something in Nick's manner finally seemed to reassure the guy, because he grinned, revealing a chipped front tooth.

'OK then, if you want I can run you back to your van with some diesel. It'll be red, mind. That's what we keep here for the tractors. You're not supposed to use it for cars, but as this is an emergency I guess it'll be OK. May not start of course.'

'Oh thanks, mate. That'll be great, thanks.' Nick thought for a moment before adding, 'How'd you mean, it may not start?'

'Diesel engines, mate. They don't like running dry. I'll bring some starting fluid.'

Oh God, Nick thought. That's all I need. 'Thanks,' he said, hoping the van wasn't going to prove too much of a problem.

'By the way, there's a bloody hornets' nest up there. Haven't got round to getting rid of it yet, so watch out for the buggers.' The guy tossed the warning over his shoulder as he disappeared between the two large steel-framed barns.

Nick looked around, immediately feeling nervous. He searched for any sign of hornets in the air. Someone had once told him their sting was much worse than a bee's. He listened, but there was no buzzing. All he could hear was the sound of an engine starting somewhere close by. While he waited he checked his mobile phone. Still no signal. A piercing pain drove through his left ear. 'Christ! What was that?'

Had he been shot? He touched his ear but there was no blood. A loud buzzing erupted as he disturbed the hornet.

'Argh! That bloody hurts.' He tried to control his panic. The hornet droned angrily around his head.

'Stay still and it'll fly away,' the guy said, as he drew up in an old Land Rover. There was a distinctive knocking sound from under the bonnet.

Nick assumed it was the engine he'd heard starting up a few minutes earlier. He didn't need a warning to stay still; his ear was throbbing and a second sting would be unbearable. He stood rooted to the spot, not daring to move. A strong smell of diesel filled the air, and for a moment he felt relieved to see an old fuel can propped on the front passenger seat. That'll be for me, he thought. But the fumes were strong. What? The guy was lighting a cigarette. Surely they'd all go up in flames? Nick braced himself for an explosion. Oh, my God, he thought as he watched the guy inhale deeply before blowing out a cloud of smoke. Any moment now….

'That might help.' The guy inhaled and blew again, watching the hornet. 'Now move slowly and get in the cab.'

Nick didn't need a second invitation. He moved as fast as he dared. He'd barely sat on the passenger seat, before his ginger-haired saviour threw the gear lever into first and let in the clutch with a jolt. The Land Rover leapt forwards.

'That should get rid of the bugger!' Ginger laughed as they sped out of the courtyard, leaving the angry hornet buzzing somewhere behind. The Land Rover bumped and swayed on the uneven track. The fuel can fell sideways, landing heavily on Nick's shin.

'Ouch!' Nick rubbed his leg. 'Are you, by any chance related to Dave, one of the carpenters at John Willows & Son? He drives just like you.'

'No, don't think so. My name's Dan by the way. Now right or left?'

Nick pointed to the right and Dan swung the Land Rover into the lane, accelerating hard. It took less than a minute to reach Nick's van and another minute or so to put a few litres of red diesel into Nick's empty fuel tank. In that time Nick's ear had swollen to the size of a large juicy red plum. He was in agony.

'Thanks, mate, I'm really grateful. I owe you one.'

'Yeah, I was going to ask for some cash. But looking at your ear, well it's worth at least a fiver in entertainment alone.'

Nick hobbled to the driver's door to step up into the van. He caught his breath as he put his full weight onto his bruised leg and pulled himself up to the driver's seat. The fuel can had packed a fair punch, right on the front of his shin where minimal flesh covers the bone. His left ear throbbed and burned, his neck was starting to feel stiff. It hurt as he pumped the accelerator. He pressed the ignition button and hoped to God it would start. The motor turned, the engine fired, and the van finally moved forwards, powered by red diesel.

'That was lucky,' Dan shouted from the Land Rover, and with a broken-toothed grin, roared back up the lane.

Nick sighed with relief and silently thanked the Gods of Diesel. It was time to get back to Needham Market and the workshop before anything else could go wrong. Most of the journey was spent rehearsing what he was going to say to his fellow carpenters, the ones who had left him with an empty fuel tank. But by the time he arrived back at the Willows workshop, the pain had overtaken his anger.

Nick stumbled down from the van and across the parking area outside the workshop. He glanced around for one of the regular carpenters, hoping to give them a piece of his mind, but Dave spotted him first.

'Are you OK, Nick? You seem to be limping. And what's happened to your ear? It's blown up to twice its size.' Dave, a kindly middle aged carpenter gazed at Nick's face, seemingly transfixed.

Nick touched his ear and grimaced, self-conscious for a moment.

'Weren't you the one they sent to see that beekeeper chap? Over Bildeston way? Crikey, Nick, did one of the bees get you? You weren't like that this morning.'

'Hornet, it was a bloody hornet. The van ran out of diesel, for God's sake. Someone didn't fill it yesterday. And then a frigging fuel can fell on my leg.'

'I see,' Dave replied. 'Well we've all had a bad day, lad. Some joker siphoned off the diesel from the vans last night and we've all had trouble. That Bildeston chap must be mad if he's keeping hornets. Better get that sting seen to!'

Nick limped into the workshop office and handed in the van's keys. The firm's secretary Pat, a middle aged lady and much the same age as John Willows' wife, dispensed sympathy and advice. Ten minutes later he was holding ice cubes wrapped in a dishcloth to his throbbing ear as he left the Willows yard in his old Ford Fiesta.

'Hope this doesn't take long,' he sighed as he drove out of Needham Market and headed for the West Suffolk Hospital's A & E department. The worst thing about the whole episode, he thought angrily, was that it was his own fault. If he'd checked the fuel gauge when he'd first set out in the Willows van, then maybe he wouldn't be driving up the A14 now with a hornet sting in his ear. He glanced at the Ford Fiesta's instrument panel; half a tank, thank God.

'Oh no,' he moaned fifteen minutes later as he checked his rear-view mirror. A police siren wailed behind. He'd already reached Bury St Edmunds and was almost at the hospital. 'Now what?' This was turning into the worst day ever. He pulled into the side of the road as the patrol car drew alongside, indicated and stopped in front. He switched off the engine hoping this really wasn't happening to him and watched as the police officer got out of the car, put on his cap and approached. Nick wound down his driver's side window as he held the dishcloth to his ear. The ice had almost completely melted and a wet patch was spreading across the shoulder of his tee-shirt. He tried to look dignified.

'Don't get out of the car, sir. Just stay where you are. I have reason to believe you've been driving while using a mobile phone held to your left ear.'

Nick turned his head to face the officer and presented his swollen left temple and cheek, now a vibrant red. He let his hand fall but the damp cloth remained suspended, as if by magic from the side of his head. The coarse dripping weave swayed gently with his movement, adding an air of crazy eccentricity to his appearance.

The officer nodded and then indicated his left ear.

Nick wearily pulled the cloth away. The last fragment of ice fell down his neck. He tried not to wince. I'm playing the lead part in a bloody farce, he thought. Dumbly, he watched as the officer's expression changed.

There was a long silence.

'On your way then, sir. You're almost at the hospital now.' The officer patted the roof of the car like a priest giving a blessing, before stepping out into the road to stop the traffic. It took Nick a few moments to realise he was being waved on but the sight of the uniform had unleashed a deep anxiety. It churned in his stomach as his ear smarted and burned. This had turned into a hellish day, he thought as he tried to banish the nightmare of a previous police interrogation still fresh in his memory. That had been entirely different, he reminded himself. He must put it behind him. This was nothing to do with being wrongly accused of terrorism.

# CHAPTER 2

Chrissie flung her car keys down on the hall table. An old mirror had been carefully placed to give an illusion of space. 'Friday. Thank God it's Friday,' she sighed. It had been a busy week and it felt good to close the front door of her modest cottage against the world. 'Hmm... not for much longer, I hope,' she said as she glanced at the plastic fob sticking up from the key-ring. It proudly announced Avis Rental and a string of numbers. The accountant in her couldn't help but try to quantify the digits and add them up.

'Stop,' she hissed. 'You don't need to do this anymore.'

*Brrring*! *Brrring*! Her mobile rang from somewhere deep within the handbag still clutched under her arm. Maybe it's that chap phoning back about the car, she thought as she rummaged in its depths and blindly felt for the familiar shape. 'Hi, hi,' she said, answering quickly, worried she'd taken too long and the caller might already have rung off.

'Don't feel well.' The volume failed, then surged. The voice sounded breathy, harsh. Unrecognisable.

'Who is this?'

Her phone hissed and crackled in her ear but there was no answer. She felt annoyed. Had some hoaxer just keyed in a random number and she was the unlucky recipient? She checked the display on her mobile. 'What? Nick? Are you OK?'

'I've been stung by a bloody hornet. On my ear.' His voice faded. 'And it hurts like hell.'

'What did you say? On the ear? Where are you?'

'I'm in A & E in Bury. My ear's swollen, half my face is puffed up and I can't open one eye. They've given me an injection - filled me up with something. What's it called? Anti-histamine, that's it. They've told me I'm OK to leave now, but I mustn't drive.' Nick's voice sputtered, cut out and then returned louder than ever. 'I've already been stopped by the police when I drove here so I can't risk it again.'

'You can't open one eye? You're puffing up? Are you sure you're all right to be let out?' Chrissie pictured Nick's head the size of a football. 'And your parents? You've phoned them, I assume.'

'They're in the Lake District for two weeks.' Nick's voice sounded strangely metallic.

'The signal's lousy. Your voice keeps breaking up. So there's no one else you can think of with a car, right?' Chrissie finished for him.

'Yeah. My old friends – some of them'll be back from uni for the summer, but… not sure who's got a car. Anyway they'll be in the pub by now.' His voice faded, then surged back. 'Probably jamming. It's a two-guitar night.'

'You sound… are you sure it's safe for you to go home?'

There was a pause. 'And I've no cash on me.'

'OK, I'll be about thirty minutes. But you are all right?'

'No, I'm bloody not; otherwise I wouldn't be phoning would I?'

Chrissie sighed as she ended the call. Poor Nick. He'd become a friend over the last year. They'd met when they both signed up for the same carpentry course; she'd been running from her past and he, well, in her book he was too young to be running from anything. It was strange, she thought, the way fate threw people together and made unlikely friends. For a start, she was twice his age. She liked to think she might pass for thirty, but she knew there'd be no disguising her forty-two years; not if she stood still for long enough in the spotlight of the late afternoon sun streaming through her window. No, it was all part of the rich tapestry of life, she told herself as she grabbed the rental keys and headed out through the front door.

Once again outside, she glanced back at her home as she aimed her key fob at a metallic-blue car. Click! The rental Peugeot responded. If only all life was so easy, she thought. She tried to concentrate, to block out the thoughts threatening to intrude. What had Nick said? He was swelling up and his voice sounded as if he couldn't breathe. Or was it just the poor signal on her mobile?

She felt a little nauseated and her pulse started to race. Was it about to happen again? Bill had choked to death. He'd struggled and gasped; fought to get air into his lungs – then lost the battle to feed his oxygen starved brain. But Nick? Surely it couldn't happen to Nick. He was in hospital. Safe.

'Pull yourself together, Chrissie Jax. Get a grip.' She spoke firmly to herself. She needed to hear a living voice, any living voice. With barely a glance in her rear-view mirror, she started the car and drew out into the quiet road. It only took a few moments to head through the sleepy village of Woolpit and then onto the A14 for Bury St Edmunds. She hoped it wouldn't take her long, but it was Friday and the traffic was heavy.

•••

Chrissie checked her watch as the automatic plate glass doors slid to one side. The journey had taken longer than she'd anticipated and the A & E department was heaving with activity. This, coupled with the trouble she'd had finding a space in the hospital car park, made her impatient and she hurried, full of anxiety through to the reception desk.

'He's over in Minors,' the receptionist eventually explained. 'It's over to the left. The nurse will show you.'

'Thank you,' Chrissie said. Even with the plate glass doors sliding silently open and closed to admit more people behind her, the fresh evening air didn't seem to penetrate. A faintly unpleasant mix of disinfectant, sweat and fear filled the air, adding to her unease. At least the receptionist's smile had seemed genuine when she realised Chrissie only wanted to collect someone.

'Thank you,' Chrissie repeated for good measure and followed the nurse. 'Minors as opposed to Majors?' she asked the nurse's back.

'That's right - minor injuries. He's in here. No sorry, we've moved him. He's on a trolley. We thought he'd be more comfortable.' She ushered Chrissie into a small cubicle bounded by curtains.

Chrissie didn't know what to expect. Nick lay with his head thrown back on the pillow, his eyes closed. She had prepared herself for the shock of a swelling the size of a football, but from where she stood he looked pretty much the same as normal. 'Hi, Nick,' she said, starting to relax, 'Sorry it took me so long.'

Nick opened his eyes and shifted a little. A sprinkling of sweat glistened in his short brown hair as it caught the light. He had a naturally round face, but the left side was pinker than the right and it was puffy near his temple. One eyelid looked swollen.

'Well at least you can open both eyes now,' she said and smiled to reassure him.

'Yeah, the injection seems to be working. My ear feels like it'll explode.' He lifted his hand and gingerly touched something on the side of his head. It took her a moment to realise what she was looking at.

'Ouch!' she gasped. 'That looks really painful.' His ear appeared to sprout from the side of his head like a huge over-ripe plum, the swollen flesh ready to burst through the taut, shiny skin. One area seemed particularly angry, almost purple. She guessed it was where the hornet must have got him. 'Ouch,' she repeated with feeling. 'All that from just a hornet?'

'Nick Cowley? Mr Cowley?' A young doctor walked into the cubicle, swishing the curtains with a flourish. He wore blue theatre fatigues and his stethoscope was slung casually around his neck. 'May I have a closer look?' He bent over Nick's ear and touched the stiff, almost polished skin. 'Yes, that's much better. Good - you can definitely go now. We don't need to keep you any longer.'

'It's still throbbing, but my face at least feels more normal. It's been bloody painful!'

'Well hornets' stings are.' The doctor smiled before continuing, 'They're much worse than a bee or your average wasp sting. They contain more acetylcholine and that's what stimulates the pain receptors. That's why they're so painful. Unfortunately it got you on the ear. The same amount of swelling on your leg wouldn't have been half so dramatic. I've written you up for some antihistamine tablets to take over the next 24 hours and if it's still painful after that, then a simple painkiller like paracetamol should be sufficient.'

'Thanks, thanks again, doctor.'

'And no alcohol with the antihistamine tablets. If the swelling gets worse, or you have any problem with your breathing, then you must come back immediately.' The doctor looked cheerfully at Chrissie and then was gone.

'Well that's all right then, time to go home. You can tell me all about it on the way.'

Nick swung his legs off the trolley and stood up.

'Woa… careful!' Chrissie put out a hand to steady him, but she was five foot two and she knew she'd have trouble catching him. Twelve stone fainting would have crushed her. 'Slowly, now!' she squealed as he started to topple against her, his shoulder pushing up one half of her neat blonde hairdo, Mohican style.

'Did he just say no booze, Chrissie?'

'Yes, looks like a quiet night in for you.'

Outside the cubicle Chrissie became aware of a shift in the atmosphere. Earlier it had felt busy in the department, obvious from the general bustle in the minor injuries bay, but now she sensed a heightened tension in the air. As she led the way back towards the desk, she heard sirens wailing and howling in the distance like a pack of coyotes.

'It's going to be a busy Friday night, by the sound of it,' the nurse remarked as she handed Nick a paper bag containing his tablets and then smiled at him.

Chrissie caught a voice behind her, urgent, hurried; 'There's been a massive fire. Some fuel tanks 've gone up. It may be a major incident. We're waiting to hear.'

A man in a short-sleeved shirt spoke to a couple of nurses. 'We've alerted the medical and surgical teams from the wards. The first of the ambulances should be here any moment now. Remember - if it's really bad it may just be a case of stabilising and sending straight on to Addenbrooke's or Broomfield.'

She didn't usually make a habit of eavesdropping, but his voice was urgent and the information shocking.

'Broomfield? That's miles away,' Nick said, echoing Chrissie's thoughts.

'I know,' Nick's nurse answered. 'But it's the regional burns centre. Now remember, any problems - come straight back or contact your own doctor.' She smiled at Nick again, blushed and hurried away.

'I don't know how you do it. Even with a plum for an ear and a puffy eyelid, you've got them falling over themselves,' Chrissie whispered to Nick.

They exited through the automatic sliding doors and stood outside in the warmth of the early evening. The ambulance bay had its own separate entrance into the A & E department and was less than twenty yards off to one side of the sliding doors. Chrissie was curious. She paused and stared. Sirens still screamed in the distance but an ambulance had just parked up. The rear doors were flung open and paramedics dressed in green jumped out. Within seconds they hauled out a collapsible trolley laden with something Chrissie hardly recognised as a human form. They let down its wheels and then trundled it in through the separate entrance.

'Oh my God, that looked like a heap of rags,' Chrissie whispered. She felt her blood drain as she added, 'I can smell the smoke from here.'

'The poor bastard.'

Chrissie thought for a moment. 'There was an oxygen mask, so let's assume he or she's still breathing.' The sirens grew louder and another ambulance approached with flashing lights. 'Come on; let's get out of here before this one arrives. It's starting to....' It came back to her - the smell of her burning car, the unmistakable fumes of petrol as it went up in flames. And with the scents and the sirens, so came the images. She closed her eyes for a moment, but they were still there, playing out across the back of her eyelids. She saw her bright red MGB roadster, heard the massive bang of the explosion, felt the heat as the flames licked the air.

'Are you OK, Chrissie?'

'It's, it's the smell. It brings back losing my car, that's all. I just got a hint of burnt diesel and petrol, nothing more.' She turned to catch Nick watching her face. 'You know I wrote *freak accident* on the insurance claim? At least no one was burnt, no injuries. Not like this here.' She swallowed back a raw pain, a kind of ache in her throat. Was it really the car she missed so badly or was it a sudden memory of her husband Bill?

'You aren't all right are you, Chrissie?'

She ignored his question. 'Come on, now where did I park my car?'

'Still driving the rental Peugeot?' Nick asked quietly.

'What d'you mean?'

'Just wondering. So we're looking for a metallic blue?'

'Yes, and that reminds me. I was going to ask if you'd come with me to look at a car I've seen. Well, I haven't seen it yet, just the advert. I left a message. I'm hoping the chap 'll get back to me soon.'

They walked in silence, Chrissie lost in her own thoughts about fire and blistering paintwork.

'So what's caught your eye?' Nick asked as they passed the first row of parked cars.

'What? Oh, I see.' Chrissie dragged her mind back to the present. 'I thought I might get something younger and more modern this time.' She waited for Nick to make a comment, but when all he did was grin, she blurted, 'I thought maybe a Triumph TR7 convertible. I've seen an advert for a rather nice one somewhere out towards Hadleigh.'

'Awesome. I suppose it'll only be about thirty years old. I'd expected you to go for something more modern like the rental Peugeot this time. Hey, there it is.' Nick pointed to a metallic blue Peugeot 207 squeezed into a space between a 4x4 and a large Mercedes saloon. 'I'll wait here while you get it out.'

Chrissie pressed between the parked cars and tried to edge her petite body into the driver's seat. 'Hell,' she moaned as she brushed her bottom and thigh against the grubby bodywork of the neighbouring Mercedes. 'Why do people park so close?' A dusting of grime covered her pale blue linen trousers and she swiped at the material ineffectually. It was annoying, but then a thought struck. With a TR7, she could just climb over the door and into the driver's seat. It had, after all been the convertible driven by Joanna Lumley's Purdy in *The New Avengers*. Perhaps changing her MGB to a TR7 wouldn't be quite so bad after all.

It didn't take her long to reverse out and drive up to Nick. He stood with his back to her, staring at something in the distance. Now what's he seen, she wondered. In fact he didn't seem to be aware of her at all. She thumped the horn and felt some satisfaction when he jumped. 'Are you all right, Nick?' she asked as he got into the car.

'I'm sure I've just seen… Dan. Yes that was his name. Dan.'

'Who's Dan?'

'He's the bloke who gave me the diesel this afternoon. I suppose you could say he rescued me.'

'Do you want to speak to him?'

Nick ignored her question. 'It was his place where the bloody hornet stung me.'

'Ah! Mixed feelings about Dan, then. So where is he?' Chrissie glanced left and right but there didn't seem to be anyone nearby.

'Over there.' He pointed towards the ambulance bay. 'I waved but he ignored me. Why'd he do that?'

'Maybe he didn't recognise you. Or maybe you're too far away and he didn't see you,' she said as he did up his seat belt. 'Now come on, let's get you home to Barking Tye. So what happened? Tell me.'

'It started while I was over at Bildeston,' Nick began.

Chrissie listened as she drove, but found she couldn't concentrate on the intricacies of beehive design at the same time as focusing on the traffic. She lost the thread of Nick's tale as she joined the A14. 'Rookery Farm?' she asked. 'Out towards Bildeston? He assumed you'd come for diesel? How strange.'

'Hey, what's that over there?' Nick leaned forwards against his seat belt, ignoring her questions and pointed.

Chrissie took a moment to realise he meant somewhere west of the motorway. The evening was still light and she caught a view of smoke billowing into the sky. 'Woa, do you think that's the fire the pretty nurse was talking about? It looks horrendous.' She glanced at Nick but his face was already pink and it was difficult to tell if he was blushing.

'I reckon that's somewhere like Blackthorpe or Rougham.'

'I didn't know there were any fuel depots out that way.'

'There are always farm tanks….' Nick paused as he rummaged in his pocket for his phone. 'Well, what d'you know? It's Matt. Hi Matt….'

Chrissie stopped listening and concentrated on driving while Nick chatted to Matt. She'd shared her workbench at Utterly Academy with him over the last year, and just like Nick, they'd become friends. It was all chance, she thought, the way you met people like Nick and Matt.

As she drove with the hint of smoke in her nose, her thoughts returned to her MGB. Her emotions were usually kept deeply buried but smells often brought them back, like a key unlocking a door and releasing memories. And once they came back, they stayed with her for hours. Her mind drifted. It had been five years ago, perhaps longer. She had been the one driving the MGB, otherwise they would never have got lost. She could still hear Bill's voice as he laughed when she missed the turning to Rougham Park and instead headed to Blackthorpe. But there had been nothing out that way, just quiet rural lanes and farms hidden down rough tracks. She didn't remember noticing any fuel depots, so what exactly had gone up in flames today? Perhaps it was just a farm storage tank. She gave her head a little shake. Something felt wrong about it all. Maybe it was just the past unsettling her. It set another cycle of thoughts spinning as she imagined billowing black smoke.

If Bill hadn't inhaled a sudden out-belching of rubber fumes from a re-cycling plant two years ago, then his airways wouldn't have gone into constrictive spasm, his circulation wouldn't have collapsed and she would never have known what fatal anaphylactic shock meant. More importantly, Bill would still be alive and she wouldn't be a widow training to be a carpenter.

# CHAPTER 3

Matt was on vacation. It wasn't a true holiday, not like going to Great Yarmouth or away to Spain, but the term had ended and Utterly Academy in Stowmarket was on its annual break. He'd heard they were running some summer schools. He glanced at his left arm. If it wasn't for the plaster cast he'd have started at Hepplewhites by now. How he wished he was like his best mates Nick and Chrissie, already a couple of months into their apprentice placements. But for the moment he was free and he was going make the most of it.

Matt made a decision. He would wear shorts and tee-shirt as befitted the vacation mood. He only had one pair of baggy styled cargo shorts and he reckoned they made him look like an explorer. The tee-shirt warranted choosing with particular care. He tugged the cotton fabric over his head. The Hawaiian theme stretched across his chest as he rolled it down. Elongated fronded palm leaves, parrots and fruits had been printed as if to mimic a pattern on a loose linen shirt. A pretend collar and buttons had even been incorporated into the design. He stood back from the mirror to inspect the look. 'Cool,' he murmured, as he patted his chest and smoothed the tight, busy design over his ample belly. This should pull the birds, he thought as he practised his winning smile. He tried to raise one side of his mouth, curling his lips in what he hoped was a sexy but subtle half smirk. He checked the look in profile and the light shone through his short, dark-sandy hair. 'Not bad!' And then he noticed the spot on his small stubby nose. 'Zit!'

Matt frowned and remembered the real reason he had bothered to get up and dressed by the unearthly hour of 9:30 am on a Monday. Ever since talking to Nick on his mobile on Friday evening, he'd been thinking about Jim Mann and the incident with the shotgun, or did he say air rifle? For a start, he knew an air rifle only had an effective range of about fifty yards, at least that's what his older brother Tom said, and yet Nick hadn't seen anyone. So had it really been a simple air rifle pellet, he wondered. It had niggled and worried him over the weekend, so by Monday he knew he had to make a visit to the Utterly Academy library to look up some stuff. But the real reason he'd chosen the Hawaiian tee-shirt was the Playwriting Summer School. It would be in full swing by mid-morning and he hoped there might be some attractive birds on the course. With any luck they might stray into the library, and if they did he'd be looking casual, a knock out.

It was time to catch the bus to the Academy and he slammed the front door as he left the modest bungalow he'd called home for all of his nineteen years. He needed to get a move on, or else he'd have to stand around for ages before another bus came. For once he was in luck. Twenty minutes later Matt stepped down from the bus and looked up at the old Academy building. Why anyone would want to build it in that pale-yellow Suffolk brick was beyond him. He'd always thought the colour more suited to a public toilet than someone's home, but a hundred years earlier, a wealthy businessman had actually chosen those bricks. What had once been the original Edwardian mansion now made up the central block of the Academy and that was where he was heading – past the visitors' car park and to the library on the first floor.

'Loads of cars,' he murmured. 'Should be plenty of 'em at the playwritin'.' He spoke with a soft Suffolk accent, the sounds far back in his throat and the vowels sometimes flattened.

Inside the main entrance someone had written, in bold capitals: WRITING DRAMA FOR RADIO: 10:30 WORKSHOP. The notice was pasted on a board and a huge arrow pointed along the main corridor. Matt started to follow the arrow, but then turned off to the right, up the main stairs and headed for the library. He patted his student card somewhere in a cargo pocket. If the library had been opened for the Summer School attendees, then he'd be OK.

'Morning. I didn't know you wrote plays.'

Matt stopped dead in his tracks. He'd found the library doors unlocked and thought no one had seen him as he sidled quietly past the librarian's empty station. He swung around, looking for the owner of the disembodied voice.

'H-hi, I'm just…,' he spluttered.

'I wasn't expecting anyone from the Summer School up here until about twelve o'clock. Like the tee-shirt, by the way.' The young library assistant smiled. She was dressed in a pale linen top and jeans and her long auburn hair fell loosely, framing her face.

His cheeks burned with pleasure as he glanced down at the fronded leaves and parrot captured on the stretched fabric of his tee-shirt. 'Yeah, I thought it'd….' It was difficult to sound casual mid-blush and the words died in his mouth. Rosie, the library assistant, always seemed to have this effect on him.

'Very Suffolk,' she finished for him and still grinning, turned her attention back to a pile of books on a small trolley.

‘No, it’s Hawaiian.’ How strange, he thought. Surely she knew there weren’t any parrots and tropical flowers in Suffolk. He made his way past the large windows. They overlooked the Academy gardens with their well-manicured lawns. Scarcely glancing, he headed on for a secluded computer station.

So where to begin, Matt wondered and switched on the computer. He wriggled his fingers in anticipation as he surveyed the keyboard. ‘Come on, come on,’ he breathed as the screen flickered and flashed through its start-up sequences. Yes, we have take-off, he thought as he finally leant forward in his chair, logged into Google and typed *Jim Mann, Suffolk*. He didn’t have to wait long. Forty-seven thousand and three hundred results! ‘Who’d ’ve guessed there’s a Suffolk in Virginia, USA?’

After wading through seventeen screen-pages of Jim Mann links, he gave up. Perhaps it had been a bit of a long shot. There wasn’t even a sniff of anyone who could possibly be Nick’s Jim Mann of Bildeston in the UK’s Suffolk. He didn’t fare any better on Facebook or Twitter either. Matt decided it was time for a different approach. Could someone hold a grudge against Jim, he wondered. After all, the incident with the air rifle pellet didn’t sound like an accident, and weren’t most grievances through work? Matt didn’t know what Jim did, other than keep bees of course. Maybe he traded under a name like BeeMann, HiveMann or HoneyMann?

Matt typed in every permutation of words he could think of that referred to beekeeping, honey and Mann, but he drew a blank. Even on the Companies’ House website there wasn’t a liquidated company registered in his name. It’s strange, Matt thought, it’s as if he’s hidden his identity from the internet. It's almost as if he doesn't exist or doesn't want to be found.

There was nothing else for it but to look through the local independent newspaper websites. Matt typed: Eastern Anglia Daily Tribune, leant forwards and read the Monday morning headline news.

*Local man found dead.* That in itself wasn't particularly earth shattering, but as Matt read on, he could hardly believe his eyes. Someone dressed in beekeeping clothes had been found dead somewhere out Bildeston way. He read it again, this time more slowly.

*The body of a man was found close to a footpath by local resident Mrs Smitt while out walking her dog early on Sunday morning.* 'But that was yesterday,' Matt whispered, the S sounding like a Z as he drew out *was* in his gentle Suffolk accent. He skipped through the next bit about the footpath running through a small orchard close to the Bildeston Road, east of Monks Eleigh. *At first I thought it was just a bundle of rags, you know, some fly tipping. But Digger wouldn't leave it alone.* 'Digger?' Matt wondered. 'Course – the dog.' A family name for the champion Schnauzer, he discovered as he read on.

*I kept calling him away from it, but in the end I had to go and see what was exciting him so much.* 'What's she on about? Oh yeah, the dog,' Matt sighed and then sucked some air through his teeth, making a low whistle. *At first I thought it was just paint on the rags, but then I realised it was blood. I could tell it was a body, but I never saw the face; there was a beekeeper's hat and veil in the way.* The standard phrases about the police being unable to give further details until the body had been identified and the family informed, rounded off the report. 'Shoot!' Matt sat back in his chair.

'Everything OK?'

Matt looked up from the screen to see Rosie standing in front of his computer station. 'Yeah, sure. Why?'

'The Playwriting Summer School should be here any moment. I'll be showing them round the library. There's some books I've laid out – a little exhibition.' She moved towards him as she spoke and then frowned. 'Your arm's been in plaster for most of the summer, hasn't it?'

Matt felt a sudden panic. He'd logged onto the newspaper website using the Academy subscriber's code. He was pretty sure he wasn't supposed to know it and he was milliseconds from discovery. Click! He closed the site.

'Yeah, but it's me other wrist. Just as me right mended I bust me left.' He spoke rapidly, frowning at the blank Google webpage and bringing his hand up to his face to cover the zit. He hoped it looked as if he was displaying his plaster cast for inspection.

'I thought you might be attending.' She turned away.

'Hey, wait.' But he'd spoken too late and his voice was muffled. The plaster cast, in covering his nose, had also covered his mouth. Matt sighed. How had he managed to mess that up, he wondered. He turned his attention back to the screen and brought up the newspaper site again. He typed Jim's name in the newspaper's search box. It seemed that Jim had featured, but only in so far as there were reports of his success with honey at the Edible Garden Show earlier in March and past triumphs at the national Honey Show the previous year, 2009. The search wouldn't go back further than 2008. Could honey be a motive for murder?

Bildeston was hardly the set for Midsomer Murders, Matt reasoned.

The library door swung open as the aspiring playwrights from the Summer School entered noisily. Matt looked up from his computer station and eyed the girls in the group. He couldn't believe his luck. In his imaginings he'd conjured up some tasty literary birds, but even in his wildest dreams he hadn't envisaged a pair of twins.

'Cool,' he murmured, but something on the screen caught his eye and distracted him from the playwrights. Jim Mann had written to the editor and the newspaper had printed the letter. He'd used angry words to oppose an application for planning permission to erect a mobile-phone mast somewhere near Alderman's Point. Matt wasn't too sure where that was, but it was obvious Jim held strong views. Why else would he use words like: *hateful*, *monstrous*, *ugly*, *destroying*, *killing* and *giant bird-slayers*? A whole paragraph likened it to the environmental effects of diesel and cars. At first Matt thought the letter was directed at a person, not a mast - but he couldn't see a name. So what was so special about Alderman's Point and why had Jim been so vehement in his opposition to the mobile-phone mast? Everyone knew more masts were needed. Matt checked the date. It had only been a month ago; 23rd July 2010.

'Passion.' It was the word that sprang to mind as he read the letter. 'Passion,' Matt repeated. He hadn't had much experience with emotion in his relatively short life, but he presumed if you were passionate in one aspect of your life, then it followed your passion might spill into other areas as well. Jim Mann had been passionate about bees, and now it would seem phone masts. Or was it Alderman's

Point? Could this be a reason for an unnatural death? Matt looked up from the screen and gazed across the library.

'Awesome,' he whispered, letting the word drag like a sigh as he watched the twins. 'Get an eyeful of them bird playwrights!'

All thoughts of Jim Mann flew out of the window as Matt stood up, intent on crossing the library to join the group. But his chair failed to slide away from him. Instead it tipped backwards. When he turned from the computer station, his thigh caught the seat-edge. He reached out to catch it but instead knocked the backrest. The chair skidded across the polished boards and crashed to the floor.

'Shit!' He lost his balance and sat down hard.

The background chattering from the budding playwrights, their voices already muted and hushed, stopped abruptly. Matt could have heard a pin drop. He sat on the floor, his cheeks burning and his face on fire. All eyes turned towards him.

'Are you OK?' Rosie broke away from the group and hurried across the library.

He nodded. If he could have curled up and died, he would have.

'What happened?'

One of the twins adjusted her glasses and gazed at him.

He tried to find the words to answer, 'I-I'm… fine.'

Rosie looked down at him and frowned. 'Are you sure? I'm giving a tour of the library, but do come and join us when I show the playwriting group the little exhibition I've set up. It might interest you.'

Matt smiled, not the sexy half smile he'd practised, but the watery one he felt inside. As he sat on the library floor, the humiliation of his childhood came flooding back. In his mind he was again the eight year old kid, looking up from where he sat on the pavement. He'd wanted to be like his older brother Tom and learn to skateboard. He'd even dreamt of mastering the finer points of tricks such as *Walking the Dog, Slides & Grinds and 360s*. He imagined being cool and impressing his brother with his agility and speed. It had been in the days before anyone had thought to mention dyspraxia in the same breath as Matt's name.

Matt winced as he recalled what had turned out to be Tom's final attempt to teach him. Even aged eight he had a bulky torso with a low centre of gravity like a fat, squat, skittle. He'd skated straight over a dog's turd, left on the pavement by a thoughtful hound and so fresh it steamed. That had been bad enough, but then he lost his balance and toppled backwards into the offensive pile, too soft to cushion his landing but peculiarly adherent and mind-blowingly pungent. Matt closed his eyes as he pictured the audience of Tom's friends. Boys can be cruel at any age. After that, the kids on the Flower Estate, its very name evoking fragrance, followed him for weeks, willing him to fall into something. It was an unfortunate end to what could justifiably be described as an innovative interpretation of a *Walking the Dog* trick. He would forever be the younger brother sitting in metaphorical shite.

Rosie picked up the chair and carried it back to the computer station while Matt struggled to his feet, shaking off his nightmare and returning to the present. Ambition, when eight years old, had ended in tears, but at nineteen he was better equipped. He pulled at his tee-shirt, adjusting the tense fabric so that a full parrot was displayed across his shoulders. He set his face into a slight half smile and looked across at the group. The twin with the maroon framed glasses and curly dark hair grinned. Matt's equilibrium was restored. He'd wait, he decided, until the library tour was over and then saunter across, casual and confident, to join the group for Rosie's exhibition.

Matt settled at his computer station and typed the word *diesel* in the Google search box. His mind was really on the group, but he had to do something while they toured the library. He could hear them as they chatted and laughed, pausing at intervals while Rosie explained or pointed to something. Half-heartedly he read about the red coloured dye added to automotive diesel, not to improve performance but purely for tax reasons. It was quite a simple concept; if it was dyed red it was taxed less, cheaper to buy and destined for off-road agricultural vehicles. 'So that's why Nick got red diesel at Rookery Farm,' he muttered. But what's green diesel, he wondered as he watched Rosie lead the straggly group to see something near the book return station.

A bit more unenthusiastic reading and he learned green diesel was extracted from sustainable vegetable oils such as rape seed oil. Its name was a reference to its green credentials. Clever people tweaked and refined it to resemble automotive diesel, but no one coloured it green. Hmm, he thought. From deep fat fryer to vehicle fuel tank - not bad.

'And that just about covers most of it.' Rosie's voice floated above the background babble.

Matt looked up from his screen. The group had congregated near a table on the far side of the library. 'Exhibition time,' Matt whispered. This time he stood up more slowly, as befitted his cool Hawaiian tee-shirt style.

‘Ah good, you’ve joined us,’ Rosie said as he approached.

‘Hi!’ he said, smiling at the twins standing next to each other on the edge of the group. Their features looked identical apart from the different coloured frames to their glasses. One was dressed in jeans, the other in a floral cotton skirt.

‘We have to thank Sir Raymond Utterly for these wonderful books. They’re part of his collection. He was an avid theatre goer.’

Matt hardly listened to Rosie as she explained the exhibits of old books and papers lying open on the table. Someone shuffled forwards to look more closely at a tattered theatre programme and Matt made his move. ‘Hi, Ginny,’ he said as he edged closer. Her name was printed on a badge clipped to the strap of her shoulder bag. No surname.

‘Hi,’ she replied.

He stood as near as he dared, his Hawaiian parrot on fronded palm leaf decoration strangely out of place next to her print skirt - a cottage garden, flower-mix design. The maroon glasses gave a finishing splash of colour, perched on the end of her nose.

‘Yes, that’s a programme for Pygmalion – May 1914, His Majesty’s Theatre,’ Rosie explained. ‘I assume Sir Raymond must have attended.’

‘George Bernard Shaw!’ Ginny spoke in hushed tones, ‘Awesome.’

Matt nodded but he wanted to get her attention back.

‘What you writin’, Ginny?’

'A drama about Guy Fawkes, I'm hoping it'll be ready for Bonfire Night. It's to be a mix of song and poetry with special effects.'

'I like musicals,' Matt whispered.

'It's more of a laser-light show, but against a bonfire backdrop. Nothing high-tech. You must come; there'll be notices nearer the time. I'm a drama student here. What about you?'

'Carpentry. Second year.'

Ginny glanced at Matt's plaster cast and frowned.

'So,' she said slowly, 'are you writing something?'

It was Matt's turn to frown, his mind a blank. 'Fuel!' he blurted, and when she didn't say anything, he added, 'Well… diesel.' He watched as she started to turn away. 'Green diesel?'

'Sorry, I must speak to Lil, my sister. She's up for the Summer School from RADA.' Ginny pulled a face at her twin, the one with green spectacle frames and jeans.

Matt stared at Ginny's back as she inched a path through the other aspiring playwrights, her attention now on the table and the Pygmalion programme. The group shifted and she seemed to disappear, as if she'd been swallowed. Well that had gone rather well, he thought, and as if on cue, his voluminous stomach rumbled as an older man in a cheese cloth shirt caught Matt with his elbow. It was time to break away from the exhibits and head for lunch.

The canteen was on the same floor as the library and a few moments later Matt pushed on its swing doors. The smell of sausage and chips met his nose, and he inhaled deeply as he strode in. 'Awesome, the canteen's servin',' he murmured and savoured the grease laden scents. This time he had enough money for a plate of chips.

While he waited at the service counter, Matt scanned the dining area. He found it difficult to recognise anyone against the dark, midnight blue walls. 'Hi,' he called, smiling when he finally spotted Chrissie and Nick. They were already sitting at a table on the far side, near a modern plate glass window which echoed and magnified the effect of the Edwardian sash windows on the end wall.

A few minutes later he bumped his fully laden tray down on their table. 'How's the ear, Nick?'

'OK thanks. You can still see where the bugger stung me, but the swelling's gone down.'

Matt bent over Nick's ear. 'Can't see nothin' mate, not in this Goth's light.'

'If you look really close, screw up your eyes and really concentrate, you can just about see a little purple spot,' Chrissie said between mouthfuls of egg mayonnaise sandwich.

'Oh yeah?' Matt looked again, 'I got it now. I reckoned that were from holdin' your ear when you sing, mate.'

Chrissie coughed, choked and swallowed hard. She dropped some seeded crust back into her plastic container as she croaked, 'Didn't expect the canteen to be open. I wouldn't have bothered bringing these in if I'd known.'

Matt noticed Chrissie's eyes had watered. He frowned. It was mixed messages again. 'Hmm. So what you two doin' here?'

'Blumfield, mate. He never stops. The apprentice release day is every Monday right through August.'

'Yes,' Chrissie added, 'and when he's away we're supposed to Skype him. It's his take on a tele-conference.'

'Are you kiddin'?'

'No, we have to be here, we've no choice. What's your excuse?' Nick asked, looking up from his plate.

'And in holiday attire. Very fetching!'

'Thanks, Chrissie. Yeah, I thought… well it's the Playwritin' Summer School, aint it.'

'That'll be why the canteen's open,' Chrissie interrupted.

'Didn't know you wrote plays, Matt.'

'Yeah well, two birds with one stone, Nick. I've been lookin' up stuff in the library. An' I've also met some of them playwritin' birds in there.' Matt tapped the side of his stubby nose.

'And?' Chrissie pulled a face.

'No, I'm serious. I've been readin' 'bout someone found dead in a beekeeping outfit on Sunday mornin', over Bildeston way. In an orchard on the road to Monks Eleigh. It's all over this mornin's news site.' Matt filled his mouth with chips and chewed.

'What?' The colour drained from Nick's face. 'I didn't hear it on the radio this morning. You're kidding me, right?'

'My God!' Chrissie stared at him. 'I didn't hear anything either. Was it Jim Mann?'

Matt nodded as he swallowed hard. 'They aint released the name yet, but it's what I'm wonderin'.'

'But I was talking to him on Friday. He can't be dead.'

'Talking to someone on Friday doesn't stop them from dying on Sunday,' Chrissie said quietly.

'As I were sayin', I've been readin' stuff an' I've a feelin, there's somethin' fishy 'bout Jim Mann – dead or not.' Matt pushed his tray away. Summer School bird watching had given him an appetite and the chips hadn't taken long to eat. He was still hungry. He glanced across at Nick.

'When will they release the name, do you think?' Nick's voice seemed to rise.

Matt liked it when they looked to him for answers, but how should he know, he wondered. He shrugged.

'If the name hasn't been released by tomorrow, maybe I'll hear something at Willows. There's always someone there who knows what's going on.' Nick frowned and pulled his plate closer.

'If it's Jim Mann who's dead, I know it's dreadful but at least you won't have to make the prototype beehive for him, will you?'

Nick looked at Chrissie as she spoke. This was the moment Matt had been waiting for. He had opportunity; now he needed speed. Like greased lightning, he thrust out his hand to snatch a lonesome chip from Nick's plate. But Nick was faster.

'Oi!' Nick brought the flat of his fork down on the back of Matt's hand, trapping it against the plate.

'Argh!' Matt squealed, 'That bloody hurts.'

Nick's eyes were on Chrissie. He seemed unaware of Matt squirming beneath the fork as he asked, 'So, when are you planning to go and have a look at this TR7, Chrissie?'

'Shit, let me go!'

'Oh, do you want to come and look at the car as well, Matt?' Chrissie asked mildly.

Matt felt the pressure from the fork ease a little. 'Did you say a TR7? A triumph TR7? Aint they got them pop-up square headlights, a shovel nose an' a wedge shaped rear?' Matt caught her expression. 'Sorry, Chrissie. Hey let me go,

Nick. Ouch!' Matt rubbed the back of his hand; no chip but he at least he was free again.

'So what are you doing the rest of the week, Matt?' Nick leaned back in his chair and grinned.

'I'm hangin' in the library an' lookin' up stuff.'

'Does the playwriting thing run for the rest of the week then?' Nick still grinned.

'Yeah, need to find out more 'bout Alderman's Point an'–'

'And write a play?' Chrissie finished for him.

'No, but them birds….'

Nick laughed and pushed his plate towards Matt. 'Tell us about it on Friday, unless of course you're otherwise engaged. Here, have the last chip.'

# CHAPTER 4

'*It's the 7 o'clock news, brought to you from Radio Suffolk....*' Chrissie covered her head with her pillow as the strident tones burst from the radio alarm by her bed, the time displayed in decimal read-out. '*Tuesday the 24th of August, and yesterday a freak....*' She didn't need to hear how a tornado had torn through a sleepy village near Bury St Edmunds, uprooting trees and damaging buildings for thirty seconds before dissipating as rapidly as it had struck. Of course she was sorry for the residents of Great Livermere, but she was still too drowsy to want to feel anything.

She had always preferred her transition from sleepy oblivion to wakefulness to be slow, and like a cat she could doze for hours. 'Hmm,' she sighed, 'just ten more minutes.' The feline qualities in her nature metaphorically stretched, as the newsreader's voice cut through to her ears again.

'*A petition to review the safety of unmanned level crossings in Suffolk is gaining momentum following the crash last week that left a man fighting for his life....*' She pushed the pillow aside and emerged. It had been an automatic crossing near Sudbury; a train had collided with a sewage tanker. Chrissie sat up; it was no good, she'd have to get out of bed.

'*The police have named the man found dead in an orchard just outside Bildeston on Sunday morning....*' Chrissie froze and listened for the name. '*Jim Mann, a resident of Bildeston....*'

'Oh my God!' she whispered. 'Matt was right.' She switched off the radio as the weather forecast got underway. She'd heard enough and anyway, all thoughts of further sleep vanished as her mind went into overdrive. Throwing the duvet back, she stood, barefoot on the waxed floorboards, and for a moment looked at the water stain near the window. Bill had left the old sash open during a storm some years before, and the rain had driven through. She remembered being annoyed at the time, and hadn't tried to disguise the discoloured patch. Instead she'd left it as a reminder to close the window. There's always a mark, always something left behind, she thought. 'I wonder what this Jim Mann has left behind?' she murmured. 'Matt seems to think he was invisible on the internet… hmm.' She padded across her bedroom and headed for a morning shower.

As Chrissie stood under a torrent of hot water and lathered shampoo into her hair, a sudden thought struck. Nick had nearly been shot when he visited Jim Mann on Friday. Was it a warning, or a clumsy attempt on Jim's life? Either way, Nick should tell the police. But which police station was dealing with the suspicious death? Ipswich or Bury St Edmunds? Chrissie let her mind run on. Clive Merry would know – she'd met the police inspector nearly two months ago when her car had been stolen. He'd been very kind, nothing more, but it would be an excuse to contact him. Hmm…, she thought, but first she'd check with Nick and make sure he was happy to go to the police about it. She could phone him later.

Having made a decision, Chrissie turned her attention to the day ahead. If she dawdled much longer, she'd be late for the Clegg workshop. She considered she'd been lucky to be assigned the apprenticeship with Ron Clegg and she didn't want to mess it up. She had fifteen, maybe twenty minutes maximum before she needed to leave, if she was to get to Wattisham on time. She threw on a pair of lightweight cotton jeans and a long sleeve tee-shirt and gulped scalding tea as she blow-dried her hair. Munching on a slice of toast, she searched for her car keys. She found them on the kitchen table. They'd slid under the electricity bill. Snatching them up, she grabbed her handbag and sprinted through her small hall, slamming the front door as she aimed her key fob at the hired metallic-blue Peugeot. 'It's like competing in a pentathlon,' she puffed. 'There must be an easier way to get going in the morning.'

Chrissie let her mind wander as she drove on the A14 from Woolpit, past Stowmarket and then left the dual carriageway at Needham Market. It wasn't the most direct route, but it by-passed some of the network of small lanes. She breezed past earthy fields of harvested rape seed. The plough-in had missed some of the dead stalks and they pointed upwards, broken and at angles. They were a testament to what had been; a distant memory. She slowed as she neared the Wattisham airbase. The Clegg workshop was easy to miss – a small turning off the airfield perimeter lane. It was poorly signposted despite the notice announcing *Ron Clegg, Master Cabinet Maker and Furniture Restorer*. She'd got hopelessly lost the first time she'd driven out that way. Sometimes she thought Ron Clegg didn't want to be found. Was he hiding from the world too, she wondered.

It was dead on 8:00 am as she rattled and bumped the Peugeot down the rutted track that led to a concrete courtyard. It was surrounded on two sides by a wooden barn and an old brick outbuilding. A cedar tree trunk stretched on the concrete like a felled giant.

'Morning, Mrs Jax,' Ron called across the barn workshop as Chrissie opened the old wooden door.

She returned his greeting with a smile. He sat in his usual place at his workbench, a mug of steaming tea close to his right hand. The joints of his fingers were enlarged and misshapen. Years of work had taken their toll and she noticed, when he raised the mug to his lips, how slowly he moved. She didn't know his age exactly, but she guessed he must be in his sixties.

'Have you heard the morning news, Mr Clegg?' Instinctively she touched her head. Her hair felt like a pile of cut grass, pointing in every direction. Had she forgotten to brush it after she'd used the dryer?

'I haven't listened to the radio this morning. What did you want to know, Mrs Jax? Low pressure weather fronts approaching from the north? Concerns about the local celery crop? Current outrage over speed bumps in Ipswich?'

'No, no. I meant have you heard? They've named the dead man. The one found on Sunday in the orchard, close to the Monks Eleigh road, just out of Bildeston.'

Ron didn't answer for a moment. He frowned as he gazed across the workshop, seemingly concentrating on a rack of cramps hanging on the far wall. Chrissie could see he wasn't focused on them; he was looking at something far beyond. A memory, perhaps? 'So did you know this man, the one they found dead, Mrs Jax?'

'No, but Nick did. I mean he didn't know him exactly, but he was talking to him only on Friday. I know we should have come round here yesterday after the day-release teaching, to work on the carvings. But Nick was still a bit shaken after Friday. Sorry, Mr Clegg. I should have....'

'That's all right, Mrs Jax. The apprentice release day is meant to be just that – a release day. You know I'm always pleased to see you all if you come on a Monday, but I don't expect it.' The fine creases near his eyes turned into furrows as he smiled.

Chrissie felt dreadful. Ron knew Nick and Matt. They'd both volunteered to help her carve the ten-years-late millennium project for Utterly Academy. The project was the cedar tree trunk she'd just parked alongside in the courtyard. With Ron's tutoring, it was to be transformed into an eighteen-foot totem pole, or so they all hoped. But she should have phoned Ron and told him they weren't coming. After meeting Matt in the canteen yesterday and hearing about the dead body, they'd all felt a bit anxious and opted to go home rather than practise their carving skills. It was no excuse. She should have phoned.

'Mrs Jax? Are you all right?'

Chrissie looked up to see Ron watching her. His attention wasn't intrusive, just a calm stillness. It was his way. She could never tell whether it was down to his arthritis or his quiet manner.

'Perhaps a mug of tea might help? Make one for yourself and, well I'll have another. Then, after you've told me all about it, Mrs Jax, we can get on with the work of the day.'

This wasn't sexist talk; this was just trainer and apprentice talk and Chrissie couldn't help but smile as she made a particularly strong brew. By the time she settled on her work stool with a mug of dark tea clasped in her hands, she felt more in control, more the usual Chrissie. She'd even flattened her hair into some semblance of a style.

'The dead chap was called Jim Mann.' Chrissie paused as she watched Ron slowly nod. 'Do you know, sorry, *did* you know him, Mr Clegg?'

'The name sounds familiar, I can't think why. But, carry on. Don't let me stop you.'

Chrissie recounted Nick's Friday. It seemed simpler just to tell it as Nick had, although it lost a little of its drama when told from a workbench stool rather than a hospital trolley. Finally she fell silent and waited for Ron to say something. He seemed lost in his own thoughts, gazing at the concrete floor. 'Nick should go to the police,' he said quietly.

'That's what I think too.'

'I also think… well I remember now. I believe I did some work for a Jim Mann, or rather his wife Minnette, many years ago.'

'Really? What kind of work, Mr Clegg?'

'A Queen Anne walnut veneered tallboy. The drawers weren't running properly and some of the veneer had split from the oak carcass. It wasn't a particularly big job, as I recall. I also replaced a lower drawer base and sides. I've probably got some of the original wood in the store.'

'So what was Jim Mann like?'

'I don't remember. It was over twenty years ago. I think I only met him the once. If I'd known he was going to get murdered one day, Mrs Jax, I'd have taken more notice. Most of my dealings were with Minnette Mann.' Ron paused for a moment before adding, 'I seem to recall there was some talk about her.' He sipped his tea. 'Yes, that's it. She went one day. I'm not sure exactly, but I think they said she just upped and left him.'

'Can you remember what she was like, Mr Clegg?'

'Very pretty, in a French sort of a way. She even put flowers in the drawers. Bright blue… yes, strikingly blue with star shaped heads. I remember her saying it was common borage. The words just rolled off her tongue, full of R's in her French accent. She made the borage sound anything but common. Why are you laughing, Mrs Jax?'

'It's the way you tell it, Mr Clegg – very exotic for round these parts. I wonder where she went and if there's a second Mrs Mann.'

'Folk said she'd gone back to France, but who knows. Now that's enough speculation for one morning. Time to get on with some work, Mrs Jax.'

Chrissie was dispatched to the small brick outbuilding that ran along one side of the courtyard. 'Find me some suitable veneer,' Ron had said. He was repairing a small writing bureau and she relished the task. The smell of wood and oils hung in the air, and she inhaled deeply as she opened the door. The building was old, with a yellow Suffolk bricked floor. The chimney breast held a copper still, disused and dulled with time. Wood, discarded or salvaged from broken furniture, was stacked against the walls.

She headed for a wide shelf where she knew a dusty pile of veneers was stored between sheets of board and brown paper. 'How much does he need?' She looked at the names written neatly on the brown paper. 'Walnut?' but her thoughts drifted across to the wood stacked against the wall.

Hadn't Ron said something about Jim Mann's bottom drawer and the wood pile? And why put borage in the drawers? It seemed a slightly odd choice of flower. Lavender or rose; flowers with a stronger perfume were more common. Borage was pretty, but as far as she knew, it wasn't particularly fragrant. Chrissie remembered reading somewhere it was popular with beekeepers; but if that was the case then it should have been alive out in the garden, not shut away in a drawer. Perhaps it was a French custom?

Chrissie turned her thoughts back to selecting a piece of walnut veneer. It looked rather unpromising in its unpolished state and she carried the fragile brittle slice on its board, as Ron had instructed. She made her way back across the courtyard to the barn workshop, and as she nudged the old door open with her knee, Ron asked, 'Any luck? Did you find anything suitable?'

'I think so. See what you think.'

Ron stood slowly and limped over to look at the walnut writing bureau and the veneer she'd selected. Chrissie knew he must have approved because he made no comment about the match of the walnut. Instead he started to explain how to go about the repair.

'Some of this,' he touched the veneer lifting up from the carcass, 'can be re-stuck down. Look, this bit here isn't too badly damaged. We start by cutting back to the salvageable bits. Remember a larger repair may be less obvious than a smaller patch.'

'And we cut following the swirls and curves of the walnut grain?'

'To begin with.'

'It all seems so.... I mean it's only a pine carcass underneath.' To Chrissie it was like a modern day celebrity masquerading as something desirable; judged by a beautiful exterior while the inner crudeness remained hidden. Shallow, that was the word she was looking for. 'Shallow.'

'What's shallow, Mrs Jax?'

'I always think of furniture, like people, Mr Clegg. There are three types in the world: firstly, the solid oak chests – what you see is what you get type of people; then there's the walnut writing bureau type – with an outer skin hiding something beneath.'

'And the third type?'

'Onions, Mr Clegg – onions.' When Ron didn't say anything, she continued, 'People with many layers hidden beneath their outer skin. A bit like Jim Mann. I mean… he finds an exotic French woman to marry and then mysteriously mislays her? He has to be an onion, Mr Clegg.'

'You'd have to call him one of those wooden Russian dolls - one hidden within another and another - not an onion, if you're sticking to the wooden theme. Now, enough chatter. Don't forget the repair veneer must be completely flat. You've got some work to do before we can use it.'

Chrissie held the veneer, still resting on its board, up to her eye level. 'Oh no, it's all curled and warped when you look at it like this.'

'Steam, Mrs Jax. Steam it.'

Fifteen minutes later Chrissie stood, her face framed by damp strands of hair sticking to her forehead and cheeks. She felt flushed. 'It isn't working, Mr Clegg.' The kettle hissed and whistled as steam mushroomed out of the spout.

'Then try brushing it with wallpaper paste, or hot weak animal glue. Then press it flat between those boards. Hey, and turn the kettle off.' She couldn't see him but his voice drifted through her foggy microclimate. 'Don't forget to use polythene sheets so it doesn't stick to the press. It'll need at least 24 hours.' Ron made it sound like a recipe. 'The celebrity writing bureau will have to manage without Botox, this time.'

Chrissie smiled. He might move slowly, but his brain was as sharp as a Stanley knife. She switched the kettle off.

Later, on her lunch break, she stood in the courtyard and stared at the cedar tree trunk. How the hell are we going to turn that into a totem pole, she wondered. Ron was a brilliant teacher, but eighteen feet of carvings? 'I've bitten off more than I can chew,' she moaned as she visualised the drawings for her practice piece – a World War II plane. She gazed up at the sky as she imagined it standing at the top of the totem pole, splendid like a bald headed eagle. Her thoughts were disturbed by a thumping rumble. It seemed to start from nowhere and then build up to a crescendo as the underside of an Apache helicopter came into view, flying low. Maybe she should be carving a helicopter? The neighbouring airbase was full of them. And as she let her mind drift on, she heard a branch crack as brambles and long grass rustled. The sound came from somewhere behind her back. She whipped around, scanning the vegetation near the rough entrance track. Her pulse raced.

'Oh my God!' she screamed as something broke from the hedge, crashed through the foliage and streaked across the track. 'What the…?' Her words evaporated as terror changed to wonder. She stood, rooted to the spot as a four legged creature with light brown fur bolted, as if for its life, from the Clegg boundary and across the open field. 'Was that a Roe deer?'

She'd passed one that very morning. It lay dead on the A 14 dual carriageway, poor creature. Deer had become a common sight at this time of the year – small groups with their heads down, grazing the farmers' crops. She supposed they were pests, and then a thought struck. Had someone really been aiming at squirrels near Bildeston on Friday afternoon? Could a bullet chosen to kill a deer kill a man, even on a Sunday?

# CHAPTER 5

Nick sat alone in the modern kitchen. He was already up and dressed, ready for work in a light stone-coloured tee-shirt and blue jeans. His parents were still away on their annual two week break in the Lake District and he had the house to himself. Barking Tye was usually quiet, but in another twenty minutes the first rumblings of early morning traffic would vibrate through the double glazed windows, and the wide lane transecting the village would turn into an artery feeding the Wattisham airbase, or in the opposite direction, the A 14. He rested his head in his hands. Matt had been right. Jim Mann was dead. He'd just heard it on the radio. Nick pushed the Jamie Oliver designed mug away, his tea half drunk, and sighed. He no longer had the appetite for it, in fact he felt sick. Breakfast was out of the question.

The shiny steel work surfaces reflected the colour of the kitchen wall tiles, a pale blue. Not cool, but cold. He felt sure if Jamie designed wall tiles, his mother would have chosen those instead and it might have looked better, warmer. And that decided him - he had to get out; out of the kitchen, the house, Barking Tye and to work. He needed to be with other people and then his stomach might stop churning.

It didn't take him long to drive the few miles to the Willows workshop. He found a parking spot on some rough ground to one side of the bay reserved for customers, and still deep in thought, locked his old Ford Fiesta. A large prefabricated structure stood at the front of the site. It was the new workshop complex. Nick walked to the side entrance.

'Morning, Nick. You're looking very thoughtful. You OK?' A voice greeted him as he stepped through the doorway.

Nick looked across the carpenters' restroom-cum-office, with its tired furniture and worn chairs. The unexpected question startled him from his thoughts. 'Yes, yes… good morning.'

Alfred Walsh, the elderly foreman held Nick's glance for a moment before gazing back at a worksheet on the desk. 'Now where're you meant to be today, lad? Let me see.' He ran his thumb down the paper and frowned. 'You were with Henry, weren't you? 'Fraid he's off sick all week.'

'Yes, I wanted to talk to you about that, Mr Walsh. You see–'

'What? About Henry?' His voice was sharp.

'No, no, Mr Walsh. It's… it's Jim Mann. I've just heard it on the news. He's been found dead.' Nick let his eyes wander across the ubiquitous brown carpet tiles.

'Ah yes… sorry, lad. I should've thought. The boss told us yesterday. He's known the family most of his life.' Alfred shook his head and frowned. 'Dreadful business… of course you weren't here yesterday. Away at that training day of yours, otherwise you'd 've heard.'

Nick hid his frustration. Old Walsh never seemed to miss an opportunity to take a dig at the apprentice release day teaching. It was a generation thing.

'But what happens now? Is the beehive project still on?' As soon as the words were out, Nick realised he sounded trivial and self-centred. He hadn't said what was really on his mind – the bit about the air rifle pellet and being shot at. Somehow Mr Walsh didn't invite chatter or intimacies and certainly not first thing in the morning.

'Ah well, that's a bit tricky, Nick. We'll have to leave it at least a week before phoning his wife – out of respect. Can't go being insensitive.' He turned his attention back to the worksheet before adding, 'She's having a lot of alterations done. She's his second wife and they haven't been married long. We don't want to upset her and miss out on any contracts now, do we?'

Nick slumped onto a dark-brown plastic stacker-chair placed neatly against the wall. He stretched out his long untidy legs and hunched forwards, crossing his arms and hugging his stomach. He'd thought being with people would help, but Alfred Walsh wasn't helping at all.

'I think, yes, I think this'd be good for you.' The foreman looked up and smiled. 'Dave could do with some help. He's working on a job over at Hadleigh. If you go with Dave, then… yes that would be OK. You're with Dave for the rest of the week.' Mr Walsh nodded and scribbled something on the paper.

Nick smiled. He'd worked with Dave before.

'What you waiting for, lad? Better get moving or you'll miss him.'

'Yes, Mr Walsh.'

Outside, the weak morning sun warmed the air and Nick's spirits rose as he walked to the yard behind the workshop. He was looking for Dave, a tubby middle aged carpenter with aspirations to be a rally driver. He was a good teacher and an enthusiastic talker. It was just a shame about his driving. Nick found him where he'd expected, fussing around one of the Willows vans. Old Mr Willows liked the carpenters to drive the firm's vans, so in the morning they left their own cars at the workshop site, spoke to the foreman and collected a van, tools and supplies. It usually worked well.

'The boss is going to organise a proper lock-up area for these vans. It'll stop anymore diesel being stolen,' Dave said as he spotted Nick.

The sunlight made streaks across the yard and Nick idly read the writing suddenly bright on the side of the van. The letters were in swirling green italic and the double L in *Willows* looked like a D. 'Now that would be insensitive, us driving over to Mrs Mann with *Widows* written on the side of the van,' Nick murmured.

'Don't just stand gawping, Nick. Make yourself useful. Load up some of this wood,' Dave shouted.

'Sure. The foreman's put me with you for the rest of the week, that's if I survive the journey.'

'What's that you said?'

'I said if I arrive early.'

'Arrive early? He wants us to arrive early? Why didn't you say that in the first place? Come on, let's get going then.'

It was as if Nick had fired a starting pistol. Dave leapt into action, glad for any excuse to jump into the van and rev the engine. Nick slammed the rear doors shut and ran to the passenger side, his gripey stomach forgotten. He was lucky to get both feet inside before Dave let the clutch out with a jolt. No chance to sit, Nick crouched and faced sideways. The van shot backwards in reverse, swaying him into the windscreen. His left ear smashed against the rear-view mirror.

'Argh!' Pain, twice as sharp as the hornet's sting burned and fizzled on the side of his head.

He struggled to maintain his balance as Dave braked. Now the van moved forwards. Nick plunged towards Dave and grabbed at the only thing in his path – the steering wheel.

'Oi! What you doing, Nick?' Dave glared at the extra hand clinging to his steering wheel. He slammed on the brakes and the van lurched to a halt. 'What's got into you, Nick?'

'I-I–'

'Don't go grabbing the steering wheel. And I can adjust my own rear-view mirror, thanks. It's pointing at the roof now.' Dave stared at Nick. 'That ear of yours don't look too good. I thought I'd told you to go and get it seen to.' Dave let the van move forward slowly, and as the tyres scrunched over gravel, his excitement seemed to deflate. 'Just stop messing about, Nick and get your seat belt on. You'll have to sharpen up if you're with me the rest of the week.'

Nick crumpled into the passenger seat.

'What's the matter, lad? You were over at Jim Mann's on Friday, weren't you? Expect you know by now.'

Nick shook his head. 'I can't believe it. I was talking to him only three days ago.'

Dave turned out of the Willows yard and the quiet sound of the engine was strangely soothing. At last Nick felt he could talk about what was on his mind. Slowly, he recounted his Friday afternoon in Bildeston: the heat, the protective overalls, the beehive design, and the air rifle pellet.

'You're sure it was an air rifle pellet, Nick? I think you should go to the police. It could be important.'

Nick sat in silence. Dave had said what Nick already knew. He had to go to the police, but it helped to hear it confirmed by someone else. He gazed out of the window as they crossed the gently undulating countryside on quiet B roads 'Where are we going in Hadleigh?' Nick finally asked as they turned off the bypass.

'Gallows Hill.'

'Oh?'

'A warehouse on Gallows Hill. The client's a Mr Rake. That's Richard Rake. He's branching out into the storage business. You may have heard of him. He runs a removal firm.'

'Rakes Removals has a catchy ring.'

'No, he calls it Fens Removals.'

'And now a storage facility as well? Logical progression, I guess.'

'Yeah, he's quite a businessman round these parts. Mind you, the family's loaded.' Dave changed into a lower gear as they shot down Gallows Hill. 'His older brother Davie owns the farm where you said you got some diesel. Yup, the two Rakes! Ricky and Davie. Big round these parts. Are you sure you haven't heard of them?'

'No, I don't think so.' Nick looked ahead. They'd reached the cricket ground. 'So where's this warehouse meant to be?'

'Damn, I've missed the turning. It's back up the hill, virtually on the bypass.' Dave braked and with some grunting and muttering, turned the van around.

Five minutes later they drove into the entrance of what looked more like a bomb site than the forecourt of a business. There was a huge hole in the ground and beyond, a concreted area. Off to one side the main construction had been completed and consisted of a metal framed outbuilding of hangar proportions, and alongside, a single storey brick building. Nick guessed the more modest sized brick structure was for offices. But the warehouse? 'Is he planning on storing Concord here?' Nick asked as he jumped down from the van. 'And the hole in the ground? What's that for d'you think?'

'Maybe he's planning to keep his removal vans and lorries here, and he's installing tanks so he can fuel them himself.'

They both watched as a black Porsche approached, picking its way between the ruts and potholes. 'Low clearance on those Porsches,' Dave remarked.

'Ah! Maybe a *Widows* van can outstrip a Porsche… off-road.'

'Don't bet on it, lad.'

The Porsche drew up next to the van and Nick had an immediate feeling of déjà vu as the driver got out.

'Good morning, Mr Rake,' Dave said and then smiled.

The man had red hair, but it was unusually long for his age. A light breeze caught it from behind and he raised his hand to stop it blowing forwards into his face. His hand cast a shadow across his features, but Nick could still make out the freckles staining his sharp nose. He had a languid manner, and he stood for a moment, watching Dave and Nick before speaking. If he'd blown cigarette smoke, Nick wouldn't have been surprised. He looked the image of Dan, twenty years older maybe, but there was no mistaking the resemblance. 'Good morning,' he said, drawing out the words as if he had all the time in the world. 'You're from Willows, I presume?'

Nick left the talking to Dave as he followed Mr Rake into the brick building. They entered a complex of offices behind a modest doorway, their footsteps echoing as they walked over bare concrete floors. Mr Rake led the way, speaking to the air ahead as he pointed out various features, finally halting when they reached a much larger room well away from the front of the building. He switched on the lights. Nick gazed at the blank canvas of plastered walls. The electricians had already run the cables and fitted the sockets. It was a windowless room; there would be no natural light. Now why would that be, he wondered as he glanced over Dave's shoulder to look at the plans. The room they were standing in was definitely called *office* on the drawings. So why did Richard Rake want bespoke wooden fittings for what was, after all, just the administrative centre of a storage and removals firm? Nick shook his head. Perhaps he wasn't your average businessman after all.

Dave confirmed the heights and dimensions of the fittings and then Mr Rake left them to meticulously measure up.

'These units are going to come quite high against this wall, and out to here,' Nick remarked as he scribbled down the measurements in a notebook. It was a much larger area than one would usually allow for four-drawer filing cabinets. Nick noticed a bank of plug sockets close by on the wall. 'What's going here? Wine cooler… or a safe, d'you reckon?' He looked upwards at a shaft in the ceiling, maybe twenty by thirty cm in size. 'Air vent?'

'Hmm, don't know. These plans are only wall and floor. The ceiling isn't on here. Just remember what they say, Nick. Measure, measure and then measure again.'

'And it'll probably still be wrong.'

'Now you're really starting to sound like a carpenter,' Dave said, laughing as he put the tape measure back in his pocket and studied the plans again. 'No, we've got to put some wooden fixings on that wall there.' He pointed to where Nick stood. 'I guess it could be for a bank of wall mounted monitors or something like that.'

'What did you say this building was for?'

'Offices.'

It took well over an hour. Dave measured, calling out the lengths and Nick wrote them down. And then they checked some of them again.

'Come on, we're just about done here now,' Dave said as he scratched his thinning hair and looked up into the ceiling vent.

They retraced their steps back to the entrance and out into the bright late morning sun. Nick was surprised to see the black Porsche still parked near their van. Mr Rake stood with his back to them, leaning against the side of the car and speaking into his phone. He'd pulled his shirt sleeves back and Nick caught a glimpse of a fine crepe bandage covering his right lower arm and secured with pink Elastoplast. Mr Rake turned his head slightly when their boots scrunched on some rough gravel. He straightened quickly and faced them as they approached. Frowning, he snapped his phone shut and rolled his shirt sleeve down, covering the bandage. 'Got all your measurements now?'

'Yes, we're all sorted.'

'Good. I'll expect to hear from you next week then, Dave and… Nick?'

They nodded, smiled and opened the van doors to climb in. 'This place gives me the creeps,' Dave confided.

'Why's that?'

‘One of my distant relatives was hanged up here.’

‘What, really?’

‘Well, it was seventeen-something-or-other. John Biggs was hanged on Gallows Hill. Ever heard of the Hadleigh Gang?’

‘The Hadleigh Gang? John Biggs? I thought Ricky and Davie Rake sounded bad enough. You know, like Reggie and Ronnie Kray… but you’re kidding me, right?’ Nick was surprised to see Dave laugh.

‘No, Nick. Back in those days it was a career choice – smuggling or farming.’

Nick shook his head. ‘But your name isn’t Biggs. You’re not Dave Biggs. You’re a Townsend, right?’

‘Yeah, but my grandma was a Biggs.’

Nick thought for a moment. ‘So, is Ronnie Biggs a relative? The great train robber?’

‘You cheeky bugger! I’m not related to every criminal with the name Biggs.’ They both laughed as Dave started the van. ‘I think smuggling and contraband was in the blood round here. Everyone was at it. Probably still are, for all I know.’

‘Were a lot of people hanged?’

‘No, not many, at least not for smuggling. John Biggs was a smuggler but he shot someone. A customs officer or a soldier. It was damned poor judgement to kill a customs officer.’

Nick watched Dave as he steered the van around the potholes and deep ruts on the building site. It was hard to believe it would soon be a forecourt. For a moment he imagined Dave as one of the get-away waggon drivers of the past, with reins instead of a wheel and a whip instead of an accelerator. But Dave’s words set Nick thinking. Was everyone still at it – evading the tax man? What was the modern equivalent to tea and brandy from the continent, he wondered. And then another thought struck him. 'Do all the Rakes have red hair, Dave?' he asked.

'Now how would I know? Come on, time to head back to Willows. We've got a lot of work to be getting on with, making those carcasses off site.'

Nick checked his watch 'Is it OK if I phone the police about that air pellet when we get back?'

'Good lad. Have I ever told you about…?'

Nick stopped listening. He closed his eyes but the image of that large hole in the ground floated in his mind.

# CHAPTER 6

Matt stood at the library window and gazed into the Academy gardens below. He didn't know the names of most of the flowers. The roses in beds near the old kitchen-garden wall were easy to recognise along with the ox-blood clematis blooms, but some of the pinks, whites and blues in the far bed? What were they? It struck him that vegetables were more to his taste. What about runner beans to pluck and chew straight from the frame, and potatoes preferably chopped and deep fried? You could always rely on a potato.

His first floor vantage point gave him a sniper's view as he watched the Summer School take its coffee break. The weather had been glorious, and the blokes in the group gravitated towards the sunny patches of grass to pose like lizards in warm rays. He resented those guys. They were lucky bastards to be on the course. He turned his attention back to the birds. They clumped together in twos and threes, chattered, laughed and then moved into another kaleidoscopic pattern as if directed by some unseen hand. He stepped back from the pane of glass, not wanting to appear too obvious. Ginny glanced up and pointed at something high above the library. If she'd noticed him, she didn't let on. Matt felt disappointed.

The playwriting only ran for six days and he'd made sure he'd been there each day so far. But the week was slipping away and Matt knew if he didn't make his move soon, it would be too late. Ginny, the drama student in the floral cotton skirt and maroon framed glasses had caught, if not his heart, certainly his imagination and he was determined to meet her again. If that meant sitting in the library pretending to write a play on… what had he said to her? Yes, that was it, Green Diesel, then so-be-it. Unfortunately she hadn't come into the library again, not since that first day, so he reckoned the lunch break was his best opportunity. He hoped to casually bump into the twins and drop a sheet of his play-in-the-writing material. Ginny would have to notice him and say something.

Matt had planned his approach with care. He didn't know exactly what the right chat-up line should be when he saw Ginny, but he realised he had to wear the right tee-shirt - something to attract her attention and further reflect the creative playwright struggling to escape from within. He looked down at the yellow cotton clinging to his torso. He liked its snug fit, but more importantly, it was topical. The words SNOW PATROL, a favourite band, were printed in black across the upper arm to give an official, almost military feel. Unfortunately the launderette had wreaked its magic on the design. Not only had the fabric shrunk with the first wash, but a pair of black jeans had found their way into the load, spewing out dye and blotching the yellow. The A in patrol now read as an E and the S had been lost forever. The name of the alternative rock group had transformed into PETROL, or more accurately NOW PETROL, and *A Hundred Million Suns 2008* was only just legible across his chest against the yellow background with black blotches. The whole effect was reminiscent of an impressionist wasp. Matt smiled. He hoped it would prove a winner in the Ginny stakes, but if he was going to carry this off then he'd better get on with his scheme.

He had to look the part. There was no point in dropping a page printed from the internet. It would be so much more effective if it was something hand-written and almost illegible - the inky words wrung from a tortured eco-warrior. Yes, he liked that idea. He smoothed down his waspish tee-shirt with *A Hundred Million Suns 2008* printed across the front, reached for a stray sheet of A4 lying on a table, pulled a biro from his pocket and drew a chair back from the computer station desk, squeaking its legs on the old wooden floorboards. He slumped down. Everything in the library seemed to absorb the natural light and despite the summer sun, it felt dark and gloomy. Behind, he sensed the heavily stacked bookshelves with their weight of books; he smelled the dust. In front the bright computer screen beckoned and beyond that, the view through the window was laced with possibility. Rosie appeared to be working on a digital catalogue and so for the next hour or more, it would be just Matt and diesel with nothing to distract from his mission.

He started to write; he didn't like writing. Better keep it simple, he thought. His internet search the day before had told him diesel was easier to refine from crude oil than petrol. It was also more efficient in terms of power released per litre. He wrote, *Diesel - cheap and efficient*. It was hardly a play, but it was a beginning. Matt frowned. Diesel wasn't cheaper than petrol, least ways not the stuff sold for cars on the Stowmarket petrol station forecourt. 'Hmm….' He chewed the end of his biro and crossed out the word *cheap* before writing, *Red Diesel* in the margin and then continuing, *is white diesel but with coloured dye, or is it*? He lined up the words *Green Diesel* beneath *Red Diesel* and sat back to inspect the effect. He scribbled, *mixed with vegetable oils to give it 'green' credentials but vegetable oil may have slight water content. Water*, he lined the word up – *bad, may separate out and sink to bottom of tank. Bugs may grow in the water and block the filters*. Yes, he thought, it could pass for a script with dialogue.

For the next hour and a half, Matt bit on his biro, scratched his short, dark-sandy hair and wrestled with his self-imposed task. He had no problem spewing out facts but when it came to making things up and using his imagination, there was just a blank. What had Mrs Critchlow, his primary school teacher said? Yes, that was it, he was a parrot repeating what he'd read, not what he'd heard. He supposed they'd call it a photographic memory now, but back then the eight year old Matt thought she meant he was a noisy bird with bright feathers and a poly-beak for a nose. He had no idea she was referring to his memory skills. And that had been the problem all through his school-days; no one communicated with him in a way he could understand. He'd have stuck out his A levels if he'd been allowed to work in his own way. Chemistry, with its symbols and compounds denoting logical predictable reactions was easy for him, but he was clumsy and school didn't like the spillages. He was considered a health and safety hazard. In the end it just didn't work out and with a distinct lack of support from home, disapproval killed his curiosity. He lost confidence and interest. The rest was history.

The sound of voices and laughter drifted through the window. Matt checked his mobile. 12:45. It was time to drag his mind back to the present and make his move. With a flutter of excitement, he clicked his computer off and grabbed the sheet of A4. Outside, the Summer School students were already gathering in the garden and he didn't want to miss a moment.

He hurried down the main staircase and along the ground floor corridor. It had once been the elegant entrance hall of the original mansion building, designed to impress the visitor with its pale marble flooring and feeling of space. Nowadays it stretched on, elongated and extended by more recent additions. Matt kept his eyes focused on the ground as the cool marble gave way to wooden floorboards and then grey heavy-duty carpet. His mind buzzed, spurring him on as he headed for a side door. Soon he would be out into the sun. A passageway between out-buildings would take him past the delivery area at the back of the sprawl. From there he planned to approach the lawns from the far end of the old kitchen-garden wall. He'd have plenty of time to search out Ginny and then amble towards her, as if chance had placed him there.

He walked past two green tanks near the delivery area and in a flash of clarity, realised what they were for. How could he look at something, maybe a hundred times and never see properly? Was it a trick of the mind or the eye? Of course, those green structures were storage tanks for the Academy's heating fuel. You didn't see fuel tanks on the Flower Estate. They'd be a target for thieves and arson. All the houses there used mains electricity or piped natural-gas for heating. Here, those huge green containers were tucked out of sight, and safe. Or were they? Matt shook his head and breathed out with a low whistle. His internet searches had told him one thing. Heating oil was fair game if you were a thief and intent on stretching the definition of recycling. There would be thousands of litres stored in there. But was it even heating oil? Someone might have filled it with red diesel instead. Throw in some cooking oil for lubrication and it'd probably work OK. His reading had told him heating oil carried 5% VAT; red diesel carried none. You could sell or pass off the red to the punters as if it were heating oil, keep the VAT and make a tidy profit. Illegal of course.

He stepped round the garden wall and scanned the lawns, searching for the twins. He spotted them, standing near the rose beds. Lil had her back to him but Ginny faced into the sun. He waved.

'Hi,' he called, and waved again. He hoped he looked like a young Mel Gibson in Mad Max 2, stepping out of the Australian sun. The twins didn't seem to notice, so he hurried forward, eyes fixed on Ginny, willing her to look at him and smile.

'Woa!' he yelled as one foot slipped off the grassy boarder. 'Argh….' His ankle twisted into a flowerbed. 'Shit!' he yelped and landed on his knees. He flung his arms in the air. The sheet of A4 floated into the roses. He was six yards short of the twins.

'Are you OK?' Lil asked as she turned to stare.

'I know you, don't I?' Ginny moved towards him, frowning, serious. 'You were in the library.'

Matt flushed as he nursed his plaster cast. His wrist was fine, but he didn't fancy struggling into the roses to retrieve his play. He needed Ginny and Lil to see it and be impressed.

'Wait, don't get up. I'll get it for you.'

Matt watched as Ginny hitched up her floral cotton skirt and stepped amongst the roses. From his vantage point low on the grass, he caught a flash of bare thigh before the summery fabric swished down and covered her leg. He dropped his gaze to her ankles. The bed had been roughly weeded and broken flint pebbles winked in the sun on the clay-rich topsoil. Her fine leather sandals sank in the earth. He didn't need encouragement to stay where he was and rested back on his heels. 'Thanks, Ginny.' This was working out better than he'd hoped.

'How do you know my name?' she asked as she stretched to reach into a rosebush. Tangerine petals showered down on her arm as she disturbed a wilting bloom.

'You… your name badge in the library.' He was nervous and the Suffolk in him altered his vowels and sharpened the word *you* so that it sounded *yew* with a W.

'Hey look!' She smiled and turned to her sister. 'It's a script, the words for a play.' She backed out of the rosebush grasping the crumpled sheet, her cherry-coloured nail varnish glowing in the sun. 'I'll be Red Diesel; you can be Green Diesel, Lil.'

'No, let me have a look. Let me choose,' Lil said, and plucked the paper from her sister's hand.

'What did you say your name was? You can be Green.'

Matt closed his eyes. This was meant to look like a play, not to be one. Hell! What was he going to do? 'I'm Matt,' he said, opening his eyes and trying the slight smile he'd practised in the mirror.

'Bloody funny names,' Lil muttered as she scrutinized the script. 'DERV, Heating Oil, Red & Green Diesel – oh and Petrol!'

'I don't know. It sounds quite original to me.' Ginny smiled at her sister before sitting on the grass next to Matt. She flicked her dark curly hair back from her forehead, looked up at Lil and then slowly turned her gaze on him. 'Tell me about them,' she commanded, drawing out her words.

Matt's throat went dry. 'Well, they're all derived from crude oil an' they got different numbers of carbon atoms in 'em.'

Lil and Ginny stared at him.

'See, they're like brothers an' sisters – different heights but still similar. They got different length carbon chains for backbones.' Matt paused. He felt nervous. 'See, heatin' oil's got a longer carbon chain than diesel, an' petrol's kinda got less. It's shorter.'

'So? Hey, Ginny, he was that carpentry guy in the library. He isn't a chemist.'

'No, but I like hearing him talk chemicals.'

'Watch out, Matt. She'll have you talking Italian in a moment. She's a great fan of that *A Fish Called Wanda* film. She thinks she's Jamie Lee Curtis.' Lil's tone harshened, 'It's time to go, Ginny.'

Matt willed Ginny not to get up. Her cheeks and neck flushed red as she shifted her position to look at him straight on. She'd somehow managed to block Lil out with her shoulder. 'Like your tee-shirt,' she said and smiled. 'So come on, Matt, what's the difference between red and white diesel?'

'See, they're like you two. Twins. Identical underneath.'

Lil snorted.

'No, honest. They're the spittin' image of each other. A bit like you two but one's 'ad some dye an' more sulphur added.'

Lil laughed. A harsh, barking sound. 'God, that's boring.'

'Ignore my sister, Matt. She's… well tell me, how do you change red diesel back to white? You could sell it on, couldn't you? Make loads of cash. That's what your play should be about.' Ginny smiled and waited for him to answer while Lil stared at the roses.

'Kitty litter. You could filter it through kitty litter… well it's really Fullers Earth. A bit like oil-dry granules for spillages.'

Ginny giggled. 'Not very chemical, Matt. Try harder.'

'Well, if you're sure. See the red dye's an azo dye. It's derived from aromatic amines. If you add a strong acid, say hydrochloric acid, them tertiary amines form solid ionic compounds an' out it comes. That's a different way to kitty litter.'

'Amines, azo dyes and hydrochloric acid… hmm.' Ginny rolled her eyes, looked heavenward and smiled at the sky.

'Don't take any notice, Matt.' Lil almost spat the words. 'She's playing the part in that film. Come on Ginny!'

'No, no. I aint pullickin'.'

'What's that you said?' Lil frowned at Matt as she handed the scrunched paper back, her dark eyebrows a continual line across her forehead.

'No, I aint complainin', you don't 'ave to leave. Please don't, least not coz of me.' Matt wished he hadn't broken into pure Suffolk. Perhaps saying pullicking was a mistake but his nerves were taut. He felt silly. He was still kneeling on the grass.

Ginny slowly got to her feet and glanced down at him. 'Well, *A Hundred Million Suns 2008*, as my sister says, it's time to leave.'

'No, please don't….'

'See you around in September, Chemistry Dude. Just keep the names tripping off your tongue,' and then she was gone.

'Quaternary ammonia salt,' Matt called after her, but it was too late, she was out of range. He watched as she walked with her sister, the cotton skirt swinging as she moved. Roll on, September, he thought. And then he remembered his plaster cast would be off and he'd be starting at Hepplewhites. Azo hell!

Matt didn't bother to retrace his footsteps. It was quicker and more direct to head past the flowerbeds with the dolly mixture blooms and back into the main corridor. From there he'd nip up to the library. What had she called him? Chemistry Dude! He liked that. All in all, it had gone rather well. He'd need to watch *A Fish Called Wanda*, though.

Back in the library, Matt logged onto Google. Ginny had been occupying his mind for most of the week, along with diesel and heating fuels, but she'd just said, 'See you in September,' so he supposed that's what he'd do – wait until September. He checked his mobile. 14:08. Rosie would be closing the library in an hour and a half. Summer School hours ruled in August and if he didn't get a move on he'd be out of time. Chrissie had asked him to find where Alderman's Point was, the proposed site for a phone mast and the subject of Jim Mann's angry letter. She had some idea it might hold important memories or significance for him. He didn't know why she thought it but sometimes Chrissie got these strange obsessions. He couldn't put off the search any longer. He was supposed to meet Chrissie and Nick in the Nags Head, his local pub, that evening, but Ginny had proved rather a distraction. Even now, he'd chosen the computer station with a view of the gardens instead of his customary one in the corner, well hidden and with restricted outlook.

Matt dragged his mind back to the task in hand and concentrated on the Google map site; but there wasn't anything for Alderman's Point. He keyed in Bildeston. The pale greens and amber-browns drew him to the screen. He zoomed in like a fighter pilot and clicked on the photo option. Pow! The image was blurry; too magnified on his screen to focus. He zoomed out, and like a swooping bird he rose to the heavens and everything was too small. There didn't seem to be an Alderman's Point marked on the map. Perhaps it was just a local name and not official, least ways, not Ordnance Survey recognised. He rubbed at the grubby plaster cast on his left wrist and keyed in the Eastern Anglia Daily Tribune site and the Academy's membership number. The newspaper's search didn't take long to find some articles about the phone mast. There were no maps but he found a description of a track leading beyond a small copse, and a *panoramic view* from the *Point* - north-east, looking across to the church on the hill west of Bildeston. He hoped the Point referred to Alderman's Point. He clicked on his Google map and looked again. Yeah, he thought, I've got it!

He rubbed at his plaster cast, but no amount of scratching on the outside could relieve the persistent itch on the inside. It was as if he'd plucked a hairy caterpillar from a juicy leaf and it was crawling over his skin. He tried to distract himself by looking at the day's local news headlines on the site: *Police announce clampdown on red diesel motorists*.

Matt read on as the caterpillar inched its way up his arm. *Police spot-checks last month found an increase in the number of motorists with illegal red diesel in their fuel tanks.* 'Yeah, well that'd follow,' he sighed, 'it's a bloody sight cheaper than DERV.' *The fire that destroyed storage tanks near Rougham last week....* Hadn't Nick and Chrissie passed that on the A14? He skimmed on. *Fire investigators suspect the fire may have been started deliberately. Preliminary tests suggest the tanks contained red diesel.* Well, the motorists had to be buying their red diesel from somewhere, Matt reasoned. But arson? Was there an underworld out there with fuel barons, gangs and turf wars? Did they have names like: the Bitumen Boys; the Tar Twins or simply, Paraffin Pieheads, and all with more than twenty carbon atoms in their chains? He grinned.

'You look happy.'

Matt glanced up to see Rosie. She'd crept up on him. Her long auburn hair was held back into a careless knot; a clasp high on her head struggled to keep it there while wispy strands escaped. It seemed to Matt her neck went on forever, just like her legs. He smiled; the one using only half his mouth. 'Hi, Rosie.'

'Haven't you got anywhere else to go? You've been here most of the week.'

'So 've you.'

'Yes, but I'm the library assistant. What's your excuse?'

'I....' He rubbed at his plaster cast. The caterpillar was on the move again.

'Come on, I need to lock up.' She stood for a moment, her attention diverted to his tee-shirt. 'What's it say? NOW

PETROL, *A Hundred Million Suns 2008*?' She spoke under her breath as if her words weren't meant for him.

He watched her sigh, shake her head and walk back to the librarian's station. Matt didn't know what to think. Maybe she didn't like Snow Patrol. It was a bit of a strong reaction though. He checked his mobile. 15:30. It was time to leave.

# CHAPTER 7

Chrissie squinted at the screen. Her laptop sat in front of her on the small pine table in her kitchen, a mug of tea near her right hand and a shaft of late afternoon sun spotlighting her left, as it rested on a sheet of paper. She ran a finger along the address and read out the details. She'd written it down herself, but it still didn't seem to make sense. The man she'd spoken to on the phone had said Hadleigh, but as far as she could make out the car was in Kersey. 'But it has a Hadleigh post code,' she muttered, irritation threatening to take over. Maybe she should get a satnav. That's what Nick had said. But getting one would be like giving up and admitting she was hopeless at finding her way. She peered at the computer screen again and shook her head.

The Google map made it look so easy, but the balloon teardrop with its apex pointing to the spot like a bloated stinger, didn't seem to tally with the directions the man had given. She looked at her watch. Six o'clock. She had at least two hours before she needed to think about getting ready to meet with her friends in the Nags Head.

Chrissie shuffled the papers around and checked the printout from the TR7.co.uk website. The photos looked magnificent. Just wait till they see this, she thought as she read out the details: 'Make – *Triumph*; Model – *TR7 convertible*; Year – *1981*; Colour – *yellow*.' It was the last bit that really made her smile break out. She repeated, 'Yellow. Bright yellow. Vibrant, almost luminescent yellow. And yellow's good because I'll be able to knock down the price.' She knew British Racing Green could fetch at least £500 more. 'Tomorrow, you yellow peril, tomorrow,' she whispered. The only snag in her plan was actually finding the seller's address, but Nick had offered to come with her. It would be Saturday and they'd have until midday to find it. She clicked print on the screen showing the Google map, something whirred on a shelf above her head and a sheet of paper wafted down onto the table. 'Sorted!'

She sipped her tea as she gazed at the map. It should be so obvious and logical to find places, she thought, but somehow it wasn't. Take Alderman's Point; she'd typed the name in the search box but there'd been no results, nothing. It didn't seem to exist. That had been three days ago and in the end she'd phoned Matt. He liked a challenge, but he'd seemed distracted when she spoke to him and said something about writing a play. It must be that Summer School thing, she decided. Hopefully he'd have found the Point for her by the time they all met at the Nags Head. She checked her watch. And then she thought of Bill.

The little kernel of excitement died. Sadness replaced it and for the first time guilt tinged her emotion. She'd gone almost a whole day without thinking of him once. She closed her eyes as she pictured the scene over ten years ago. She could still see it as clear as day - a red MGB, polished and gleaming in the sun. While Bill had looked under the bonnet, checked the engine and the bodywork, she'd lost her heart to it. They'd gone for a test drive and the deal was done, the car was hers. How could she have ever guessed it would be taken from her? And now here she was but without Bill, contemplating buying another car, something that would fill a small space in her heart. For a whole day she'd forgotten the person who occupied the rest of it. Did the fact it was a TR7 this time and not another MGB weaken her link to the past? Was it what she wanted?

Chrissie opened her eyes and blinked away the moisture threatening to film across her view. She could almost hear Bill's voice. 'Come on Chrissie, you need a new car. Be bold; life's for living!' She shook her head. Was she just imagining what she wanted him to say?

'Activity; come on, keep yourself busy,' she muttered and reached to the shelf above her head for a sheet of A4. It was time to marshal her thoughts into a list. *Check documents*, she wrote and then listed: *logbook, service history and previous MOT certificates. Check Vehicle Identification Number: it should be visible somewhere at base of windscreen, under bonnet and stamped into chassis*. And then she added: *look for rust, mileage, and mismatched paint*. Her neat handwriting filled most of the page. It's unbelievable, she thought, all this just to buy a twenty-nine-year-old car. Even organising the car insurance wouldn't be entirely straightforward. She knew from her experience with her old MGB, she'd have to send photos before the company agreed an insurance value.

She tipped the tea dregs from her mug into the old-styled white porcelain sink. At least she didn't have to worry about Nick and the gunshot any more. The conversation played in her head, his tone calm and reassuring as she remembered it.

'I spoke to someone on the phone, gave my name and contact details. They said an officer connected with the case would get back to me,' he'd told her.

'And have they?'

'Yeah, a few hours ago. Someone rang and I told them what had happened. I agreed to go to the police station on Monday and give a statement; four o'clock, Raingate.'

The conversation had been two days ago and Monday was a weekend away. The police should have had a chance to check out the beehive and corroborate his story by then.

'I wonder if he spoke to Clive Merry,' she sighed and felt guilty again.

By 8:15 she'd showered and changed into a clean pair of summer weight jeans and a fresh tee-shirt. She grabbed her natural-look undyed loose linen jacket from where it hung on the back of her chair, bundled the Google map printout and address into her handbag and cast around for her keys. They were still on the narrow hall table where she'd flung them when she'd arrived home. They'd slid across the polished surface and lay against the heavy pewter photo frame. The one holding Bill's smiling face. She paused as she picked up the keys and caught a fleeting glance of her reflection in the mirror on the far wall. Was she over dressed for the Nags Head, she wondered as she smoothed back her short blonde hair.

Chrissie made good time, the roads were quiet and within fifteen minutes she was manoeuvring the Peugeot into the unusually busy Nags Head car park. She was lucky to find a space. Her windows were down and the sound of noisy chatter and a discordant rock ballad carried on the warm humid air. For a moment she wondered where all the noise was coming from. She pressed the automatic closing switch and the glass slid up and the sound of drinkers and music faded. It was only when she got out of the car that she noticed the blue and white striped awning of a marquee.

'Oh wow, the beer festival!' A blackboard was propped against the front wall of the pub and someone had written in white chalk: *15 cask beers + selection of local ciders.* A roughly drawn arrow pointed towards the marquee along with the words *BEER TENT*, and then almost as an afterthought, *Live Music.*

Oh dear, she thought, as she edged her way through the old front door and into the crowded bar. She clutched her handbag close, looked across the low-beamed room and jostled into the wall of sound.

'Chrissie, over here!'

Somehow she heard her name and looked towards the familiar voice. 'Hi! It's a mad house!' she shouted back.

Nick replied with a grin. He was taller than the average drinker and it was easy to spot his flushed face amongst the chaos. He waved, beckoning to a small table in the snug bar and sat down.

Chrissie brought her sharp elbows into play and winged her way through the throng. 'I didn't think I was going to make it across the bar. How d'you get a drink round here? There's hardly room to lift a glass to your mouth.'

Matt sat with his legs outstretched, seemingly oblivious to the crush. He smiled and shifted along the pine bench to make room for her. 'Hi.' He gulped at a pint of straw coloured liquid.

'What are you drinking?' she asked.

'Golden Newt.' Matt set the glass down and passed the back of his hand across his mouth.

'And?'

'Yeah, it's OK. Kind of hoppy an' fruity.'

Chrissie pulled a face. 'And yours, Nick?'

'Wild Mule.' He held the glass up for inspection. 'Bitter and fruity, and 3.9%.'

'So, still some kind of kick to it, then?'

He grinned. 'If you want to try one of the cask beers it's probably easier to get served in the marquee. There's a refundable glass deposit.'

'Oh great!'

Nick upended his glass and drained the Wild Mule in a final gulp. 'I'll go and get some refills. What'll you have, Matt? Chrissie?'

Matt handed over his empty glass. 'Something more like Carlsberg, mate.'

'And I'd like something light and hoppy. Just a half, I'm driving.' Chrissie turned her attention back to Matt. 'So, what've you been doing all week?' She watched as he frowned, pulling his dark-sandy eyebrows together. 'Go on, you said something about a play when I rang,' she prompted.

'Yeah, well I reckoned it might impress Ginny.'

'The girl at the Playwriting Summer School?'

'Yeah. Not easy, this playwritin'. I listed some facts so it looked like dialogue. I think she were impressed. Said she'd see me in September.'

Chrissie laughed. 'I'd say that's a result. What's the play meant to be about?'

'Diesel. It's interestin'. Take that fire you passed comin' back from Bury. Bet there's somethin' shady 'bout it. They've likely been sellin' red diesel to motorists. There's gangs out there. It's big business.'

Chrissie looked up as Nick struggled back into the snug bar. Drinkers stepped away to avoid beer slopping from his brimming glasses. The scent of sweat, hops and malty bitter pervaded the air. The old wooden floorboards were damp and sticky.

'Didn't spill too much,' Nick said as he thumped three glasses onto their table. 'I'll tell you what though. They've got a bloody useless singer in there. Matt, yours is a Golden Bolt and Chrissie, it was either the American Blonde with 5.5% or Bombshell with under 4%. I got you the Bombshell.'

'Thanks, Nick. And you?'

'The Dog Father. It's malty.' Nick sat down before reaching for his pint. Straw coloured beer dripped from his glass. 'Hmm,' he murmured between sips. 'Tastes good. Jumping Jack Flash, my arse - that chap's no Mick Jagger!'

'Matt was talking about red diesel and the fire we passed near Blackthorpe.'

'Oh yeah? I heard the police 've been stopping cars and checking the tanks for red diesel. Let's hope that Willows van doesn't get stopped.'

'But it was only a small amount and it'll have gone by now, surely, Nick?' Chrissie sipped her Bombshell, it had a kick to it and it was starting to lighten her mood.

'Yeah, kind of,' Matt grunted. 'You wouldn't see it naked-eye now, but the dye sticks around an' can show in the testin'. If you want to get rid of all traces, the internet suggests runnin' through with vegetable or biofuel an' changin' them filters.'

'Really?' She was impressed. 'You're not spending the weekend in the library as well, I hope.' Chrissie set her glass back on the table. It was covered in wet circles of beer, and like footprints, they'd left a trail of their sips and slurps as they progressed through the evening's drinking.

'Weekend? Thought I were comin' with you an' Nick. You know, to look at the car.'

'Of course, if you want.' Chrissie rummaged in her bag and pulled out the folded Google map along with a rather crumpled set of instructions. 'Here, what d'you think?' She handed it to Nick and passed the sheet with the TR7 details to Matt.

'Gross! What you thinkin', Chrissie? It's blindin' yellow. If you spin into one of them fields of flowerin' rape seed, it'll be weeks before anyone finds you. Hey, but the front bumper looks kinda sharp when them pop-up headlights are down.'

'Yeah, fit to split firewood,' Nick added.

'Now come on you two, it's a brilliant car. And it's a convertible.' She searched their faces, looking for signs of approval.

Nick muttered, 'Shovel nose and big bottom. It'll suit you. The shape was ahead of its time, Chrissie.'

Matt grinned.

'I'll take that as approval then.'

'Yeah, I'm comin' tomorrow, wouldn't miss it for anythin'.' Matt gulped his Golden Bolt.

'It looks straightforward to find,' Nick said reaching for his Dog Father. Chrissie caught the smile he hid behind the rim of his glass.

'Good. Well that's settled then. And talking of finding places, any luck, Matt with tracking down Alderman's Point?'

'Yeah.' He drove his hand into his jeans and produced a grubby, crushed sheet of A4. Chrissie opened it out and they huddled over the map. She focused on a smudge Matt had made with a biro; more of a loopy circle than an X marks the spot.

'It's on our route, tomorrow,' Nick said. 'Do you think it's important, Chrissie?'

'It might be. I've a feeling it meant more than a phone mast to Jim Mann. If it's a nice day and we're passing, why not take a look?'

'Great. Make a day of it. Your TR7 and then Alderman's Point.' As if to signal approval for the scheme, a tone beeped from somewhere in Nick's pocket. 'Now what?' He pulled out his mobile and read the text message.

'Everything OK?' Chrissie asked as she watched him frown.

'Just Mel. She won't leave me alone.'

'I thought you said she were history, mate.'

'She is. It was ages ago. Exeter - my first six weeks there.'

'Sounds deep, mate.'

'Not really, but she's....'

'Possessive? Needy? Controlling?' Chrissie sipped her Bombshell. Nick spoke about Mel sometimes, usually after a few pints. It was strange, but she'd noticed he never smiled or looked happy when he mentioned her. What had she done to him? Exeter was almost two years ago now and since then, as far as Chrissie could see, Mel only seemed to contact him when she sensed his attention was wandering or he was getting serious about a new girlfriend on the horizon. Fast and loose. That was the term tripping off her tongue. It summed Mel up perfectly. Fast and loose. 'What are going to do? Ignore the text?'

Nick shrugged. 'Last I'd heard she'd found someone else. I guess it's fallen through.'

'She's only doing it because you react. Stop reacting and she'll leave you alone.'

'Yeah, find another bird, mate.'

'Matt's right.'

'Yeah, Ginny's got a tasty sister if you're–'

'Shut it, Matt!'

It was time to change the subject. 'How are you going to get to Hepplewhites, Matt?' Chrissie asked. 'Can't be much longer before that plaster comes off.'

'Next week for the plaster. A couple of weeks an' then it's Hepplewhites. Hadn't thought... maybe bus... or train?'

'Why don't you get a scooter?'

Nick coughed on his Dog Father.

'I see you on a Vespa. A bit retro, to match your taste in tee-shirts.' Chrissie eyed the current tie-dyed yellow and black example hugging his torso. She struggled to keep her face straight.

'Isn't Vespa Italian for wasp?'

'Yes, Nick.' She couldn't hold back any longer. Her laugh exploded across the table.

# CHAPTER 8

Chrissie drove, Nick map read and Matt sat in the back humming a tuneless riff. The day had passed remarkably smoothly so far and Chrissie buzzed with excitement. They'd found the TR7 surprisingly easily. Within seconds she'd lost her heart, and as Matt said, maybe her head as well. While Nick listened to the engine, she ran her hand over the mohair hood and yellow bodywork. The test drive was a dream. There'd been no complaining from the manual 5-speed gearbox as she'd slipped through the gears effortlessly. The two litre engine purred – not overly powerful, but she wasn't a boy racer, she reminded herself. Matt had stood waiting for them, grinning when they returned fifteen minutes later. 'No oil spots. No fluid leaks,' he'd said, pointing to the concrete where the car had previously been parked. And then the deal was done. She paid a cash deposit, wrote a cheque and shook hands with the owner. Secretly, Chrissie didn't know how she was going to contain her impatience until after the weekend when the classic car insurance had been finalised and she could collect the car.

'Come on, this calls for a drink,' she'd said. 'Kersey has a pub and it looks OK to me.' She'd smiled and laughed as she linked arms with them both before steering them into the bar. Chrissie stuck to her usual ginger beer. Matt seemed desperate for Carlsberg after the previous evening of Golden Bolts and Newts, while Nick settled for whatever bitter was on tap. The happiness barometer read high. Forty minutes later and suitably refreshed, Chrissie checked her watch. Two o'clock.

'Alderman's Point? We've plenty of time. Is it still OK with you two?'

And so, while Chrissie drove, Nick studied the crumpled sheet with the Google map and Matt hummed. She was buoyed with the success of choosing her TR7, exhilarated and excited. She knew they'd find the Point. This day, of all days, was going to be a winning day for her, and as she turned east out of Bildeston she corralled her thoughts. That's when she recognised the tune. 'If you hum *Yellow Submarine* once more I'll kill you, Matt.'

Nick looked up from the map and grinned. 'That's right, up this hill. Follow the road for a bit and then we should see a track on the left.'

Chrissie glanced at her rear-view mirror and caught Matt's grinning face. 'I'll concentrate on the driving; you two keep your eyes skinned for the track.'

'Slow down, slow down! We're coming up to it... now!'

She lifted her foot off the accelerator as they cornered and then slowed to a crawl.

'Look there! The grass verge is all flattened. People have parked there before.'

'Hey, well spotted, Nick.' Easing the Peugeot forwards, she saw the marks left by cars pulling off the road, their tyre-treads printed in the dried mud. 'I don't see a track, though.'

'Let's park and have a look, anyway.'

Chrissie drove onto the rutted verge, the car rocking and bumping in complaint.

'Over there. One of them footpath signs, see? 'Spect you'll notice they're usin' *yellow* arrows for public footpaths.' Matt pointed to a dirt track. It wasn't obvious from the road - a little off-set.

Nick was out of the Peugeot first and holding the map, headed up the track. Chrissie hurried after him, making sure she kept his pale khaki tee-shirt in view as he began to blend with leafy bushes and trees ahead.

'What's the hurry?' Matt puffed behind. 'Slow down, can't you?'

Chrissie looked back. 'Come on, Matt. Think of it as pay-back for all those yellow jokes.'

Matt held up his plastered forearm. 'OK, no more yellow. Now slow down, will you, Chrissie.'

She waited for him to catch up. 'The car's golden-cream to you, not yellow. Got it?' She watched him nod. 'Come on, then.'

The track ahead was wide enough to take a small tractor. They walked, following the old grooves and troughs worn by heavy tyres, a central grassy strip separating them. A slight breeze lifted Chrissie's hair, working its way over her head like delicately massaging fingers. She found it strangely calming and happily slowed her pace to suit Matt. Ahead, she could see Nick already waiting, sitting on a wooden gate with oaks, birches and elder behind him.

'Looks like the track takes us through those trees,' she said. 'Who'd have guessed there's a wood up here?'

'Copse. That's what I read. If it were right it's only a copse.'

Nick jumped off the gate as they approached and opened it for them, waving his arm in an extravagant flourish.

Above, a pigeon disturbed by their presence, flapped noisily as it took off from a branch. Chrissie couldn't help but notice how the temperature dropped as they followed the track deeper into the trees. The gentle gusts no longer fluttered at her legs and the air stilled close to the ground. Twigs scrunched underfoot. Her mood started to match the dappled light. Clunk! She nearly jumped out of her skin. Leaves moved and rustled as Nick slammed the old gate shut.

'Look! We could've driven here.' Matt pointed at a shiny black four-by-four.

At first she could hardly make out the Lexus, its outline broken by patches of light playing over its luscious dark surface. Someone had driven it off the track. How strange, she thought. It's almost as if it's been hidden and instinctively she quickened her pace. Matt followed suit. A few more yards and then the trees thinned, the path rose gently, took a bend and they broke cover.

'Wow!' Chrissie stood and gazed ahead. They'd reached the plateau of a large flattish hill.

'About 85 metres above sea level according to the map,' Nick said behind her.

'It feels higher. You can see for miles. Look, across the valley – beyond Bildeston.' Chrissie stepped onto natural meadow. The ground had been left uncultivated and as she walked further through the rough grass she noticed a clump of little blue flowers with hairy leaves and a drop down stems. She stooped to take a closer look.

'What you seen, Chrissie?' Matt called from somewhere off to her right.

'Don't know,' and she picked a star-shaped blue flower and held it to her nose. The delicate petals touched her face and as she ran her tongue over her upper lip, she detected a sweetness, almost like honey. Something tingled in the back of her mind, but for the life of her she couldn't think what it was. She walked on, noticing more of the blue flowers. They were everywhere.

'You can see why they'd want to put a phone mast up here, can't you.' Nick stood with his back to her, gazing out across the valley.

Chrissie looked up from the meadow flowers and turned to admire the view. High above her a sky lark hovered, chirping its long complex song. She glanced around for Matt. Where was he, she wondered, and then she spotted him, still less than ten feet from the tree line. He seemed to be transfixed by something on the ground. Typical, she thought, all this way, a stunning view and all he can do is stare at the soil. She sighed and made her way slowly through the long grass back towards the trees. 'What's so fascinating, Matt?'

He didn't answer. He didn't seem to have heard.

'What've you seen?' she asked when she finally stood next to him. She'd reached a small area where the meadow melted away and underfoot, the earth lay bare. It looked dry and clumpy, but not like the earth-works left behind by a particularly industrious mole or burrowing rabbit. It looked dug over. 'Why are you…?'

Matt indicated more patches of recently disturbed earth and then walked closer to the tree line. This time he pointed with more urgency. Chrissie followed the direction of his finger. All she could see was a bank and ditch, the old fence on the copse boundary. Nothing very remarkable in that. 'What've you seen?'

'Look….'

'A rabbit hole?' She looked again, this time focusing on the entrance. Some furry creature must have tunnelled, flicking the soil behind as it worked into its burrow. And then she saw it. Glinting. 'My God!'

Three white curved roots joined an enamel crown – the sort used for chewing. It lay on the dirt as if surfing on the crest of an earthy wave. Half of Chrissie's brain saw the gold filling, and the other half didn't want to recognise it. Animals don't have gold fillings, she told herself. She started to bend to take a closer look, but Matt touched her shoulder and pointed to the ground near his feet. 'Now what…?' she started to ask.

Crack! A shot rang out. A crow cawed and Chrissie's heart missed a beat. Beside her, Matt dropped to his knees.

'Matt?' She braced herself, expecting to see blood spattering the ground. She felt rather than heard Nick's pounding feet as each footstep vibrated through the dry topsoil.

'Are you OK? Have you been shot?' Nick yelled as he ran across the meadow. He threw himself down next to Matt and gasped as he caught his breath.

'Yeah, I'm OK, mate. But watch out, you're kneeling on it.'

'I heard a shot. You went down! Didn't someone just shoot you?' Nick panted.

'No, you daft bugger. That'll be for crows, I reckon.' Matt looked at the ground again. 'Grut lummox, you're kneelin' on a tooth, Nick.'

'What?' Nick rocked back onto his heels. They all peered at the imprint left by his knee.

'A front tooth, d'you reckon?' Chrissie whispered.

Crack! Another shot rang out, and this time dirt flew up in the air a few yards to the left of Nick.

'Shit!'

'C'mon – run for the trees!'

Chrissie didn't remember thinking anything, just reacting. She saw leafy branches in front of her and ran. Nick and Matt followed.

# CHAPTER 9

Nick crouched in a leafy elder bush on the edge of the copse. Matt and Chrissie lay on the ground close by, sheltered below its branches. No one spoke. Nick tried to control his breathing and slow it down so he could listen better. He strained to pick up the tiniest sound, his ears almost hurting with the effort. It was as if his life depended on it. Half his brain was in reflex survival mode and the other half threw up questions at the rate of a spinning fly wheel. Had someone just tried to kill them? Was that person still out there? And why? He steadied himself and reached silently for his phone. No signal!

Alderman's Point stretched wide and exposed on one side. He knew the trees offered the only cover. It was a no-brainer. They'd have to work their way through the copse, then somehow run the gauntlet of the open track if they were to reach the Peugeot. The alternative was to stay hidden. But for how long?

Clunk! The sound bounced off the trees and reverberated in the air. It took a moment for Nick to work out the direction. It was from the far side of the copse. He caught Matt's look: eyes wide open, jaw clenched and deadly still. Chrissie lay motionless, eyes tight shut. Of course, the gate! Someone had opened the gate.

A soft rustle and then a deeper, heavier clunk! A car door, perhaps? An engine purred into life. Nick maintained his squatting position but steeled himself to move. He felt an overwhelming need to see what was happening. Matt must have sensed it because he shook his head, an unspoken plea to stay put. Nick dithered as tyres crackled over twigs on the leafy track. Curiosity tried to pull him to his feet while self-preservation froze him to the spot, and then it was too late. Silence.

Matt let out a long slow breath.

Nick summoned his courage. 'Stay where you are. I'll go and have a look.' His pulse raced as he stood up and still hidden by the large elder, he pushed aside its shrub-like branches and stepped between the nettles and brambles. Within seconds he was out into the dappled light filtering between the trees. Picking his way through the sparse undergrowth, he concentrated on stealth rather than directness. The movement helped to steady his nerves and it took a few moments to work his way towards the path. Once on the trail he kept his eyes skinned for the Lexus. But where was it? He looked again, scanning the undergrowth. It had vanished.

Keeping to the edge of the track just in case the Lexus came roaring at him out of nowhere, he dared to hope the danger had passed. But he still needed to check the gate. He moved on. A few more steps and he rounded a slight bend. The gate was in full view and wide open. 'Thank God,' he sighed. The driver must have been in a hurry to get away and hadn't stopped to close it. In his mind, the gunman and the Lexus were one and the same thing. If one had gone, so had the other.

Nick took his time retracing his steps back to the elder bush. As he walked he was infused with a sense of relief, and as he allowed himself to relax and believe he might be safe, so the reality of what had just happened bubbled to his conscious level. It threatened to engulf him. Emotion struck at his solar plexus. He almost stumbled as nausea gripped his stomach. That's twice, he thought. Twice someone's taken a shot at me. What the hell's going on? He crossed his arms over his midriff.

Chrissie's voice cut through the air. She'd broken from the cover of the elder bush, ignoring his advice to stay hidden. 'Has he gone? Are you OK, Nick?'

'Yeah, sure. I just felt....' He felt stupid. 'The Lexus has gone.'

'Thank God!' Her face was ashen and a fragment of dead leaf clung to her blonde hair.

Matt followed close behind her, his faded tee-shirt riding up and a roll of pale fat breaking the line between baggy jeans and washed-out cotton. 'D'you think that were just bad crow shootin', or were he tryin' to warn us off?' He brushed at his plaster cast with his good hand.

'But why would anyone do that? It's bloody dangerous. Come on, let's get the hell out of here. Matt and I can't get any signal on our mobiles. What about you Nick?'

'Nothing. I tried earlier when we were hiding. I guess that's why they want to put a mast here.'

'Come on, I'm not hanging around any longer.' Chrissie led the way and Nick brought up the rear, his mind in turmoil. Had someone really tried to shoot him or was he just over-reacting? He was living through a recurring nightmare with bullets flying through the air and once again no bloody phone signal. At least this time I'm with friends, he thought and quickened his pace, almost breaking into a run by the time he reached the Peugeot. He waited, catching his breath as Chrissie unlocked the car and they bundled in, slamming the doors as if it would emphasise its impregnability.

'Now what?' Matt asked from the back seat.

'We drive till we get signal. Then we phone the police.' Chrissie started the engine.

'Why the police? What can they do? They'll just say we got too close to someone shooting crows.' Nick swallowed back the bile threatening to rise in his throat.

'I don't know how much you saw before the second shot, Nick but someone's been digging there recently and I'm bloody sure those teeth were human.' Chrissie threw the car into gear and accelerated off the rough ground.

Nick rocked and jolted forwards. He gripped the dashboard as Chrissie's words spun through his head. Teeth? What was she talking about?

'Yeah, someone's missin' an ivory or two.' Matt rummaged in his jeans and pulled out his mobile. 'Right, I'll say when there's signal but you do the phonin', Chrissie. OK?'

Nick glanced behind, expecting the Lexus to appear. Matt concentrated on his phone. 'I reckon we'll get signal if we head towards Needham Market,' he said.

While the car swung and swayed along the lanes, Nick thought back to the moment he'd knelt beside Matt and earth kicked up when the second shot struck. He hadn't seen what he'd knelt on, he'd been too busy looking at Matt and searching for signs he'd been hit, like splatters of blood. If he'd realised he was kneeling on human remains he'd have… he'd have what?

'Signal!'

Chrissie jammed on the brakes.

'Here.' Matt thrust his mobile at Chrissie.

'It's OK, Matt. I'll use my own. I've got the number.'

Nick watched as Chrissie slid her mobile open and tapped at the compact key pad. His heart pounded. He could feel it up into his neck and ears. How did she manage to look so calm and composed? And then he remembered how he'd felt when he'd been in the thick of it. There'd been no time to register his anxiety. So why give in to it now? Chrissie would likely tell him to get a grip and move on. He dragged his mind back to the present as Chrissie's voice cut through his thoughts.

'Hello? Is that DI Clive Merry?'

Nick held his breath, willing it to be Clive Merry.

'How did you know it was me? …. My name came up when I rang? …. So you'd kept my number on your phone?'

Nick watched as colour returned to Chrissie's ashen face.

'Look I, we need your help …. You're not on duty? …. No, it's just I don't know who to report this to. I don't even know if it needs reporting …. Tell you anyway?'

It took less than five minutes but it felt like twenty to Nick. Finally Chrissie slid her mobile closed.

'And?' Matt asked.

'He'll meet us there in about half an hour.'

'What?'

'Come on, it'll be OK. That shot was like bullying us, and I don't like being bullied. And anyway, this time Clive'll be there.'

Nick was about to make a comment about the DI, but he caught Chrissie's expression and thought better of it. Instead he settled for, 'We better get going then, Chrissie.'

•••

They decided to wait in the Peugeot, parked on the verge near the beginning of the footpath, but still in clear view of the road. Chrissie had smoothed down her hair, but neither

Nick nor Matt was going to tell her about the dead leaf sticking out at the back

'It's spot on thirty minutes since you spoke to 'im, Chrissie. Man of 'is word,' Matt said, as the DI's black Ford Mondeo pulled off the road and parked close by.

Nick watched Clive Merry get out of his car. He wore lightweight charcoal walking trousers, high-tech walking shoes and a short-sleeved checked shirt. His face looked more tanned than Nick remembered, and judging by his sun streaked auburn hair, he'd probably spent a summer break hiking in some warm and sunny clime. Nick guessed Chrissie's phone call must have dragged him from an afternoon he'd planned to spend rambling.

'Hi, Chrissie,' Clive said as she opened her car door. 'And it's?'

'Nick Cowley and Matt Finch, but you've met before. That business with….'

Yes, yes, I remember. After your car was stolen.'

Nick smiled. This DI was sensitive. No mention of the attack that followed after her car was stolen a couple of months back. 'Hi,' he said and smiled again as they got out of the Peugeot.

'So where did this happen? You'd better show me.'

'This way.' Chrissie pointed. 'We have to follow the track. It leads to a copse and then Alderman's Point. Thanks for coming, by the way.'

'No problem. Shall we walk then?'

They made their way back along the track. The gate still stood open, just as the Lexus driver had left it. Nick expected to feel anxious but somehow he'd got on top of his fear. There were four of them and one was a policeman, he told himself. The DI exuded a quiet confidence and it was contagious. It was as if by revisiting and facing where it happened he was confronting his own terror. Nick began to feel better about himself. He could see from the way Chrissie moved that she felt comfortable walking next to her DI. And Matt? Judging by the grin on his face, he was enjoying himself.

'Somewhere here. It were parked… yeah, see them marks?' Matt said.

'Keep back and be careful where you tread. Those marks may be important.' The DI squatted to take a closer look. 'The ground's very dry. Come on, show me where you found the tooth.'

They walked on, following the track through the trees as it rose gently, turned a bend and then broke onto open meadow.

'Wow! This is a well-kept secret, Chrissie. I've walked most of these parts but this is spectacular.' From then on the DI turned his attention to the ground, rather than the view.

'The tooth, actually there were two of them, was somewhere near this bank, just a few feet from the fence line. Rabbits, at least I assume it's rabbits, have burrowed into the bank. Now where were they? Hey here, Clive. Look!' They all moved to where Chrissie pointed.

The DI's manner changed almost immediately. It was as if someone had flicked a switch. He was no longer relaxed and off-duty, he'd slipped into professional policing mode. He asked them to stand back as he moved between the areas of freshly disturbed soil, the easy smile replaced by a rather set expression.

'Look, this could take some time. I need to make some calls. We'll need to get a team out here to look at this more closely.'

'So it does look suspicious to you, Clive?'

'It doesn't look like the work of a metal-detector enthusiast, if that's what you mean. But it may be perfectly innocent. There's no point in you all hanging around. You might as well go. But before you leave, just point out where you were hiding.'

'The elder bush, there.' Nick waved towards a leafy tree-like shrub.

'Ah yes, I see it. OK, I may need to get in touch. I've got Chrissie's number, so I guess I can contact you both through Chrissie. Make sure you keep the shoes you're wearing, just in case this turns out to be anything and we need to exclude your prints.'

Nick glanced at Chrissie. She seemed to hesitate, as if she felt she should stay. 'If you're sure, Clive.'

He checked his phone. 'Come on, I'll walk back with you to the car. I've got to make those calls and there's no decent reception for my mobile here.'

Of course, Nick thought, he's probably got a radio in his car. They started to walk back in silence. Chrissie picked some wild flowers from the edge of the meadow – nothing special, just the pretty star-shaped blue ones. For a moment it made him feel like a Sunday afternoon stroller foraging for blackberries, not part of a group of traumatised innocents returning from a grim discovery. So what's with the flowers, he asked himself. Is she trying to appear a bit girly because Clive's here? She doesn't usually bother with that sort of thing.

‘Magpies!’ Matt broke the silence. ‘Magpies pick up shiny things… gold fillin’s and the like.’

‘And then drop them,’ the DI continued. ‘Yes, let’s hope it all turns out to be nothing.’

‘I’m really sorry if we’ve wasted your time, Clive. But when those shots went off, well maybe we stopped thinking straight. I hope you don’t mind I phoned.’ By this time they’d reached the cars and Chrissie unlocked the Peugeot.

‘No, no, I’m pleased you…. I’ll call and let you know what happens.’

Nick bundled into the car and slammed the door as Chrissie said goodbye to Clive. It was time to put some distance between them and Alderman’s Point. The dreadful anxiety had settled and he felt almost back to normal. ‘Try not to knock off the exhaust,’ he said as Chrissie bumped and rattled the car off the grass verge.

‘Yeah, but just think; you can dig your way outa this kinda stuff with a TR7 nose,’ Matt mumbled.

‘Oh shut it.’

Nick smiled. Harmony had been restored. There was no point in saying more and the first few miles passed in silence as they headed back towards Needham Market.

‘How old’s your DI, Chrissie?’

‘Don’t know. I hadn’t thought about it, and anyway, he’s not my DI, Matt.’

‘Well I reckon at least fifty-five.’

‘No! He’ll be in his forties… early-forties.’

‘So you ’ave thought ’bout it then.’

Chrissie ignored Matt and Nick tried not to smile.

‘Give her a break, Matt. She hasn’t got us home yet.’ But it set him thinking. ‘If we keep going on this road,

Chrissie, we pass a gun shop before we reach Needham Market.'

'Do we? Chrissie frowned as she drove. 'Why are you interested in a gun shop?'

'I-I need to understand what happened back there. I mean twice, twice someone's shot at me and I don't even know if an air rifle pellet could have hurt me. I don't even know if it was an air rifle this time. I'm just assuming.' Nick watched Chrissie's face.

She glanced in the rear-view mirror, indicated, pulled off the lane and killed the engine. He waited for her to say something, felt stupid and looked at Matt in the back seat.

'Sorry, Chrissie, I aint meant nothin' 'bout your DI. I were just thinkin' out loud.' Matt hung his head.

'I've already told you he's not my DI.' Chrissie shifted her position in the driver's seat so that she was almost facing Nick. 'Look, you're being paranoid. The first time… whoever fired that shot, it was about Jim Mann, not you. And this time… well, we were all there, not just you. If someone had wanted to hit you this afternoon they would have. We were all sitting ducks. No one followed us there. The Lexus was already there.'

Nick wanted to say something about the pellet hitting the ground closest to him, but she cut across before he could speak. 'No, Nick. We disturbed someone. If it was anything other than an accident then it was meant to achieve what Matt said. We got out of there bloody quick.'

'So, it was because we interrupted someone out there?'

'Yes. Now, if you want to visit the gun shop, fine. But get it into your head, what happened out there this afternoon wasn't personal. No one's stalking you. Got it?'

Nick worked through Chrissie's logic. It made sense. He nodded.

Matt broke the silence. 'I've never been to a gun shop.'

'Come on then. It's been a day of firsts. Let's finish with another.' She turned to face the steering wheel and started the engine. 'Before we reach Needham Market, you say?'

'Yes. Take a left, signposted to Somersham, but it's only a few hundred yards along that road.'

•••

Nick was the first out of the car. Since voicing his fears he'd regained his sense of proportion and some kind of equilibrium. His naturally cheerful nature resurfaced as he peered at the shop front. Was it open? He couldn't tell. It wasn't a conventional, high street kind of store - more of a work shop at one end of the village with a newly built single storey extension on the side. A fishing rod and tackle basket made up the window display, and judging by the layer of dust, they'd been there a while. He pushed the door. It swung open and he stepped down into a vestibule. The air felt cool as he followed worn carpet through a second door and into the body of the shop. Shelves were filled with Wellington boots, waders, waterproofs and waxed hats – the insignia of country pursuits and the colours of a shade-card in greens, muds and sludge. He felt strangely reassured by the rural, timeless nature of it all. A trace of machine oil perfused the air. Guns, he thought, it must be the smell of guns.

'Can I help you?'

Nick spun on his heel, startled by the girl's voice. Chrissie and Matt were still out at the shop door and he'd thought he was alone.

'Sorry, I didn't mean to spook you.'

'No, no I….'

Nick smiled as the girl moved to the counter area. She looked much the same age as him and rather shapeless in an engineers' overall coat. The brown blended with the rural colours on the shelves around her.

'Hi.' He smiled in what he hoped was a reassuring manner. 'I was hoping for some advice. I'm not really looking to buy. More just to….'

'Sure. That's OK.'

Nick didn't know where to begin. He searched for the right words. 'Air rifles?'

'My Dad's the gunsmith. I'm still training, but what d'you want to know about air rifles?'

'Well….' He searched her face. She seemed to transmit a kind of stillness as she waited for him to speak. For a moment he imagined her waiting motionless to take a shot, but her light hazel eyes looked too kind. Sniper? Huntsman? No, he thought, more likely a competition target shooter, but she'd need to tie back that riot of long curly hair before she ever aimed a rifle. He smiled again. He was starting to lose track of what he wanted to say. 'It was more what you'd use one for?'

'Round here, most people use them to shoot small game – rabbits, squirrels, pigeons and things like that.'

'So, you couldn't harm or kill a person with one?' Nick watched as she pushed her gloriously toffee-coloured hair away from her face as she frowned.

'It's rare, but it only takes two and a half foot-pounds of energy for a pellet to penetrate a human skull if it enters through the eye. You see it depends where it hits you. Somewhere soft like your neck might injure you more than in the arm, and of course if it hit you in the chest and went through….'

'So they're pretty powerful then?'

'Not really. An air rifle, unless it's been modified in some way, delivers less than twelve foot-pounds of energy to the pellet, say a ·22 calibre pellet. To put it in proportion, a bullet of similar diameter but fired from a rifle – well you're talking 1,000 foot-pounds of energy.'

'That's awesome.'

'Yes it is. Why d'you ask?'

'Well,' Nick paused as Chrissie and Matt entered the main body of the shop, 'I think we've just been shot at by someone with an air rifle. An accident, I'm sure, but–'

'That shouldn't happen. Sounds like a matter for the police. Where was this?'

'Alderman's Point,' Matt answered as he moved closer to the counter.

'Hmm, don't know it. Are you all together?'

'Yeah.' Matt nodded. There was a silence as he stared at the girl.

'How far away would you have to be to kill something?' Nick let his voice trail.

The girl turned her attention back to Nick. 'Well, if you were a really good shot, you could just about kill a rabbit at a little over 50 metres with a ·22 pellet and an unmodified air rifle.'

'And you can tell if it's an air rifle by the sound when it's fired?' He'd finally asked what had been bugging him for days.

'Usually. If you're using a pneumatic one there may be a whip crack sound - the sonic bang. That's if the pellet's travelling near the speed of sound. Of course you might confuse it with the short explosive bang you get from gunpowder when a shotgun or bullet is fired. Generally though, with an air rifle it's just the sound of the air pressure releasing, which is a softer sound.'

'Hmm….'

'You might also hear a whizz as the pellet passes you and then a ping.'

'A ping?'

Before she could explain, Matt interrupted, 'If 'e weren't wantin' to shoot crows with an air rifle, what'd 'e use instead?'

'Maybe a shotgun with, say, size 6 shot.'

'An' then there'd be lots of shot landin'?'

Nick wasn't sure this conversation was helping. He hadn't heard a spattering of shot landing but he'd heard a bang. That suggested a bullet. The more he learnt, the worse it sounded. The girl must have sensed it because she ignored Matt and smiled. 'Look, if you want to talk about it again or ask more questions, I'm here most days.'

'Thanks. What's your name? I'm Nick, by the way.'

'Kat. Well, Katherine, but everyone calls me Kat.'

'I've got to give a statement on Monday so you've been really helpful with all that stuff about the sound a gun makes when it's fired. Thanks, Kat.'

'That's OK. Let me know how you get on.'

Chrissie tapped his arm. 'Time to leave,' she whispered. Outside, she unlocked her Peugeot and added, 'I don't know how you do it. All we've done is ask about air rifles and within seconds you've as good as picked up a gorgeous gunslinger.'

Nick grinned. Perhaps it hadn't turned out to be such a bad day after all.

# CHAPTER 10

Matt stared at the wall. He lay on his bed and focused on the grubby blue paint. He knew he needed to stick up more posters to hide the colour of fading Mediterranean smog. If he covered the last few patches escaping from above his wardrobe, peeping from behind the bedroom door and hiding close to the window where the curtains swung back, then he could pretend he'd never been anything other than nineteen. He could forget there'd ever been a past, a time without friends and he could… he could what? Wipe out those early teenage years, all the loneliness along with the walls of pale grimy-blue? He'd read somewhere, probably the wisdom of a fortune cookie, that you were shaped by what you'd been through. He rested his hand on his ample stomach. Did it mean he'd been shaped by all the comic-strip books he'd read or merely rounded by calorific take-aways? He held up his left wrist with the plaster cast. Maybe they meant things like his arm?

The toilet flushed, water hissed in the pipes as the cistern filled, and heavy footsteps passed the door. His mum was awake. He checked the time on his mobile. 7:30. That's early for her, he thought. Maybe she's planning to come to the fracture clinic with me. She didn't say anything yesterday, but maybe this time?

If it wasn't for his appointment, he'd have nothing to do. The Summer School was over, the apprentice release day had gone electronic for the next two Mondays and he didn't have anything planned. The Utterly Academy library didn't open again until two weeks' time, so until then he was a loose agent. But the word agent conjured an image.

For a moment he was transported back to his comic-strip books and agents with double 0 prefixes. What had Chrissie said? A Vespa? It was Italian for wasp and wasn't there a girl with the same name in *Casino Royale*? Italian was sexy; he knew that because Lil had said so. That's why Ginny liked the film where the bloke kept saying words in Italian. And the bloke with the Italian got the girl. The more Matt thought about it, the more he liked the idea. He had barely two weeks before he'd need regular transport to Hadleigh. With a Vespa he'd nail the journey and Ginny would be mesmerised as well. It was time, he decided, to try out the power of the Italian word.

Fired with purpose, Matt dressed for the hospital. If his mum was coming too, then she'd want him in a clean plain tee-shirt, fresh underwear in case he got knocked down on the way and the jeans without the rip in the knee. He'd have to ditch his preference for shorts. Why didn't she like him showing his knees, he wondered.

'Mornin', Mum,' he mumbled twenty minutes later when he sauntered into the chaotic kitchen. She sat with her back to him, her elbows on the breakfast bar. She still wore her faded dressing gown, an apology for pink candlewick. Her bleached hair looked flattened where she'd rested her head on her pillow all night. 'Thought you were up, Mum.'

'I'm up aint I? It's me 'alf day, so why'd I be dressed yet?' She didn't turn to speak but maintained a solid expanse of hunched shoulders, blocking him out along with the sink spilling yesterday's plates, and the frying pan still on the cooker with its faint smell of bacon.

Matt shifted his weight onto one foot and leaned against the draining board. A fork clattered down and skidded across the floor. 'Sorry, Mum. Vespa!' There, he'd tried out the Italian.

'You grut lummox!' She sounded cross. 'Pick it up then.'

Had she heard, he wondered as he bent for the fork.

'Vespa, Mum.'

'What you sayin'?'

He felt the frown in her tone. 'Vespa, Mum. It's Italian.'

'You alright in the head?' She turned slowly. 'Since when d'you speak Italian? An' how'd I understand it?' She stared at him for a moment. 'You're all prinked up. Where you goin' today?'

'I, we… it's the clinic. Don't you remember?' He held up his arm with its plaster cast.

'Oh that. 'Bout time it were sorted. No, you'll be fine on your own. Anyone who can speak the Italian'll be able to understand them doctors.'

'Please, Mum.'

'What gave you the idea I'd come?'

'I just thought, Mum.'

'Too much thinkin' and too much dreamin'. That's your trouble, an' now it's the Italian!'

'No, Mum. Vespa. It's the name of a scooter. Italian make. Italian name, that's all.'

'What you want with a scooter?'

'Two weeks' time an' I'll be startin' at Hepplewhites, in Hadleigh. I'll be an apprentice, Mum.'

'Hmm,' she frowned again before adding, 'Tom, that useless brother of yours, might know where t'get a cheap scooter. Not seen 'im for weeks, mind. Try phonin'. He'll know.' She turned back to her mug of tea and the breakfast bar. 'I 'ave to be at work midday.'

Of course, it was her half day. She'd worked at the Co-op for as long as he could remember. She blamed his dad; said he shouldn't have left, shouldn't have walked out on them. She was the martyr. 'It's your dad's fault I need a job, an' your fault 'cause you need feedin'.'

He knew from experience the conversation was over. He should also have known she'd never come with him to the clinic, but at least the Italian had worked. He'd said Vespa and although she hadn't exactly melted and gone soft on him, she'd taken an interest. Just her speaking to him was a plus.

•••

Matt leaned against the bus stop outside the West Suffolk Hospital. Thank God the plaster cast is off at last, he thought. He'd glanced at his wrist in the clinic, been horrified to see it looked strange, almost alien and hadn't dared look again. Now, outside in the non-threatening summer air, he held it up for inspection. Even to him his left wrist looked pale and thin and the skin dry and flaky. The hairs reminded him of strangled blades of grass, deprived of light and struggling to grow from under a heavy stone. His hand was a different colour – grimy where he'd spared the soap and water, not wanting to soften the plaster cast. He compared it with the other. The right was tanned from the sun, but the more he looked, so the shock lessened. At least the nails were neat, not like the right. He'd never mastered using scissors with his left hand and when doubly hampered by the plaster cast, it was a miracle he hadn't hacked off more than a nail. He moved his wrist cautiously. It seemed to bend OK and it didn't hurt.

He still had the Eastern Anglia Daily Tribune tucked under one arm. He'd found it discarded in the clinic waiting area and as no one seemed to want it anymore, he'd picked it up. Now he reached for it gingerly with his poorly hand. So far so good, he thought and opened the newspaper. He folded the pages back, patting the sheets flat, flexing his temporarily pale withered wrist. It felt fragile, but it worked. It was definitely part of his body again. He began to relax as he scanned the pages and waited for his bus back to Stowmarket. A headline grabbed his attention. *Man dies after fuel tank fire.*

Matt frowned. Hadn't there been an article only the other week about the police cracking down on motorists using illegal red diesel in their cars? At the time he'd wondered if it was anything to do with the fire, the one Chrissie and Nick passed on the A14. He read on. The man had been in his fifties, a local farmer out Blackthorpe, Rougham way. *He suffered severe burns to his head, face and upper body, as well as smoke inhalation injuries*. That's horrible, Matt thought. 'But how'd he get all them burns? Did the tank explode?'

'Pardon, what did you say?'

Matt glanced up from the paper. A middle aged woman waiting next to him stared into his face. Instinctively he repeated what he'd just said. 'Did it explode?'

She frowned and looked away. He wished he'd kept his mouth shut.

He turned his attention back to the paper. It appeared the man, named as Jonas Nunseon Rivett, had *lost a brave battle to survive his injuries, despite the care of the regional burns centre in Broomfield, Chelmsford.* But what kind of a name was that, Matt wondered as he rolled the word

Nunseon over his tongue. It sounded as if he should be a God fearing man from the Bible Belt, not a Suffolk farmer trying to save his red diesel storage tank. Matt searched for more details, but there weren't many. The report implied the fire was started deliberately. 'How can they can tell?' he murmured. The police were now *treating the man's death as either a case of aggravated manslaughter or murder.*

'What's aggravated manslaughter?' He peered over his newspaper and the middle aged woman edged further away. Now what had he done? He shrugged and turned his attention back to the paper. The police spokesman was quoted as saying *there'd been a recent spate of farm diesel thefts and they might in some way be connected with the fire.* Now that was interesting.

Matt felt someone jostle his arm. The newspaper print jumped and he lost his focus. 'Shit!'

'Watch your mouth,' the woman hissed.

Matt stepped back and the queue disintegrated. It changed from an orderly line to a bunched group as the bus drew up, air brakes hissing, hot exhaust fumes filling the air. Matt crushed the newspaper into a semblance of its original folded form and elbowed his way forwards. Only then did he notice it was the wrong bus. 'Vespa!' he looked around, but the middle aged woman hadn't heard. The shelter and pavement emptied.

Left alone once again, he watched the rear of the bus as it pulled away. How he hated bus journeys. If he was going to survive his apprenticeship in Hadleigh, he needed to find some wheels, and that meant wheels of his own. Inspiration struck. 'Of course, the Scooters for Sale section.' He opened the crumpled hastily folded paper. The inner sheets dropped to the ground and a loose half page caught the light breeze. He flapped at it with his weak wrist and the print took flight. It scuttled across the road, wafting into an oncoming car before gambolling between the tyres. It was closely followed by more pages as passing cars whisked the air into gusts.

'Litter lout,' someone shouted from the other side of the road.

Matt reached for his phone hiding deep in the pocket of his baggy jeans. It was after 12:00. Maybe it was time to speak to Tom. He tapped the mobile and released it from its sleep mode. 'Hi, Tom.'

'Wotcha, mate!'

'I don't s'pose you know of a scooter goin' cheap?'

'Who's askin'?'

'Me.'

'Christ, Mat; you'll kill yourself. Why?'

For a moment Matt had forgotten how Tom could put him down, always make him feel small. 'I start Hepple-whites two weeks' time. How d'I get there?'

'Bus?'

Matt didn't bother to answer. Tom hadn't anything useful to say after all.

'Look, if you're serious I might be able to help but you'll have to do somethin' for me.'

Matt waited.

'Are you still there? Matt?'

'Yeah, yeah. What you wantin'?'

'Don't know yet. I'll think of somethin'. So, any particular scooter?'

'Yeah, a Vespa. I fancy a Vespa.' Matt thought for a moment before adding, 'Well, somethin' Italian.'

'OK, I'll ask around, see what I can find. It won't be cheap, mind and you'll have to do the compulsory basic trainin' course. You'll need it to get your licence. It's all money, you know. So how you plannin' on payin', Matt?'

'I'll be an apprentice. Workin'. Thought maybe you'd help. I'd pay you back.'

There was a long silence and Matt checked the signal indicator on his mobile. Tom was still there. 'I'll pay you back, Tom.'

'Yeah, sure you will, Matt. Look, mention my name at the trainin' centre. It might get you a reduction, and….'

'And?'

'I'll get back to you. Give me a couple a days, mate. OK?'

'Yeah, OK – an' thanks, Tom.'

Matt slipped the mobile back into his pocket and smiled. Tom was seven years older than him. His big brother. He had the same dark sandy hair, but that's where the similarity ended. He'd always had friends, and as if that wasn't enough, in the last few years he'd broken free from Tumble Weed Drive and their mum. An uneasy feeling took hold and the smile faded as he recalled Tom's conditions for lending. They usually ended in some form of humiliation for Matt and the price was always high. Sometimes too high.

# CHAPTER 11

Chrissie turned off the ignition and pulled out the key. She caught her breath as she gazed at the shock of yellow paintwork stretching ahead, the bonnet plunging downwards and dipping out of sight. The colour was a wake-up call, jolting her out of her daydreams and forcing a reaction. Would she ever get used to it, she wondered. There was no point in locking the TR7. She couldn't imagine anyone wanting to steal it, and with that thought filling her head she gathered up her handbag and headed for the old wooden door to the Clegg workshop barn.

'Morning, Mr Clegg,' she called as she stepped onto the cool concrete floor largely taken up with workbenches and stacks of old wood. The band saw and planer were off to one side. Near the door, shelves, weighed down with bottles of oils, stains and glues, threatened to fall from the walls. 'Morning!'

'Good morning, Mrs Jax.' Ron's voice wafted on the scent of wood-dust from the far end of the workshop.

Chrissie couldn't see him but the sound of gentle tapping followed by a heavier thump gave her a clue. She followed the percussive notes. 'What are you doing, Mr Clegg?' And then she spotted him, bending over something on the floor.

Ron straightened up stiffly. 'I'm trying to get these joints apart.' He flapped an arthritic hand towards a heavy Victorian dining chair lying on its side. Chrissie saw the problem straight away. The wood was split and the legs splayed where they extended, as if in a continuous line, past the corners of the seat and up into the back of the chair.

‘Someone’s rocked back on it. The old wood couldn’t take it,’ he explained. ‘There’re five more like this and they’re all in a dreadful state.’

‘So, what are you doing, Mr Clegg?’

‘We’ve got to get all the joints apart, take the chair to pieces and clean away the old glue. We’ll replace or mend this.’ He let his fingers rest on a battered wooden leg. ‘And then we re-assemble it again, but with modern glue.’

Chrissie liked the way he said we rather than I. ‘That’ll be six times. I mean, for the whole set.’ In her mind she started multiplying by the number of legs. Part of her would always be an accountant. ‘Twenty-four,’ she predicted.

‘Twenty-four what, Mrs Jax?’

‘Joints.’

‘Ah! Well there’ll be many more than that, believe me,’ and Ron smiled.

‘Mug of tea, Mr Clegg?’ She knew the routine. He’d have been up for hours and her first task of the day was to put the kettle on for a strong brew.

He nodded. ‘How’s that new car of yours running, Mrs Jax?’

‘It’s great, just great.’ She might have known he’d call it new. He dealt with antique furniture, and to him, something from a production line almost thirty years ago wasn’t old. Admittedly the last owner had fitted an electronic ignition as a nod to recent technology, but by most drivers’ standards the car was ancient. She hadn’t been surprised when Ron didn’t mention the colour. It was typical of him to be frugal with his words. When he’d first stepped outside to see it earlier that week, he’d merely raised his hand to his eyes, as if to shield them from the dazzling glare. He'd laughed and said he thought it would suite her just fine.

Chrissie put the mug of tea on a workbench close to his customary stool. 'That reminds me. I've left something in the car. I-I wanted to show you. See what you think? I won't be a minute.' She hurried back into the sunny courtyard, and feeling a little foolish, she reached into the open top TR7. To be honest, she'd acted on impulse that morning. Hadn't really thought it through.

Earlier at home, as she'd rinsed her breakfast plate and set it to drain on the rack, a bunch of dying flowers caught her eye. She remembered stuffing them into a small vase and setting it on the kitchen windowsill when she'd first got back from Alderman's Point - but she'd forgotten to top up the water. Over successive days of neglect the thirsty blooms must have wilted and the heads dried so that as she'd stood at her sink and gazed, she saw them as if for the first time. They looked dead. Star shaped, desiccated but strikingly blue. Wasn't that how Ron had described the dried flowers in Jim Mann's tallboy all those years ago?

On a whim she'd plucked them out of the vase, shedding crisp leaf-fragments across her kitchen. She'd cursed as she left a trail to her front door and then tossed them into the TR7's passenger footwell. Now she cursed again.

Damn, she thought as she lifted them out, knocking blue petals from the distinctive heads. She took a little more care as she carried the disintegrating bunch into the Clegg workshop barn. 'What d'you think, Mr Clegg?'

'For me, Mrs Jax?'

Chrissie looked down at the lifeless bouquet fit for the compost heap. 'For you? Of course not, Mr Clegg.' She felt her cheeks redden. 'No, I didn't mean....'

Ron sipped his tea and waited for her to say more.

'When we were at Alderman's Point, the other day, remember I told you about the teeth and the gunshot?'

Ron nodded.

'Well, there were hundreds of these blue flowers. I think its borage and it set me thinking, except of course, I forgot about them until this morning. The colour's so striking and when I saw them like this–'

'Like what, Mrs Jax? From here they look dead.'

'I forgot to top-up the vase, and well, in this weather they died.'

'Ah! You'd missed out that bit. So, you picked a bunch?'

'Yes, and as I said, when I saw them dead this morning I wondered if you'd recognise the flower? Do you remember if they were the same as the ones in Jim Mann's tallboy? The borage Minnette Mann collected?' Chrissie paused for a moment, as she struggled to put into words an idea so shadowy she hardly knew it was there. 'I wondered if it meant Minnette Mann is still up there and that… maybe she didn't just disappear but died.'

Ron stared into his mug. For a moment Chrissie wondered if he'd heard her. She watched, almost holding her breath as he frowned and then asked, 'Have they found anything more than a tooth, do you know?'

'I've not heard anything.' It was something else niggling her. Clive Merry had said he'd phone and she'd not had a call from him, not even a text. She tried to focus her thoughts. 'So do you think they're the same, Mr Clegg? These flowers?'

'Let me have a closer look. Bring them over here, will you.'

Chrissie waited as Ron touched the star-shaped flower heads, turning them over and setting them back down on the workbench. Finally he spoke. 'The flowers are so striking,' and then he smiled. 'You're quite right. That was the word I used. This blue.... It was many years ago, but this is definitely borage, common borage and that's what she'd put in the drawers. But it doesn't mean anything. The borage could have come from anywhere. She could have grown it in her own garden.'

'I know, Mr Clegg but it was more than a feeling up there. Someone had disturbed the ground. They'd been digging. It set my imagination–'

'Running wild,' he finished for her. 'I imagine finding a tooth and the gunshot must have spooked you. But come on, where's your common sense? One tooth doesn't make a body just as one swallow doesn't make a summer.' He shook his head. 'I think it's time to get on with some work and fill your mind with something useful.'

'Yes, of course but I just needed to know. And it was more than one tooth, Mr Clegg.' Chrissie tried to banish the memory of the gold filling as it glinted in the sun. 'I hope you didn't mind me bringing the borage to show you?'

'I can't remember the last time anyone brought me a bunch of flowers. Now let's concentrate on getting this chair apart.' As an afterthought he added, 'If your imagination is running in the direction of bodies, perhaps you should speak to that policeman again. Maybe he'll settle your fears.'

'DI Merry?'

'Yes. From what you've said he sounds like a sensible chap. He should be able to set your mind at rest. Now come on, you've got me chatting again and wasting time. I don't know; women and workshops. Next you'll be wanting to put up curtains in here, Mrs Jax.'

Chrissie laughed, despite herself. She knew he wasn't being serious, just trying to nudge her from her morbid thoughts; make her rise to his chauvinistic dig and forget her suspicions. But he'd planted an idea. Perhaps she should phone Clive Merry.

By lunchtime they'd got the first chair in pieces and Chrissie was busy scraping away the globules of ancient glue from the depths of a corner mortise-and-tenon joint. At first she didn't hear the ringtone, she was picturing an earlier carpenter. The one who'd chiselled out the mortise sometime in the nineteenth century. Judging by the rough marks on the wood, he might have been an apprentice like her – well not quite like her of course because there wouldn't have been women apprentices back then. *Brrring*! *Brrring*! The sound cut through her imaginings. *Brrring*! *Brrring*!

The shrill notes were urgent, demanding. Chrissie scanned the workbench for her handbag. Where the hell had she left it this time? She needed more pockets and then she wouldn't have to go through this drama every time her mobile rang. *Brrring*! *Brrring*! With the chisel still in her hand, she followed the sound, almost breaking into a run. She spotted the familiar soft grey leather, exactly where she'd thrown it down on a bench stool.

'Hi, hi!' she said, grabbing her mobile from somewhere deep in her handbag and answering without checking the name of the caller.

'Chrissie?'

For a moment she wasn't sure if her ears were playing tricks. 'Yes, hi!' She smothered her surprise.

‘Ah, glad I caught you.’ He sounded business-like, in a hurry. ‘I thought I ought to let you know before you heard it on the news first.’

‘Yes, you said you’d phone and let me know.’ She tried to copy his detached style, ‘Thanks for getting back to me, Clive.’

‘That’s OK. I’m phoning because there’ve been some significant findings up on Alderman’s Point and it looks…, well, the forensic anthropologist has been looking at the bones and it seems they’re human remains.’

‘My God!’ Chrissie felt her legs weaken as her head started to float. She sat down hard on the stool and crushed her handbag. ‘Any idea who?’

‘Much too early to tell.’ His voice sounded as if he was smiling. ‘Only skeletal remains, I’m afraid. At this stage we’re waiting on the anthropologist’s report.’

‘But can’t you distinguish? I mean, is it a woman?’

‘Yes, they can tell it’s a female skeleton and an adult. But we’re waiting for more details.’

‘And her age?’

‘As I said, Chrissie, we’re waiting on the report. We don’t even know how long the bones have been there.’

‘You mean it could be archaeological. A Roman gold filling?’ She tried to keep the sarcasm out of her voice.

There was silence on the line and then Clive’s voice emerged, softened. ‘Sorry. Of course, you were there. But please, you must keep the details to yourself.’

‘And the gunshot? Did they find a bullet, any shot or pellets?’

‘Ah, that could take longer. There’s quite a large area of ground to cover, so….’ His words trailed away and she got the impression a voice was talking to him somewhere in the background. 'Look, it's mad here. Really busy. I'll call you when I've more time to speak. Bye, Chrissie.' The line went dead.

'Bye… and thank you,' but she knew he couldn't hear her. He'd already rung off.

Chrissie closed her eyes and tried to gather her thoughts. It was as if a lightning bolt had thrown her with the violence of a punch to the solar plexus. She'd been contemplating the handiwork of a Victorian apprentice and then the skeletal horror of death and decay had burst back into her day. It was one thing to imagine a body might be buried on Alderman's Point, but very different actually knowing. 'My God! And I nearly touched the tooth.'

'Are you all right, Mrs Jax?'

Chrissie opened her eyes to see Ron standing a few feet away, a rubber headed hammer in one hand and a disarticulated chair leg in the other. 'I came over all…. I feel sick, Mr Clegg.' He didn't say anything, so she continued, 'That call. It was from DI Merry.' She looked down at her lap, eased her grip on the chisel and switched her mobile to sleep mode. Echoes of Clive's voice still rang in her head. *Human remains*. 'Human remains,' she repeated, trying to keep her tone steady. 'They've found human remains up on Alderman's Point.' Chrissie waited for him to say something, but he seemed lost in his own thoughts. It was as if a thick cloud had descended. The air felt leaden.

She watched as Ron placed the hammer and chair leg on the work bench, his movements deliberate and unhurried. Finally he spoke. 'When they said Minnette Mann left all those years ago I assumed… well, I assumed as she was French, it made sense when they said she'd gone back to

France. There's no reason to think it's Minnette Mann up there.'

She didn't answer. What could she say?

'Weren't Nick and Matt with you when you found the teeth?'

She nodded, and that reminded her. Clive hadn't said if he'd phoned them. Did he even have their numbers? Somehow she'd got the impression it was rather fraught at his end of the call. 'Yes, I'd better let them know. Is that OK?'

'Of course. It's lunchtime. You probably need a bit of a break. Maybe you'll feel more yourself when you've spoken to your friends.'

It was so like Mr Clegg to show her the way or point out what she should do without actually saying as much. 'I think I'll go outside, if that's all right, Mr Clegg.'

Chrissie opened the old barn door and blinked as she stepped into the brightness. Her TR7 blazed, the colour almost luminescent in the midday sun, and she automatically moved towards it. Leaning against its warm metal bodywork, she scrolled through her contacts and rang Matt. She'd chosen to speak to him first because she guessed his reaction would be excitement. It would be easier to dwell on the upbeat side of the discovery and ignore the drama and tragedy behind the gruesome find. She wanted to shake away the image Clive's words conjured up. In her imagination she pictured an unknown woman callously bundled into an earthy grave, the deed shrouded in darkness. She shivered despite the summer day.

Matt answered on almost the second ringtone and when she heard him say the anticipated *shit* and *cool* as she recounted Clive's call, her mood started to lighten. He asked the questions that also bugged her. *How long ago did the woman die? How long had she been in the ground up there on Alderman's point*? It was probably one and the same answer.

'I don't know. They're still working on it, Matt,' she sighed, and then she voiced her fears. 'I wondered if it could be Minnette Mann.'

Matt didn't miss a beat, just accepted her suggestion and said something about it being difficult to find out about Minnette if it was too long ago, least ways if he was only using the computer.

'So what are you doing with your week of leisure?' she asked.

'I were readin' the highway code.'

Chrissie laughed. She assumed he was joking. 'Speak to you soon. Bye!' She rang off. She'd been right. He'd made her feel better, not because he'd tried to, but because he was Matt. Straight, literal and funny. It was Nick's turn next and she predicted an altogether different reaction.

'But have they found anything else? You know; shot, or a pellet or bullet?' he asked when she phoned.

'Clive said they're still looking. It's a large area to cover.'

'But they only need go over it with a metal detector. How difficult is that?'

Chrissie had guessed his main worry would still be the gunshot. 'They will, but it takes time, apparently.'

'If human remains were buried on Alderman's Point, then we disturbed someone and the gunshot wasn't a coincidence,' Nick said. The implication was uncomfortable, even for her.

'The police are involved now, Nick. We've told them everything.' She wasn't sure who she was trying to reassure. 'None of us know anything the police don't already know and the gunman could've been aiming at any of us. We were all there, remember, not just you. And thank God the body's been found.' She couldn't quite bring herself to say bones. 'Look, we didn't see the gunman. We just found something suspicious and alerted the police. There's no reason to single you out.'

She didn't expect he'd be receptive to her suspicion it might be Minnette Mann up there, so she bit her tongue. It wasn't the moment to share her qualms. They could wait. If it was Minnette, the police would find out soon enough.

'Nick? Nick, are you still there?'

'Yes, and of course you're right. But it was still bloody scary.'

'I know. But look, it was probably only imagined danger, not real danger. There's a difference.'

She heard him sigh.

'Yes, of course. Thanks, Chrissie.' His voice seemed to relax. 'Sorry, I haven't asked. Are you OK?'

'I'm fine,' she lied.

'Good. Look, we'll speak later. Bye,' and he was gone.

Chrissie switched her phone back to sleep mode and idly ran her hand over the car's glass-smooth paintwork. It felt warm, solid, reassuring. It was time to get on with the business of the living. A mug of tea wouldn't go amiss, she thought as she headed back into the barn workshop.

# CHAPTER 12

Nick slipped his mobile back into his pocket. What had Chrissie just said? They'd found human skeletal remains on Alderman's Point and the police were about to make an announcement? It took a moment for the meaning to sink in. He shuddered. It was horrible, macabre even - but Chrissie was right, of course. There was nothing to be afraid about. He tried to re-focus his thoughts. He'd been working with Dave on the fittings for Ricky Rake's office, his mind filled with the finer details of drawer-joints and sliders, interspersed with images of Kat's hazel eyes. Until a few moments earlier he'd been relaxing, sipping bottled water on his lunch break. But then Chrissie's call crashed in on him, her gruesome news intruding like a juggernaut.

Dave sat next to him on one of the brown plastic chairs he'd pulled out into the sun. They lounged at the rear of the Willows workshop, looking onto the works van parking area. Dave bit into a doorstep sized sandwich, oblivious to the drama playing out in Nick's head.

'There you are. Might've known you'd be somewhere near the vans, Dave.' Alfred Walsh's voice brought Nick back to earth with a jolt. He watched as the foreman walked slowly, his forehead creased, his eyes half closed against the sun.

'D'you want to sit down?' Nick asked, starting to stand.

'No, no. Much too hot for me out here. No, I've just had a call from Mr Rake, Hadleigh. He wants the office fitted by the end of next week!'

'What? You must be kidding. I thought we'd several more weeks. That's what we'd agreed wasn't it?' Dave's voice cracked and faltered, as he choked on a fragment of bread.

Nick glanced at Dave before turning his attention back to the foreman. Surely he must know they weren't even half way through making and assembling, let alone ready for fitting.

'Said as much to Mr Rake, but you know what he's like. He even threatened to cancel the work and take it elsewhere. All polite-like in that slow voice of his.'

'He's bluffing. No one else'll get it finished. Not from scratch. Not by the end of next week.' Dave's face reddened. 'He must be bluffing.'

'I know, but he's a good customer. I've spoken with the boss and well, there's some overtime in it for you.'

'Why the sudden hurry?' Nick asked.

'He says he's moving the storage units in and business'll be up and running. Says he needs his office. Look, I can't spare anyone to help you this week, but maybe by next Thursday?'

'Well, at least we've got all the maple now. It came on Monday's delivery.' Dave grimaced. 'Looks like you'll be as good as living here for the next week or so, lad.'

Nick grinned. He didn't mind hard work.

'And this way someone'll be in the workshop till late. It'll put off them diesel thieves,' the foreman muttered, 'Goodridges were hit last week!'

'Now hang on. We aint night watchmen, Alfred. I'm having none of that.' Dave's round face contorted into a scowl.

'OK, OK. But you'll still be here.' Alfred let his voice drift as he began to limp back to the main workshop. 'You may not have time for the sunbathing though,' he tossed over his shoulder.

Dave grunted by way of an answer.

'Mr Walsh, just before you go,' Nick called after the foreman. 'Any more news on the beehive job?'

Alfred paused in his tracks. 'I spoke to Mrs Mann yesterday. She said she'd let us know after the inquest. Beehives… that were always a crazy job anyroad.' He resumed his slow walk. The conversation was over. The lunch break terminated.

Nick sighed. It was probably just as well. If he was concentrating on his work, he'd forget about everything else, well not quite everything. He'd planned to call in at the gun shop on his way home and speak to Kat again but now it looked as if he'd be finishing too late. He couldn't tell if the combination of guns and her toffee-coloured hair created the frisson, or simply she was bloody attractive. Either way, he knew he was hooked. He recognised the feeling. Now he'd have to wait till Saturday to try and speak to her again.

'I thought Ricky Rake seemed an easy-going kind of a guy,' Nick said to Dave as they made their way back into the workshop.

'That's how he catches people out, but he's sharp. Don't be fooled, he's a sharp businessman. Always has been.'

Nick nodded. He thought about the office plans. The design could be described as anything but standard. Take the piece he was currently working on. The typical width for a kitchen unit was 60cm and filing cabinets 47cm, but this was closer to a metre wide, relatively shallow, tall and with a frame thick enough to take a mortise lock. A booze cabinet? Hardly.

The afternoon flew as Nick planed and smoothed wood for perfect butt joints and then applied long cramps to press the boards tight as glue bonded one edge to another. He was so absorbed he hardly noticed he'd worked on for a couple of extra hours, long after the other carpenters had returned the Willows vans and gone home. Dave kept an eye on him, making suggestions and corrections, but always teaching. Nick was secretly pleased he didn't have to decide which piece abutted which so the panels in the cabinet doors blended and matched as the grains ran vertically. Dave had the last word on that, just as he was the one who finally called time.

'We've done enough for today. Tomorrow we'll start working on the frames for the panels. By the time we're done you'll be living and breathing stiles, cross rails and muntins, even blindfolded,' Dave chuckled. 'And if you get it wrong, I'll bloody kill you.'

Nick ran a hand over the finely sanded wood. 'It looks good, really good, doesn't it?' He was pleased with his efforts. 'I've enjoyed it, learnt a lot.' He could have added he was shattered.

'Yeah, might even make a carpenter of you yet. Now get these shavings swept up, lad.'

Fifteen minutes later Nick threw his sweatshirt into his Ford Fiesta and settled into the driver's seat. His tee-shirt felt sweaty and his jeans were covered in wood dust. Winding down the window he sat back and let the balmy summer air waft across his face. Somewhere in the distance the sound of an engine cut into the evening. He listened, absentmindedly to the urgent, rhythmic notes as the London-to-Norwich fast train hurtled along the Needham Market section of line, out beyond the confines of the Willows grounds. A silence followed and Nick automatically waited, enjoying the emptiness. And then he heard the faint strains of an engine. A car engine with a knocking sound. He frowned. He'd heard it somewhere before. Where? Tiredness descended. He couldn't think. 'Time to go home,' he murmured. His mind must be playing tricks, he decided as he started the Fiesta.

Nick slipped the car into gear and slowly edged forwards. He glanced in his rear-view mirror. Behind he could see the Willows vans safely corralled behind the newly installed security fencing, their white paintwork transforming them into a motorized bovine herd parked-up to chew their cud overnight. Dave had already zoomed away, accelerating home for his over-late tea, but Nick took his time. He coasted past the prefabricated workshop and braked at the exit to the site. Checking to the right and left, he pulled out onto the tarmac. There were no other cars; the road was deserted, just an old Land Rover and that looked as if it had been dumped by the side of the kerb. No driver in sight. He changed up through the gears and headed for Barking Tye and home. Somewhere behind him a burglar alarm started to wail. Strident beeps shrieked.

But Nick chose not to listen. His thoughts ran in an altogether different direction. The extra hours of work needed to meet Ricky Rake's new deadline had messed with his plans. At this rate it was going to be an age between first meeting Kat and following up on her invitation to drop by the gun shop again. He knew he should play it cool. He only had to think back to what happened in Exeter to be reminded. There he'd worn his heart on his sleeve and been too obvious. What had Mel called him? Transparent. She'd played him like a fool. This time he'd be wiser and anyway, fate had stepped in to help. He shook his head and imagined what he could say. Gun shop chat-up lines were a new category and he really didn't want to have to buy a gun. 'I could pretend, I s'pose,' he murmured.

The remaining weekdays flew as he worked with Dave on the units. Like oversized Lego sets, tenons were fitted snugly into mortises. 90° angles were checked and corners squared up. Small adjustments were made, and when Dave was satisfied, Nick reassembled the units, but this time applying glue to the joints and long cramps to the sides. Piece by piece, they worked their way through the plans.

'I heard there was an attempted break-in the other night,' Dave muttered as he checked Nick's drawer sides made a true rectangle. 'Sometime after we'd left here, thank God. I wouldn't have wanted to confront them. They probably had crowbars, bolt cutters and Christ knows what else.'

'What? Was anything taken?'

'No. Seems they were interested in the lock-up. Probably after diesel again. Lucky the boss fitted alarms when the fencing went up. The noise must've put 'em off.'

'But why? They've already had one go at the tanks. Surely they'd guess it wouldn't be so easy a second time round?' Nick reasoned.

'You'd think so. The trouble is it's as simple as taking candy from a baby – impossible to trace and difficult to prove it's stolen unless you're caught sticky-handed.' Dave paused. 'That looks OK. Just slide the drawer bottom in. No glue for that bit. Need to allow for some movement in the wood, otherwise it'll just split. Yeah, seems they were just after easy pickings and the locks and the alarms were too much trouble.'

Nick tried to concentrate as Dave effortlessly moved the conversation between the finer points of drawer making and diesel thieves. 'I think I heard an alarm going off when I reached the Barking Road the other night. I never thought it could've been from here, though.' A shadowy memory of a battered Land Rover and the sound of an engine knocking flashed through Nick's mind, the recollection so faint and transient it almost disappeared before he'd registered it. No, can't be relevant, he thought and immediately dismissed it to those subconscious areas of his brain that only ever re-emerged in dreams.

Nick felt he'd scarcely have time to blink before he'd be in *deadline* week. The Willows workshop filled rapidly with the assembled and glued units. 'Ready to go,' as Dave called them but Nick thought they looked anything but ready to go. There were no desk tops or kick-boards and the pieces looked strangely naked, showing their innards and modern, screw-design, height-adjustable feet. The whole point about bespoke carpentry, as Dave kept reminding Nick, was that some things had to be fitted on site.

'However well we've measured,' Dave announced like a well-worn mantra, 'you can bet the floor aint flat, and the walls are slightly out. A millimetre or two doesn't sound much but it'll look dreadful if you get it wrong.' Dave made it sound like a threat, but after the best part of a week in the Willows workshop, Nick was actually looking forward to returning to Ricky Rake's office. He was surprised by how much he wanted to see the units fitted with the cut-to-measure desktops and kick-boards, and he found himself curious about the relaxed, easy-going man with the convincing mask that apparently disguised a sharp businessman.

•••

Music floated on the warm humid Friday night air. Nick couldn't help but start to hum, harmonising with Elton's *Crocodile Rock*, and then he remembered he wasn't alone and internalised his voice. Should have sat outside, it's cooler, he thought for the second time in half an hour, but he hadn't the strength to move. It had been an exhausting week, both mentally and physically and he'd struggled to find the energy to shower and change before setting out for the Nags Head. And here he was almost drifting off, lulled by his first half of Land Girl and the jukebox. Someone shouted, the barman tossed some ice into a glass, missed and the slippery cubes rattled and banged as they skidded over the wooden boards. A cheer went up somewhere near the dartboard and Nick momentarily dragged himself back to his surroundings as he glanced around the bar. No sign of Chrissie or Matt yet, he thought and then turned his attention to his beer. He'd almost been tempted by the specials, still left over from the beer festival, but in the end he'd settled for a familiar brew.

His mind wandered back over his day in Hadleigh. He could still picture Ricky Rake with his thin smiling lips and the crepe bandage on his arm, peeping out as his shirt sleeve fell back, cuff unbuttoned and the fine cotton flapping across his face as he pushed his hair away. Every movement had appeared slow and measured but elegant in a Suffolk kind of way. He'd seemed genuinely prepared to speak to Nick, almost amused by him, and Nick for his part had found it a bit unsettling but at the same time secretly flattering. He'd even felt emboldened enough to ask him about the office, but maybe that was Rake's trick; to lull you into letting your guard down and showing your cards. That's exactly what Nick had done, he remembered. He smiled into his glass as he recalled how he'd been encouraged to reveal his curiosity. What had Mel called him? Transparent, and that's how he'd been.

'Is that a safe in the corner?' he'd asked as he stared at a dark green metal door five foot high with a central handle and digital lock. It was wide and narrow. He'd never seen a safe before and this didn't look the shape of the ones regularly busted in the movies.

Mr Rake had smiled and then drawled in his languid way, 'Yeah, easier to fit the wooden cabinet around it after it's been installed. The safe has already been bolted to the floor and,' he'd patted the plaster, 'two abutting walls. It won't be going anywhere.'

'Really?'

'Yeah, no one'll get that out in a hurry. It weighs over 600 lbs.'

'Awesome! I couldn't work out why I was making a unit that shape. Now it make's sense. It's to hide it.'

'No point advertising. And no, in case you're wondering, I don't keep money here.'

Nick remembered glancing at Mr Rake, the next unspoken question obvious.

'It's a gun safe. Far more secure than a simple cabinet with a padlock. Yeah, I subscribe to the American way. No one with a wrench or bolt cutter will get my guns.' He'd driven his hands into his pockets and leaned against the wall. He'd looked unthreatening, passive even next to his gun safe.

'But why keep guns here at work, in this office?' Nick realised what he'd said, but it was too late to retrieve his words. The implications were out. If there'd been a stone to crawl under he'd have squeezed into the tiniest, darkest space. 'Sorry, I didn't mean… anything.'

Mr Rake hadn't answered. He'd just fixed Nick with an unblinking stare; straight, unemotional, impossible to read.

Nick's cheeks had burned as he'd turned away to hide his embarrassment.

'The Hadleigh Rifle Club – it's how I relax after work sometimes. It's conveniently close. Maybe you should try it,' he'd added sweetly. He still leaned against the wall, but now smiling and seemingly amused by Nick's discomfort.

'Come on, Nick,' Dave had barked. 'Stop yakking, there's more to unload from the van.' And so the conversation had ended.

Nick gazed into his empty beer glass, torn between weariness and thirst. Thirst won. He struggled stiffly to his feet. The jukebox pounded out another song, *We Are The Champions*; inappropriate in a World Cup loosing year, he thought as he made his way to the bar. Where were Chrissie and Matt? He elbowed his way through the scrum and ordered a pint. Something hard nudged against his back, almost knocking him into a bar stool. He spun round. 'What the hell?' but his words died as he took in the sight of Matt embracing a motorbike helmet. 'What the hell?' he repeated.

'Hi, mate. I aint got nowhere to put it,' he said indicating the helmet as someone jostled behind, propelling him towards Nick again. Thump! The chin guard connected with Nick's arm.

'For God's sake, Matt, go and find somewhere over there and I'll get you a pint. Carlsberg?'

'Cheers, mate.' Matt backed away.

What was Matt up to now, Nick wondered. It was unbelievable. To be honest, he'd been so busy at Willows he hadn't spoken to him for days. 'See the plaster's off your arm, at last,' Nick remarked moments later as he thumped two overfull glasses down on the small wooden table. 'So did the hospital suggest you wear a helmet in case you broke your head next time?'

'Hi!'

They both looked up. Chrissie had arrived. 'Crikey, Matt. What's with the helmet? Don't tell me you're a nervous pedestrian now.' She threw her handbag down on the table and then headed for the bar, small-change purse in hand.

Matt sipped his lager. 'I reckoned I needed wheels.'

Nick froze, glass halfway to his mouth. 'Matt, you haven't…?'

'I've spent the last few days trainin'. Got me CBT today.' When Nick frowned, Matt sighed and continued, 'Compulsory Basic Trainin'. So, now I can ride me scooter on the road.'

'Ride your scooter,' Nick echoed. 'You've got a scooter?'

Matt nodded, a wide grin dimpling his cheeks. 'Sure. I wanted a Vespa, somethin' Italian. Tom said he'd see what he could do.'

'You've got a Vespa, Matt?' Chrissie arrived back from the bar; wisps of blonde hair stuck to her moist forehead. 'Did I hear right?'

'Yeah an' no. Tom found me somethin' Italian. It's a Piaggio. They make Vespas but–'

'But it's not a Vespa?' Chrissie finished for him.

Matt shrugged.

'C'mon, c'mon. So what is it?' Nick asked, impatience catching his throat as he swallowed a mouthful of Land Girl.

'A Zip!'

'A Zip?' he coughed.

'Yeah, a Piaggio Zip. 49 cc. Almost two years old.'

'Wicked! Does it mean you'll always be walking around with a helmet, or can you stow it somewhere on the scooter?' Chrissie settled on a pine bench, shifting the cushions to get comfortable.

'Yeah, well Tom got me a good price. But I got to fix the lock, then it'll stow under the seat.'

'So how's the Yellow Wedge driving?' Nick asked, but Chrissie didn't seem to hear. He watched as she stared at Matt's tee-shirt.

'But that isn't the name of your scooter, Matt.'

Nick read out the words printed across Matt's chest, '*Casino Royale*.' He was about to say, 'So?' but then realised there was more, in smaller lettering. '*Vesper*.' He didn't attempt to voice the *007* logo or hum the iconic theme tune. Nick started to laugh. Usually he tried to ignore Matt's tee-shirts.

'Yeah, I know – it's a Bond bird; Vesper with an ER. It aint a scooter but it's close enough, an' there weren't nothin' else at the charity shop. Thought I'd try….' Matt glanced down at the cotton stretched across his stomach.

'Irony?' Chrissie murmured.

Matt looked up and grinned. 'You told me I aint no good at irony, Chrissie.'

'Well, you are now.' She frowned and asked, 'How're you paying for it?'

'I owe Tom. If I do 'im some favours there'll be no interest. Not sure what he'll want yet. Once I'm at Hepplewhites I'll start payin' back. It'll be OK. He's lent me cash before.'

'Well, it makes sense. You'll be saving on travel to Hadleigh.' Chrissie drained her glass. 'God, it's hot in here. Come on, let's go outside and see this scooter.'

Nick gulped the last of his beer, and followed Chrissie as she dodged past elbows and dart players. He tried not to laugh as she pushed the old wooden door open for Matt, both his arms now fully engaged in hugging the helmet.

'C'mon, Nick, keep up,' she called over her shoulder.

Outside a slight evening breeze cooled his face and the jukebox sounded muted. He knew he had to ask; he couldn't stop himself, but did he want to hear the answer? Why spoil the relaxed humour of the evening? 'Any more news from Clive Merry?' There, he'd done it.

'Nothing, I'm afraid. He said he'd ring when he'd more to tell, but I've not heard from him again, yet.'

Nick frowned. He could have sworn the DI had an interest in Chrissie.

'What about you? Have you caught up with your gun slinging Kat?'

'Afraid not. It's been mad this week, but I'm hoping tomorrow. They said she's usually in the gun shop on a Saturday. Hey Matt, is this it?'

They stopped next to a brown scooter. Nick thought it looked quite modern with its sloping front wind and leg guard, an aerodynamic design suggesting the promise of speed. The generous seat and wide footrest were somehow absorbed and disguised by its styling.

'Cool! Matt, it's awesome.'

Matt glowed as he moved round it, pointing out its features, touching the grip handle and then resting his helmet on the seat. 'Yeah, I....' A beeping jingle sounded from deep in the cargo pocket of his shorts. 'Yeah?' he said as he groped for his mobile and then frowned as he put it to his ear.

It struck Nick that Matt was holding his phone as if it might bite him. So who's the mystery caller, he wondered as he watched Matt's face break into a grin.

'Yeah .... Yeah, Gloria .... I'm tryin' but it's so temptin' .... Yeah .... No .... Thanks, Gloria.' Matt switched his phone to sleep mode and slipped it back into his pocket.

Nick and Chrissie waited for him to say something, but when he ignored them and ran his hand over the glossy brown paintwork, Nick couldn't hold back any longer.

'Gloria? Who's Gloria, Matt?' he murmured.

'Ah - she's from the Quitline. I were hopin' you'd ask.'

'Quitline? What Quitline?'

'Smokin' Quitline.'

'But you don't smoke, Matt. How can you quit something you don't do?' On the face of it Chrissie's question seemed pretty logical.

'Ah, but see, when I were up the hospital....' He tapped his arm where the plaster cast had been, 'I had to do a bit of waitin' around. I read this notice 'bout...,' he drew himself up as he continued, 'smokin' cessation strategies.'

‘And what’s Quitline?’ Chrissie asked.

‘It’s a telephone support to help you quit. You get at least three follow up calls. I reckoned they’d be birds phonin’ me. An’ I were right!’

‘But it’s Friday evening. Why are they phoning at this hour?’ Chrissie reasoned.

‘Yeah, well I told ’em it were like a cravin’ when I were out of an evenin’, an’ Fridays were real hard. Hope it’s Gloria next time, she sounded nice.’

Nick started to laugh. For the first time since Chrissie’s call about the skeletal remains he felt completely relaxed. Hard work helped but, Gloria? And a Zip?

# CHAPTER 13

*Ping*! A text arrived. There was no caller's name. Matt's phone didn't recognise the number but the sequence looked strangely familiar. 'Yeah, of course the administrative sec. It'll be old Blumfield wantin' to know if I'm OK to start at Hepplewhites.'

Matt read the message. He was right. *Please attend meeting with Mr Blumfield in his office at 13:30 today, Monday*. Well that'll be easy, Matt reckoned. Utterly Academy was about to open again. The summer break had ended and it was back to business as usual. *Please confirm*, the message ended. God, he thought, it's not even nine o'clock yet and they're already on my back.

Matt flung his head back on his pillow. He didn't need to get up yet. No one would notice if he didn't go to the apprentice release day teaching that morning. Officially he was still off sick with his arm until the 13:30 meeting with Blumfield. He closed his eyes. Yes, it had been a great Friday evening, and Chrissie and Nick - their reactions had been priceless. He could still picture their faces when they'd seen his Zip. Perhaps in future he'd call it his Piaggio. It sounded more Italian, especially if he let his voice lilt over the soft G's and then draw out the O. Chrissie had even said he could do irony. Now that was something. Trouble was, he knew he hadn't quite got it – the irony bit. He'd looked it all up over the weekend. Vespa with an A was Italian for wasp and an iconic scooter, Vesper with an ER was Latin for evening. So where was the irony in that? He'd even wondered if it was a reference to him being like James Bond, but in that case he reckoned it was just a compliment. But Chrissie had been impressed, so he'd worn the tee-shirt all weekend while he'd scootered around Stowmarket looking ironic. Now he'd have to find something else to wear for the meeting at 13:30.

*Beep-itty-beep*! *Beep-itty-beep beep*! Matt's mobile burst into life. He squinted at the screen. Tom. For a horrible moment he'd thought it was the Academy again.

'Hi, Tom. How's it going, mate?'

'Wotcha, Matt. Come off the scooter yet?'

'You're kiddin' – course not.'

'I need you to do somethin' for me. Show someone round the Academy. One-thirty today, OK?'

'No-can-do, mate. Got to see the Course Director one-thirty. Sorry.'

'Hmm. Think you'd better do one-thirty, Matt. That's what the bloke wanted.'

In Matt's world there were only a few people scarier than old Blumfield and this unknown bloke wasn't one of them. 'Sorry Tom. Later, OK?'

'Don't know. It'll be on your head if my bloke's upset. He said he'd meet you in the car park, one-thirty, mate. Don't keep him waitin' more than ten minutes. He'll be standin' next to your scooter. Be there. Just be there, OK?' The line went dead.

Matt sat up and swung his legs off the mattress. On the face of it, Tom's request didn't seem too difficult, apart from the double booking aspect. But why did everything have to happen at lunchtime? He'd hoped to meet up with Chrissie and Nick in the canteen, and there was always the possibility he might spot Ginny as well. 'Shoot!'

•••

Matt closed Mr Blumfield's office door on the first floor of the Academy main building and sighed. The meeting was over and he'd escaped into the relative safety of the corridor. All things considered, Matt thought it had gone pretty well. Blumfield had seemed pleased when he'd assured him the doctor said he was OK to start work, and when he held up his arm it was obvious the plaster cast was off – evidence enough for the Course Director.

Matt dug in his jeans for his mobile and adjusted his tee-shirt, pulling it down to cover his pocket. It seemed to have a natural tendency to keep riding up and exposing an expanse of bulky flesh. He checked the time. 13:35. What had Tom said? *The bloke will wait ten minutes. Don't be late.*

He started to walk; his black tee-shirt had a giant exclamation mark almost dividing his chest into two. Small white lettering filled its outline with words like: *one*, *someone*, *one day* and *oneself.* He'd never really understood it. Was it making out the exclamation mark was the number one, or simply an artist's idea of design? It was probably that irony thing again, he decided, but at least it was clean. Tom had once said it looked like a giant bird's dropping and that appealed to Matt. Well, at least Blumfield had been OK, so the bird's shit must have worked.

He checked his mobile. 13:36. He didn't do fast, but he quickened his pace. Why was Blumfield's office so far from the car park? A long passageway and a flight of stairs later, and he'd broken into a sweat. He wiped his moist palms on the exclamation mark and checked the time again. He started to run. A few moments and he was outside. He reckoned if he took the most direct route then he could slow down a bit and catch his breath. His trainers thumped a rhythm on the paving stones as he rounded a corner. On the other side of a low hedge the bike parking area was in sight.

His Piaggio, as he'd now decided to call it, stood beautiful and shiny-brown amongst the other scooters and motorbikes, but he couldn't see anyone near it. He'd hurried for nothing. 'Tom'll kill me!' He checked his mobile. 13:41.

Perhaps the bloke had left a note on the scooter? He stood, panting as he rubbed his forehead with the back of his hand. And then he remembered his helmet. He'd left it in Blumfield's office. 'Shoot!'

Matt turned on his heel, all interest in notes and Tom's bloke driven from his mind. His only thought was to fetch his helmet.

'Hey! Where you going? Supposed to meet me here, weren't you?'

Matt glanced over his shoulder. A student lounged against the Piaggio. It was as if he'd appeared from nowhere. 'Careful, mate! You'll have it over,' Matt squawked, his voice rising. He knew it was an object of desire, but that didn't mean every Tom, Dick and Harry with ginger hair could touch his scooter. 'Look, I aint stoppin'. Left me helmet somewhere.' Before he could add something about coming back to show him the scooter if he was really interested, the penny dropped. 'Are you the bloke I'm meant to be showin' round?' To Matt he just looked like a student: young, tee-shirt, jeans and trainers.

The bloke didn't answer, just watched him as if he was sizing him up. A coil of cigarette smoke rose from one hand and then something seemed to jolt him into action and he raised it to his mouth and inhaled deeply. 'Are you Matt?' he asked, blowing out smoky fumes with each word.

'Yeah.'

'Then I'm the bloke you're showing round, mate.' He threw the butt on the ground and crushed it, twisting his foot in a languid manner seemingly laced with disdain.

'C'mon then. Outside first.'

'Sure. So what subject you thinkin' of studyin'?' Matt couldn't guess. He looked kind of rough with a couple of day's stubble on his face. It was a slightly browner shade of red than his head and considerably paler than the grime under his nails. 'Car maintenance? 'Orticulture?'

The bloke laughed. 'C'mon. Round the buildings and delivery areas first. Nice scooter by the way.'

Matt didn't get it. Why was he showing this guy around? Where was the favour in that? He led the way to the entrance to the main block – the three storey old mansion building, but when he made as if to head through the doorway, he felt a light tap on his shoulder.

'No, mate. Outside.'

Matt shrugged and followed the gravel drive as it wound off to the right. They traced their way between the end of the old mansion building and a new prefabricated block that was home to the performing arts. He trudged on, past the delivery bay and round behind some single storey additions, car maintenance and then carpentry.

'So where're the oil tanks for the heating fuel?'

'Round here,' Matt grunted. He was mildly surprised, but turned back towards the delivery bay. He followed a wide concreted route between some outbuildings and then pointed. 'There, tucked to one side. There's two of 'em, see?'

'Clever. Not obvious till you drive down this way.' The bloke pulled out his mobile and took a photo.

They moved towards the tanks. Matt noticed they were made of some kind of plastic with indented ridged sides, a bit like polystyrene packaging but coloured green. He supposed the ridges gave strength to the structure.

'Double shell,' the bloke noted and took another snap, this time concentrating on a padlock on a circular topped lid.

'Looks like a man'ole cover or one of them entrance hatchways of a Sherman tank,' Matt joked. He felt a little confused. 'So what's your interest in 'em?'

'Urban photography, industrial scenes, mate.'

Matt nodded. 'Cool.' He could relate to that. 'Want to see inside now?'

The bloke looked at his watch. 'No time, mate. We started late, remember?'

They retraced their steps back to the car park, taking their time as the bloke looked up at the buildings, staring and squinting against the sun. Matt noticed the poor bugger had a chipped front tooth. 'What you lookin' for?' he asked.

'CCTV monitors. It's a kind a sport, takin' shots of them watchin' us.'

'Cool.' Matt liked posters of things rather than scenery. He'd once Blu-tacked a close-up of skateboard roller wheels to his bedroom wall. It had been there for so long it left a clean patch when it fell away. The bloke must be into photography, he reckoned. 'The courses are startin' this week. So, what you think you'll sign up for? Photography?' He wasn't sure if there was such a course at the Academy.

'No, mate. You're a right nosey bugger, aren't you? And there was me thinkin' you'd know how to keep your mouth shut.'

Matt closed his mouth. This was rapidly turning into something unpleasant. He should have guessed. Tom was involved so there was bound to be something dodgy about it. If he'd stopped to think for a moment he'd have known this bloke was never going to be a prospective student, and now as he looked at him more closely he saw the mean, hard swagger for what it was. He'd seen guys like this wandering around the Flower Estate; they hunted in packs like feral dogs. Usually it was obvious and they didn't speak, but this bloke had started off OK. Hell.

'If I need to know more I'll be in contact. Like the tee; it's a kind of bird shit statement!' He turned and started to walk away. 'No, don't follow me,' he said over his shoulder and then as an afterthought, 'Helmet! Better look for that helmet. You might need it, Matt.'

Matt froze, rooted to the spot. He closed his eyes. Too many mixed messages. He needed to think. He reckoned actions spoke for themselves. The bloke wanted to know where the heating fuel storage tanks were and he'd probably even checked how full they were while Matt was imagining Sherman tanks. This wasn't about urban art. The bloke was casing the joint. What should he do? Tell someone? But what if they didn't believe him; thought he was setting up a heist and then grassing on his mates in case he didn't get his cut? He didn't even know the guy's name. The only link was Tom. Bloody Tom. What should he do? He looked around but Tom's bloke had already vanished into the car park. Lunch. That might help and Chrissie and Nick might be up in the canteen. It was the apprentice release day, after all. He checked his mobile. Almost two o'clock.

‘Helmet! Get me helmet.’ That’s what the bloke had said and Matt decided it made good sense. He headed back into the main building, all enthusiasm evaporating with the sweat on his face and neck. The stairs up to the first floor seemed steeper than ever, and half way up he stood to one side to catch his breath. A torrent of scruffy last-minute diners hurried down towards him, already late for their various lectures and practical sessions.

‘Hi Matt,’ someone called, and he spotted the back of Nick’s head disappearing down the stairs.

‘Maybe catch you later?’ Matt called after him, his voice blending with the heavy footfalls. ‘Over at Clegg’s?’

Nick raised a hand above the bobbing heads and then he was gone.

•••

Matt found his helmet on the floor outside Mr Blumfield’s office. He must have put it down when he knocked on his door at one-thirty. It looked huge, bulbous and shiny white, like a robotic cleaning device out of some futuristic film set. He snatched it up and hugged it to him. ‘Need to get that seat lock fixed,’ he muttered as he wandered along the corridor and up another flight of stairs to an administrative office on the hot, pokey top floor. He needed to hand in the doctor’s certificate saying he was fit to return to work and he also wanted Hepplewhites address and instructions on where and when exactly to turn up the following morning. He felt his life was starting to change.

•••

The wind blew against his arms. It was difficult to get the full force-ten effect with a top speed of only 30 mph when flat-out and on the level, but Matt did his best, grimacing behind his smoked Perspex visor. He’d almost reached 33 mph on the hill down into Bildeston but the scooter's two-stroke engine complained and struggled as it pulled his thirteen and a half stone out of the valley and onto the road to Hadleigh. It was Tuesday morning and Matt felt fantastic. He still wore his black tee-shirt, the one with the exclamation mark / bird shit design, but he reckoned he'd be working so it wouldn't matter if it wasn't exactly fresh. His full-helmet with chin guard, all white, topped off the exclamation mark. Somewhere in the stowage compartment under his seat, firmly held closed by the weight of his ample bottom, were the instructions and paperwork to hand into Hepplewhites.

'Don't be late; not on your first day, Matt.' The memory of Chrissie's voice reverberated inside his helmet.

He'd enjoyed himself over at the Clegg workshop the previous afternoon. They'd met there at about four o'clock. Chrissie and Nick had come hot-foot from the apprentice release day, but he'd skipped the afternoon teaching and got there earlier. He could do that sort of thing now he had the scooter. They'd drunk mugs of tea and then Ron supervised their practice carvings. Matt wondered if they'd ever get the totem pole completed. He'd wanted to say something about Tom's bloke but the right moment never came up, so he'd dismissed the uncomfortable thoughts to some silent, uninhabited part of his brain while he'd tried to get his head around the three-dimensional aspects of carving.

It didn't take Matt long to find the Hepplewhites workshops. He'd studied the Google map after he left the administration office the previous afternoon and now he pictured it in his mind and simply followed the route. For once he felt superior to his comic-strip heroes. They needed special electronics to project a map onto a helmet's visor screen whereas he just conjured it up.

'Oh hell,' he muttered when he saw Friars' Hill rising ahead. The Piaggio finally stopped complaining as he rode across a concrete ramp and into a tidy forecourt. He parked and pulled off his helmet. His dark sandy hair was part crushed, part standing on end and he grabbed his paperwork out of the under-seat compartment. A smart green door seemed the obvious entrance and he hurried inside, still hugging his helmet and temporarily clamping the paper-work between his teeth.

'Good morning.' A middle aged woman looked up from her computer screen. She sat at a desk, presiding over a deserted office with filing cabinets along one wall, a few scattered office waiting chairs and a water dispenser.

'Mornin',' Matt mumbled, grabbing the papers from between his lips whilst still embracing the helmet. 'For you....' He shuffled towards her, proffering the documents. Saliva discoloured the edges where his teeth had indented and crinkled the paper.

She stared at him without speaking.

'For you,' he repeated.

'And you are?'

He dropped the paper on her desk. 'It's all there. Matt Finch, apprentice.'

She frowned and with well-manicured finger and thumb, grasped the pile and pulled it towards her. 'Matt Finch,' she murmured and then read for a moment. 'Oh yes, I remember - the apprentice arrangement with Utterly Academy. Weren't you supposed to start sometime in June? You're almost three months late.' She tapped the desk, her polished nails flashing like blades.

'Yeah, but I bust me wrist.'

She pulled a face.

'So where'd I go now?'

'I don't think Mr White is expecting you. In fact he may have already left.' She checked her watch. 'Yes, you're too late.' She frowned and looked at her computer screen. 'That leaves… Alan. If you're quick you might catch him. He's round the back.' She pointed over her shoulder with an unhurried movement loaded with disdain.

Matt stood his ground. He hugged his helmet and waited for more specific instructions.

'I suppose I'll have to show you.' She combined a sigh with a grunt and stood up. 'You won't need the helmet. I expect Alan'll take you with him in the van. Leave it here if you like. Come on.'

'Thanks.' Matt balanced it on the top of the water dispenser and grinned at his reflection in the visor. Cool! It looked like something from Doctor Who.

Outside, Matt heard a diesel engine starting up, and ducked as something swooped from the overhang of an old stable block, part of the workshop premises. A moment later a van appeared from the back of what had once been an old cowshed. The woman stepped into its path and waved both hands as if she was marshalling a plane.

'Hey! Alan stop!'

The van, the same green as the entrance door and with side windows open, drew to a halt. 'What now, Janet?'

'There's an apprentice here for you. From Utterly.'

'What?'

'Mornin'.' Matt ambled forward and grinned.

Janet stood with her hands on her hips. 'There's no one in the workshop this morning and you can't leave him hanging round me.'

Matt watched as Alan's face changed from an earthy colour to a muddy red. 'Oh, for Pete's sake,' he hissed. 'No one told me.' He stared at Janet for a moment before turning his attention back to Matt. 'Suppose you'd better come with me then, lad.'

Matt didn't need a second invitation. The thought of being left with Janet for the morning was enough to spur him into movement. He reached for the passenger door handle, let the weight of his arm pull it open and heaved his leg up to climb into the van, at least he would have if his foot hadn't slipped. Alan, oblivious to Matt's lack of agility, began to draw away. 'Y-ouch!' The door swung closed, catching Matt across the back of his calf.

Alan stopped the van. 'Are you all right? It looks like those house martins got you as well.'

'I'll be OK,' he said, rubbing his leg. 'Come on, just get goin'. I'm Matt, by the way. Matt Finch, the new apprentice.'

'Well, Matt, we're heading over to Bildeston. You must've guessed by now, no one's expecting you today. I'm Alan.' His weathered face seemed to crease into deep folds as he smiled. 'Are you from round here?'

'Yeah, Stowmarket. So what we doin' today?' Matt sneaked a sideways glance. He reckoned Alan could be any age over forty.

'Well, if she'd told us, then some kind of introduction. You know, health and safety stuff. As it is you're in the deep end. Bloody woman.' He paused to indicate and then turned onto the A1141, heading away from Hadleigh.

'We're fitting out a walk-in-wardrobe. One of those old houses with a roof space and gables like a maze. It's proving tricky. How'd you get here, then?'

'Piaggio,' and when Alan didn't seem to react, he added, 'On me scooter. It's a Piaggio.'

'That's handy.' They drove in silence for a few miles and then Alan frowned. 'We're working in someone's home remember, so don't make a mess, and watch your language.' After another silence he added, 'And no chatting up the lady of the house.'

Matt grinned. He was secretly flattered. Alan must think he was some kind of red-blooded guy. To be honest, he'd never considered chatting up a middle aged bird. Take Janet, he couldn't think of anyone less fanciable.

'Not much further,' Alan muttered as he slowed to give way for a car where the road narrowed in the centre of Bildeston. 'It's out the other side. We're almost there now.'

A few moments later he turned into a gravel driveway. It wound into a large circular expanse of gritty stones, hidden from the road by tall hedges. The house was slightly offset, old and beamy. The roof was its most striking feature. Peg tiles, like fish scales seemed to coat the steep inclines, roof ridges joined at angles and brick chimneys pointed to the sky.

'There's more roof than 'ouse,' Matt muttered. 'Wow, it's.... Do many people live 'ere?'

'I don't know, exactly. I've only seen Mrs Mann. Her husband died recently. You may have heard about it. Now come on. Time to unload the van.'

'Mrs Mann? Jim Mann's wife?'

'Yeah, why? D'you know him? Dreadful business. Are you OK, lad?'

Matt sat glued to the seat. He couldn't believe his ears. This must be the place where Nick came to see the beehive; where bad things happened, like being shot at. He cast around. Was someone aiming at him? Could he see the muzzle of a gun or was it just part of a birdfeeder near the hedge? He began to sweat. The words died in his mouth so he kept his thoughts to himself and nodded.

'Good, we've work to do. Can't stay sittin' in the van all day. Fresh air'll clear your head. Come on.'

'What time are we meant to start, then?'

'Now. We were lucky to get this job. It should've gone to the Willows lot in Needham. So look a bit lively and help take some things in.'

Matt swung the door open and gingerly lowered himself out of the van. He wished he was one of his comic-strip superheroes with eyes in the back of his head. Instead he was wearing a bird shit design tee-shirt and exposing his rear – an easy target for the ready-to-assemble sniper's rifle disguised as a birdfeeder. Meanwhile, Alan threw the van's back doors wide open and started pulling out lengths of timber.

'Here, take the other end, Matt. We'll stack 'em up and then you can bring 'em in as I need 'em.' He looked past the van, towards the house and smiled. 'Mornin' Mrs Mann. I've got Matt here to help me today.'

Matt twisted to see Jim's widow, she must have come out from somewhere while he was watching the birdfeeder, but the van door blocked his view.

'Tea OK for both of you? Any sugar, Matt?' The voice was almost musical.

'Yeah, two sugars, thanks.'

'I'll leave the mugs in the kitchen. The one with a spoon in's got the sugar. I'm a bit busy so maybe you can carry them upstairs yourselves. OK?'

'Yeah, that'll be great. I'll send Matt to fetch the tea when we've unloaded the van and got our stuff inside.' Alan halted while he spoke and Matt, still holding the other end of the timber, found himself pinned against the rear of the van. He'd heard her soft lilting tones, but it might as well have been the bird table speaking, for all he could see past the van door. He felt like a lump of meat stuck on the end of a grill-stick. Footsteps scrunched on the gravel and Alan started moving again. Matt shuffled forward, linked to him by the timber, and caught his first glimpse of Mrs Mann as she strode back into the house. He never saw her face, just her dark, loosely-plaited hair and the cornflower-blue skirt as it swirled around her calves.

'Argh!' He scuffed his trainer on the gravel. If he hadn't been holding his end of the wood he'd have gone flying.

# CHAPTER 14

Chrissie looked up from the screen. She was finding it hard to concentrate. That in itself was not unusual but she'd logged onto a Rennie Mackintosh website and was reading about the Glasgow School of Art. It should have interested her, grabbed her imagination and then held her. The ground-breaking designs still looked as fresh and clean to her now as they must have when first seen in the early nineteen-hundreds, but for some reason her mind kept wandering. Perhaps it was time to redecorate her living room? She wondered how an art nouveau rug would look on her old pine floorboards. She glanced around the small room with its narrow Victorian fireplace and mean sash window. She'd squeezed an armchair into the space behind the door and the rest of the room felt swamped by the two-seater sofa.

She sat with her laptop balanced on her knee. It had felt cosy when Bill was alive and then safe after he died, but now it was starting to close in on her. The photos and knick-knacks pointed accusingly, reminding her of Bill and a past life already beginning to fade; a time capsule she could only revisit in her dreams. It was early evening and a Wednesday, neither the beginning nor the end of the week; the day trapped equidistant between the weekends. A non-day. 'And it's already September,' she murmured. 'I must answer Sarah's email.'

If she left it any longer she'd end up offending Sarah beyond what could be brushed off as being busy or depressed. They'd met at the Ipswich fencing club six months before Bill died, both new members and complete novices.

Their friendship had blossomed, born of similar interests but totally different personalities and both living in Woolpit. Chrissie had dropped out of the club, devastated by Bill's death, but Sarah had become quite skilled with a foil and rather enamoured with the instructor. She was bubbly and outgoing and at first tried to offer support by trying to jolly Chrissie out of her misery. Then, when that didn't work, she left it to occasional meetings for coffee and a pep-talk. They hadn't seen each other for a few months and Chrissie knew she needed to make an effort; she didn't want the friendship to die. The trouble was she didn't know if she could face Sarah's animated chatter, not this evening. It was probably best to just reply with an upbeat email and fix a meeting soon. Chrissie sensed she was changing, moving on from Bill and finding herself again. But for the moment she was still caught; caught between summer and autumn, Bill and life without Bill.

Her thoughts drifted back to the now. She wondered how Matt had got on at Hepplewhites. And Nick? Had he asked his hot-haired Kat out on a date yet? She closed her eyes and more questions popped into her mind. What of Clive Merry and Alderman's Point? Why hadn't he phoned her and why should she care?

Her mobile rang, fracturing her solitude.

'Hi!' she answered, hardly taking in the caller ID.

'Hi! Chrissie?'

She recognised his voice immediately. Had she summoned him up simply by thinking of him? It certainly hadn't worked before and anyway, she wasn't going to admit he'd entered her thoughts for more than a fleeting second. She felt surprised, slightly anxious, but also a little excited.

'Chrissie? Are you still there? It's Clive. Clive Merry.'

'Yes, and I know which Clive you are. So hi and how are you?'

'I'm fine, thanks. Look we've had the analysis back on the bullets and bullet casings we found at Alderman's Point.'

'Bullets? You never said you'd found bullets. Teeth and human remains. That's all you said.' Chrissie tried to keep her voice steady.

'Well, I can't tell you everything.' The line seemed to go dead for a moment and then Clive's voice broke back onto the airwaves. 'Look, I wanted to speak to you myself. There've been some developments and the forensic ballistic boys have been busy.'

'The forensic ballistic boys?' she echoed. 'They sound like the name of a pop group.'

'Yes, I suppose they do. They're firearms identification boffins. Look, I think this might be easier if I talked to you face to face. Can we meet? It's only six o'clock. I'm on my way home.'

Chrissie's stomach did a flip. What did he need to tell her that couldn't be said over the phone? 'It's nothing terrible is it?' she asked, her voice threatening to slide into falsetto.

'No, nothing for you to worry about, but it's police business and I'd rather speak to you face to face.'

'But I'm.... Why...?'

'Is it inconvenient? Sorry. I didn't think. I'd hoped to catch you earlier. I didn't want to intrude on your evening. You can come into the station tomorrow, if you'd prefer.'

'No, no. You've got me really curious now.' Curious was an understatement, terrified would have been closer to the truth. 'Is there some kind of danger?' Her pulse stepped up a gear. It had been racing since he mentioned the bit about police business.

'I don't think so, but I'd like you to tell me again exactly what happened at Alderman's Point. There may be something you don't realise you've left out. It may be important.'

Chrissie didn't know what to say. She hardly dared voice her deepest fear. 'It's not... you don't think it's anything to do with Valko Asenov?' She almost choked as she said his name.

'No, no. Nothing to do with the psychopath who stole your car a few months ago.'

Chrissie wasn't convinced. Clive's voice didn't hold enough conviction and he'd answered too quickly. It was just like him to try and spare her feelings, but the theft of her car was the reason she'd ever met the DI in the first place. It had barely been more than a couple of months ago and he'd been in charge of the case. Valko Asenov had turned out to be a Bulgarian criminal loose in Suffolk. The memories came flooding back. She closed her eyes, trying to shut out the image of her burning car.

'Look, I'm sorry. I shouldn't have phoned. He's in a Bulgarian jail. We've checked he's still there. And he'll be there for years to come.'

'Thank God for that. Yes, you must come round. I have to know what you've got to tell me. Do you have my address?'

'Yes, from your statement when your old MGB was stolen. It's number three, Albert Cottages isn't it? I'll be about thirty minutes.' The line went dead.

Chrissie didn't usually swear. 'Oh my God!' she yelped, but it didn't help.

•••

Twenty-five minutes later the doorbell rang. The electric buzzer had lost its resonance and the best it could do was feeble, like the noise of a dying rattle snake. Chrissie moved slowly, a dreadful foreboding weighing on her shoulders. She'd just had time to change out of her work clothes and throw on a clean tee-shirt and jeans, but the mugs and breakfast bowl would have to stay on the draining board in the kitchen and her laptop, still open, rested on half the sofa.

She released the lock and pulled at the old front door handle. 'Hi, so you found it OK.' She immediately felt stupid. Of course he'd found her house OK, he was standing outside her front door and had arrived sooner than she'd expected. Her cheeks started to burn. 'Come on in, Clive.'

'Sorry to intrude like this but it's best you know what's going on before the papers get hold of it.' He closed the front door behind him and followed her through the small hall and into the sitting room.

Last time he'd phoned, it was in case she *heard it on the news first*. Was this going to be the only reason he'd ever contact her, she wondered. 'Just say what you've got to say. Tell me and then I can cope with it. As it is I'm imagining all kinds of dreadful things. Sorry, where are my manners? Do sit down.'

Chrissie watched as the tall DI shoe-horned himself into the armchair behind the door. He'd left his jacket in the car and his cotton shirt looked crumpled. He smiled at her, but he looked distracted, as if his mind was working overtime. 'The bullet?' she prompted.

'Ah yes. It seems the bullet that killed Jim Mann may have been fired from the same gun as the bullets and casings we found at Alderman's Point. The marks on the casing we retrieved in the orchard match the grooves and indents on the one's we found close to where the Lexus was parked.'

'Oh my God!'

'And although it's difficult to be 100% certain with the bullets–'

'Why?' she interrupted.

'Because bullets get distorted when they're fired into something. It messes up the marks - the striations. But what they have been able to look at on the bullets seems to match, or rather the striations do. So you see it's the same gun.'

'But we walked past that Lexus. We were close. Are you saying a killer shot at us? At me?'

'Yes, but I don't think he, or she was intending to hit you, just to frighten you all away. You were getting too close to something important. What it tells us is the evidence is mounting up and we don't think Jim Mann was shot accidently. The Coroner's handed it on to the Crown Prosecution service. We're probably dealing with a murder.'

Chrissie didn't say anything while she processed the implications. Finally she voiced the hunch which had been gaining strength since she'd seen the common borage. She spoke slowly. 'What it tells me is Jim Mann wasn't the only person who didn't want people disturbing Alderman's Point.'

'Whatever do you mean?' He frowned and then added, 'Why do you say that?'

'Jim Mann didn't want a phone mast put up there. He wrote letters objecting. They were in the local paper. Maybe he knew something… something about what was buried up there.'

'Now slow down Chrissie, you're usually so logical. This is just pure speculation.' Then he added, almost under his breath, 'I didn't know about the phone mast business.'

Chrissie felt stupid. He'd said she was being illogical and the humiliation drove a hot glow to her cheeks. She stared at a knot in the old floorboards.

'Look, we're still trying to identify the skeleton. I said human remains, but really there were only bones. It's not much to go on and it's a painstaking business. We know she was female and her approximate age was twenty-five to thirty years old when she died. But how long she's been in the ground? That's more difficult and it'll take longer to find out. We're working on about twenty years. We can look to see who was registered missing around that time.'

'But you can get DNA from the bones, can't you?'

'Not really. But those teeth are good. We can ask the lab to look at some pulp from a tooth, but we still have to match it against someone. It's only recently DNA samples are taken routinely when relatives register someone missing. They give a bit of hair from a brush or something.'

Chrissie nodded. 'What about Jim Mann's first wife, Minnette? She has to be a candidate, for a start.'

'Why? And anyway there's no hope of getting any of her DNA. Not now, not after all this time.'

'But she was reported as a missing person and her age would fit.' Chrissie was guessing now. Fishing.

'She wasn't reported missing for a few years. According to our inquiries Jim Mann thought she'd walked out and returned to France. About ten years ago he applied to dissolve the marriage and she couldn't be traced. The French authorities were involved and it took time. You can imagine. And then as part of that process she was reported as missing and then finally registered as presumed dead.'

'And so he was free to marry again?'

'Yes, he married last year. You seem very interested. Why?'

Chrissie felt calmer when she was talking facts with the DI, but she didn't want to seem illogical again. Those blue flowers had caught her imagination; she knew it was only a flight of fancy, but she couldn't shake off the conviction it was Minnette buried on Alderman's Point. She ignored his question. 'So you could end up checking the bones against every female of the right age who was reported missing around twenty years ago?'

'Yup! Now, what can you remember about the Lexus?'

'Nothing much, really. It was black, looked newish… yes that's about it. We were all talking. We'd just had lunch and, well I was thinking about Alderman's Point. I never saw anyone, just heard the two shots. You know the rest. That's all.'

'Hmm, well you'll need to make a statement and see if you can identify the Lexus model. Also, if you could bring in the shoes you were wearing then we can exclude some of the foot prints.'

'Just me, or Nick and Matt as well?'

'All of you, but I'll get one of my chaps to contact them. We got Nick's number but if you could give me Matt's?'

Chrissie couldn't help smiling. 'So I've had special treatment with you coming to speak to me personally. And there was me thinking it was all part of the service and you visited everyone!'

Clive smiled, and this time it reached the creases near his eyes. 'No, I was just on my way home.'

'Are you sure you won't have tea or coffee?' Chrissie knew she hadn't offered any earlier, but it sounded better if she said it that way.

'No, no thanks. I must be getting home. It's been a hell of a day.'

She checked the knot in the floorboard near her foot. She sensed he was looking at her.

'Maybe some other time though,' he said as he stood up. 'Let me know when you come in to make your statement. Perhaps I could treat you to a police cuppa? Or, if you'd prefer, they do a nice lunch at the Rose.'

'Thanks. The police cuppa sounds almost irresistible, but I expect we'll all end up going over together on Monday. It's easier on the release day.'

'Sure.'

She followed him out into the hall, confused. Was he making a play for her or just being polite? More to the point, was he available? He paused in the hall. Bill's photo, the one in the polished pewter frame, smiled up at Clive. In fact Bill smiled at anyone who passed the hall table. He'd sat there for over two years, captured in pixels with legs astride a gate and the wind catching his hair.

'Bill?' he asked.

It wasn't fair. Clive knew she was widowed but she knew nothing about him. 'Yes, do you have the equivalent of a Bill at home?' She felt stupid again. Why did she say such crass things when Clive was around, she wondered.

'No. Mary and I divorced a few years ago.' He looked back at her and frowned. 'I'm not gay, if that's what you meant.'

Chrissie felt her cheeks burn. If the ground had opened beneath her feet, she'd have dived in. But it didn't, so she stood, searching for the words to say it wasn't at all what she meant. 'No, no... I didn't....' She closed her mouth. She was making it worse.

'I have to get home. I promised to feed a neighbour's cat. The old boy had to go into hospital at short notice yesterday. Now don't forget, phone me when you come in to give your statement.' He turned and then he was gone, the old front door clunking as it closed behind him.

Chrissie waited for a moment, not wanting to move. Her stillness was at odds with the turmoil in her mind. Thoughts buzzed back and forth, colliding with emotion as logic struggled to gain control. Clive was right. She needed to be rational but she couldn't help feeling a little flattered as well.

# CHAPTER 15

Nick arrived late at the Nags Head on Friday evening. He should have been meeting Chrissie and Matt earlier, but an old mate had begged him to help out. The singer in Jake's band had been laid low with a nasty bout of tonsillitis. It was short notice, but the band had fought long and hard for a prestigious Saturday night spot in the line-up at the John Peel Centre in Stowmarket and they were desperate not to cancel. It would be months before the chance came around again. At first Nick was reluctant to sing with the band. Jazz-folk wasn't really his style, but after Jake cajoled and flattered him, he'd agreed. It was an emergency, at least in the life of the band. The evening practice session in the drummer's garage had gone well and now he'd had a chance to run through the numbers with them, he felt confident. Secretly he suspected his voice was better than their usual singer. Why else would he have overheard the base guitarist suggesting they ask him to sing for them regularly?

Nick checked his watch. Ten o'clock. The Nags Head exuded a discordant mix of noise. Chattering voices, clinking glasses and jukebox greeted him as he pushed his way through the door and elbowed a path to the bar. He was dying for a pint and hoped to get a quick one in before searching out Chrissie and Matt. He guessed they'd be somewhere in the quieter area in what had once been the lounge bar before the pub was opened out a little. He could have gone for a drink with Jake at the Crown but he preferred the Nags Head and anyway, he'd be spending Saturday evening with the band at the John Peel Centre.

‘Hi!’ He spotted the back of Chrissie’s head. There was no mistaking her short blonde bob.

Matt looked up and grinned. ‘Wotcha, mate!’ His white helmet sat next to him on the bench seat and two half-full glasses stood like soldiers on the small pine table.

‘I see you haven’t fixed the lock on your scooter seat yet.’ Nick set his pint on the table and pulled up a stool. He nodded at the helmet. It felt like a fourth person at the table, a kind of presence.

‘How did the practice go? Voice holding out OK?’ Chrissie smiled and reached for her glass.

‘Good – it was good.’

‘Yeah, we were thinkin’ of comin’ to the gig tomorrow.’

‘Might not be quite your thing, but... that’d be great. Kat said she’d come as well.’

‘You’ve finally asked her out?’ Chrissie said.

Nick felt his face flush and nodded. ‘Went out on Tuesday.’ He looked at his friends and grinned. ‘Well, I s’pose you’d call it a date. She took me to the Hadleigh Rifle Club.’

‘What?’ Chrissie held her glass mid-way to her mouth, arrested in motion as her eyebrows threatened to disappear behind her fringe.

‘Cool dude, mate!’ Matt’s reaction was much more predictable.

Nick concentrated on his beer as he thought back to the evening. They’d parked near the Drill Hall on George Street and he’d followed her, pulse racing, onto the firing range. It had proved difficult to chat much but he’d managed a few one-liners, despite the ear muffs. Later he listened mesmerised as she talked about her ·22 rifle and her ambition for the fifty metre Olympic rifle event. He'd felt as if he'd been allowed a glimpse into another world, but something had surprised him. It had niggled afterwards like an itch. When he'd mentioned Ricky Rake and his gun safe, Kat said she'd never heard of him and certainly never seen him at the Hadleigh Rifle Club. She didn't think he was even a member. So why had Ricky Rake said he was? Nick shook his head.

'Why are you shaking your head, Nick?' Chrissie's voice jolted him back to the present and the Nags Head.

'Nothing, nothing.' There was no point in telling Matt and Chrissie; he didn't think they'd understand. 'So, what've you two been talking about while I was at band practice? I assume you've both had a call from the police to make a statement?'

'Yeah, it's an offer you can't refuse, mate. Are we all goin' together on Monday?'

'It makes good sense. I think they want us to remember some details about that Lexus.'

'Why d'you say that Chrissie?' He watched her face redden. 'The bloke who phoned me said just to come and make a statement. He didn't mention the Lexus. Has your DI spoken to you, then?'

'No. I imagine I've had the same call as you guys.'

He watched as she sipped her ginger beer, hiding her face with her glass. He was puzzled, but when she didn't say anymore, he shrugged. 'Don't suppose you can remember the number plate, Matt?'

'Sorry, mate. Didn't look. There's somethin' been botherin' me since last week though.'

'Oh yeah?'

'Yeah. Tom asked me to show some bloke round Utterly. See, I thought he were wantin' to be a student, but all he looked at were the oil tanks.'

'The oil tanks?' Chrissie echoed.

'Yeah, the heatin' oil. I think he's settin' it up. To nick it.'

'You'd better tell the Academy about it, Matt.'

'Can't, Chrissie. Tom'll kill me.'

'I could come with you.' The words were out. Nick hadn't really thought before he spoke. 'We could say we'd seen some dodgy characters hanging round the tanks and… the Academy needs to improve the security.'

*Beep-itty-beep*! *Beep-itty-beep beep*! The jingle burst into life as Matt grabbed at his pocket.

'Gloria?' Chrissie and Nick asked in unison.

Matt grasped his mobile, covering the microphone as he mouthed, 'Smokin' Cessation.'

Nick watched, trying to guess Gloria's half of the conversation as Matt spoke into the phone. He imagined her, sincere and intense on the other end while Matt angled to keep her talking and her calls coming. He really was a toe-rag sometimes.

•••

Monday was dull and breezy. It made Nick feel as if summer was already on its way out as it wheezed gusts of wind before making way for autumn. Even the midday sky looked gloomy. Another week or two and the Academy would need to switch on the heating. So where was Matt?

'He should be here by now,' Nick muttered, trying to control his irritation as he scanned the teeming throng. He knew Matt tended to slip some of the release day sessions, but this was getting ridiculous.

They'd arranged to meet before lunch in the main corridor near the notice boards. After the evening in the Nags Head on Friday they'd agreed it would be sensible if Matt at least showed Nick the fuel tanks, but he hadn't turned up.

'Bloody slouch,' Nick muttered, and then he spotted him. 'What the hell are you wearing, Matt?' Irritation sharpened his voice.

'Tee-shirt. Put it on specially coz of you, mate.'

Nick stared at Matt's chest. The print of a large ginger globe filled the centre of the black cotton. It resembled an orange and seemed to unravel at the top as if someone had started to peel off its rind. 'An orange? Orange - the mobile network provider? For me?' he nearly added, *are you mad*? But he stopped himself when he saw Matt's face.

'No. It's bein' peeled, mate. Kind of says John Peel Centre to me. You were brilliant.'

'But it doesn't say anything on it, nothing about the Centre.'

'Yeah, but I thought you'd guess. Best I could do.'

Nick closed his eyes for a moment. Irritation, frustration and disbelief chased an overwhelming desire to laugh. He shut his mouth and struggled to regain control of his emotions. 'Thanks, Matt. Now get a move on. I don't want to waste the whole of my lunch break on this.'

Dodging between groups of students, they followed the marble floor, as it blended into the wooden boards and then finally the grey heavy duty carpet. The busy corridor seemed to stretch forever, but at last Matt zigzagged towards a side door, and then they were outside. Nick followed him between outbuildings and through the service area.

'Over there,' Matt said pointing.

It took Nick a moment to spot the tanks. 'I don't think I've come out this way before. They're quite well hidden. So, was it just the one bloke?'

'Yeah, no one else. He met me in the car park. I aint seen his car. Don't know how 'e got there.'

Nick took a closer look at the tanks and then they re-traced their route in silence. As he walked, Nick tried to work out what he was going to say when they reached the administrative office. In the end he decided he'd leave Matt to do the talking, after all he was the one who'd seen Tom's bloke. 'Ready?' he asked as they shoved and jostled their way up the stairs to the second floor.

He barely caught Matt's mumbled reply as he pushed at a half open door and looked into an open-plan office.

'Come on, Matt,' he hissed over his shoulder.

'Can I help?' A face dominated by heavy frame fashion glasses peered over a computer screen.

'Yes.... Hi! Umm, we were wondering who we should speak to about,' he paused and smiled.

'We?' She looked above his head and then to one side in a deliberate, slow move. 'We?' she repeated and adjusted her glasses.

Nick glanced behind him. There was no one there.

'Where the...?'

'Yes?' She stared at him. Recognition flashed across her face. 'Weren't you... weren't you singing at the John Peel Centre on Saturday?'

Nick studied his trainers. Where the hell was Matt?

'I'll kill the toad,' he muttered.

'*Still on the Road.* Yes that's the song. You were great, really!'

Nick looked up. He had to think fast. Her cherry-coloured lipstick was rather tantalizing so he reckoned there was only one option. He smiled slowly. 'I've got a small problem, something I feel I should report. But I'm not sure who I should speak to. Perhaps you could advise me?'

She leaned forwards.

Nick's brain worked feverishly. Where are you Matt, you bastard, I'll kill you, he thought. 'Maybe it's a matter for security?' he continued without missing a beat.

He smiled again and she simpered. Nick began to regain his composure as he basked in her attention. He even started to relax a little as one half of his brain concentrated on her fashion glasses and lip gloss; the other less primeval half planned retribution for Matt's desertion. It didn't take him long to explain his suspicions about the fictitious character he'd supposedly seen and then he froze as she lifted the phone and made a call.

'I've spoken to Donald.... Ah, Don,' she said looking past Nick as she replaced the phone, 'That was fast! This is Nick.'

A middle aged man strode into the office. He wore black trousers and a blue shirt with *Security* embroidered on the epaulet. Close-cropped hair topped his head. It reminded Nick of the bristles on a toilet brush. Sanitation sprang to mind, not security.

'Hello, Nick. I'm Donald. I'm in charge of security.' He held out his hand and Nick winced as his own was crushed in an iron grip, an unspoken signal that he was in Donald's safe hands. 'So, you've seen some bloke hanging round the Academy's fuel tanks and asking lots of questions.'

'Yeah, that's about it.'

'Ex-police,' a voice whispered from behind the computer screen, as if it would explain everything.

'Can you describe this person?'

Nick swallowed hard. He'd guessed this might happen. That's what Matt was supposed to be here for, the little shit. 'Well, he was mid-height, average build... nothing out of the ordinary.'

'Age?'

Nick glanced at the ceiling for inspiration. 'Difficult to be sure. Maybe twenties.'

'But you'd recognise him again?'

'Oh yeah, of course,' he lied.

'I've been thinking about those tanks. We're vulnerable here. As you say, an easy target. Lucky you caught me. Well thanks, Nick. I may get back to you.'

Nick saw his opportunity to get away. 'I'll leave my number with...?' He smiled at the eyes behind the fashion glasses.

'Glynnis.'

'With Glynnis,' he continued. 'But I've got to go now.' He checked his watch as she reached for a ballpoint.

He wrestled briefly with his conscience as he gave Glynnis the mobile number. He'd planned to give her Matt's details and land him with the security guy if more information was requested. It would serve him right, but there was a chance Glynnis might phone Nick anyway. He'd been the singer in the band, and maybe she fancied him. It would never do if Matt got her call. Reprisal, not reward was on Nick's mind.

Five minutes later Nick hurried to the canteen. He wasn't surprised there was no sign of Matt or that he didn't show up for the afternoon teaching session. Part of him didn't care. He was too annoyed, but irritation turned to concern when, at the end of the afternoon, he waited by his battered Ford Fiesta in the student car park and Matt didn't turn up.

'Where the hell is he?' he muttered.

They'd agreed, when they'd parted on Friday night, to share a car and all go together to make their statements at the end of the release day. Only ten minutes ago Chrissie had said she'd check in the library, Matt's favoured hiding place, but there still wasn't any sign of either of them.

'Where the hell are they?' Nick muttered again.

# CHAPTER 16

Matt bolted. He didn't think. He just reacted. 'Sorry, mate but Tom'll kill me if he finds out,' he mumbled.

He hoped Nick had heard him, but he didn't wait to find out. He hurried back along the corridor. When no footsteps thudded behind him, he slowed his pace. Nick must have gone into the office without him.

The scent of peperoni pizza wafted up the stairs, flirting with his nose and enticing him down to the first floor canteen. He was sweating and his breath came in wheezy gasps as he held the handrail and descended. He wiped his forehead and stood for a moment. Should he retrace his steps and join Nick, he wondered. If he turned back now, would Nick have had time to tell the office about the fuel tanks? Matt could pretend he'd been taken short by the irresistible call of nature and needed to pee. There'd be no need to say he'd lost his nerve. But if Nick was still in there talking about Tom's bloke, then he'd be drawn in. What if Tom found out?

Matt hovered, consumed with indecision.

'Hi, Chemistry Dude!'

He whisked around, almost overbalancing. 'Hi. Ginny! Ginny?'

She had her back to him, her tie-dye cotton skirt flouncing as she headed towards the library. He followed like a hungry hound, ignoring the lure of the canteen and pursuing the faint bouquet of flowers and precious woods. He'd never spent any time at the women's perfume section in Superdrug and had no idea what was responsible for Ginny's exotic trail. She moved surprisingly fast and Matt lagged behind, all thoughts of Nick and Tom's bloke replaced by the vision in front. Optimism propelled him through the library door and hope pulled him towards her as she stood, her back towards him and already in conversation with Rosie.

'Hi,' he said as he made a mental note to check if any of the charity shops in Stowmarket sold perfume. Cancer Research and the National Heart Foundation never let him down with his tee-shirt selection, so maybe it was the place to look for a bargain fragrance. He tugged at the dark cotton fabric hugging his stomach, smoothing the orange with its unravelling rind as he remembered the girl in Help the Aged.

Rosie looked up and smiled. 'Hi,' she mouthed and then turned her attention back to Ginny.

Matt waited for Ginny to speak to him, but nothing happened so he lingered like a bad smell, impossible to ignore and no one wanting to acknowledge the warm odours. Eventually she half turned her head. 'Better get working on your own play, Chemistry Dude!'

'Chemistry? I thought you were carpentry.'

Matt grinned at Rosie. 'Yeah, but it don't mean I don't know some. I'm global in me interests.' He touched the orange sphere unpeeling on his chest.

Rosie looked at his tee-shirt. Something in her expression must have caught Ginny's attention because she turned more fully to face him.

Matt waited, holding his breath in an attempt to pull in his belly as she stared, the soft folds of her skirt still swaying from her movement.

'Is that a firework? A kind of Catherine-Wheel? Good for bonfire night. Maybe you could help hand out some flyers for my play?'

Matt glanced down at his chest and glowed with pleasure. 'Yeah, sure.' He thought for a moment before adding, 'What, now?'

'No, fool. Nearer the time!'

'Yeah, OK.' Matt's cheeks burned. 'Cool perfume,' he said, groping for the name of a scent, 'Avon?'

'No. Issey Miyake.'

Her sharp tones stabbed his ears. He dropped his gaze and studied the scuffs on his trainers. When he looked up again, she'd moved away and her back didn't invite further conversation. So why had she called him a fool and who was this Malarkey bird anyway? All he'd done was offer to help now. What was wrong with that? It was tricky, this business of talking to birds. Google might not offer the same buzz, but at least it never derided him.

'I've got a Piaggio now,' he whispered, but the Italian didn't work its magic. He sighed and turned his attention to the other attraction in the library – the computers. His favoured station near the corner was free and the screen seemed to beckon.

Chrissie found him there a few hours later.

•••

Tuesday morning washed in on a curtain of rain. Matt hadn't slept well and the persistent drizzle suited his mood. The words *bloody fucking useless* still rang in his ears. He reckoned Nick must have been pretty mad to have shouted at him like that. If it had been Tom, he'd more than likely have punched him as well. 'Shoot,' he breathed as he remembered Nick's anger and his own feelings of confusion.

The silence had been worse still. No words were spoken as they travelled to Ipswich to make their statements and Matt's misery had slowly grown, filling his evening and spilling into his dreams.

It was a relief to get up. Matt pulled on Monday's stale tee-shirt and a pair of baggy jeans. A sudden gust of wind hurled raindrops against the window and like a drum-roll it promised a soaking. He supposed his helmet would at least keep his head dry. He'd read somewhere that if you ran through the rain you'd get less wet than if you walked. He reckoned if he rode his scooter fast enough he might not get a drenching. But at 28 mph uphill? Probably just fast enough to drive more rain into him. He could hardly kid anyone he had the aerodynamics of an aeroplane wing but, he consoled himself, in his comic-strip books it would have been possible. He reached for his faded denim jacket as a concession to the weather.

Outside, the rain formed rivulets on the Perspex visor. It was almost impossible to see where he was going, but he revved his scooter and with a leap of faith worthy of Indiana Jones, launched himself out of Tumble Weed Drive. Wind drove the water from the front of his helmet so that it fell in a steady stream onto his shoulders. With his second breath, moisture condensed on the inside of his visor.

At least he only had to ride his scooter to the Mann's house in Bildeston. Alan had suggested he go straight there. It made more sense than riding all the way over to Hadleigh just to get a lift back to Bildeston with Alan in the Hepplewhites van. And besides, it saved on fuel.

Twenty minutes later he slowed down to turn into the Mann's driveway. His tyres spat gravel and he braked hard, almost skidding to a halt. It was as if he'd created the soundtrack for his own hailstorm. He wrenched off his helmet and rubbed his eyes. No green van. 'Bugger,' he muttered as he realised he'd arrived before Alan. 'Well, I'm not standin' out in this bloody rain.' This was the garden where people got shot at, he remembered, so there were two reasons to get inside and under cover and certainly nothing to be gained by standing on ceremony. He headed for a door on the near side of the house.

He knocked, but when no one came, he pushed at the old handle. 'Hello,' he called as he stepped onto polished flagstones.

'Hello?' a musical voice echoed his call. 'I'm just coming.' Mrs Mann appeared, tall and willowy, a bundle of men's clothes grasped in both arms and shadows beneath her watery blue eyes. 'You've caught me in the middle of.... Good heavens, you're soaking wet. It's Matt isn't it?'

They both looked down at the floor where a puddle was growing at his feet. Rain dripped from his sleeves and leached out of his trainers. His faded denim jacket was drenched, the pale blue darkened and the fabric stiffened by the deluge. He moved his limbs like an automaton as he shifted his helmet to his other hand. 'It's bloody pissin' it down - I mean it's bucketin' down out there, Mrs Mann,' and then as an afterthought, 'Sorry.'

'Come in, come in and take that wet jacket off. Didn't Alan bring you in the van?'

'No, I rode me scooter. It's a Piaggio.' There, he'd said the magic word. Maybe the Italian would work on her.

'A Vespa?'

He wondered if she'd ever ridden one; she looked just about young enough. Water trickled down the back of his neck and he tried not to pull a face as he answered, 'Wanted one but I could only afford a Zip.'

'They're great fun, but not in this weather. Don't you have any waterproofs?'

He shook his head.

'I was just sorting through some of Jim's, I mean my husband's clothes. He won't be needing them now. Maybe I can find some waterproof trousers or jacket for you if it's still raining when you go home. Come on, you'd better come to the kitchen and dry off a bit.' She led the way along a narrow corridor and then down one step into a large room stretching almost the width of the house. Dark beams straddled the ceiling and a large pine table filled most of the space at one end. She dumped the pile of clothes on its scrubbed wooden surface without ceremony.

'Hey, off there, Marmaduke!' She brushed at a fat tabby, caught him as he fled and briefly held him to her face before releasing him onto the floor.

Matt left wet trainer marks with each step. He knew the kitchen well. To be honest, most of his time had been spent fetching cups of tea and carrying them upstairs for Alan and then back to the kitchen. When he wasn't doing that he'd watched Alan work in the eaves, then held one end of a tape measure or swept and cleared up. So far apprentice work had been pretty boring.

'You can hang up that wet jacket on the Aga rail.'

Matt placed his helmet carefully on a rush-seated breakfast chair and tried to flex his cold fingers. They were too stiff and numb to undo his jacket so he stood and waited.

'People may think it's heartless but I can't live here and keep looking at his clothes.' She rummaged through the pile as she spoke, sorting garments into types. 'If he could come back and be alive again, he wouldn't understand.' She selected a corduroy shirt and laid it flat. 'Take his first wife's things. Nothing was moved, nothing was thrown away. He kept the house like a museum for years. Then I came along. Well I wasn't going to put my clothes alongside a dead predecessor's. It wouldn't have been right.' She paused as she folded in the sleeves to lie along the length of the shirt's back, smoothing the fraying cuffs. For a moment Matt was reminded of someone stroking a cat.

'He wouldn't even hear of her clothes being given away. In the end I phoned a storage facility in Hadleigh. It took the best part of a day to pack it all away. And I insisted they remove some of her furniture as well.'

'Me mate's doin' work fittin' out an office for a storage an' removals firm in Hadleigh.'

She folded the back in half, turned the shirt over and straightened the collar. Matt wondered if she'd even heard him as she searched in the pile and tugged at a chequered cotton-twill sleeve. 'It felt better once all her things were cleared out. I was hoping this'd make me feel better as well, but….'

'It aint?' Matt blurted out in a rare moment of correct guesswork.

'What a wise head on young shoulders.' She let the chequered sleeve fall back into the tumult. 'I didn't even want the carpentry firm from Needham Market doing this job. Jim knew John Willows, the boss and I couldn't face having him here being sympathetic. It would have kept reminding me of Jim.' She bit her lip. 'That's why I got Hepplewhites. That's why you're here.'

‘Me mate’s….’ The words died in his mouth. He never got a chance to mention the beehive. Beads of moisture glistened in her eyes and when she blinked a droplet trickled down one cheek. Jeez, he thought. Either it’s bloody rainin’ in here or she’s cryin’. ‘You OK, Mrs Mann?’

‘Yes, yes. I’ll be fine. Just need to get this lot sorted.’ She turned her attention back to the table and lifted up a sludge-coloured lamb’s wool sweater. Silence, heavy and oppressive, filled the room.

Matt shifted his weight from one foot to the other. Air bubbled through the rainwater trapped in his trainer and escaped through its seams. Squelch! Even to Matt it sounded obscenely loud.

Something in the quality of the noise must have affected her because she stilled for a moment, then pushing some wisps of dark hair away from her face, worked them back into her loose plait. She began to speak, one hand still grasping the lamb’s wool knit. ‘I know Jim was quite a bit older than me but I’d expected more time together. A year. That’s all we had. One year.’ She flung the sludge-coloured sweater back into the pile.

Matt didn’t know what to say so he kept his mouth shut while his brain worked overtime. Finally he asked, ‘So what did Jim, I mean your husband, do? Were ’e into telecommunications, phone masts an’ stuff like that?’

‘No. Whatever makes you say that?’

‘Don’t know. Alderman’s Point, maybe.’

‘Oh that – no, he didn’t mind phone masts as long as they weren’t on beauty spots; special places like Alderman’s Point.’

Matt waited, hoping she’d say more.

‘It’s funny but we never walked up to the Point together. It was his special place.’ She smiled briefly and then another thought seemed to strike her. ‘I remember now. I’ve seen some oilskins hanging in the shed. I’ll look them out for you later.’

‘No, I’m OK – please.’ He didn’t want to wear a dead man’s cast offs. It was one thing to buy stuff from charity shops like Help the Aged; he could pretend no one had died, but these waterproofs would be completely different. For a start, he knew about this particular stiff. He might even start to imagine Jim inside the oilskins with him. It was sick. His computer search on Monday afternoon was still fresh in his mind - *the police are treating it as murder* - the man wasn’t just dead, he’d been wasted.

‘Mornin’!’ A voice boomed into the kitchen from somewhere up the corridor. It seemed to resonate around them, breaking the spell.

‘That’ll be Alan; I’ll put the kettle on.’

‘Yeah, I’ll go an’ help unload the van.’ Matt was pleased to get away. It had been exciting asking the second Mrs Mann some questions, but it had been horrible when she produced those tears. He’d felt nervous, almost panicky. What was he supposed to do when a bird started to blub? Tom had said something about offering a tissue in an emergency, but then Tom had been talking about chicks watching sad films, what he called tear-jerkers, not recently widowed birds.

‘You’re here early, Matt. I see the rain caught you.’

‘Yeah.’ There was no point in saying more. It was obvious he’d been soaked. ‘Anythin’ to bring in from the van?’

'The spirit level and hanging rails. When you've done that I could murder a cup of tea, if Mrs Mann's brewing up.'

Matt grinned. Alan had a way with words, but so did Nick. If he'd been here he'd have known what to say to Mrs Mann, known how to get more information out of her and avoid the tears. The thought caught his breath. For the last hour he'd forgotten about Nick and his angry words, but as he remembered, emotion cut deep. He'd never found it easy to make friends, but with Nick it had been different. He was a best mate, and you don't let best mates down. That's what Nick had said and Matt agreed. But he'd still bailed out and scarpered when he shouldn't have.

'Chrissie; she'll know what to do. I'll ring 'er later,' he murmured.

# CHAPTER 17

Chrissie slipped the car into gear and pulled gently away from the junction. She'd owned the yellow TR7 for less than a month but it still gave her a thrill, lightening her mood and making her smile. The daylight was starting to fade as the evening drew in. She switched on her headlights and glanced at the clock. It displayed the time as midnight from its place in the plastic moulded dashboard. She reached forward with one hand and tapped the glass – nothing happened, it never did. She'd need to get a replacement or live with the wrong time. She knew it was 6:30 pm; late to be leaving the Clegg workshop, but it had been a busy few days and Ron had required more help than usual to complete the restoration of a Davenport writing bureau.

'What a week,' she sighed as she thought back to Monday. What could she have done or said to alter anything, she wondered. Nick was convinced Matt had behaved like a snivelling wimp. Yes, those were the politer words he'd used, and Matt had insisted no one would believe how violent Tom could be when roused. Nick said he'd have behaved differently if he'd been in Matt's shoes, no matter how vicious Tom's temper.

It hadn't helped when Chrissie pointed out, 'You're not Matt so of course you'd behave differently. And if you were, Matt wouldn't be Matt!'

Chrissie shook her head as she remembered the atmosphere. One had been angry and the other upset, all of them miserable. 'Too much testosterone,' she murmured as she flicked the indicator and turned left towards Stowmarket. So, what with the trouble between her friends and her own natural reticence, she hadn't phoned Clive when they finally went to make their statements in Ipswich. Would he be offended, she wondered.

She drove on in silence, lost in her own thoughts. 'I should have contacted Clive. He's bound to find out I was at the police station and now he'll think….' But what would he think? What did she want him to think?

It was almost 7:00 pm as she passed the entrance turning to Utterly Academy and it would be another ten minutes or so before she'd be home in Woolpit. Her phone burst into life, startling and irritating her. She grabbed in her handbag on the passenger seat.

'Yes?' she hissed as she braked and steered the car with one hand to the side of the road, her mobile held to her ear along with an errant shred of a sweet wrapping from the bag. 'Matt, is that you? I'm just pulling over.' She put the gear stick in neutral and switched off the engine. 'Speak up. I can hardly hear you.'

'Hi! Didn't want to bother you….'

'It's OK, you've caught me on my way home. I was just passing the Academy.' She turned off her headlights to save battery and plunged the road ahead into darkness. The street lighting shone dimly from a lamp post somewhere far behind. 'I've stopped the car now.'

'I been thinkin' 'bout Monday,' his voice trailed away and she let the silence stretch. She guessed whatever Matt wanted to say would come out in its own time, but if she prompted him he'd only get distracted.

'Chrissie? You still there?'

'Yes, I was just waiting. I didn't want to break the flow.'

‘Ah… well I can’t stop thinkin’ ’bout Monday. I reckoned you’d know what to do. You know, to put it right with Nick.’

Chrissie sighed. How was she supposed to have any idea? She doubted even Nick would know. ‘Talk to him. He’s had time to cool off. Buy him a pint! He can’t stay cross forever.’

‘Reckon so?’

‘Look, I’m only a few minutes from the Nags Head. I’ll stand you a pint if you like. It’s easier than talking over the phone like this. OK?’

‘Yeah, knew you’d know what to do.’ The line went dead.

‘See you there then,’ she said into the disconnected airwaves. Typical, she thought. It was just like Matt to assume things would sort themselves out without doing anything. Why couldn’t he speak to people? She restarted the car and flicked a switch, grinning as she watched the headlights pop up from the sloping bonnet. She pulled out into the road.

A horn blasted.

‘Christ!’ She stamped on her brakes and the car stalled.

A pick-up truck appeared as if from nowhere, taking up her side of the road. It moved fast, its lights heavily dipped and heading straight for her. At the last moment the driver swerved. It was too dark to make out any faces, but the side window was down and his angry voice cut into the night.

‘Dozy bitch!’ he yelled. He poked a finger from his clenched fist and jabbed upwards into the air. ‘Look where you’re driving that bloody piece of junk.’ He leaned out of the window to make sure she'd heard. Almost as soon as it had begun, it was over and the pick-up had passed.

Frozen in shock, Chrissie looked into her rear-view mirror. She watched as the tail lights travelled into the darkness and then for an instant a street lamp shone onto the driver's cab. In that fleeting second she was sure she could see another person, someone in the passenger seat. A moment later and the pick-up vanished from sight as it turned into the Academy driveway.

Chrissie waited. She couldn't move until she'd collected her thoughts. Her pulse skipped a beat as part of her brain told her: *I nearly died. A second sooner and…*, but her plucky heart was incandescent with rage. *He called me a dozy bitch. His headlights weren't on and he was the one driving too fast.* She started the car. *Bloody piece of junk* – how dare he?

'My car is wax-oiled and under-body protected. If I drove over him he'd soon find out.' She spat the words as she imagined the driver trapped under her wheels, his crude hand-sign caught in the oil sump. Perhaps a drink with Matt in the Nags head wasn't such a bad idea after all. It might calm her nerves.

•••

Chrissie leaned back in the chair and sipped her ginger beer. The Nags Head was quiet. Too early for the regulars and for once the jukebox was silent. She took her time as she studied Matt's face. His naturally smooth forehead creased as he frowned into his glass and he worked his mouth as if he was about to speak but then changed his mind and gulped his lager. He'd done this several times and she waited, wondering what he was struggling to say.

'Thing is, Chrissie, I don't reckon this apprentice business suits me. I aint done much. Just fetchin' an' car-ryin'.'

'It's early days, Matt. Give it time.'

'Yeah, but,' he paused as another thought seemed to strike him, 'the customers are OK. Take Mrs Mann.'

Chrissie tensed. With the first mention of Mrs Mann she felt alert, slightly uneasy. 'The current Mrs Mann?'

'Yeah, Jeanette. Yeah, that's what Alan called her. Tried to palm off his oilskins on me.'

'Really? Alan's?'

'No, Jim Mann's. Well it were rainin' and I were on me scooter.' He swigged at his lager again. 'It's joggled me. I should've said.' He looked across at her, hardly rais-ing his head. He reminded her of a hound dog with mourn-fully heavy eyelids.

'Said what? You should have said what?'

Matt slowly recounted his conversation with Jeanette. The more he spoke the faster it came, the words spilling out as Chrissie sat engrossed, hardly believing her ears.

'You realise what this means, don't you?' she said when he finally ran out of steam.

'Jim knew 'bout them bones at Alderman's Point?'

'No. Well maybe. It means there could still be some of Minnette's DNA in existence. A hair on a hairbrush, or something like that.'

'You think it's 'er up there, don't you?'

'If the DNA matches.' Chrissie didn't say more. She knew it was just a hunch. There was no evidence Minnette had disappeared in Suffolk rather than in France and Clive had made that pretty clear to her, in fact he'd been irritated by her suggestion.

'If we could find out which storage firm in Hadleigh.' She spoke softly, more to herself than Matt.

'Do you want another ginger beer, Chrissie?' Matt's voice dragged her back from her musings.

'No, no thanks but don't let that stop you getting another lager.' She watched absent-mindedly as he gathered up his glass and headed for the bar. And then realisation struck. Matt and Nick still didn't know the bullet in Jim Mann and the ones found on Alderman's Point were all fired from the same gun. The newspapers had only said the police believed there might be some link - nothing more specific, no details. Should she tell Matt, she wondered. She'd only kept quiet about it in case it made Nick panicky.

Matt made his way back from the bar. He'd tried to sip his lager as it slopped from the overfull glass, but judging from the marks on his tee-shirt, more had spattered down his front than passed down his throat.

'You're smilin'; you must be happy,' he remarked as he set the glass on the table and sat down.

'Was I?' She hadn't realised. Her thoughts had been following their own path. For a moment they'd escaped from the tyranny of her cool logic and they'd wandered into a compartment labelled emotion. She was grasping something she hadn't allowed herself to think about too deeply. Clive had been treating her differently to Matt and Nick. He'd given her privileged information. If she'd been getting special treatment then it had to mean something.

'So, do you reckon they'll test the DNA?'

'I think they might if they find some, but I need to give Clive a call.' Her thoughts wandered into the compartment labelled organisation. She tried to ignore the ones still lingering in emotion. Opposite, Matt sipped his lager, seemingly less desperate now he'd already a pint inside him. 'So what did the bloke who wanted to know about the Academy's heating oil look like?' she asked.

'Ordinary. Short hair. Reddish, yeah, that's right. And a wonky tooth.'

'A wonky tooth?'

'Yeah, must've bust it some time.' Matt tapped one of his front teeth to illustrate. 'Seemed… twenties, maybe younger. Why d'you ask?'

She told him about her near miss with the pick-up truck.

'D'you reckon it were the same bloke?'

Chrissie shook her head. 'It was too dark and there were two of them. I didn't notice the driver's hair, or even if he had any. They could have been wearing woolly hats. Yes, it would explain why I didn't register their hair. I'd recognise his voice though.' The driver's rough tones replayed in her mind.

They lapsed into silence.

'D'you think Nick'll come for a drink this evenin', Chrissie?'

'Why don't you ask him? Of course he might be taking Kat out.'

The bar was starting to fill and Chrissie checked her watch. 'Look, I'm knackered. It's been a busy week and I think I'll get on home if that's OK. I need an early night.'

'Yeah, sure. Thanks, Chrissie, an' careful with the Wedge. Don't blunt your nose; you've almost pranged it once this evenin'.' He grinned at her over his glass. 'I guess I'll stay on here.'

'Cheeky!' She flicked at his head as she left.

•••

Chrissie tucked the newspaper under her arm. A week had passed since she'd phoned Clive, initially buoyed with courage after leaving the Nags Head. She'd been bursting with Matt's account, eager to share his information and filled with newly found confidence. She hadn't been surprised when Clive made some non-committal noises in response to her suggestion he hunt through every storage unit in Hadleigh, but there was no mistaking the warmth in his tones when he'd suggested they meet for coffee.

Saturday morning had seemed a safe time and far enough ahead so as not to appear too keen. She'd bought a morning paper on the way to the Costa coffee shop. It would be something to read, company if Clive was late. The market always made the town busier and added to the weekend shoppers, and this morning outside the large plate glass windows, Bury St Edmunds seemed to be buzzing. She took her place in the orderly queue for service and glanced around to see if there were any free tables. It felt as if half the town had dropped into Costa for a coffee. Perhaps she should have suggested somewhere quieter? No sign of Clive yet, she thought.

She found a table in the back of the shop. It felt darker, almost gloomy, but at least it was away from the bustle of the service counter and till. She sipped her coffee and opened the paper. It was something to hide behind while she tried to calm her nerves. This was the closest thing to a date she'd been on since her marriage. It's been ten years, Chrissie thought and she was terrified. She'd phoned Sarah who'd said, 'If you do nothing else, at least get your nails done.' So she'd splashed out on a manicure.

‘Plum,’ the girl in the nail shop had said. ‘That’s what everyone’s wearing. It’s very now, if you know what I mean.’

Chrissie had no idea what she meant, but nodded anyway and said yes because she liked the colour and hoped it would make her look modern and fun.

Now, in the cool light of Costa, she wasn’t so sure. Against the newspaper print, her fingers at least looked feminine. He probably won’t even notice, she thought and turned the page.

‘Hi, Chrissie. Sorry if I’m late.’ Clive’s voice blended with the background murmuring chatter, and for a moment she didn’t realise he was standing in front of her, next to the vacant chair. She looked up and almost jumped with surprise.

‘Clive! You startled me.’

‘Sorry, you were buried in your paper. Something interesting?’ He leaned forward to see what she was reading. ‘Oh that. It’s getting like Chicago in the prohibition. If the numbskulls who made these laws had to enforce them, then maybe they’d come up with something better.’

She let the paper rest on the table. ‘You mean this?’ She pointed to a headline. *Clampdown on Motorists Buying Illegal Fuel.* Further down on the same page was an article entitled: *Home Owners Step Up Security, as thieves target domestic fuel tanks*.

‘Yes, it’s like a war out there, a gangland turf war.’

‘You make is sound… well it’s only fuel.’

‘Liquid money, more like.’ He grinned at her. ‘Would you like another coffee? I looked to see if you were here first before joining the queue.’

‘What, in case I hadn’t shown up?’

'No, detective. I was running late. I didn't want you to think I wasn't coming and I didn't know if you'd already bought a coffee. Needed to take your order.' He grinned again and this time she felt her cheeks burn.

'Well, since you're offering, a black Americano, small, please.' She felt wrong-footed. She should have waited for him to arrive before she'd bought her coffee. Now he probably thought she was greedy and self-centred. She folded away the newspaper and gulped down what remained in her regular sized cup. She pushed it away and tried to decide what she'd say when he returned. Something light and without innuendo; no mention of the search for Minnette Mann's possessions, no immediate enquiry. She'd give him a chance to settle first.

It didn't take him long to return with a tray.

'Were you being serious when you said there are gangland turf wars over fuel?' She tried to bite back the words but her question was out before her brain caught up with her tongue. It was hardly the light chatty opener she'd planned.

He didn't answer for a moment as he unloaded the tray and then sat down. 'It's not really on my case load. There's a team liaising with the Norfolk and Cambridgeshire police over it, but yes, that death from the fire near Blackthorpe last month – Jonas Rivett.' He paused and glanced at her, smiling when he caught her eye. 'That's thought to be a reprisal for venturing into the Stowmarket area and onto someone else's patch.'

'Really?'

'And so the tit-for-tat continues. The thugs caught emptying the Academy tanks last week are trying to implicate the Hadleigh lot!'

'The Academy tanks? Utterly Academy? I hadn't heard there'd been… last week? Why are you laughing?'

'You sound, well, as if you think the Academy should somehow be exempt or it couldn't happen without you knowing.'

She bit her lip. Of course she didn't think anything of the sort, but then he'd no idea how close her brush with those thugs had been, possibly the same thugs he'd just mentioned. He'd misinterpreted her shocked surprise and she felt stupid. 'Last week? You don't mean a week ago last Friday, do you?'

'Not sure the exact day. As I said, it's not my case. Why? Is it important to you?'

She watched him frown. Oh dear, she thought, this isn't going well. I'm digging myself into a hole. She certainly didn't want to risk opening a can of worms, ones which could land Nick or Matt in trouble. She gulped at the steaming coffee and cast around for a suitable answer. Out of the corner of her eye she caught him checking his watch and her heightened emotions stepped into overdrive. He's bored with my conversation, she thought and the implied insult sparked a flash of anger.

'Am I keeping you from something?' she snapped.

'Not at all. Just wondering how long it would take you.'

'How long it would take me to what?'

'To get round to asking if I'd followed up on the storage units in Hadleigh.'

She relaxed and smiled, and waited for him to say something, but he just sat and met her gaze.

'So have you?' she finally asked, annoyed because he'd forced her to ask, and doubly annoyed because he'd presumed to know her and been right.

'Actually, I should thank you.'

'Thank me?' Now he was messing her about. She didn't want to play this game. She folded her newspaper. 'Come on, Clive, tell me. You know I want to know, you're teasing me,' and she tapped him with the paper.

He grinned before answering, 'I should thank you because now we've got some more leads to follow. When we interviewed Jeanette Mann again, apart from giving us the name of the storage firm, she remembered something she hadn't told us before.'

Chrissie waited, but when he didn't continue she had to ask. 'And? What hadn't she told you before?'

'She said someone came to speak to her husband the following week.'

'From the firm?'

'She doesn't know. She'd never seen him before and it was quite soon after the visit that the air rifle pellets started straying into the garden. So it may have been important. She said the man wore a medallion, although she described it as being like a locket. She remembered being surprised because men don't generally wear lockets.'

'A kind of Suffolk version of a medallion man perhaps? But why is she only telling you this now?'

'Maybe she's had time to recover from the initial shock of learning her husband's been shot, and talking about putting Minnette's things into storage must have jogged her memory. People react differently to dreadful news. Not everyone is blessed with total recall like you, Chrissie.'

She ignored his last remark, not sure if he was being sarcastic. 'And the name of the storage firm?'

'Fens Removals, in Hadleigh.'

'And you've been over to check it out?'

'Not yet, but we will. We're still going through the missing persons register, but nothing's come up so far. No ID on the bones yet. Any more questions?'

She sighed. 'I suppose I must sound like an interrogator. Sorry. And it's your day off.'

'Not for much longer. Got to pick up the kids in half an hour.'

'Kids! What kids?'

'Ellenor and Josie. They're Mary's, from her first marriage. We didn't have any. She said two were enough. Perhaps it was just as well as it turned out.'

Chrissie couldn't think of anything to say as she sat, reeling from his bombshell.

'The kids took it badly when we split and as they don't see much of their real dad, we agreed I keep up some contact. Come on Chrissie, this isn't like you. Any more questions?'

'No, no – I should have realised. Of course you'd have children.'

'Well, kind of.'

She nodded. 'But that's nice.'

Chrissie didn't remember much of what was said after that. She was too taken aback. But why not children, she asked herself. Of course he'd come with baggage. Anyone of his age would. After all, didn't she? The difference was he seemed at ease with himself and at ease with the way things were.

# CHAPTER 18

Nick was bored. He put the chisels back, placing each one in the box so they were arranged in size and the sharpened edges protected. The Ricky Rake office project had been long since completed and currently he was helping Henry in the Willows workshop.

'Have you finished sharpening them chisels yet, Nick?' Henry's voice sounded hoarse. He'd been a twenty-a-day, roll-your-own type of man before he went off sick, but he'd stopped smoking since he'd come back to work and he seemed irritable.

'Yeah, do you want to check them?'

'Nah! I trust you.'

Nick tightened the bench vice, ensuring the wood was held firmly. He'd already marked where he needed to chisel out the place for each hinge to be let into the frame.

Henry walked across and looked over Nick's shoulder. 'Hmm,' and then he coughed, a series of grating noises from deep in his chest.

'Sure you're OK?'

'Don't worry, you can't catch what I've got.' The conversation ended, while Henry hugged his side and wheezed.

This reminder of someone else's mortality disturbed Nick and since he wasn't being challenged by his work, his concentration naturally wandered beyond the workshop. Take the business with Matt, he thought. Has he been avoiding me?

Matt's absence had become a perverse irritation. When he didn't turn up for the release day session Nick hadn't thought too much about it, guessed he was probably in the library. But when he failed to materialise for the next one it started to niggle at him. If he was being brutally honest with himself, Nick would also have admitted to being a little distracted by Kat. One or two of the Friday get-togethers at the Nags Head had been missed so as to give more time to focus on her. But he didn't want to make the same mistakes he'd made in Exeter. He'd come on too strong too soon with Mel and he'd suffered for it, hanging like a piece of bait, wriggling on the end of a hook. He had no intention of repeating that experience. No, his friends were important and he'd been neglecting them. For the moment Kat could wait. He needed to put things right with Matt.

'Time for coffee, Nick,' Henry announced, breaking into Nick's thoughts.

Nick looked up from the frame. He'd chiselled out the imprint for each flange so the hinges were inset and the fit was snug. He smiled. He was pleased with his handiwork.

'Milk and two sugars?'

'Yeah.'

Nick went to make the coffee. 'He won't notice if I slip in more than two sugars,' he muttered as he heaped in four loaded teaspoons, sugar spilling onto the counter.

'Have you lost some weight?' he asked as he settled the overfull mug next to Henry.

'I've had to tightened me belt a few notches.'

Nick took that as meaning a yes, but Henry was coughing again so he didn't say more.

It was a relief when Nick's ringtone interrupted the coffee break. 'Sorry Henry, but I better take this,' he said as he pulled his mobile from his pocket. He read the caller ID: Utterly Academy. 'Hi?'

'Hi, is that Nick? It's Glynnis here.'

He smiled. So he'd been right. The girl with the fashion glasses was calling. He knew she probably would, but why had it taken her more than a couple of weeks, he wondered. 'Hi, Glynnis.'

'Look, I'm just phoning to warn you. The police may contact you.'

'What? Why?' His stomach summersaulted.

'You must've heard about the attempted raid on our heating fuel tanks a few Fridays ago. We got one of the thieves but the other one ran off. Donald's given the police your number, so you may be getting a call. I think they've found the one who got away and now the police want to see if you can identify him. You know, the bloke you reported to us.'

'What? Shit!'

'And I was also wondering when you're next singing with that band?'

•••

Nick walked into the Raingate police station waiting room in Bury St Edmunds. The police constable's phone call had come soon after Glynnis's warning and at the time he'd been too shocked to say much. So it was only now that he formulated a plan. It was obvious. He'd say there'd been a dreadful mistake. He'd explain it was his friend Matt who'd seen the guy poking around the fuel tanks. And because Nick fancied Glynnis, Matt had pushed him into the office without him so he'd have an excuse to speak to her, and well, the rest was history.

But Nick hadn't reckoned on the strength of his reaction when he entered the police station. He hadn't expected the memories to come flooding back, quickening his pulse and making him breathe in fast shallow bursts. He'd thought he was over it; after all, nearly three months had passed since he'd been wrongly held in police custody for twenty-four hours. He'd survived an explosion that blew up Chrissie's stolen car only to be thrown into police cells and interrogated. God it had been terrible. A trip to hell and back and the trigger for his panic attacks.

The longer Nick waited the more physical his reaction became. By the time he was called to give his name and address and answer a few questions, his tongue stuck to the roof of his mouth and he was unable to form coherent words.

'Are you feeling all right, sir?' The question was simple enough. All he had to do was nod or shake his head.

'Water, please.' His throat felt dry as he fought to get the words out.

'Water? Yes, sure.' The uniformed policeman smiled, but all Nick could see was *good cop, bad cop*; a replay of his twenty-four hour detention.

*The police will never believe me*, he thought as he gulped at the proffered glass. *They'll never believe the stuff about Matt and probably think I was in on the job and one of the gang.*

He closed his eyes in an attempt to stop the room from spinning. There was only one thing he could do, he decided. Go through with it. If he nodded and grunted his way through the identification parade and then failed to identify anyone, what harm had he done? The police weren't going to convict anyone on his say-so alone. They'd also need concrete evidence to link this bloke to the crime: fingerprints, CCTV footage, that type of thing and anyway, from the sound of it, no real crime had been committed. The thieves had been stopped before they'd made off with the fuel.

'Thanks,' he whispered, pulse racing. He wiped the sweat from his brow and stood up. 'I'll be OK now, thanks.'

Nick followed the uniformed policeman along a corridor and into a room with a large one-way viewing glass panel. He hardly listened as the policeman went through the procedural instructions again. He didn't need to hear because he wasn't going to recognise anyone. He just wanted to get the whole thing over with and escape as quickly as possible.

On the other side of the glass four men stood in a row. Nick didn't hurry; he'd got himself under control now. It was too late to turn back. He concentrated on appearing as if he was taking the identification seriously.

Nick looked again. The third man in the row seemed familiar. He must have been in his early twenties and as Nick watched, the man shifted his weight from one leg to the other. Shoot, Nick thought. I've seen him before. There's something about the way he stands, but last time he wasn't clean shaven. Those freckles peppering his cheeks, I've not seen those before.

'No, he wasn't any of these men,' Nick said firmly.

'Are you sure? Take another look, please.'

Nick composed his face, daring any expression to break through. He concentrated on his breathing. Slow and calm, he told himself.

He looked again, ignoring the close cropped ginger hair topping the man's head. 'No,' he repeated, 'he wasn't any of these men.'

•••

Afterwards in the police car park Nick took long deep breaths. The thumping in his chest slowed. For a moment he'd been sure his heart was trying to escape through his ribcage, heaving and beating against the skeletal bars. He hurried to his car and leant against the old Fiesta's door. The metal struck a welcome coldness through his sweatshirt while he closed his eyes and tried to clear his mind. 'What happened in there?' he murmured. Had he got away with it?

He must have stood there for a while because he felt chilled when he opened his eyes. It's time to go home, he thought. He felt calmer; he'd be able to drive back to Barking Tye now.

Nick eased the Fiesta through the rows of parked cars, most of them police. He slowed and waited to turn into Raingate Street. As always, Bury St Edmunds was busy and he wound down his window. He needed fresh air, something to blow the cobwebs from his mind.

'Hi!' A young man stood on the pavement alongside the tarmac. He grinned down at Nick. 'Hi, we've met before, haven't we.' It wasn't a question, it was a statement. He shifted his weight in a languid manner before asking, 'So why're you here?'

Nick nearly stalled the car. 'Hi.' His pulse started to race. He'd thought the police would somehow separate their witnesses from the identity parade characters. 'Hi, Dan.'

'So, why're you here?'

Nick had to make a decision. 'I was… I was failing to identify you in an identity parade, Dan.' Nick waited.

‘I thought they’d pulled in Tom’s kid brother. Thought he was the one on the other side of that frigging viewing room.’

‘Well, it was me.’

‘Yeah, you’ve said. But why?’

‘Because Matt’s bloody scared of Tom, that’s why.’

‘And you aint?’

‘Something like that, Dan.’ Nick watched as Dan pulled a face, the chipped front tooth showing for a fraction of a second. ‘Look, I don’t know what you’re bloody up to and I don’t really care, but Matt’s a mate and I owed you. So now we’re straight. OK?’

Dan stared at Nick and then slowly nodded. ‘Yeah, I think I get it. You realise the bloody Rivetts are trying to stitch me up, the bastards.’

Nick didn’t answer. He was getting out of his depth. A car drew up behind and tooted its horn.

‘Look, I can’t stop, Dan.’

‘Yeah, sure – and thanks, mate.’

Nick pulled away. It was time to phone Matt and put things right.

# CHAPTER 19

Matt waited in the Nags Head. Forty minutes earlier he'd been riding home from work when he felt his phone vibrate in his pocket. He'd stopped his Piaggio, wrenched off his helmet and then stood by the side of the road to answer it.

'Hi, Nick!'

'Matt, I'm in the car so I can't really speak properly. I'm about to drive back from Bury, so meet me at the Nags Head, six-thirty. I've got some news and it's time we had a pint together. Be there.' The phone cut out. The message was short and to the point and it left Matt reeling.

So Nick had some news for him. What news? They hadn't spoken for the best part of three weeks and now there was something so urgent to say, it couldn't wait. But more importantly, he'd said, over *a pint together* and that sounded quite matey, so maybe he wasn't cross any more. I should buy him a beer, he decided. So, forty minutes later he sat on the bench seat in the Nags Head with his legs sprawled under a small table. Two glasses were lined up on its stained surface; a pint of lager and a pint of Land Girl.

He glanced up as the pub door swung open. Nick hurried in, grinned and raised a hand in greeting as a blast of cold air cut through the scent of stale beer.

'Got you a pint of Land Girl, your favourite,' Matt announced. He reckoned Nick's smile was a good sign.

'Great, thanks Matt.' He threw himself down onto a stool.

'So what you want to tell me?'

'Thought it was time we started talking to each other again and….'

Matt listened, curiosity changing to disbelief, only to be replaced by fear as Nick told him about his visit to the Raingate police station and the identification parade. 'You mean, they really tried to drain them tanks? And they were caught before they got away? Tom'll kill me, Nick. He'll bloody kill me. You said the bloke thought it were me doin' the identifyin'. The bugger'll tell Tom.' Matt gulped his lager.

'I reckon Tom's bound to hear about it and then he'll contact you, Matt. That's why I'm telling you everything now, right away. Look, I made sure the bloke knew it was me at the identification parade when I saw him afterwards. I spoke to him as I left the car park. He knows it wasn't you, Matt. He even hinted he thought it was the Rivetts who'd landed him in the shit. He reckoned they'd set him up. God knows who the hell they are.'

Matt thought for a moment, his head spinning with Nick's information. It helped to try and focus on something.

'Jonas Nunseon Rivett,' he said, reading out the name as he recalled the news print from his photographic memory. 'He were the bloke who died followin' that fire out Blackthorpe way.'

'How d'you know that?'

Matt looked at Nick's pale face. 'Coz I read it on the newspaper's website.'

They both fell silent. 'So how come you hadn't heard about the attempted fuel theft till now, Matt?'

Matt wiped his mouth with his sleeve. The lager moustache transferred to his denim outer skin as he considered his answer. 'Don't know. S'pose it weren't on the website. Been concentrating on Ginny. She's asked me to distribute flyers for her play.'

'Look, Matt, if you don't start coming to the release day teaching you may find yourself kicked out at the end of the year. Have you thought of that?'

Matt stared at his hands. Sausage fingers, his mum called them. 'Thing is, Nick… I don't know if carpentry's for me.'

It was only on the way home that Matt remembered he hadn't thanked Nick for saving him from Tom.

•••

Matt was in a good mood. He was lying in bed, so when he opened his eyes on this particular morning, the patch of blue paint on the wall near his wardrobe looked like a Caribbean sea, and his mushroom-coloured sheet, a white sandy beach. He'd never been to such exotic places except in his dreams, but he felt happy. He supposed it would be like wearing rose coloured spectacles on Great Yarmouth beach. For a moment he couldn't think what was so good about life, and then he remembered: Nick was talking to him again, there'd been no word from Tom, and today he planned to distribute the first of the flyers. It wasn't long now until the Guy Fawkes play.

He threw back his duvet and rolled out of bed. What had Ginny said the other day? Yes, that was it; 'You're based in Hadleigh, aren't you? That's where you said you worked. It isn't much longer till the play, so put one of these in every shop, every pub, through every letterbox, and anywhere you can think of.' He remembered watching her, transfixed as she put her arms in the air and twirled around as she held a glossy sheet of printed paper.

'But them's loads of flyers. It'll take forever,' he'd said.

'So you're not going to help then?'

He'd been in the Utterly mansion building at the time. He'd almost bumped into her as they'd passed each other in the main corridor, the artery running along the ground floor. He hadn't known what to say, so he'd hung his head and bitten his lip. It must have been OK though, because she laughed.

'They're in the library if you're still interested, Chemistry Dude.'

Of course he was still interested. 'How many d'you want me to take?'

'Two, maybe three hundred,' and then she'd flounced away. 'That's just for starters,' she'd tossed over her shoulder as she disappeared into a throng of other students.

Matt smiled at the memory and turned his attention to the important matter of what he should wear. The black tee-shirt with the large orange globe symbolising the John Peel Centre to Nick and a firework to Ginny, was clean and roughly folded. He was saving it for bonfire night, the night of Ginny's play. Instead, he rummaged through a drawer and pulled out a plain white tee. He spread it out on his bed, selected a black marker pen from a jar on the windowsill and set to work.

He stood back and read out, '*U A* D A D.' And then he repeated it but this time saying a word for each letter. 'Utterly Academy Dramatic Arts Department.' Whichever way he looked at it the word, DAD seemed to leap off the cotton. It shrieked uncool. There was only one thing to do. He turned it inside-out, pulled the tee-shirt over his head and smoothed down the fabric where it rucked and crinkled above the expanse of his belly. Viewed from the wrong side, the letters were uneven and patchy where the ink had penetrated the fabric in an erratic manner. Inside-out and back-to-front hardly seemed to matter. Now he was mysterious and super cool. He reckoned the smudges on his forehead just complimented his look.

Twenty minutes later Matt set off for the Hepplewhites workshop in Hadleigh with three hundred flyers in his under-seat stowage compartment. The Piaggio whined as he finally climbed the last hill before slowing to turn into the workshop forecourt. He parked his scooter and flipped the seat back. The flyers filled most of the space so he kept his helmet on, pulled out a couple of sheets and headed for the green door.

Janet looked up from her computer screen and scowled. 'Don't come in here wearing that helmet. You'd take it off if you were in a church or restaurant.'

Matt dropped the two flyers onto her desk and pulled off his helmet. What was she talking about, he wondered. How could her office be likened to a church or cafe? 'This aint a hold-up, Janet.' He didn't bother to explain it was either wear the helmet and carry the flyers, or bite the flyers and carry the helmet. 'Thought you might be interested,' he said as she pulled the glossy paper towards her.

'Guy Fawkes?'

'Yeah, it's a play, with pyrotechnics on Bonfire Night.'

'I can read, Matt.'

He watched as she pursed her lips and ran the tip of a polished nail along the title. 'Your name isn't on here, Matt. Pity.'

Matt shook his head. 'No, I aint no drama student. I'll go through to the workshop now if that's OK, Janet.' He balanced his helmet on the top of the water cooler and headed for the door.

He ignored her shriek of anger as the words, 'I've told you not to put it up there,' ricocheted off the back of his denim jacket.

Matt sauntered past the old converted stables and in through a side entrance. 'Mornin', Alan.'

'Mornin'.' The sound of a Beatles hit from the past floated in the background.

Magic FM must be playing stuff from the sixties, Matt thought as he watched Alan cut a long piece of wood into shorter lengths on the table saw. 'Right, Matt. I want you to plane these edges so they're flat and at right angles, and this time make sure the plane blade's good an' sharp!'

'Can't I make coffee first?'

'When you've got these edges planed, lad.'

Matt struggled through the morning. It wasn't that he didn't enjoy the carpentry, it was more a problem of engaging with its physical aspect. This, added to his lack of inherent skill with the hand tools was probably the reason he'd been told he wasn't a natural. The pile of wood shavings built up at his feet as he laboured, smoothing and levelling the edges for Alan. But despite his effort with the hand planer, the wood remained stubbornly lopsided.

'Better give it a rest, lad,' Alan grunted, finally releasing Matt from his task. 'Looks like those wrists of yours haven't mended properly yet.'

Matt nodded, thankful for an excuse.

'Here, sweep up the mess on the floor instead,' and Alan handed him a broom.

By the time they took a break for lunch Alan seemed pleased to let him go. Matt knew he had an hour and he'd planned to use it for distribution. Luckily, Janet wasn't in the office, so retrieving his helmet was easy. He paused as he contemplated the water cooler and after a short deliberation, took off his denim jacket and placed it around the water bottle so it looked like a headless torso. That'll please Janet, he thought as he rammed on his helmet, and a few moments later zipped away on his scooter. He decided to start from the top of Gallows Hill and work his way down into the town.

A placard on the side of the road caught his eye. The name *FENS* leapt off the white board and beneath in smaller lettering, *Removals & Storage*. That's where Nick had fitted an office, he remembered. Without too much thought he turned his scooter into the newly concreted entrance drive and headed for a brick building located to one side of a huge metal-clad warehouse. He hoped it was somewhere he could leave some flyers, but the place looked deserted. Still optimistic, he pulled out a dozen glossy sheets from his stowage compartment, balanced his helmet on the seat and walked to a glass panelled door. A hand written notice read: *Sorry, closed for lunch. Back 2:00 pm.*

'Shoot, now wha' d'I do?' Matt ambled back to his scooter. 'I'll just 'ave to dump 'em,' he muttered and wondered where exactly. He realised the sliding doors of the warehouse were partially open. They stretched almost to the roof. He guessed they were tall enough for the removal vans to pass through and if they'd been left ajar like that, he reckoned someone might be inside.

Matt strolled to the warehouse and stepped from the bright autumn daylight, through the dark opening and into the dim coolness. He caught his breath as he gazed upwards. The space was open to the roof, like a huge barn or hangar. 'Wicked!' But he choked on the word as a harsh noise broke the silence. It pounded and echoed far above.

He ducked. Heart in mouth, he scanned the air overhead for the source of the sound. He spotted a pigeon. It flapped its wings and landed on a roof girder. Silence settled on the warehouse. Matt looked around to see if the noise had alerted anyone, but the place appeared to be deserted. Had everyone gone to lunch?

The greater part of the space in front of him was given over to removal vans. At least two were parked nose to tail with *FENS* printed in huge lettering along their sides. He walked past them but he couldn't see any drivers or loaders. The temperature seemed to drop as he went further into the warehouse, and he hugged his cotton tee-shirt close and wished he'd worn his denim jacket.

Matt turned his back on the vans and faced the side wall. Huge oblong containers, like giant metal building bricks, were stacked three high and painted blue. It reminded him of the ones he'd seen on the Felixstowe docks waiting to be loaded onto the container-ships. Metal walkways ran along the front of the containers creating staging, and stairs linked each deck. A huge forklift with tall uprights stood in front of the container second from the end, ground level and near the back wall. Matt tried to take it all in. It was awesome, but at the same time desolate.

What should he do, he wondered. He headed towards the forklift as a harsh screech rent the air. Metal scraped on metal as a container door swung open, its steel hinges complaining. Matt closed his mouth on the scream bursting from his throat. If it had been another pigeon taking flight, then he'd have been prepared, but this was a new sound. Eerie. It had come from the container near the forklift.

So maybe there's someone here, Matt thought as he moved carefully, instinctively treading softly. He noticed a beat-up Land Rover parked beyond the forklift and tucked close to the back wall of the warehouse. As he moved closer, a faint murmuring drifted towards him. He paused to listen, recognising the sound of men's voices. Should he get closer?

'Well, that's all fitted in quite well,' said a bloke's voice straying through the air.

'Yeah, it aint easy to hide it. We only got the tip-off a couple of hours ago. I better get back and help Dad drain the last tank before the surprise police raid. Bet they can't wait to swarm over our barns and poke their bloody fingers where they've no business.' The tones were younger. Matt frowned as something about the voice struck him as familiar.

'Don't worry, it'll be safe here. The police'll need a warrant before they search this place.'

'Yeah, well hopefully they won't want to. I made bloody sure no one saw me coming here with the stuff. You switched your security cameras off after Dad called to say I was on my way, didn't you?'

'Yes, of course. I'm not a ruddy fool. And I've closed the office and sent everyone for lunch. I've thought of everything.'

'You heard the police tried to pin the Utterly Academy heist on me?'

Matt caught his breath. The Academy heist? The name jogged something in his memory and a face started to take shape, a face he'd seen before. Of course, it was Tom's bloke. His pulse raced.

'Yes, your Dad said. The Rivetts got there first and then that bloody apprentice with Willows tried to finger you.'

'Yeah, but the identity parade turned out a friggin' shambles. Dad thinks that's why they're raiding us. Determined to pin something on me and Dad. The bastards!'

Matt stepped back. The shock of hearing the older bloke mention Nick slammed the wind out of him. He needed to get away. Sod the flyers.

'Come on, let's lock this lot up. Then you go an' get the next load, Dan.'

Matt knew he needed to get out of there fast, but as he turned to leg it, a flyer slipped from his grasp. It floated towards the container.

'It's getting out of hand. We shouldn't have torched their place,' the familiar voice whined as the container door juddered on its hinges. Matt stood like a thief caught in security lights as two men stepped out and stared at him.

'Shit!'

'Who the hell are you and what're you doing here?' A man with shoulder length hair spoke slowly, his tone oozing menace.

Matt felt impaled by the man's unblinking gaze. 'Hi! I've got some f-flyers. For Saturday.' Matt held out the remaining glossy paper sheets.

No one spoke for a moment, and then the man flicked back his hair with an unhurried movement 'Who is this, Dan? Why's he here? I thought you said no one followed you.'

'Well, who'd of thought? It's Tom's kid brother.'

'So he's Tom's kid brother. But what's he doing here?' He glared at Matt. 'How long've you been in here?'

Matt looked from one to the other as both stared at him. Tom's bloke, or Dan as he now knew he was called, stood with his weight on one leg and slowly smiled. The older man, the one with shoulder length hair scrutinised Matt from head to toe and then gazed at his chest.

Matt's mouth felt dry, but he forced himself to speak.

'I've only just walked in 'ere. As I said, I'm handin' out flyers for the Bonfire Night show. Look.' The older man didn't react, so he handed the glossy pages to Dan.

'It's me lunch hour and I can't hang around. These doors were open so I reckoned someone were about – an' I were right, you appeared.' Matt smiled mechanically and moved as if to pick up the flyer on the ground. Behind the two men, the container stood gaping, the metal door wide open.

Dan stepped closer to the older man, blocking Matt's view into the container.

'OK?' Matt said, proffering the dusty flyer as he stood up again. He made to walk away, but in that second he'd seen what they were hiding.

'Wait!' The voice cut through the air. 'Why would Tom's kid brother wear a tee-shirt with *cadeau* written on the front?'

Matt gazed down at his white tee-shirt and put a sweaty hand over the inside-out and back-to-front marker pen letters.

'You've spelled it wrong of course; missed out the E, but I can see it's French for a gift. C A d *A U*. Is it a message from your brother?'

Matt felt his face burn. He'd written something ubercool and in French without even knowing. Who'd have guessed Utterly Academy Dramtic Arts Dept could stand for anything back-to-front?

'What are you talking about, Uncle? Look, I can't hang around. You're wasting time. Just let him go, he's harmless. Anyway, why would Tom send a message? And in French? Dad said you were getting, what did he call it? Yeah, that's it – paranoid. Just let him go.'

The older man narrowed his eyes.

'And you're the only one round here who can speak French,' Dan murmured.

'OK, but I'm not sure about the apprentice from Willows. He's trouble.'

Matt didn't wait to hear any more. He put one flat foot in front of the other and ran, his footsteps echoing through the warehouse as his heart thumped in his chest. He didn't stop until he reached his scooter. He didn't dare look back to see if he was being chased. He simply rammed on his helmet, switched on the ignition and accelerated away.

Matt rode down Gallows Hill, took the corner past the cricket ground at speed and skidded off the main road and onto the rough lane alongside the river Brett. He drew into the bushes and waited. He listened, but encased inside his helmet all he could hear was the pounding as blood rushed through his head. He fought for breath. What the hell had happened back there?

As the minutes ticked by and no beat-up Land Rover came tearing down the hill, Matt began to relax. Maybe he'd got away with it? Part of him wondered if he should phone Tom, but the wiser part knew it would be a mistake. Best leave it to Tom to do the contacting, he decided. After fifteen minutes, Matt was able to breathe normally and his mind had started to clear. He figured it should be safe to break cover and make his way back to Hepplewhites. He felt shaky, his stomach grumbled and he still had over two hundred flyers under his seat as he pushed his scooter out from the bushes. What kind of a mess had he got Nick into, he wondered, and then he asked himself, 'What the hell do I do about it?'

# CHAPTER 20

It was mid-afternoon and Chrissie was finding it difficult to concentrate. Normally the smell of the wood and the dusty atmosphere in the Clegg workshop barn kept her fully engaged with whatever she was doing. She gazed at the simple pine dresser. It was a challenge, standing in front of her with its battered surface and broken hinges. Ron had set it as a project for her, saying she should try and do all the work herself as a kind of apprentice restoration piece. There would be plenty to occupy her, he'd explained. For a start the back and bottom boards would need replacing. She'd have to repair the cornice, which would be a first for her and she'd also need some glazing skills. She eyed up the broken glass panel. All that, she thought, and there's still the refinishing and polishing. The pine dresser seemed to return her glance with a raffish sadness.

'What are you thinking Mrs Jax?' Ron asked from his work stool. 'You've been staring at that dresser for the last ten minutes.' He laid his Japanese saw on the work surface and blew the sawdust off a length of teak held firmly in the bench vice.

Chrissie didn't answer for a moment as one thought chased another. The dresser? Did it look French Country style? Not really, she decided, but just the thought of France reminded her of Minnette Mann. Had Clive or one of his team chased up Minnette's possessions yet, she wondered. But thinking of Clive reminded her of Bill.

'I suppose I was wondering if you can ever truly get over someone.' She turned to face Ron and when he frowned she continued, 'I mean, take Jim Mann. Do you think he ever got over his first wife? It took him ten years before he applied to dissolve the marriage after she'd walked out on him, and then a whole lot longer before he married again.'

'Where ever did you hear that, Mrs Jax?'

'Clive told me.' She felt self-conscious and turned to look at the dresser to hide her burning cheeks.

There was a long silence before Ron answered. She sensed the surprise in his voice. 'I still don't see how looking at a pine dresser made you ask a question like that, but since you ask, I think it rather depends on the manner of the parting.'

'How d'you mean?'

'Well, just suppose he felt responsible in some way. Say there'd been a row and he'd said things he didn't really mean; cruel things just to hurt. How would he feel afterwards? That he'd driven her away?'

'Remorse?' Chrissie frowned. 'Yes, and then not allowing yourself to move on would be a way of punishing yourself. A kind of penance.'

Chrissie waited, but when he didn't say more, she asked, 'And if you never see the body, like in a plane crash or those poor people who died when terrorists attacked the Twin Towers, or when someone just goes missing, what then?'

'That happened to families after the last war. Sons, husbands, fathers missing in action somewhere like Singapore or Thailand. It's difficult to accept your kinfolk are dead if you haven't nurtured them through an illness, never seen the body. It's easier to hope they're alive but drifting around with some kind of memory loss and one day they'll walk back through the kitchen door, home at last, memory restored. Not easy to be certain they're dead, let alone get over it, Mrs Jax.'

'So, you've got to believe it before you can get over it?'

'Yes, something like that.'

Chrissie watched Ron as he spoke. He seemed to be focusing on something far beyond the pine dresser. She wondered if his words came from personal experience. Could his father have served in the Second World War and gone missing, presumed dead? She tried to work out his age, doing the maths in her head. Could he be sixty-five? Perhaps he was referring to another family or a relative more distant than a father but lost in 1945.

'So, if you're talking about Jim Mann, I suppose he may have felt responsible for his wife's disappearance, or refused to accept she wasn't coming home. Guilt, denial or both. They're powerful emotions, Mrs Jax.'

Chrissie dragged her mind back to Jim Mann. Guilt. Now that was something she hadn't considered. 'If you felt guilty, would you keep all your wife's possessions?'

'Are we still talking about Jim Mann?'

'Yes, of course. Apparently he kept all her things like a mausoleum. His new wife got rid of them quite recently, but he wouldn't hear of anything being thrown away so everything went into storage. So why would he do that, Mr Clegg?'

Chrissie watched as Ron frowned at the workbench and then slowly shrugged his shoulders. 'In the beginning, maybe he thought she was coming back and later… just an inability to let go.' He looked at her and smiled. 'You heard that from your DI?'

Chrissie hoped her cheeks weren't flushing again. 'No, Mr Clegg. Matt was working over there.' Another thought struck Chrissie, something much closer to home and more personal. 'I keep photos of Bill and things to remind me of him. Does that mean I'm…?'

'No, it's normal to keep reminders like photos. But I think with Jim Mann you're talking about extremes of behaviour.'

Chrissie tried to imagine her home without the photos of Bill. She decided it wouldn't seem right. They'd shared eight years of their life together and after his death the little reminders had initially been more bitter-sweet than a comfort. That had been two years ago and slowly, almost imperceptibly the pain had mellowed. Now she mostly felt sadness and regret for what might have been. If all Bill's things had been left exactly as when he'd been alive, his clothes in the wardrobe and his shoes by the door, it would have overwhelmed her. It would have prevented any kind of recovery.

Chrissie turned her thoughts to Jim Mann again. Was his behaviour a way of punishing himself, making time stand still, controlling his environment and his emotions? She didn't like the picture she was building. It seemed unhealthy. 'So Jim was likely to have been a man who couldn't let go and possibly felt guilty about something. Perhaps he liked to control the things and people around him?'

'Good Heavens, Mrs Jax. You seem to have turned into a profiler. That pine dresser was only meant to be a restoration exercise.'

Chrissie laughed. 'Well I'd say,' she studied the dresser, 'it's a country piece without pretentions. It lacks ambition. The glass panels suggest openness, although I don't think they were original and the broken cornice–'

'Suggests a home with low ceilings. Now come on, Mrs Jax, that's enough. It's time to get some work done.'

Chrissie walked around the dresser. 'I'll take the damaged back boards off first, if that's all right, Mr Clegg.'

'Good, but before you do that you'll find it easier if you take the doors off. You've got to repair and rehang them anyway and while they're off it'll open up your access to the back boards.'

Chrissie set about her task. If her hands were busy, then maybe her mind would stop wandering. She knew from watching Ron that the screws she removed needed to be put in little pots, along with the old hinges so as not to lose them. She worked carefully and methodically, crouching on the concrete workshop floor.

*Brrring*! *Brrring*! Damn, she thought as she cast around for her handbag, now what? She'd only just focused on the repair project. *Brrring*! *Brrring*!

'It's on the workbench over there.' Ron pointed to a soft leather hobo-style bag.

'I'd lose my head if it wasn't attached at the neck,' Chrissie muttered as she fished for her phone. It *brrring*ed again in her hand. 'Matt, is that you?'

Chrissie frowned as she took the call. It wasn't like Matt to phone during the day. He spoke fast, words tumbling out, disconnected and seemingly meaningless. She listened hard and concentrated, but she still couldn't make any sense of what he was saying. Even gobbledegook has a tone and this one was fear. 'Stop, stop,' she said. 'Just answer yes or no. Are you able to get yourself over here or do you need me to come and collect you?'

‘Yes, no, yes, yes. I’ll leave now.’ His words came like Morse code. She knew it had to be something bad to have freaked him out so much.

‘Take your time and ride carefully. No accidents now.’

What the hell’s happened, she wondered as she checked her watch. Four o’clock. She slid her phone closed as a tight fist seemed to grip her stomach. She reckoned it would take him about half an hour to get from Hadleigh to the Clegg workshop.

‘Everything OK, Mrs Jax?’

‘I don’t know, Mr Clegg. That was Matt. Something’s come up. He’ll be here in about thirty minutes.’ She closed her eyes as she tried to unravel what he’d said. ‘Nick, yes I think he said, Nick may be coming as well.’

•••

Chrissie switched the kettle on. It was an excuse to give herself a moment to think. Her head was buzzing and she needed to get her thoughts into some kind of order. Nick had only just arrived and Matt was going through it all again for him. Across the old workshop voices murmured, rose, fell and sank into silence as Nick and Matt talked to Ron. Their body language spoke volumes. Nick kept shifting his position; sitting forwards, standing and then restlessly sitting again. At least Matt looked a little calmer now. He thrust his legs out as he hugged his denim jacket close. When he’d first stepped into the Clegg workshop, having ridden his scooter from Hadleigh, she remembered how he’d kept glancing behind and listening. ‘You’re safe here, Matt. No one’s followed you,’ she’d said. ‘If they’d wanted to get you they wouldn’t have let you out of the Fens warehouse, or they’d have chased you at the time.’

'You must tell the police, Matt.' Ron's words drifted towards her. His measured tone and unhurried words cut through the kettle's agitated rumble.

She didn't hear the answer but she knew what Matt would say. He'd already said it once and it was unlikely he'd changed his mind. She flicked the kettle's switch and poured boiling water into the coffee mugs.

*Brrring*! *Brrring*! Her arm jumped. Scorching water slopped around a mug, splashing her hand as steam billowed into her face. 'Damn!'

She hurried to search out her phone, flapping her hand like a broken wing. 'Yes?' she hissed, sliding the mobile open as her skin smarted and stung.

'Hi, Chrissie. Are you OK? You sound–'

'As if I've just spilt boiling water on my hand, detective?' She laughed despite her pain. 'Hi, by the way.'

'Hey look I didn't mean to catch you at a difficult moment but I don't suppose you'd want to go out for a bite to eat this evening? I've no food at home so I was thinking of going for a curry and… well it would be nicer to share a meal. Were you being serious about your hand?'

'Yes, and yes a curry sounds nice.' The words just came out. He'd caught her off guard and she'd answered without thinking. Anxiety stripped away her natural reserve and his voice spelled safety. 'Look, something's come up. I'm still at the Clegg workshop. I don't suppose you'd call in on your way home? I think you should hear what Matt's got to say. We're all here, in the old barn. Would that be OK?' She waited for him to answer, wondering if she'd said too much.

'Yes, that's….' She could almost hear him checking his watch. 'Yes, I've a few ends to tie up here first and then… yes, I'll be at Clegg's in about forty-five minutes. Is that OK, Chrissie?'

'Thanks, Clive. And don't let on I asked you to come.' She ended the call, not wanting to say more. If Matt realised she was speaking to Clive, he'd more than likely take fright and hurry back to Stowmarket, only to disappear into the murky darkness of Tumble Weed Drive. It was best to spring Clive on him, she decided, just as Clive had sprung his call on her.

Chrissie carried the mugs of milky coffee over for Nick and Matt while Ron sipped his tea. She felt steadier, more focused as they all chewed the fat for a while. Just knowing Clive was on his way eased the griping anxiety threatening to erupt in her stomach.

'He called him Uncle, you said?' Nick's voice sounded puzzled.

'Yeah, "Uncle" and "Dad" were mentioned loads.'

'And you're sure he was called Dan? Did he have a chipped front tooth?'

Matt nodded.

Nick frowned and stared into his coffee mug.

'What are you thinking, Nick?' Chrissie asked.

'Well, Dave from work said something about the Rakes. Two brothers, Davie and Ricky. Big round these parts.'

'And?' Chrissie prompted, not following where this was leading.

'It sounds like the Dan Matt showed around the Academy is the same Dan who gave me red diesel when I had an empty tank. Remember I told you I got help at Rookery Farm on my way home from Bildeston?'

Chrissie tried to piece the jigsaw together. There was a long pause before Nick broke the silence. 'He's also the same Dan the police hauled up for the identity parade. The first time I saw Ricky Rake he reminded me of someone but I couldn't think who. Now it all makes sense. I guess Ricky Rake is Dan's uncle.'

'And you think Davie Rake is his dad?' Chrissie finished for him, slotting a piece into the puzzle.

'I guess so. You said he went on about police raiding the farm, Matt. D'you suppose it could be Rookery Farm?'

'Shoot!' Matt looked as if he'd driven over a favourite tee-shirt.

'What, Matt?'

'It's what I clapped me eyes on in the lock-up, you know, one of them storage containers. Now I get what they're up to.' He nodded his head, a mix of wisdom and anxiety.

They stared at Matt and waited for him to explain. Chrissie had never had patience with guessing games. Why couldn't he just say it? She bit her tongue; she wasn't going to be the first to ask.

A distant scrunch of tyres on the rough track cut the silence. An engine purred as a car approached and pulled into the courtyard. Fear bit; it was hard to breathe.

'They've found me,' Matt yelped, his voice a blend of terror and vindicated *I told you so*.

Chrissie recognised the sound of the Ford Mondeo's engine, but it didn't stop her pulse racing; Matt's fear was contagious. 'Clive said he might call in to see me on his way home to Lavenham. It'll be his car,' she tried to sooth.

She glanced at Ron and caught him looking at her, as if he was trying to read her mind. For a moment he looked anxious and then he smiled. 'That was the call you took when you were making the coffee, wasn't it Mrs Jax?'

She nodded as the sound of the engine cut out and a car door slammed.

'You better be friggin' right, Chrissie.' Matt's face had a pale unearthly quality.

Chrissie stood up. It was time to show the courage of her convictions. She walked to the barn door and pulled on the old handle. The ancient wooden panels creaked and groaned on their hinges. 'Hi, Clive,' she said, hoping to God it was him.

'Hi!' He stepped into the pool of light cast from the open door.

A rush of blood flushed her cheeks. For a millisecond she didn't care if she'd let her guard down and her face showed emotion. But it only lasted for a flicker before she'd marshalled herself. He didn't need to see the depth of her relief and attraction to him. She tried not to register how good she thought he looked in his faintly checked lilac shirt, as she mouthed a warning to him. She continued in a slightly over-loud voice, 'What a nice surprise! Come on in. Coffee? Tea?'

Relief and embarrassment flowed through her in equal measure as he brushed past, his eyebrows raised and a smile threatening to break. 'Hello, Mr Clegg. I hope I'm not intruding. Just called in on my way home. I often pass this way. Matt! Nick! I had no idea.'

Ron smiled a welcome. 'Hello, Inspector.'

'You can't guess how pleased we are it's you,' Nick said as he grinned at Chrissie and perched back on a work stool.

'For a moment we thought some thugs had followed Matt back from Hadleigh,' Chrissie explained. She smiled at Clive. 'But it was you.'

'Sounds as if it's just as well I dropped in, then.' He glanced across at Matt who seemed to be studying the concrete floor. 'Are you OK, Matt?' Silence filled the old barn as he waited for him to answer.

For a moment Chrissie thought Matt was about to make a run for the door as he stood up, red blotches on his moon face, his eyes moving restlessly. Then he pulled at his denim jacket, forcing it back from his shoulders. He shook and dragged his arms from the sleeves, much as one might draw a prawn-tail out of its shell. But instead of the prawn's pink flesh, rolls of pink skin were exposed as his tee-shirt rode up with the effort.

'Are you OK, Matt?'

Matt didn't speak. He smoothed down his tee-shirt, jabbing and yanking at the thin cotton fabric. Finally he seemed satisfied and straightened up to face Clive. 'Do it look French to you? Were that Ricky Rake bloke jokin' or just messin' with me? What you think?'

Chrissie caught a glance from Clive, both concern and surprise. 'He wrote over you with a marker pen? Those letters on your tee-shirt?'

Chrissie stared at the black hieroglyphics and spelt out the letters, 'C A d *A U*.'

'French for a gift, but without an E? Is that what you mean?' Clive said slowly.

The sound of Clive's voice, the French word, just the mention of something French made a nerve fizz somewhere in the depths of Chrissie's mind. All thoughts of Hadleigh thugs evaporated as the kernel of an idea began to form.

She tried to hold onto it, but Matt's voice broke her concentration and cut the thread.

'Yeah, 'e said somethin' like that as well. I thought you'd know some French, bein' a DI.'

'I think you should start at the beginning. Just tell the DI, nice and slowly what happened over at the Fens Storage facility today, Matt.' Ron's voice, calming and unhurried, floated across the air like oil poured onto troubled waters.

Chrissie thought she'd heard it all before and twice, but this time when Matt recounted his lunchtime visit to Rake's outlet he came up with another detail, as if his memory was refreshed by the frequent telling of the tale. She knew he'd miss out the bits about Tom and Dan's reference to the tour of the Academy fuel tanks. There was nothing to be gained by letting Clive in on that nugget of information, but when he casually dropped in the bit about seeing into the storage container, she almost gasped with surprise.

The look on Clive's face suggested it came as a bit of a bombshell to him as well. 'Just say it again, and slowly, Matt. Blue plastic drums?'

'Well, it weren't metal or glass. Blue coloured drums – medium size, about half a dozen of 'em. They had white labels. Yeah, that's right, *25 litres* and *ACID* printed on the outside. And them hazard signs for corrosive liquid.' Matt closed his eyes for a moment. Chrissie knew he was trying to recall the image of it all, draw on his photographic memory for words and numbers. 'See the drums were curved so the writin' on them labels were curved. It were difficult to see the ends of them words, but I'd guess – *HYDROCHLORIC ACID – 28%.*'

‘Six, 25 litre drums of acid? What in hell’s name are they up to?’ Clive spoke for them all.

‘Well, it aint all there were. Some large metal drums, large enough to need the forklift to load ’em in there, and then some smaller white coloured plastic containers, ’bout five litre size. He said he had to get back to the farm an’ bring the rest of the stuff. Seemed in a hurry.’

‘The thing is,’ Nick spoke for the first time, ‘if the farm they were referring to was Rookery farm, they could be dealing in red diesel. But why the acid?’

‘Yeah, dealin’ in red an’ also usin’ the acid to get the dye out the diesel.’

‘So you think that’s what the acid’s for, Matt?’

‘Yeah, mate. Unless someone’s got a huge swimmin’ pool.’

‘A swimming pool?’ Chrissie asked, incredulous.

‘Yeah, you can use acid to reduce the PH of the water in your pool.’

‘Then you wouldn’t need to hide it would you? And he said they’d been tipped off about the police raid?’ Clive’s voice sounded more serious than she’d heard it before. She sensed he’d moved into professional mode.

‘I think operation Nancy will want to hear about this, Matt.’

‘Operation Nancy?’ Nick chipped in.

‘Yes, we give the tactical, cross-force investigations names; like hurricanes. In alphabetical order. It’s not my patch but I think they’d be very interested to hear what Matt has to say. We can contact them in the morning.’ He turned back to Matt. ‘No one need know the information came from you. The Rakes are well known to the police round these parts. We’ll find a reason for a warrant to search the new Fens storage unit.' He was about to say more but he glanced at Chrissie and his expression changed, as if a cloud had blown in front of the sun.

'What's the matter Clive?'

'It reminded me of something I wanted to tell you, but it can wait. Now's not the time.'

If it was another guessing game, Chrissie didn't want to play. Something in his tone didn't invite further comment. He'd become Clive the policeman, almost a stranger. The frisson of warmth and humour, a kind of understated intimacy she'd sensed between Clive and herself, evaporated. When he took a call on his phone a few moments later and apologised because he'd have to leave, no mention was made of the curry. Perhaps she was just tired and oversensitive, but the pang of disappointment hurt more than she'd expected. She didn't hear his text message arrive, twenty minutes later.

# CHAPTER 21

Nick switched off the ignition and leaned back against the head rest. He'd parked his old Ford Fiesta in the Willows car park but he was still too early for work. Normally he slept well, but after yesterday's evening in the Clegg workshop, he'd passed the night in a state of half-wakefulness interspersed with dreams and nightmares. By the morning he felt exhausted, and with the logic born of disturbed sleep, he got up. It was dark, his bedside clock had read 05:15 but at least he knew by getting up, the dreams would stop.

He'd stood in the shower, hot water beating down on his head while steam misted the glass cubicle walls. He'd closed his eyes and for a moment Ricky Rake's twisted sneer appeared. When the image seemed to back away its arms were wrapped in bandages like an Egyptian mummy and its burial-mask was a flaming gold, cast like a curtain of shoulder length red hair. But instead of jewels, it was draped with an amulet made from steel bullet casings with little brass tips. Nick stood helpless as the mummy raised a swathed hand to its death-mask, its fingers uncurling to reveal a gun, shaped like a mobile phone.

In his nightmare Nick had tried to run, his feet leaden as bullets whistled past, but there had been no escape. Awake and smothering a scream, Nick looked up at the cascading shower and waited as it drove away the spectre.

It had taken him half an hour to get dressed and leave the house. He'd no stomach for breakfast but he'd scribbled a note for his mother and slipped its edge under the Jamie

Oliver mug on the kitchen table for her to find later. She'd be bound to see it there, he'd reckoned.

But getting up hadn't really helped. The anxiety still churned deep inside and he knew it wasn't going to feel any better until he was busy, working and joking around with the other carpenters. There'd be at least another hour and half to wait before Willows opened for the day. He'd reached for the Amy Winehouse *Back to Black* CD and slid it into the player. That's better, he thought as her smoky voice and mellow tones drove out the image of Ricky Rake's faintly smiling face. And so, once he'd reached the Willows car park, Nick had switched off the ignition, leaned back and waited.

'What the hell am I doing here?' Nick asked himself as Amy's voice soothed in the background. 'Running away?' He sighed as he replayed some of the previous evening's conversations in his head. He'd known about the fuel gangs, but the reality of gangland threats and violence had never been tangible before. The penny dropped when he'd realised the harmless Dan of Rookery farm was Tom's sinister threatening Dan. He'd felt deceived. He'd been duped and it made him feel vulnerable and stupid.

Even Ricky Rake wasn't how he appeared. Dave had warned him, and according to Matt, Ricky had said Nick was trouble. Now what the hell did that mean? He'd hardly exchanged more than a few words with the man, hardly seen him. What had he ever done to upset Ricky Rake?

As always, it seemed to Nick there were more questions than answers. He leaned forwards and pressed the radio button. He'd had enough of Amy. The seven o'clock news would be more distracting. It's funny, he thought, how Kat could listen to Amy for hours. For him, half an hour was enough, but then Kat had a stillness about her. Perhaps it was a skill that lent itself to target shooting. He remembered how she'd explained the slightest movement could upset the shot, direct the bullet to one side of the bull's-eye. There was an art to controlling the breathing, she said, so that chest expansion didn't move the position of the arms, not even by a fraction. He laughed when she'd told him and playfully tweaked her in the ribs. She'd jumped of course, and tickled him back. He smiled at the memory. Then something else struck him. Ricky Rake had a stillness about him as well. Nick had thought it more a languor or foppishness, but if he was picking a shooting team, then those were the qualities he'd be looking for.

Nick's mind wandered between Kat, the radio news items and Amy Winehouse. Little by little he started to relax and as the daylight dawned he drifted into a light sleep.

*Tap*! *Tap*! *Tap*! The sound propelled Nick like a missile into wakefulness. His throat felt dry, his eyelids heavy.

Where am I? God, my neck hurts, he thought as he tried to focus on Alfred Walsh's weathered face. It took him a moment to orientate. Of course, he was in the car park. He might have guessed the foreman would be the first to arrive. He attempted a smile and fumbled to open the car door as Alfred raised his hand to knock on the windscreen again.

'You all right, lad?'

'Yeah. I just got here a bit early, that's all, Mr Walsh.'

Alfred looked at him and nodded slowly. 'Well I hope you're not going to keep falling asleep all day.' He turned and limped towards the workshop office door.

Nick switched off the radio and followed the foreman into the office. He felt stiff, cold and hungry. He'd left his lunchbox in the car so after filling the kettle he rummaged in the biscuit tin. The last digestive was stuck at the bottom of the packet, ready to break into a thousand fragments.

'I had a call from Mr Rake yesterday, late afternoon.' Alfred said and leaned against the desk.

'Ricky Rake? In Halstead?' Nick tried to keep his breathing even. Nightmares were nightmares not reality, he told himself.

'He said one of the unit doors was sticking. He wanted someone to go and fix it.' The foreman pulled the work-sheet towards him and bent to read. 'Specifically asked for you.'

'What? Me?' The digestive shattered as Nick tried to release it. He's setting a trap, Nick thought and his appetite vanished.

'I was surprised too. He said Monday, the later the better.' He ran his finger down the list of names and shook his head. 'Not often we have people asking for an apprentice. A compliment to you I s'pose. But that don't make it right. Dave's over that way today. You can spend the day with him an' both of you drop in to Rake's office on the way back.'

'But didn't he say…? I mean shouldn't we leave it till Monday, like he said?' Nick knew he'd be at the apprentice release day on Monday and Dave would have to go by himself. It'd let him off the hook.

'No, he should be well pleased to have you both a few days early.' Alfred looked up and smiled, as if the matter was settled. 'Two sugars in mine, Nick.'

The foreman's bombshell exploded inside Nick's head. The shards of his nightmare blasted through him, as indiscriminate as shrapnel.

•••

Dave seemed genuinely pleased to have Nick with him for the day and kept up a steady stream of chatter, distracting him as he drove the Willows van over to Hintlesham. He was fitting book-shelves, almost to ceiling height in a room aptly named the library. From the outside, Nick had thought the Victorian house too small to accommodate so much space solely for the storage of books. But then size was deceptive.

'Can't judge a book by its cover,' Dave quipped.

'So what was the last book you read?'

'Car workshop manual.'

Nick frowned. He was about to say the contents would be pretty obvious from the title, let alone the cover, when Dave interrupted his thoughts.

'We'll aim to finish here at about three. That'll give plenty of time to get over to Mr Rake's Hadleigh emporium and fix whatever's sticking.'

The familiar churning started in the pit of Nick's stomach.

'Come on, Nick. Don't look like that. It's not your fault something's dragging or catching. Everything was OK when we finished, and that was weeks ago. Wood moves, you know.'

Nick swallowed hard. It was impossible to explain his real fears. 'Yeah, sure.'

Time passed quickly as they worked on the book-shelves. Too quickly, and it didn't seem long before Nick found himself packing up the van, ready to head over to Hadleigh. The churning had become rawness, fleetingly doubling him over. He hugged at his stomach.

'You all right, lad? Something you ate?'

‘Maybe. I don’t know. I’ll be OK. Just take it easy round those corners, will you.’

‘If you’re going to be sick, for God’s sake don’t throw up in the van.’

By Dave’s standards, the journey was slow. He braked hard before each bend and then accelerated away, straining to reach the Hadleigh bypass and hit 60 mph. A quick left turn down Gallows Hill and Nick’s head spun like a gyroscope. His stomach couldn’t take any more and he closed his eyes as the familiar single storey office building came into view. Despite his fears, he was thankful when the journey ended. Forcing back the bile, he waited for his breathing to settle. He flung open the van door. It was time to face his demons.

‘We’ll go and see what the problem is first,’ Dave tossed over his shoulder as he headed for the office. ‘Then you can fetch whatever we need from the van.’

Nick followed close behind, glancing to the right and left. It felt safer with Dave. The afternoon sun, typical for that time of the year, sat low in the wintery sky, the rays seemingly directed straight into his eyes. He put up his hand to block out the dazzle and almost missed seeing Ricky’s black Porsche. It was parked to one side of the massive warehouse. Nick shivered in the cold bright light.

Inside, the building smelt of new carpet and Nick kept close to Dave as the receptionist led them along a corridor. She hesitated at the innermost office door, the organisational headquarters. ‘Just wait here a moment, please,’ she said, before knocking.

The place felt deserted. They stood, listening to the murmur of voices, as the receptionist spoke to someone inside. 'Mr Rake will see you now,' she announced, opening the door wide.

The last time Nick had been in the office, the floor had been bare concrete and the walls raw plaster.

'Wow!' His reaction was automatic. 'It looks….'

'Different?' Ricky swivelled round on his deluxe office chair. Behind him, a computer screen flickered. Static images of doors and metal gangways stared from a bank of monitors. The office furniture and cabinets glowed in rich colours of wood, their patina achieved with clever staining. The result was a hoax, achieved without depth of beeswax or elbow grease.

Nick looked up at the ceiling. 'So that's what….' Above, some kind of window shaft led to a grey-blue sky.

'Have to have some natural light,' Ricky said, following the direction of Nick's gaze. 'You realise this isn't convenient, don't you? I wasn't expecting you till Monday.'

'The boss said we were to come straight away. He said you're finding some of the doors or drawers are sticking.'

Ricky twisted his neck slightly to look at Dave. He didn't speak but just watched him for a moment, as if he was trying to decide whether to answer. Nick felt uncomfortable and shifted his weight from foot to foot. He could imagine him fixing Dave in his rifle sights and then slowly squeezing the trigger – bull's-eye!

'I'm sorry if you've had any trouble, Mr Rake. But this happens with new builds. It takes time for everything to settle, for the plaster to dry out completely. It only needs a few millimetres.' Dave's voice trailed away as he met Ricky's unblinking gaze.

'I wasn't aware there were any problems with the plaster. I don't see any cracks.'

'And the wood tends to move and shift a little as the central heating–'

'You may have noticed I keep this room cool. Most of the heat comes from the computers. Look, I don't want excuses. I want it fixed. Do you understand, Dave?'

'Of course, Mr Rake. If you could just show us what's sticking?'

Nick watched as Ricky drew in his legs, put a hand on the desk top and stood up. The movement reminded him of a snake uncoiling, graceful and silent. He gestured to the corner close to the door, and his shirt cuff flopped back. No crepe bandage today, Nick thought as memories of his nightmare flashed through his mind. Hell, even his skin looked reptilian, but it was the wrong colour; red and shiny. Nick wasn't sure he'd seen anything like it before. Could it be a burn, he wondered. But why would he have a burn on his arm?

'Over here?' Dave moved towards the office door.

Nick kept quiet. The atmosphere was becoming frostier by the minute. The wooden gun cupboard door stood ajar and the drawers in the unit alongside were not pushed back fully into the frame.

'Yes, if you wait a moment, I'll show you.'

They paused while Ricky walked over to the gun cupboard, his movement fluid. 'You see, the door's jammed. I can't move it unless I put my shoulder to it. And if I do manage to ram it shut, I can't get it open again. I can't get at my guns and I'll end up damaging the door.'

Dave put his hand on the cupboard door and moved it slowly, looking to see where it was catching. 'I can see where the trouble is. And these drawers, you said?'

Nick edged closer to see as Ricky bent to pull on a drawer handle. There was a moment of resistance and then it shot open. Something glinted in the bottom, a warm, orangey gold.

'You can see the problem, can't you?' Ricky's attention was on Dave. For the moment he seemed to have forgotten Nick, who stared into the drawer.

Nestling in the depths, a gold chain coiled in a careless heap. Lying at its centre an oblong of gold caught the light. It was clearly a locket, but not like anything Nick had seen before. The face was hinged. It had a central panel of filigree, like an ornate grill but not in gold. It was made of a different metal, possibly silver, platinum or pewter; he couldn't tell which. It was beautiful. The contrast in colours and the delicacy of the craftsmanship held him, transfixed.

'Hey, you nosey bastard!' Ricky's hand darted into the drawer. He grasped the necklace and elbowed Nick sharply in the ribs. 'Get out of the way!'

Nick stepped back, shocked by the sudden violence. He watched as Ricky wrenched the gun cupboard door open with one hand. The locket dangled from its chain in his other hand as in a flash he tossed it into the gun-safe.

'Sorry, Mr Rake.'

Either he hadn't heard or he was ignoring Nick, because Ricky seemed to direct his next words at Dave. 'This really is not a good time, you know. I've a meeting with a customer in about half an hour.'

'Well, these drawers will be quick to sort out. They just need a little adjustment on their metal sliders. The door will need to come off its hinges. If you like, we can do the drawers quickly now and come back another time for the door?'

‘OK.’ The tone was silky, ‘but come back on Monday. Now I want you gone in thirty minutes.’

Nick hurried back to the Willows van and collected his toolbox. All they really needed was a cross-headed screwdriver and maybe a spirit level, but he didn’t want to risk getting it wrong, so he took all he could carry.

The atmosphere in the central office seemed to have thawed by the time Nick returned. Ricky was sitting on his deluxe swivel chair and his body language spoke relaxed executive.

‘Thanks, Nick.’ Dave had already taken the drawers out. He selected a screwdriver, and working fast, adjusted the setting of the runners. Soon all the drawers were sliding smoothly again.

Each time Nick glanced up, Ricky, was watching. His eyes seemed to bore deep, and something in his expression made him feel uneasy. So what had been so special about the locket? Nick couldn’t think, but there was definitely something familiar about it. He couldn’t quite place why and then he remembered. It had been in his dream. The mummy had worn an amulet of steel casings with golden bullet tips. It was a nightmare version of the gold locket he’d just seen with a contrasting metal front. Nick didn’t believe in the supernatural, but this was too much of a coincidence. Something or someone must have put the idea there. He racked his brains. Was it anything Chrissie had told him the evening before?

Nick began to sweat as he recalled his nightmare. Ricky was too close. ‘Can I start loading up the van, Dave?’ He needed to escape. The last drawer was just sliding in and the familiar griping was churning his stomach.

‘Reckon so!’ Dave checked his watch. ‘Spot on thirty minutes. Come on let’s be going.’

‘Goodbye, Mr Rake.’

It was only when they were back at Willows that Nick realised he’d left his own toolbox on the concrete next to where the van had been parked outside Rake’s emporium.

# CHAPTER 22

Matt sipped his lager. Open Mic Night at the Nags Head was proving to be quite a hit. It was a new event, something to draw the punters in mid-week when the bar was slow. He'd seen the notices and persuaded Nick to come and sing. A step up from karaoke, Chrissie had said and judging by the smiling faces and number of drinkers, she was right. Nick had brought his acoustic guitar and was doing some last minute tuning in front of the microphone.

'Any idea what he's going to sing, Chrissie?'

Chrissie shrugged and pulled a face. 'As long as it's not *Streets of London* – you know, his Ralph McTell rendition. Did he tell you, Kat?'

'Don't look at me. I got the impression he was going to duet with his guitarist mate, the one from the band he sometimes sings with.'

'Jake?' Matt said, pleased to chip in a word and show he knew Nick better than anyone else. He'd wanted to chat up Kat, but didn't know what to say. She might be Nick's bird, but she was, in his book, bloody attractive and fair game. She was hardly going to get up and walk off; not when she was there to listen to Nick sing.

'He nearly didn't come. He said something about leaving his toolbox over at Hadleigh and needing to go back to collect it, but I persuaded him to go another time.' Kat didn't look at Matt. She seemed to have eyes only for Nick and directed her words in Chrissie's direction as the microphone crackled.

'If it's Hadleigh he's left it, I hope it isn't at Ricky Rake's emporium.' Chrissie's voice sounded sharp.

‘Yes, I think it might be, but what’s the big deal in that?’

‘What’s the big deal? I told ’im old Rake had it in for ’im, didn’t I Chrissie?’ Matt hoped Kat was impressed.

‘You did, only the other night.’

Kat was about to say something, but Nick tapped the microphone. The laughing and chatter in the bar quietened to an anticipatory hush for about a second before rushing back with the sound of bar orders and drinkers. Matt watched as Nick applied a clamp to the neck of his guitar and plucked at a couple of chords before clearing his throat. He looked invincible.

‘I asked about Ricky Rake at my shooting club. You know he’d told Nick he was a member, in Hadleigh?’

‘Shush. He’s about to sing,’ Matt hissed at everyone. He brushed at the lager splattered down the front of his tee-shirt and grinned at Kat.

‘*OK, let’s see if you can recognise this one….*’

The first few chords strummed out a kind of foot-tapping simple rhythmic beat. Nick’s voice, a reedy tenor, flowed above the noise in the bar and Matt swayed to the music. ‘Yeah, yeah,’ Matt yelled. ‘Kaiser Chiefs!’ and then he clapped and whistled. He’d instantly recognised the intro to *Love’s Not a Competition, But I’m Winning*. He felt on fire with the audience, the booze, the atmosphere. ‘Awe-some!’

He glanced sideways to check Kat was enjoying it.

‘Great, aint ’e!’

‘Yeah, I can see why he chose it. He said he didn’t feel so confident playing without Jake being there. Easy chords. Just bang it out. Great voice!’

‘I know, great choice,’ Chrissie said and winked at Kat.

Matt gulped his lager and watched Kat. So what was she trying to say? That Nick couldn’t play the guitar well?

‘He aint usin’ that clamp thing ’cross the strings coz he aint no good at playin’, Kat.’

‘Capo. It’s called a capo.’

He stared at Kat for a moment, trying to take in what she’d said. ‘Italian. That’s an Italian word, aint it?’ He might have guessed. It was the Italian magic again. Now why hadn’t he thought of that? Trust Nick to have known to use Italian words on her. ‘I’ve got a Piaggio, you know.’

‘Is that a make of guitar, Matt?’

‘You were saying, Kat,’ Chrissie butted in, ‘you’d asked about Ricky Rake at your shooting club.’

‘Oh yeah. It seems he used to be a member but then there was some trouble after a rifle target competition. A punch-up. Apparently he thumped the winner and supposedly cracked his jaw. Ricky didn’t agree with the result and thought he should’ve won. Not a good loser, by the sound of it. They ended up chucking him out of the club. All before my time, which is probably why I’ve never met him.’

Nick tapped the microphone again. ‘*I see my friend Jake has just arrived, so I’ll spare you the Cold Play number and if you give us a few moments – we’ll give you something new*!’ Clapping rippled through the bar.

Matt leaned across to Kat. It was his chance. ‘Are you goin’ to them fireworks on bonfire night over at Hadleigh? There’s a kinda play while they’re lightin’ the bonfire. It’ll be awesome. A friend wrote it!’ He rummaged in his jeans pocket and pulled out a scrunched up flyer. ‘See, it’s on Aldham Common, Saturday. That’s only a few days away.’

Kat smoothed out the glossy paper. 'The north side of the bypass? There's a monument up there, isn't there? For someone from Hadleigh. Rowland something. He was burned at the stake for real.'

'That's horrible. It sounds spooky.' Chrissie swigged at her glass. 'I'm still coming though. Should be fun. What about you, d'you think you'll come, Kat?'

'Yeah, you must come.' Matt tried his sexy half smile. All he needed now was a call from Gloria to check on his smoking progress and his cool image would be complete.

'Not sure what Nick....'

'Course he's comin'. Bloody said he would!'

'Well, Kat, it seems like you'll be with us all on Saturday evening then. It should be fun. I'll be bringing some friends as well. So it'll be a good crowd of us.'

Matt was about to ask who, but Nick tapped the microphone again, and the staccato tones spattered around the bar.

'*OK. I think we're ready now. Jake, d'you want to make the intro*?'

Matt shifted on his seat and checked his tee-shirt. The lager splatter had dried and what had once been plain white cotton with the words *CLEAN AIR* printed across the front was now peppered with patches of smog. He glanced up and caught Chrissie's eye. 'Irony,' she mouthed at him.

'Irony?'

She nodded.

'*Yeah, thanks Nick. Well this is a kind of unplugged version. I hope you enjoy it. So - Destiny Tuesday*!'

The first few chords rang out into a wall of chatter and clinking glasses.

‘Shush! I can’t ’ear,’ Matt grumbled as he turned to stare at drinkers near the bar, but they quietened anyway as someone dropped their loose change and coins clattered and rolled on the old scrubbed floorboards. Jake’s fingers plucked at steel strings while Nick strummed out a rhythm section and for a few moments Matt was lost in the music, all thoughts of heating fuel and red diesel forgotten. While Nick sang the melody, Jake harmonised with an earthy rumble. Tom would have described it as a character voice. No wonder the band needed a singer, Matt thought. And then it was over and Matt whistled and hooted and clapped.

‘Great, mate. You were great!’ Matt stood up to give Nick a hug and then thought better of it and thumped him on the shoulder instead. ‘Great!’

While Jake went to buy a couple of pints of Land Girl, Nick sat next to Kat. Matt watched as she smiled and whispered something in Nick’s ear. What wouldn’t he give to have Ginny whisper in his ear like that, he wondered and then he thought back to their last meeting. He’d seen her in the canteen, drinking coffee with her drama friends. He’d carried over his cola bottle, hoping to sit with her.

‘All them flyers are out now, Ginny.’ He’d smiled and stood near her chair, hoping she’d invite him to sit at her table.

‘Thanks, Chemistry Dude,’ she’d said without turning to look at him. ‘Don’t let me hold you up; I think you were going somewhere.’ A ripple of laughter spread around the table.

‘Yeah, to the show. You’re still in it aint you?’

Someone clapped. ‘Good on you, Chemistry Dude. Great one-liner!’

Matt had no idea what he'd said to earn the applause but Ginny turned and smiled at him. 'Of course I'm still in it. See you there then.'

He hadn't known what else to say or do so he'd left the canteen with his drink and a hot face. Did she mean it when she smiled, he wondered.

'Are you all right, Matt?' Chrissie's voice broke through his memories. 'You looked as if you were miles away.'

Matt dragged his mind back to the present but before he could answer, Nick butted in, 'That's reminded me. There's something I wanted to tell you, Chrissie.' Nick's eyes were fixed on the next singer standing at the microphone.

Matt followed Nick's gaze as a young woman with a generous cleavage adjusted the height of the stand. 'Well, get a load of that!'

'No, Matt. I was looking at what's hanging round her neck!'

Matt adjusted his eye line. 'The necklace?'

Nick nodded. 'Chrissie, I think I might've seen the locket you described the other day. You know, the one Mrs Mann said Jim's visitor wore.'

'What? Hanging round the next singer's neck?'

'No, Chrissie. Over at Ricky Rake's office.'

'Oh my God, Nick!'

# CHAPTER 23

Chrissie picked up her mobile. It was Friday afternoon and her nerves were on edge. They'd been jangling ever since the open-mic night at the Nags Head a couple of days before. She knew she should feel on top of the world, after all, she was going to have that date with Clive. He'd rearranged the dinner invitation for the coming Saturday night instead - the night of the Guy Fawkes play. She'd felt excited and flattered. The only blot on the landscape was Ricky Rake. He was playing on her mind and she knew she needed to get off that track if Saturday was going to be a success.

The phone *brrring*ed in her hand. 'Yes?'

'Hi, Chrissie.' Clive's voice sounded strident against a noisy background.

'Clive! Nice to hear from you, but you'll have to speak up. Are you phoning from the office or something?'

'Yes. Sorry about this, Chrissie, but something's come up. Mary's just phoned and… well, it looks like I've got the kids on Saturday.'

'That's nice.' She didn't know what else to say.

'So, how about a curry this evening, instead? We never made it for a curry last time, so what d'you say?'

'That… sounds nice.' She'd been taken by surprise and her mind was whirring, her stomach flipping.

'Great! So that's OK then. Knew you'd understand. I'll pick you up around eight o'clock. OK?'

'See you at eight, then.'

The line went dead.

Chrissie sat down on the workbench stool and stared at the lifeless phone in her hand.

‘Are you all right, Mrs Jax? You look rather flushed.’

She glanced up to see Ron watching, his eyebrows slightly drawn and forehead creased. In principle she didn’t like to talk about her private life, she’d always subscribed to a view that work should be kept separate. It was unprofessional to have it any other way but boundaries often blurred and kindly enquiries had a habit of piercing her armour.

‘That was Clive. It seems he won’t be able to make it to the Hadleigh fireworks tomorrow.’ A thought struck her. ‘I don’t suppose you’d want to come, Mr Clegg?’

‘That’s very kind but I think I’ll pass on that, Mrs Jax.’

Chrissie chuckled and dropped her phone back into her handbag.

‘I’d rather thought he was sweet on you, Mrs Jax.’

‘Really?’ His quaint phrase caught her unprepared. Her cheeks flamed again. ‘Well, he has asked me out for a curry this evening instead.’

‘There you are then. Your plum nail varnish wasn’t wasted. Now, if that’s settled, it’s time to have another go with the router. This cornice isn’t going to get made by chatting.’

Chrissie headed back to the table mounted router. The cutter ends made ridges and curves along the wood in a way that fascinated her. The skill was in adjusting the height of the shaped cutter and the pleasure was in seeing the contours in reverse, like turning plaster out of a mould. The problem was that she hadn’t quite mastered it yet. She tried to clear her mind as she picked up a length of wood. It was time to make a pact with herself. Two more hours concentrating fully at the Clegg workshop and then she could worry about Clive and her evening out to her heart's content.

She made another decision as well. She'd phone Sarah on the way home and ask if she'd like to come to the fireworks on Saturday.

•••

Clive held the door open as Chrissie settled into the passenger seat of his Ford Mondeo. She'd always thought you could tell something about someone's character by the inside of their car. Clive's was pristine. No chocolate wrappers or CD cases. She hadn't even removed a coat, scarf or heap of papers from the seat before getting in. At least he hasn't an air freshener hanging from the rear-view mirror, she thought.

'Stowmarket or Bury?' he asked as she fastened her seat belt. 'You look very thoughtful.'

'I was just thinking I wish my car was as clean and tidy inside as yours. Now what does that tell me?'

'Am I going to be profiled? I could have just had it valeted, you know.' He laughed as he closed her door and walked around to the driver's side. 'Or are you going to profile yourself?'

Chrissie tried to remember what Sarah had said. Keep it light, just relax, loosen up, be yourself. The trouble was it had been so long since she'd felt able to be herself. 'So, let me guess. You removed the nodding dog before you came to pick me up?' She hoped to God she'd read him correctly.

'Yup, along with the fluffy dice.'

She caught his smile as the inside light faded and he started the car. 'Bury, let's go to Bury if that's OK with you.'

For a moment he drove in silence. The instrument panel glowed green in the darkness. The car, the engine noise, the motion - it was all achieving what Sarah's advice couldn't. She started to relax. Unbuttoning her jacket she hoped she'd made the right choice with her silky blouse and black jeans.

'It's been a hell of a week. By the way, before I forget. We've located Minnette Mann's possessions. Over at the Fens new storage unit in Hadleigh.'

'Really?'

'Yes, it was amazing – all her things, just as if she'd nipped out for a cup of tea but expected to be back in a second. We're still going through it. There's plenty of material for DNA testing.'

'Hair? Is that what you use?'

'Yes, and there were lots of photos. Those aren't for DNA testing of course.' Clive smiled and then indicated as he changed lane on the A14. 'All of them show her wearing a curious necklace, like a locket but with a decorated mesh front, like a perforated cover. Very unusual. Gold and silver, I think.'

'It could be a vinaigrette locket necklace.' Chrissie tried to keep her voice even, light and relaxed, just as Sarah had advised.

'Sounds like a salad dressing.'

'No, it'll be an antique. It's for holding something aromatic soaked on a sponge and then put in the locket. The holes in the front allow the scent to disguise the fetid odours of the day! I think they tended to use vinegar and hence the name. Unusual. Can't be many around.'

‘Well, I never knew that. Anyway, the current Mrs Mann thinks it’s what her husband’s mystery visitor was wearing. We’ve shown her the photos.’

‘You mean our Suffolk Medallion Man?’ Chrissie thought hard before she spoke again. She didn’t want to spoil the easy harmony developing between them but she was bursting with her news. ‘Actually, Nick thinks he’s seen something like that. Over in Ricky Rake’s office on Wednesday.’

‘What the hell was he doing over there?’

‘Adjusting unit doors and drawers. But this Rake person worries me. I’ve heard he was chucked out of the Hadleigh rifle club because of his temper and a punch-up.’

‘I didn’t know that. Christ, Chrissie, have you turned detective or something? Look, leave this to the police. Operation Nancy is poised to bust the premises. Don’t any of you go making him suspicious by poking around. You do understand, don’t you?’

‘Of course.’ She didn’t dare tell him they’d all be in Hadleigh the following night. It certainly didn’t seem the moment to ask if he wanted to come as well, and to bring his kids along. That’s if he wasn’t already taking them to a Saturday night firework display elsewhere. She gazed out of the window and watched as a huge flower head of light exploded in the air, followed by another and then another, somewhere off towards Blackthorpe. ‘Wow! Did you see those fireworks? They’re starting early.’

‘They’re huge, aren’t they? You wouldn’t think there’d be enough money around to spend on something that quite literally goes up in smoke. It’ll be going on all week. I bet there’ll be loads of baked potatoes and burnt sausages eaten as well.’

Chrissie laughed. 'Yes, there's a fine line between crispy and burnt.'

'Lightly charred or turned to cinders.'

'Did you have fireworks when you were a kid?'

The conversation wandered into easy reminiscing and wove between pranks with fire-crackers and injuries with sparklers. Clive described his childhood in Norfolk where his father taught at the Norwich School for Boys. He made those early years sound like another world, kinder and more humorous.

In Bury, over chicken tikka and saag aloo, she found herself telling him about her ambition to be an accountant and then her disillusion and the need to change. Dipping into a dish of lamb vindaloo, he almost choked and with his eyes and nose streaming, tried to explain what had attracted him to the police force. She avoided talking about Bill and he didn't mention Mary. Instinct told her she needed to discover more about him before any of the other players on the field. Mary and the kids would have to wait on the side lines for now.

They were one of the last tables to leave. She couldn't believe it when she looked at her watch. Nearly eleven o'clock. Outside, Churchgate Street seemed murky despite the street lighting. Chrissie hugged her jacket close and stumbled on the pavement. He'll think I'm pissed on half a lager, she thought but when Clive grabbed her arm, she didn't care.

The firework enthusiasts had long since given up shooting rockets into the air. It was late and the night sky looked inky as they drove along the A 14.

'Would you like to come in for some coffee?' she asked as he dropped her back home.

'I'd love to, thanks but I've got to be up early to pick up the kids and it'll take me a while to get back to Lavenham. So this time I'll say no.'

She fumbled to open the passenger door, her fingers searching for the unfamiliar handle in the dark. 'Sorry, can't seem to find the....'

Clive smiled and got out. In a few strides he was around the Mondeo. He looked amused as he opened the door for her, but his courteous act flustered her as she said, 'No really, I couldn't see the handle in the dark.'

'Yes, it's a complicated business opening doors,' and he bent and lightly kissed her cheek when she stood up from the car. 'Goodnight, Chrissie.'

He waited until she'd opened her front door before driving away and after bolting it closed, she turned to look Bill's photo straight in the eye. He smiled from his heavy pewter frame on the narrow hall table. What would he think, she wondered. Would she have approved if the situation had been reversed?

•••

'There must be a curry closer than Bury,' Sarah said as Chrissie nosed her TR7 into Wolves Farm lane near Aldham Common. 'I mean, if you add it all up - Lavenham to Woolpit, then Bury, Woolpit, and back to Lavenham. It's one hell of a round trip. Clive must like you, Chrissie. Stands to reason. He's spent enough petrol on you.'

Chrissie smiled.

'I mean, isn't there somewhere nice in Haughley? It's much closer. Why not try there next time?'

Chrissie didn't answer. She was concentrating on finding somewhere to park. It was six o'clock and pitch dark. The play was due to start at six thirty and the bonfire and firework display was scheduled for half an hour after that. She'd arrived early so she could park and meet up with Matt, Nick, Kat, and their friends.

'And another thing,' Sarah continued, as Chrissie reversed off the lane onto a muddy verge. 'What do you feel about him? You've never really said.'

Chrissie killed the engine and opened her door. Before getting out, she turned to Sarah. 'I don't know. I like him. I like him a lot but I don't want to get hurt. Some days my head rules and some days my heart rules. So there you have it in a nutshell. I'm a bit of a–'

'Nut?' Sarah finished for her.

'Thanks! No, I was going to say a mess. Confused.'

'Oh hell!' Sarah's Wellington boot sank into mud as she stepped out of the TR7.

'At least it's not raining. The forecast said rain.' Chrissie wrapped her scarf an extra time around her neck and pulled on her gloves. The air felt cold. Moisture permeated the night like a dank mist. She stamped her feet on the tarmac. Her walking boots were warm and waterproof, so she figured she'd be OK as long as the mud was only a few inches deep. 'Got everything you need before I lock the car?'

Sarah nodded. Chrissie thought she looked like a Michelin Man in Hunter wellingtons and was about to say as much, but then Sarah pulled on a woolly hat with ear flaps over her glossy black bob. It transformed her from county tyre set to Icelandic chick. God, Chrissie wondered, how does she manage to look fun, relaxed and stylish, all in one.

'The main entrance is that way.' Sarah pointed back up the lane.

'Yes, but we can probably get in this way. Look, over there.' In the distance, lights shone on the common and Chrissie was able to make out a cluster of vans and off-roaders parked in a circle, like wagons in a western. She watched as people moved in and around the circle, just silhouettes in the darkness and too far away to recognise. 'I guess that's the mobile changing room and service centre for the play and fireworks. Bet you that's where we'll find Matt. Let's head in that direction.'

'Lead on Macduff!'

Chrissie found a gate in the hedge. No one seemed to be manning it, so they slipped through and walked across the damp grass. As they moved further onto the common, Chrissie caught sight of the massive pile of wood, towering high, like a two storey house. 'My God! It's like a building construction.' Old doors, wooden pallets and logs were the backbone, while broken chairs, tables and garden brushwood filled in the gaps. 'Hell! That'll go up like a....'

'Now that's what I call a bonfire!'

Arc lights had been set in front of it, lighting a grassy apron and then ropes slung between posts heralded the outer fortifications – the start of the fences and boundaries to hold back the audience, to protect them from the fire and display.

'Wow, it's quite exciting, isn't it?' Chrissie sniffed the air. Hints of damp grass mingled with sulphur and fuel. 'Come on, over this way.' A crowd was beginning to form and she pushed past a group of kids playing with luminescent bendy tubes. She headed for the circle of vehicles.

'Why's it so noisy? Have they left their engines running on purpose or something? Wooah! ' Sarah slipped on the mud as she hurried to keep up with Chrissie.

'No, that'll be the generators. They're always bloody loud, especially the ones running on diesel. Are you OK? It's lethal on this grass in the dark.'

'Yeah, should have brought a torch. So have you spotted, what was his name - Matt yet?'

'No. He must be here somewhere.'

# CHAPTER 24

'This feels weird. Why the hell did I come?' Nick asked himself. Had he been stupid?

His Saturday evening so far wasn't turning out too well. Kat had phoned him earlier to say she was delayed at a rifle shooting competition in Cambridge and he'd have to go to the firework display by himself.

'Sorry, Nick, but I just won't be back in time. Six thirty for seven is pretty early, you know.'

'Yeah, s'pose it's aimed at families and kids. Maybe we can go out later? Nine o'clock sound OK?'

'That'd be cool,' and so the conversation had ended.

Nick wasn't particularly keen to go to the fireworks, not without Kat, but he knew Matt would be offended and Chrissie might kill him if he didn't turn up. All Matt had talked about for the last two months was Ginny and her Guy Fawkes play. So, there really wasn't any choice but to wrap up in warm layers and head over to Hadleigh. He'd zipped up his fleece and thrown an anorak into his car. That's when his brainwave struck. If he set out straight away he could drop in at the Fens office and retrieve his toolbox. It would save him another journey. Kat must have thought him a real wuss when he'd struggled to rationalise his fear over collecting it. He'd tried to explain it was about meeting Mr Rake. She'd seemed dismissive.

The prospect of seeing Kat later that evening inspired and excited Nick. He felt invincible as he drove over to Hadleigh. At this hour and on a Saturday he reckoned he'd be safe. No boss was likely to be around after five thirty.

The Fens site looked deserted. The hangar-like doors fronting the massive warehouse were closed and security lights cast an eerie brightness onto the concrete. The darkness beyond looked impenetrable. The time on his dash board read 18:10.

'Je-e-e-z, this had better be OK,' he breathed, looking at the empty forecourt. What had Ricky Rake's message said? He tried to think. 'Yes,' he murmured, remembering the words. '*We're open till six, after that, the warehouse is locked but there's a security guard in the office. Your toolbox will be in the office building.*'

Nick gazed up towards the lights. The CCTV camera would be nearby, he reckoned and the security guard would probably be watching him on the bank of monitors at that very moment. He felt self-conscious, just as he'd felt when the foreman passed on Rake's message. Soon everyone at Willows would know he'd been dozy enough to leave his toolbox behind. And he'd never live it down with Dave, particularly if Dave collected it for him on Monday while Nick was attending the apprentice release day. He shook his head. He wasn't going to be known as a dozy wuss. He was going to retrieve it and he needed to get a move on. There was no point in hanging around in the car.

Outside, the air felt damp and cold as he slipped his arm into his anorak. In the distance a lone rocket whizzed and cracked as it shot into the sky. The noise stopped him dead in his tracks and for a moment he was sweating, transported back in time. In that instant the firework sounded like gunfire and he dropped to his knees. The concrete struck cold through his jeans. Something screeched far above into the night, squealing and squawking before fizzling out.

His heart beat so fast he could barely breathe as he pulled his mind back into gear. Of course, a screamer. Just another firework. He should have realised the early evening darkness would bring out the enthusiasts with their family boxes of fireworks further down Gallows Hill. It would make a good night for a shooting though, and then he nearly vomited with the thought.

Nick raised his head as he knelt and looked up at the office building. Its glass panelled door stared at him. Somewhere, deep beyond its cold surface a light flickered for a second and then was gone. Was it the reflection of a firework or something within? He caught an impression of movement. A dark shape against black shadows. Somebody was watching him from behind the door.

'Shit! What the hell am I doing here?' he hissed, his breath coming in short rasps. He glanced back at his car. Would he make it if he ran?

He started to move, pushing himself up from the concrete where he knelt. The door frame rattled as the lock turned. He froze and stared at the opening door.

'Are you OK?' The words were kind but the tone cold. 'I was watching on the monitors. I'm the security guard for tonight. You suddenly buckled over.'

'I-I….' Nick met Ricky Rake's gaze, the shadows turning eye sockets into dark holes in the pale face. 'I caught my foot.'

Ricky flicked at a switch and light flooded the corridor behind. 'It's Nick, from Willows, isn't it?'

'Yeah, I was over this way for the firework display on the common. Thought I'd just collect my toolbox. Got your message, thanks.' Nick tried to slow his speech. He'd nearly vomited with fear a moment earlier and now his words came in short bursts.

Ricky didn't answer. He looked into the sky as a firework crackled, sharp as a machine gun. 'Hmm, you better come in then.'

Nick watched as Ricky disappeared into the hallway. He'd left the door open; the light blazing behind him and an unspoken assumption Nick would follow.

•••

Matt shivered on Aldham Common. He hugged his denim jacket closer as he stood near one of the vans in the ring of vehicles. He'd been waiting since six o'clock, hoping to catch a glimpse of Ginny. Costumes and make-up were working from the van, so he reckoned he was bound to see her eventually. He stamped his feet and pumped his hands to get the circulation going while a generator hummed and throbbed nearby. He wore his favourite tee-shirt, the black one with an orange globe un-peeling from its apex. A giant Catherine-wheel, Ginny had said and so he'd chosen it for her. This time he'd added an extra twist; he'd teamed it with an under layer for warmth. With a bit of pulling and tugging, he'd stretched the thin cotton over a blue sweat-shirt, but the arms were proving a problem. It was so tight near his armpits that his hands were starting to tingle.

'Have you seen Ginny, mate?' he asked as a student bustled past carrying a wooden chair.

'Sorry, I'm props. Have you tried sound? It's the small Academy van on the other side. You can't miss it. Loads of cables leading to it.'

Matt ambled around the circle. He felt special, one of the production team. 'Matt, promotion an' advertisin',' he told a jumped-up student in a high visibility jacket when he was challenged.

He tasted excitement in the damp air as cast and crew scurried between vans and the grassy stage. People were already gathering behind the roped off areas. It can't be much longer before it starts, he thought. Where's Ginny?

'Hi, Matt!'

He whipped round. 'Shoot!'

'That's no greetin'.' Light caught the man's sharp nose, casting a shadow across one cheek. He raised a languid hand and sucked on a cigarette.

Matt felt his blood drain. 'Hi, Dan. What you doin' here? Did you… did you sign up to the dramatic arts course, then?'

'Course not, you stupid bugger.' Smoke wafted from his nose and mouth as he laughed.

'So were it the flyers I left? Is that why you've come?' Matt tried to edge away.

'Listen, Matt. What d'you hear?'

Matt stared at him.

'You can hear a generator, Matt. The sound of a big motor making electricity. I've provided it for this evening. It don't run on air.'

'Red diesel?'

'Yeah, you're fast tonight, Matt. Yeah, I supply the diesel and the generator. Nice little earner.'

Matt didn't know what to say. Something in Dan's manner still threatened so he just waited, his hands tingling and his feet cold.

*First call, first call. We're on in ten*, a PA system announced.

Dan drew hard on his cigarette and then exhaling smoke through his nose, dropped the stub on the ground.

'Better run along then Matt. Sounds like the show's about to start.'

Matt backed away.

'Look where you're going, Chemistry Dude,' a familiar voice screeched. A firm hand grabbed his shoulder and pulled from behind.

Matt twisted backwards to find himself looking into the filthy face of a seventeenth century street woman wearing maroon framed glasses.

'Ginny?' he yelped in surprise. 'I thought you'd be playin' the lead. You know, Guy Fawkes.'

'Oh for God's sake, dude - that's a bloke's part.' She flounced away, hooped skirt swinging fiercely.

'Ginny! I aint meant….' But she'd gone. And then he remembered Chrissie and Nick. Where was everyone?

•••

Nick stared at the open door. Should he go in, he wondered. For a moment he stood mesmerised by the brightness, and like the eyes of a snake, it held him transfixed. The longer he hesitated, the more the light seemed to beckon. In the end he felt powerless to resist.

With his heart pounding, Nick stepped into the hallway as another screamer shrieked into the night. He didn't close the glass panelled door, he felt safer leaving it open behind him. The corridor stretched ahead and as far as he could see it was deserted. Where had Rake gone, he wondered. Was he playing some kind of a sick game? He tried the nearest door, but it was locked. 'Where's my toolbox?' he muttered. 'Mr Rake?'

The cold advanced into the building with him and he shivered. This is weird, he thought. He turned the handle of each door as he passed, but none would open.

'Mr Rake?' He must be in his office, Nick decided, and headed on, rattling handles and calling out as he walked. A door at the end of the corridor stood ajar, light shining through the crack. 'Mr Rake?' Nick pushed and it swung open.

He knew the room; he'd spent enough time working in it. But Nick caught his breath when he saw the chaos. Drawers and filing cabinets hung open and a paper shredder whirred and whined next to Ricky's office chair. Sheets of A4 covered the floor. What the hell is going on, he wondered.

'You took your time, Nick.' Ricky sat facing a computer screen, scrolling through columns of numbers.

'Sorry to disturb you, like this, Mr Rake.' Nick tried to keep his tone even. 'What are you doing?'

'I'm, what they call, tidying up.'

'Is everything all right?'

Ricky swung his chair round. 'No, but you know that, don't you?'

Nick stared at him, shocked by his words. 'What are you talking about, Mr Rake?'

'You came here to gloat, didn't you Nick?'

'What are you talking about? I came to collect my toolbox, Mr Rake.'

'No, you came to gloat. First you informed on Dan and he was arrested. And when they let him go you told them about Rookery farm. But we were warned so they found sod all. And now I've heard they're planning a raid here, but then I expect you know that already, don't you?'

'No, no. You've got it wrong, Mr Rake. I haven't told anybody anything. How could I? I don't know anything to tell. And who am I supposed to have told?'

'Don't play innocent with me, you bastard. They? The police, the fuzz, the pigs – that's who. Why else would you be here?'

'I've already told you. I've come to collect my toolbox, Mr Rake.' Nick stepped back toward the door. Cold air wafted gently from the corridor. Should he just get out, escape while he could and forget the toolbox, he wondered.

'Hah!' Ricky laughed. 'I can move the fuel, the chemicals… all the evidence. But once the pigs are here, if they don't find anything in the storage unit, they'll be disappointed. I know those bastards.' Ricky waved his hand at the computer screen. 'They'll widen the net. They'll start going through all the figures, my accounts – everything.' His eyes darted from screen to monitors and back without blinking. A strand of red hair stuck to his damp forehead and curled like a snake. In the harsh light his skin looked deathly pale.

'I don't understand,' Nick whispered. 'Mr Rake. I haven't done anything.'

'Oh yes you have, Nick. You've been onto me from the beginning!'

Oh my God, Nick thought. The man's crazy. And in that instant an iron knuckle of fear drove into Nick's stomach.

•••

As the crowd waited, shifting and stirring like lapping water, Chrissie looked at her friends. Matt grinned and Sarah smiled. Anticipation and excitement filled the air as paraffin fumes mixed with smoke and brushwood crackled, flames leaping high. The play was over, Guy Fawkes had been carried off to the Tower and the bonfire was in the process of being lit.

'Pity, Nick didn't make it,' Chrissie said.

'Yeah, I just phoned but he aint answerin'. Ginny were great. It were wicked!' The light caught his expression and for a moment Chrissie was reminded of an adoring puppy.

'Come on, it'll take a while before that bonfire really gets going.' She checked the time on her phone. 'We've got five minutes before they start the fireworks. Let's go back to the vans and see if we can catch Ginny. She was good, wasn't she.'

Matt nodded. 'Yeah, come on then.'

Chrissie grabbed Sarah's arm and steered her in the direction of the vans. They dodged between woolly-hatted kids and booted folk in mufflers as Matt trailed behind. It wasn't far before the crowd seemed to thin and then fade away.

'Where d'you think she'll be?' Chrissie yelled back at Matt. She turned to catch his reply, but the throbbing hum of the generator drowned his words and the darkness seemed to swallow him. 'Where's he gone?'

'I think he must've nipped between that off-roader and the blue van.' Sarah pointed to the left.

'Well, if we head alongside this generator we'll be straight into the circle and near the blue van. Come on.'

'Oh God, Chrissie. Are you sure? You know what your map reading's like.'

Chrissie picked her way in the dark, reaching out every few steps to check for the van's side. 'How many blue vans can there be? Of course we'll find it all right.'

‘Do you know Ginny then?’

‘No, but it was an excuse to get Matt to go back to speak to her.’ Chrissie stopped dead. She wasn’t sure if she’d seen what she thought she’d just seen. Ahead, a dark shadow broke into three. ‘Christ! Trouble.’

Behind, Sarah bumped into her. ‘What the–’

‘Shush,’ Chrissie hissed.

The shadows moved, and Chrissie made out the shape of a man, no - two men and something on the ground.

‘Fucking bastard!’ A rough voice cut through the generator noise.

She recognised the voice. Her stomach twisted and her heart thumped. Last time she’d heard it she’d been safe in her car. She tried to step back, but Sarah was behind.

‘You fucking bastard,’ the voice snarled. The man kicked the darkness on the ground. Again and again. It was like a frenzied dance.

‘No!’ Chrissie yelled, but the sound died somewhere in her throat. She tried again. ‘No, no. Stop!’ This time her strangled cry carried through the air. Behind, Sarah screamed.

The figure stilled for a moment and turned to stare in her direction. ‘Did you hear that? Seems we got company.’

*Oh my God*, she thought. *Now they’re going to come for us*.

‘Chrissie? Sarah?’ Matt’s voice cut above the generator. ‘Wait, slow down. Where’ve you gone?’

‘We’re here, Matt. Over here. Now!’ Chrissie shouted as loud as she could.

‘Count yourself lucky, you bastard. But we aint finished yet.’ The second man kicked into the darkness while the first man looked towards Chrissie.

'Yeah, it's your uncle's turn next and we aint goin' to be so polite.'

'Chrissie? Sarah? Where are you? What's going on?' Matt stumbled into Sarah, pushing her into Chrissie's back.

*Bang…. Crack, crack, crack.*

A firework shot into the air and then burst into a fountain of explosions, raining down reds and greens and white. For a moment the night sky lit up and Chrissie saw the heap on the ground more clearly. In a flash she glimpsed knees drawn up towards a stomach and a limp hand covering a face, muddied and pale. 'No,' she shrieked, 'leave him.' Something snapped in her brain. Terror turned to rage. 'No,' she bellowed, 'Leave him!' and this time there was power in her voice.

'Come on,' the man hissed, 'there's three of 'em. Let's get the hell out of here.'

The two figures backed away and in an instant the dank air closed on them as they vanished into the night. Chrissie strained to see but there was nothing, just the darker shadow on the ground and the hum of the generator.

She didn't try to follow. Her breath came in short bursts. She turned to Matt and flung her arms around him, hugging him tight. 'Thank God you found us.'

'I didn't know what to do,' Sarah sobbed, 'I thought I'd be able to run but I just froze.'

*Bang…. Crack, crack, crack.* Another firework shot into the sky.

'Was that a mugging?' Sarah's husky voice was almost lost to the sound of the throbbing engine.

'A beating, more like.' Chrissie broke away and moved towards the body. She crouched down and touched the heap on the ground. 'Hey, are you OK?'

The heap stirred and Chrissie grasped a cold damp hand. She strained to see his face. 'Are you OK?'

He coughed and then groaned.

'I think we ought to call an ambulance,' she said, standing up to face Sarah and Matt.

'No… don't. I'm OK. Just leave me… I'll be all right.' His words came in croaky gulps. He coughed and wiped his mouth with the back of his hand.

Chrissie didn't know what to do. The man looked dreadful, illuminated every few moments as rockets exploded above, shooting bright colours into the night. She'd seen the kicking. It had been vicious. 'You can't be OK. We should call an ambulance, or the police.'

'No! Just mind your own business. Now piss off, will you.' He tried to sit, pushing himself up and wheezing.

'Shit, it's Dan,' Matt muttered.

# CHAPTER 25

Nick backed towards the door. Mr Rake had appeared calm at first, almost rational but the more he'd said, the angrier he'd become. Nick couldn't make sense of it. Danger and madness filled the air. It was palpable.

*Brr*! *Brr*! The ringtones cut into the silence. Nick reached for his mobile.

'Leave it!' Ricky stood up and moved towards him, crossing the office with the speed of a snake about to strike.

'Leave it, I said.'

*Brr*! *Brr*!

Ricky came close, his chest almost touching Nick's and his face only inches away. Nick felt his breath, smelled the alcohol.

'It's o-only my phone, Mr Rake. My friends, they'll be expecting me.' As soon as the words were out of his mouth, Nick knew he'd said the wrong thing.

Ricky flinched. His mouth twisted into a snarl, 'Friends, you bastard? You call them friends? Give me the phone.' He pushed his face closer and now there was something harder in his expression.

*Brr*! *Brr*!

'Give me the phone. Now!'

Nick looked into the cold eyes. His pulse raced as he slipped his hand into his pocket and pulled out his phone. *Brr*! He switched it off. 'There, it's off now, Mr Rake.'

With a sudden lunge, Ricky grabbed at Nick's wrist and snatched the phone. Nick pulled back, trying to resist but Ricky went with him, pushing at his chest. Nick fell backwards. He was on the ground, looking up at Ricky still on his feet. 'Shit, Mr Rake. Why d'you do that?' Nick tried to slow his breathing as shock reverberated through his body. It was obvious. He didn't stand a chance against Ricky.

Ricky didn't answer, just stared before slowly walking back to his deluxe office chair. He seemed calmer, almost relaxed, as if the physical clash had released the tension.

'Now isn't that more comfortable, Nick?'

Nick nodded as he sat on the floor. It seemed best to humour him.

'You seem different to the usual tradesmen, Nick. But I've worked it out. You are different.'

Nick watched as Ricky flicked a strand of hair back from his face. The languid elegance had returned. The old Ricky was back. He seemed in control of himself again.

'You've been planted, Nick. You're a spy. When I visited Jim – don't frown, you know I mean Jim Mann. Well, you weren't there the first time, but you were in the garden with him once the pellets started flying. He must have called you in to protect him.'

Shit, Nick thought. He thinks I'm a bodyguard or MI5 or 6, or something. He's mad.

'But you weren't very good, Nick, because you slipped up. You should've been protecting Jim in the orchard. You underestimated me. You didn't think I'd finish him so fast, did you?'

'You think...?'

'And then I find you at Alderman's Point scrabbling about where you had no business to be. I guessed you'd followed me. You must have known about the bones and you were still protecting Jim. Or rather MI6 was protecting

Jim's past.' Ricky sat back and smiled, a kind of self-satisfied smile as it he'd won Master-Mind.

Something occurred to Nick. 'So Jim was in MI6, was he?'

'He was abroad a lot, that's where he met Minnette. She never said what he did. We were close, Minnette and I. Very close.' His voice trailed away and there was a silence.

'So how do you know he was in MI6?' Nick asked, shifting his legs to tuck them beneath him, ready to spring up.

'I didn't, but when you turned up I knew.'

Nick decided to reason with him. 'Look, Mr Rake. It's post graduate entry for MI6. I'm not a graduate. I was at Exeter Uni for a year but dropped out. For the last year I've been at Utterly Academy training to be a carpenter. I'm hardly MI material.'

'Could just be your cover, Nick.'

'I don't speak any other languages and when you took my phone just now, well if I was MI trained–'

'You'd 've side-stepped me and smashed my jaw?'

'Something like that, yeah.'

'Hmm, so why d'you come sniffing round my gun cabinet?'

'I didn't. I'm just an apprentice carpenter on a job.'

'And Jim Mann's garden. What were you doing there then?'

'He wanted me to build a prototype beehive for him, that's all, Mr Rake. Honestly. You've got it all wrong.' Nick was about to say he thought Ricky'd been watching too much TV, but decided better of it as a far darker thought struck him. Ricky must have been the gunman at

Alderman's Point. 'You tried to kill me up at the Point, didn't you? You tried to kill me.'

Ricky threw back his head and laughed. 'That was a warning to stay away, a message I thought you'd understand if you were with MI6. If I'd wanted to kill you, I assure you, I wouldn't have missed. You surprised me, though. I wasn't expecting you to turn up at Alderman's Point that day.' Something caught Ricky's attention on the monitor and his body seemed to tense.

Now's my moment, Nick thought as he steeled himself to leap up. He glanced to check what Ricky had seen on the bank of screens, but the images made his blood run cold. Two men were caught on camera. The security lights cast long shadows as the figures moved in front of the hangar doors. Balaclavas covered their faces, exuding menace. They swung petrol cans, flinging liquid at the painted metal. One of them lit a rag and dropped it onto the ground close by. 'Shit! They're trying to torch the place.'

'Bastards!' Ricky yelled. 'I'll bloody show them.' In one bound he hurled himself towards the gun safe. Its cupboard door stood ajar, still waiting for Dave to fix on the coming Monday.

'No, not the guns,' Nick yelled as he pushed his heels into the carpet and propelled himself backwards. He caught his shoulder against the wooden cupboard door behind. With a sickening thud, he drove it shut as he landed sprawling on the floor.

'You bloody fool. You've jammed it.' Ricky scrabbled and clawed at the door. 'I need to get at my gun safe. Now!'

Nick struggled to his feet, his stomach churning and his shoulder throbbing. He ignored Ricky and stared up at the monitors. Flames licked at the hangar doors. 'It'll never catch will it? I mean, they've got to get inside the warehouse to get it to burn properly. It's metal.'

Ricky glanced back at the screen. 'Yeah, looks like those bastards haven't managed to get into it yet.'

Something crashed and thudded onto the carpet outside the office door. 'Oh God,' Nick hissed, 'I left the front door open. I thought I'd be safer.'

For a moment there was silence as petrol fumes and a wisp of smoke crept into the office. Then a bell rang – strident, urgent, demanding.

Ricky opened the office door wider to look into the corridor. Thick brown smoke billowed into his face. He stepped back, coughing and choking.

'For God's sake, Mr Rake, the smoke'll kill us. Shut the bloody door.' The fumes caught in his throat and his eyes smarted as he pulled Ricky sideways. He heard the roar as the petrol started to burn with a fury. He slammed the door and cast around the room for a fire extinguisher. There wasn't one. 'What the hell are we going to do?'

'The bastards! They've torched this building as well,' Ricky spluttered.

'Who are they? What the hell's going on, Mr Rake?'

'It's the Rivetts! It's retaliation. Revenge for Jonas.'

'Jonas?'

'Jonas Rivett.' Ricky rubbed his forearm.

Images flashed into Nick's mind: the red shiny skin; a crepe bandage on Ricky's arm; and before that, Dan in the hospital car park on the night of the Blackthorpe fire. Of course!

'My God! Do you think they're still out there?'

‘No, they’re snivelling cowards. They’ll have scarpered by now. If I’d had my gun….’ Ricky bent double in a paroxysm of coughing.

‘How much time d’you think we’ve got? This is a fire door, but how long will it hold?’ He looked up at the ventilation shaft connecting with a window in the roof. It obviously hadn’t been designed with escape in mind. ‘We’ll never get out through that.’

‘Yeah well, this room was created to be secure,’ Ricky wheezed, ‘and then you bloody leave the front door open so those Rivetts can torch us.’

‘For God’s sake, we need to call the fire brigade. You’ve got my mobile.’

‘Should’ve had sprinklers fitted,’ Ricky muttered as he got his own mobile out and tapped at the keys.

Nick tried to calm himself. His pulse raced so fast he thought his head would explode. In the background Ricky spoke in short bursts between rasping coughs but Nick didn’t listen. He needed to think, needed to work out a plan. How long have we got? Twenty… thirty minutes, he wondered. And then he had an idea.

# CHAPTER 26

Matt looked more closely at Dan. How the hell had he got beaten up like this, he wondered. A firework lit up the sky for a few seconds and there'd been no mistaking the trickle of blood on his lips and the mud smearing his cheek. It seemed unreal; shocking. He'd always thought of Dan as a predator, not prey. 'Shoot, you're bleedin'. Are you OK?'

'I told you to piss off.'

Matt felt Chrissie tap his shoulder. 'Is this the Dan everyone's been talking about?' she whispered in his ear, 'Careful, Matt. He seems to have plenty of fight left in him.'

'Who's Dan?' Sarah asked.

Sarah's voice seemed to stir Dan into action and with a feral groan he struggled to his feet. A rocket shot into the air, whizzing above them before shattering into hundreds of lights. The sudden flash disorientated Matt and for a moment he imagined himself in the trenches with a volley of gunfire spattering shells overhead. He was a World War I comic-book hero. He ducked as Dan lurched forwards.

'Shoot!' He caught Dan on his shoulder.

'Wooah! Careful,' Chrissie shouted.

For a few seconds Matt was rescuing a comrade-in-arms. An act of bravery in the face of enemy fire. He tried to take Dan's full weight on his shoulder and then buckled beneath.

'What the hell are you doing, you wanker?' Dan's breath felt warm on Matt's ear.

'Argh.' His face hit the muddy grass as Dan crumpled on top of him. A salvo of fireworks shot into the air, crackling and banging as they burst into flower heads of light. He was a fallen hero.

'For God's sake, you need an ambulance,' Chrissie's voice cut through.

Matt felt the weight being lifted away and then Sarah's firm hand under his arm. He staggered to his feet, catching his breath. 'Thanks, Sarah. Shoot, what you playin' at Dan?'

'Just bugger off an' watch the fireworks, will you.'

They stood in an uneasy group. Dan swayed as Chrissie kept a hand on his forearm and Sarah gazed into the night sky.

Matt pulled his sweatshirt down as icy air struck his midriff. If Dan wanted to be alone, then he wasn't going to argue with him. He may have been beaten up, but Dan was still a force to be reckoned with. 'Come on,' Matt muttered, 'let's go.'

No one made a move.

'Who were those thugs? Do you know who attacked you?' Chrissie asked.

'I said mind your own bloody business.'

'I recognised one of their voices. I've heard it before.'

'Come on,' Matt muttered again. 'Leave 'im, Chrissie. Let's be goin'.' He'd remembered Ginny and he didn't want to miss her.

'Who are they? Do you know them, Dan?' Chrissie's voice sounded calm, persistent. She stood her ground as she held onto Dan.

'Come on Chrissie. We were goin' to see Ginny, remember?' Matt was about to say more but stopped as a firework exploded above their heads. He watched as Dan shook Chrissie's hand off his arm and rummaged in his pocket. He pulled out a mobile and tapped at the keys.

'Shit,' Dan hissed and then shook the phone. He stared into his hand. 'Christ, no! The bastards have smashed it!'

'It probably saved your life. They looked like they were kicking the hell out of you, Dan.' Chrissie paused before adding, 'Better your phone than a ruptured spleen.'

Chrissie's words conjured a sudden image in Matt's mind. For a moment he was back in World War I again as he pictured a silver cigarette case with a dent from a bullet. The life-saver in a uniform breast pocket. It was the stuff of movies. Above him, the sky lit up with another barrage of fireworks. Yeah, he thought, a mobile phone was the modern equivalent.

'How am I going to warn my uncle?' Dan's voice sounded harsh against the generator. 'My mobile's bloody dead.'

'If you give me the number, I'll phone on mine,' Sarah said. She groped in her handbag and then nearly dropped it as her hands shook.

'I-I can't remember the number. It's on my contacts list.' He slapped his phone again and glared at its face. 'It's dead, the bloody Rivetts!'

Somewhere in the recesses of Matt's mind he saw a carrier pigeon. Yeah, he thought, that's what they'd have used in World War I. 'Carrier pigeon,' he blurted.

'What are you on about, Matt?'

'Wanker!'

Matt felt stupid. The darkness hid the sudden rush of blood to his cheeks.

'Did you come on your scooter, Matt?'

He stared at Dan. 'Yeah, what if I did?'

‘I’ll take that.’

‘Take what?’

‘Your scooter, you arse-hole. If I can’t phone I’ll ride over and warn him instead.’

‘Why can’t you use whatever you drove here in?’ Chrissie chipped in.

‘Yeah, why can’t you use that?’ Matt echoed.

‘Because it’s the pick-up with the generator. If I take it, I take all the power supply for this lot. They need electricity till about ten o’clock. I can’t wait till then. It’ll be too late. I’ve got to warn him now.’

Matt began to feel anxious. His throat tightened. ‘You aint havin’ me Piaggio, Dan. No way.’

‘An’ I aint plunging this lot into darkness. I’m warning you, Matt. I take the scooter or ride pillion. Either way, let’s get bloody going.’

Matt’s stomach churned. The Piaggio was his most prized possession, as faithful as a hound and pretty much the same colour. No one was going to take it, not even Dan. He had to make a stand. His breath came in short gasps.

‘No, you aint havin’ me Piaggio. If anyone’s ridin’ pillion, it’s you.’

A sharp pain seared through his shoulder as Dan grabbed him ‘You bucket of bolts. You’re wasting time. Take me to it now, or Tom’ll….’

‘Ouch, let go.’

‘Hey, leave Matt alone.’ Chrissie’s strident voice wobbled a little as she snatched at Dan’s arm. ‘Leave him, I said. We’ve just saved your life, and now you’re–’

‘I aint goin’ to hurt him. He’ll get his scooter back. Now out of the way.’ He shook her hand off his arm. ‘Come on, Matt. Move!’

Matt looked from Dan's muddied face to Chrissie and made a decision. 'It's OK, Chrissie, I'll take him. I reckon it's what Tom'd want. Ouch! Let go me shoulder.'

•••

Chrissie couldn't believe it. Had Matt lost his mind, she wondered. What was he doing taking Dan? And where was he taking Dan? 'Hey, Matt,' she yelled, 'where are you going?' Matt didn't seem to hear. He'd already started walking. She watched as he disappeared into the shadows, hurrying close to Dan.

'I don't understand what's going on,' Sarah muttered, 'Who's Dan, Chrissie?'

'It's complicated. Dan's some guy who just happens to be mixed up with Matt's brother, Tom. He's from a family of hoods, as far as I can make out. Fingers in lots of pies, according to Clive.'

'So what's this all about? Why's he rushing off?'

Chrissie didn't answer for a moment. She knew something was wrong, badly wrong, but she couldn't say what exactly. The smell of sulphur in the air, the droning generator engine, the flashes and crackles of exploding fireworks in the sky above; they were portents of doom with a sound track from a horror movie. She thought back to the vicious kicking. 'God, what thugs….'

'They're all thugs. Not Matt of course, but Dan and those other ones, they're all as bad as each other.'

Chrissie shuddered as she remembered the harsh voices, coarse words and the brutality. 'The two who ran away; I think I might have met one before.'

'You know them? Bloody hell, Chrissie, who are you mixing with these days?'

'No, of course I don't know them.' She felt impatient. 'Look, something clicked in my mind when I heard one of them speak. I recognised his voice. The raw anger. It was the same when he almost hit my car with his pick-up a few weeks ago. He yelled at me. It was horrible. God knows what he's capable of.' She shivered as the cold struck through her coat. 'And Dan seemed really frightened by what they might do to his uncle.'

'His uncle? Do you know him as well, Chrissie?'

'No, I do not.'

'Look, I'm sure Matt can take care of himself. Stop worrying, Chrissie.' Sarah rummaged in her handbag. 'I nearly didn't bring it, but now I'm glad I did.'

Chrissie caught the glint of a metal hip flask in Sarah's hand.

'I think a swig of brandy is in order, and then we can catch the end of the firework display. That's what we came for, right?'

'Yes, sure.' It tasted fiery as Chrissie swallowed, nearly taking off her head. She let Sarah guide her away from the circle of vehicles and back into the crowd. They edged their way to the front of the cordoned-off area. 'Wow, look at those colours,' Chrissie said as giant Catherine wheels spun on a frame. She tried to concentrate on the luminescent greens and blues as the display whirled and spiralled, but her mind was in turmoil. If only Clive was here this evening, she thought. He'd have known what to do when they'd stumbled on those thugs.

She checked the time on her mobile. Only a few minutes before it'll all be over, she thought. So, what's happened to Nick and Kat? He's missed the whole thing and it's not like him. She pressed the automatic dial for

Nick's number but his phone was switched off. It seemed odd. Was he with Kat? She presumed he was OK.

Then she remembered Dan's uncle was Ricky Rake. Of course: the fuel gangs, the Rivetts, Ricky Rake's storage facility, the fuel bust. It all started to drop into place. Realisation exploded in Chrissie's mind as a firework burst into glittering light. In that instant she knew. 'He's a Rivett!' she blurted.

'Is that the firework's name? It's spectacular!'

'No, Sarah. It's the name of the thug. I've just worked it out. They'll be after Dan's uncle as payback for something.'

'What did you say? I couldn't quite catch....'

'I've worked out where they've gone. Dan's uncle has a storage facility in Hadleigh. It's only a mile or so along the bypass from here. It's the obvious place. It has to be. Come on.'

'Can't we just see the last of those, what did you call them, rivets first?'

•••

Matt stumbled. Pain fired through his arm as Dan tightened the grip on his shoulder. His breath came in short gasps.

'Come on. Keep up; you're walking like a crab. Now, where's the scooter?'

'I-I,' the words almost died in his mouth, 'Where we goin'?'

'Where d'you think, pea-brain? To warn my uncle. Now where's the scooter?'

Matt didn't know what to do. Dan hadn't seemed so frightening when Chrissie and Sarah were there. Now he appeared to have recovered his strength and menace. Matt didn't want to lead him to his Piaggio but he reckoned Dan would find it soon enough, even without his help. He'd parked hoping to show it off to Ginny, and like a fool he'd left it in full view between a van and 4x4 at the edge of the vehicle circle. Between shuffling steps he tried to make a plan, but there wasn't a choice; Dan still held him by the shoulder. 'OK, OK. It's over here.'

'Keys?'

'Yeah, yeah. In me pocket. Just let go of me, will you?' He rummaged in his jeans but before he'd had time to separate the entry ticket from the keys, Dan grasped him by the wrist.

'Thanks, Matt.' In a flash, he'd snatched them.

For a moment, Matt was back in the school playground facing off the class bully and losing. Then it had been sweets but now the stakes were higher. 'No, not me Piaggio!' With a rush of emotion he ran forwards as Dan rocked the scooter off its parking stand.

In an instant Dan had the engine firing, the headlights on full beam and was mounted, ready to go.

It was now or never. With a Herculean effort and pounding heart, Matt hurled himself at Dan's back as the scooter started to move away. He flung out his arms, bear-hugging Dan as the back wheel spat mud. He ran, trying to keep up. But he couldn't. He slipped and then his feet were dragging. The scooter slewed to one side as Matt's weight pulled on Dan.

'Let go, you arse-hole!'

Matt held on, as if his life depended on it. The 49 cc engine whined and the wheels lost grip on the muddy grass. The scooter skidded. Dan braked.

'You aint goin' to take me Piaggio, Dan.'

'Let go, or I'll hurt you.' Dan jabbed his elbow backwards catching Matt in the ribs.

'Shit!' he squealed, winded. But the bear-hug held.

'You've got one second to let go. I'm warning you, Matt.'

'You aint takin' me scooter, not without me.' Desperation hardened Matt's voice.

'Then stop bloody messing about and get on the back.'

Without really thinking, Matt stepped onto the foot rest and tried to swing his leg. The scooter wobbled. He didn't expect to make it but Dan accelerated abruptly. The jolt did the rest. Matt landed, squeezed astride the saddle and hugging Dan close. 'Holy crow!' he wheezed.

Matt felt the speed riding pillion in the dark and without a helmet. Above, the sky flashed with light as fireworks exploded; cold air tore at his hair and pulled at his scalp. The 49 cc engine droned, complaining at the load. Dan wove a path over the grass and towards the gate onto Wolves Farm Lane.

'How far we goin'?' Matt shouted in Dan's ear. But the wind took his voice as they sped down the slope from Aldham Common. He gripped Dan tight and closed his eyes against the turbulence. He'd never been so close to a bloke before and he didn't like it. They slowed to turn off the bypass and onto Gallows Hill. That's when he realised where they were heading. 'Je-e-e-z, not the Fens storage unit,' he groaned, but before he could say more, the smell of smoke and burning hit his nose.

'We're too late!' Dan screamed.

# CHAPTER 27

Nick watched as Ricky ended his phone call. His shoulders sagged and his movements slowed. He looked defeated.

'Are they coming? You did get through to the fire service, didn't you, Mr Rake?'

'Yeah, yeah. I got through. Seems bonfire night's pretty busy. They thought I was a hoaxer but I think I convinced 'em in the end. Those bloody Rivetts. They knew they'd picked a good night. They've stitched me up. Bastards!'

'How long before they get here, d'you reckon?' Nick's heart pounded as his stomach plunged. He didn't want to die and not like this, trapped in a room and fighting for breath as flames licked his face.

Ricky stared at him for a moment. 'If you think I'm bloody sitting here and waiting to get roasted alive like some piss artist, you can think again.'

'Stop!' Nick yelled as Ricky headed for the office door. 'Don't! The smoke'll kill us.'

Ricky stopped dead in his tracks and spun around.

'Have you got a better plan?'

'Well d'you think you can make it to the outside door on one breath? I mean, would you find your way through the smoke?'

'Yeah. It's worth a try. Are you coming?'

'Look, I've an idea. We need something to protect us from the flames and something like a wet rag to breathe through. At least let's give ourselves a chance.' Nick knew if Ricky opened the door they'd only have a few moments before they were choking. He needed to convince him. 'If you give me my toolbox I can take some of these unit doors off.'

'What the hell for?'

'So we can hold them like shields in front and over our heads. They're good solid wood. It'll give us a chance against the flames when we go down the corridor.'

'I don't know. You with a chisel. It'd be like a weapon. If you're taking any doors off it's got to be the gun cupboard first.' Ricky faced Nick, challenging him to disagree.

Nick knew they were wasting time. He needed his toolbox and he had to persuade Ricky fast. The memory of Kat's voice rang in his ears. He could almost hear her saying, *live ammunition and flames. It's a lethal combination* and the thought of Kat fleetingly transported him to somewhere beyond those four walls.

Ricky watched as Nick's face softened for a moment.

'Hah, got you! You'll do it, I can tell.' Ricky spat out the words. 'Gun cupboard first.'

'I want my toolbox, Mr Rake.' Nick tried to keep his tone even, tried to hide his nerves. He sensed the bully in Ricky. 'How long is it since the fire started?' He didn't want an answer; he just needed to distract Ricky. Drive home the urgency.

Ricky glanced at the monitors. 'The wiring runs through the roof space. The pictures are holding so the roof space–'

'Will be filled with smoke. Toolbox, Mr Rake. Now!'

Nick's words finally seemed to jolt Ricky into action. He leant behind his desk and pulled out the toolbox.

'Thanks. Now try and find some water to soak whatever we can use to breathe through.' Nick flung back the lid and rummaged for the cross-cut screw driver. He opened one of the base unit doors and quickly released the hinges from their fittings on the cabinet's side wall. Ignoring Ricky, he worked efficiently, the activity calming his nerves. How many doors do we need, he wondered as he released a second door. He glanced up at Ricky – no he wouldn't manage to carry more than one. He was already slumped in his deluxe office chair with a bottle in his hand.

'What the hell are you doing?' Nick shouted.

'I could only find whisky. I thought it'd be more use if I drank it. No point in pouring it over ourselves.'

'What? Getting rat arsed isn't going to get us out of here. Now come on. If we're going, let's go before the fire really gets a hold.'

Ricky held his ground. 'No, now you've got those base unit doors, it's the gun cupboard next.' The tone was silky, menacing again.

Was it the whisky speaking? 'No! No guns, Mr Rake. Come on, You're wasting time we haven't got. You go in front. Hold one of these doors and I'll bring up the rear holding one over both our heads. OK?'

'Gun cupboard, first.'

'What's so bloody important about the gun cupboard? You know live ammo will be lethal in a fire.'

'It's not about the guns. It's the locket. It's all I've got left of Minnette. It was hers and I want to take it with me.'

Something snapped in Nick's head. The terror, the smell of burning, the thought of death and finally the frustration all fused together and burst into anger. 'Tough! We're going now.'

Two strides and Nick was across the office. He bent over Ricky and grabbed him by the front of his sweatshirt. Yanking upwards, he had him on his feet. He shoved him towards the office door. 'Pull that up a bit. Try to cover your mouth if you can,' he hissed, releasing his grip on the sweatshirt. Ricky coughed and whisky fumes filled the air. Nick was surprised how light Ricky seemed. 'Here, hold this door in front of you. Take it by the handle and then your hand is protected as well.' He gave him one of the base unit doors.

Ricky responded like an automaton. 'It's a shield,' he murmured. 'You're a clever boy, Nick. Sure you're not MI6?'

'Just piss off, Ricky. We've been through that. Now, you lead the way. I'll be right behind, so no tricks.'

Ricky looked across at the gun cupboard.

'No,' Nick said calmly. 'It's too late for that. We're going now. On the count of three, you open the office door. Hold your breath, put up your shield and keep moving forwards. OK?'

'Yeah, dog leg to the right. *One*!'

Nick pulled up the neck of his own shirt, held the second unit door above his head and crouched a little. His pulse thumped in his ears. '*Two*!'

Ricky reached for the office door handle. He glanced over his shoulder and looked at Nick. There was something in his expression Nick couldn't read.

'Remember to take a breath and then hold it,' Nick hissed.

'*Three*!'

•••

Dan accelerated into the Fens Removals & Storage Unit driveway, braked hard and tried to leap off the scooter. Above them, security lights shone down, harsh and bright from the hangar-like warehouse.

'Let go of me,' he yelled.

Matt hadn't realised how tightly he was holding on. 'Shoot!' but the word barely left his mouth. He'd never seen a building on fire before. He'd watched news footage and movies when things went up in flames, but the reality in front of him was shocking. 'There's so much smoke.'

It billowed out of a door; clouds of dirty brown, tumbling and cavorting as it escaped from the brick office building. It looked to Matt as if it was pausing to think while it gathered strength, and then rising upwards it became a dark swirling monster reaching for the night sky.

'Uncle Ricky! Where are you?' Dan jumped off the scooter as his voice ripped into the air, the primeval sound twisting into Matt's soul.

'What about the warehouse? Maybe he's in there,' Matt shouted, and then noticed burnt charred paint on the metal frontage. Piles of ash and smouldering rags lay on the ground at the base of the closed sliding doors. He sniffed the air. Smelled petrol fumes. 'They've torched the place.'

'Where's my uncle? What've they done to him? Uncle Ricky, where are you?'

Matt didn't know what to do. His first instinct was to turn the scooter around and escape from Dan while he could. He shifted his position on the saddle. That's when he saw flames for the first time. They flickered yellow through the smoke in the office building doorway. What would Nick do? Phone for help? He rummaged with stiff cold fingers for his mobile.

'Look, they're still here; they've left their car. They must be close by. Bastards!' Dan yelled. 'Where are you, you bastards?'

Matt glanced up from his phone. Terror froze his fingers, constricted his throat and took his breath. Were thugs hiding in the shadows with petrol cans, waiting to pounce on him? And then he saw what Dan was pointing at. A blue Ford Fiesta.

'That's Nick's car. He must be here somewhere.'

'You mean he's the bastard who did this? I'll kill him.'

•••

Nick took a deep breath and held it as Ricky pulled the office door open. Thick smoke flowed in, high on the air. He grabbed Ricky's belt and pushed forwards. He heard the spluttering as the skirting boards and door surrounds burned. He felt the heat. He held his door shield above their heads and pushed again. Ricky started to move, then broke into a springing run as the carpet beyond the door smouldered and flamed.

Nick held on and ran with him, eyes smarting. Dense smoke filled the corridor. He couldn't make anything out. Ricky led, changing direction to the right – one step, two – and then a sudden twist to the left. Nick followed, clutching Ricky's trousers and belt. Shit, Nick thought, it's the dog's leg. He's trying to shake me off.

He tightened his grip and accelerated fast. He shoved Ricky in front, almost holding him up by his belt. He couldn't see. His lungs were bursting. Christ, would he make it?

•••

'Look,' Matt shrieked, 'there's somethin' in the doorway. Look, Dan.'

Out of the smoke the "something" took shape. It was low, angular, not human form. It paused and appeared to turn into a ball as a taller thing appeared behind it. Matt rubbed his eyes. It was changing shape again and this time the "something" clattered onto the concrete. Was he really seeing this?

Dan ran towards the office door but stopped as he coughed and choked. 'Come on, Matt. Help me.' The ball had disintegrated into several parts.

Matt was afraid to go into the smoke. It billowed outside the office door. It was a monster. He wanted to zip away on his scooter, but then he heard more coughing and remembered Nick. His stomach flipped. It was as if 240 volts had discharged through the Piaggio. He leapt from it, stumbling as the force carried him forwards. Right foot caught on left and he was nearly over, but the momentum carried him onwards. He tried to dodge but there wasn't time. He collided with Dan.

'Shit!' Dan, already bent and coughing, fell to the ground.

It didn't stop Matt, he blundered on. Catching his breath, he tasted smoke. He smelled the fumes and his eyes streamed. He just about recognised the shape of the bodies. They were sprawled on the concrete; one wheezed while the other retched outside the office door where the smoke was thickest. He couldn't speak. He thought his lungs would burst. Dropping to the ground he grabbed at an arm and just pulled. He was desperate to get away from the smoke.

He tugged and yanked but nothing happened. When the body retched again and tried to roll over, he put his arms around its chest and heaved. This time they both shifted a little, and once they'd started to move, the impetus kept them going. Matt hauled fiercely and the body struggled to its feet. Together they covered some ground, at last out of the worst of the filthy air.

Matt gasped as they collapsed in a heap. Somewhere close by he heard Dan pulling at the wheezer.

The security lights shone down, and Matt caught his breath as he studied the grimy face looking up at him. No amount of smudgy soot could disguise the mucous trailing from the nose, or the saliva and bile covering chin and chest. 'Nick? Are you OK, mate?' and then overwhelmed, Matt hugged him.

Behind, he heard Dan's rasping breath as he half carried, half dragged the second body, the wheezer, out of the smoke. 'Come on, Uncle. What the hell happened here? Are you OK?'

The wheezer burst into a paroxysm of coughs as Dan laid him on the ground close by. 'Easy now. Just breathe easy, Uncle.'

Oh God, Matt thought. What do I do now? Then he had an idea. He held his position and leaned across Nick, shielding him from Dan's view.

# CHAPTER 28

'Come on, Sarah. Let's go. The fireworks have almost finished. If we leave now we can get away before the main rush and we need to get to Dan's Uncle's place ASAP.'

'What did you say, Chrissie?'

'Come on, we're leaving now.' Chrissie grabbed the woolly plait dangling from Sarah's Icelandic style hat. The ear flap dragged sideways as she pulled at it. 'Now, Sarah! We're leaving.'

They trudged through the crowd, dodging kids and pushing past adults. The ground had been worked into a muddy quagmire near the cordoned off area, but as they headed for the gate in the far hedge, they made better speed.

Sarah banged her hands together as Chrissie fumbled for her car keys. 'Well, we're out OK. I assume this car of yours will start.'

'Cheeky sod, of course it'll start. It's got an automatic ignition.' She unlocked the car, slipped the key in the ignition, turned it and prayed the modern addition to the TR7's original features would start it first time. 'See? It recognises its master's touch. Why are you laughing?'

'Its *master's* touch? Just like you, Chrissie. So what's the hurry and where are we going?'

Chrissie caught the flash of red nail varnish as Sarah took off her mitts. It was a colour reminiscent of blood. The sight struck urgency into her voice as she manoeuvred the car off the muddy verge. 'Gallows Hill. It's about a mile along the A1071.'

'What are we going to do when we get there? Have you considered that?'

Chrissie didn't answer. She couldn't think that far ahead. She just knew she had to get there fast. The empty feeling in her stomach told her. 'I think Matt's there. He won't be safe.'

'Chrissie, this could be a big mistake.'

Chrissie accelerated hard out of Wolves Farm Lane. Her pop-up headlights beamed down the hill as the speedometer read: 30… 40… 50 mph.

'Steady, Chrissie.'

She swung onto Gallows Hill. 'It's somewhere just off… here!' She took the entrance at speed, then jammed on the brakes.

'Watch out, Chrissie!'

She smelled the smoke as soon as it entered the air intake. It was obvious when her headlights caught the side wall and then front of the storage hangar. She swept around the driveway, but she knew she was too late. 'Oh no,' she moaned as she came to a halt. Matt was slumped over a body on the concrete. Behind him, Dan stooped over something else. Her headlights picked them out as harshly as a searchlight.

'Call the emergency services, Sarah. Phone now, for God's sake.'

Her heart beat so fast she thought it would explode. Her hands shook; her breath came in shallow gasps. She left the engine running and the headlights on. She got out of the car. Black smoke billowed from a low brick building next to the warehouse. It caught in her nose and her throat and made her cough. Security lights shone down from above the huge warehouse doors. They cast an eerie reality. She walked slowly, lit from behind by her car's full beams and taking in every detail.

‘It’s the nosey bitch!’ Dan shouted, his voice hoarse. ‘What the hell are you here for?’ The effort made him cough and then he spat onto the concrete.

Chrissie stiffened as the body on the ground stirred, turning its head sideways.

‘It’s the Yellow Wedge,’ a voice croaked.

‘Nick? Is that you, Nick?’ Chrissie quickened her pace. ‘You sound… are you OK? What’s happened to you, Nick? And Matt? What’s he done to you?’ She crouched to see them better. Matt mouthed something to her and she leaned closer. Out of the corner of her eye she noticed Dan move.

‘Did you just call him Nick?’ Dan took a lurching step. ‘He’s the bloody bastard who’s done this.’

Chrissie stared him down. She’d had the measure of Dan earlier at the firework display. She’d saved his life once already. How dare he threaten her? How dare he threaten her friends? Fear changed to anger. It fired through her, cold and white.

‘Don’t be stupid, Dan. This isn’t Nick’s work. It’ll be the Rivetts. Use your head. Think about it.’

Dan moved towards her.

Time seemed to slow for her as she stood up, stepping over the tangled mass of Matt and Nick on the ground. She saw Matt curl closer, like a protective doughnut. She waited, blocking Dan’s path, guarding the mound behind, daring him to make one more move.

‘For God’s sa….’ Harsh wheezy coughs blended with the crackles of fire spitting from the office building.

Dan whisked round, so fast he nearly overbalanced.

‘Uncle? Hey let me help.’ He dropped to his knees and supported the bundle on the ground as it struggled to sit up.

‘Is that Ricky Rake?’ Chrissie had imagined a very different man to the one Dan held. Smudges of soot blackened his face. Lank hair swung as he coughed, falling forwards so that only his sharp nose protruded.

‘Dan,’ he wheezed. ‘We’re wasting time.’ He paused to draw a rattling breath. ‘They’ll be here soon…. We’ve got to get rid of the evidence.’ The last word turned from a moan into a hacking cough. He hugged his sides as if to help expel the smoke from his lungs.

‘I know, I know. Just save your breath. No more bloody talking, just concentrate on breathing. OK Uncle?’

Chrissie heard her car door slam. Automatically she twisted round, turning her back on Dan.

‘The fire engines will be here in a couple of minutes.’ Sarah walked towards them, Michelin Man in Icelandic hat. ‘They’d thought it might be a hoax, so we weren’t a priority. But we’re top of their list now. Most of the emergency services will be here shortly.’

‘Thank God. I better move my car out of the way.’ Chrissie broke into a run. ‘Watch Dan!’ she yelled as she flung open the TR7’s door. She dived into the driving seat, threw the gears into reverse and accelerated backwards. She felt a slight clunk as she swung the car around and then parked it out of the way on the edge of the driveway. This time Chrissie made sure she locked it before slipping the keys in her pocket.

She was thankful Dan hadn’t moved very far by the time she re-joined the group. Sarah stood in a kind of fencing En Garde position and Dan just stared at her. Good old Sarah, Chrissie thought, but something far more worrying had struck her. ‘I caught the smell of fuel as I walked along here. Is there a tank or something close by?’

'Yeah.' Nick spoke for the first time. 'They sank a fuel tank for the removal lorries when they built the place. We're probably lying right on top of it!'

'What? But we'll go up in flames.'

'Diesel aint as flammable as petrol. We should be OK.' Matt looked up at her, grinning. 'Dye or no dye.'

A kind of wail started softly, then gaining momentum, morphed into Dan's voice. 'There's no bleedin' time left. Those bloody Rivetts. We can't drain the tanks now. The lorries….'

'Leave it Dan,' Ricky wheezed. 'No need for both of us to get mixed up in this. Go! Go while you can. I'll clear up here.'

Chrissie watched Dan cast around, his movements jerky, his look, wild. 'Where's the scooter?'

Sirens screamed in the distance.

'No time, Dan. Go! Just disappear into the night.' Ricky shifted, trying to get up. 'Get back to Aldham Common. Remember you've been there all along.'

The sirens grew louder, more urgent, more demanding.

As Ricky coughed, Dan helped him to his feet.

'You're a good boy, Dan. Now go.'

Chrissie felt as if a windstorm had torn into the driveway as the first fire engine arrived, its siren so loud it would burst her eardrums. She watched as firemen in yellow suits jumped from the cabin. A second fire engine screeched to a halt. It was bedlam. She glanced at Ricky. He stood alone, hunched shoulders, knees slightly bent. He appeared fragile as he swayed gently from foot to foot under the security lights. Instinctively she reached out to steady him. She felt his arm muscles tense under her hand. 'Shouldn't you sit down? You don't look well, Mr Rake.' That's when she noticed Dan had disappeared.

'It's too late. Everything… everything I've worked for, created… it's destroyed. I'm ruined.' He gazed at her for a moment. She smelled the whisky on his breath as he rasped, 'I must stay on my feet.' He lurched away from her, staggering forwards towards the office building.

'No!' she screamed. 'No, Mr Rake! Where are you going?'

He didn't seem to hear. It was as if he was in his own world, oblivious to her shriek. He walked on.

'No, Mr Rake. Stop!'

He paused for a moment and then straightened his back. It was as if he was summoning some kind of strength. Then, with a lolloping stride, he disappeared into the palls of black smoke, still billowing out of the doorway.

'No! Come back,' she yelled, hardly believing her eyes. Ricky appeared to have walked into an inferno. Chrissie was paralysed with horror.

A fireman shouted a warning. Fire hoses, jets of water, and men in breathing apparatus swarmed around her. She turned to Nick and Matt. They still sat on the ground. 'Did you see that?'

Nick looked up at her and nodded, his face expressionless.

'Why?' she moaned, 'Why'd he do that?' and then tears filled her eyes, filming across and blocking her view. She blinked and they fell, spilling down her cheeks. She brushed them away roughly and sniffed. 'Thank God you're….' She knelt down and gave them both a hug.

'Were it a disappearin' trick? Or did 'e really go back in?'

‘What could be so important you’d go back into that?’ Chrissie asked as she stifled a sob.

‘Here they are.’ Sarah’s voice rang out loud and clear as she led an ambulance crew to Nick and Matt.

‘I don’t need nothin’,’ Matt grunted. ‘It’s Nick here what breathed in all that filthy smoke.’ He stood up as if to demonstrate his fitness.

A paramedic crouched down beside Nick while Chrissie spoke to a fireman. She tried to explain what she’d seen. A police officer took their names and addresses and they were told they were all free to leave, except Nick.

‘Where are you taking him?’ Chrissie asked.

‘It’s OK, miss, it’ll be Ipswich Hospital. Best be on the safe side. He says he ran through smoke and out of that building. Look at the state of him. Stands to reason he’s breathed it in. He’s bound to have suffered some smoke inhalation. We’ll get him checked over.’

They’d put him on a gurney and Chrissie watched as they prepared to load him into the ambulance.

‘You’ll be OK, Nick.’ Chrissie tried to read his face. He seemed completely out of it. ‘Look, switch your phone on, for God’s sake and then we can ring you.’

‘It’s…. Ricky took my phone.’

Chrissie leaned in closer to catch the words. His oxygen mask seemed like a barrier, swallowing his voice.

‘Look, take mine. Yes, I know the directory won’t have the numbers you need but at least we’ll be able to get hold of you.’ She dug into her handbag. ‘Here, take it.’ She thrust it into his hand.

‘Thanks.’

'Don't lose it!' She stood, watching as the paramedic slammed the ambulance door. 'Poor Nick,' she whispered to the night and anyone who'd listen.

'It's been a hell of a fire.' Sarah touched her arm. 'Come on, Chrissie; there's nothing more for us here. Let's go.'

'Yeah, but where's me Piaggio?'

Chrissie frowned. What was Matt on about, she wondered. 'It'll be where you parked it, of course.'

'Well it aint.'

'D'you think Dan took it?' Sarah chipped in.

'Would've heard the motor. Nah, it's gotta be here somewhere.' Matt swung his arms and then hugged his denim jacket close as he wandered into the shadows and away from the security lights. Chrissie and Sarah followed.

'Oh no! Bleedin' hell!'

'What, Matt? What've you–'

'Me Piaggio. Some joker's knocked it over.' Matt squatted to look. 'Hey help me, will you?' His voice rose to a whine as he jumped and heaved and tried to rock something.

Chrissie broke into a run, Sarah a stride behind. The scooter lay on its side, its brown bodywork camouflaged by the darkness. Its wheels and under carriage exposed, as blatant as a dog lying on his back, displaying his most private parts. 'Is it damaged?' she asked.

They all set to, but it was only when the Piaggio stood upright again and in the security lights that Chrissie spotted the smudge from a black rubber bumper on its rear wheel guard. Matt seemed too busy checking there weren't any dents to notice the tell-tale mark.

'Seems OK,' Matt mumbled and started the engine.

'I need a drink,' Sarah announced. 'In fact I think we could all do with a drink. What d'you say?'

'Yeah, first sensible thin' anyone's said all evenin'.' Matt grinned as he revved the engine, demonstrating the sound of all 49 cc of its power.

'We could all come back to my place. I've a bottle of wine in the fridge. Good idea?'

'Yeah, Chrissie!'

Chrissie hoped she looked casual as she brushed her leg against the TR7's rear rubber bumper. The flecks of brown paintwork were barely noticeable.

•••

Chrissie sipped her second glass of wine. She suspected Matt would have preferred lager, but he seemed happy enough to make do with the wine, judging by his empty glass.

'This room's cosy,' Sarah murmured. 'You've got a nice home here, Chrissie.'

Chrissie nodded. She felt mellow. It had been two years since so many people had sat in her living room. Last time it'd been after Bill's funeral.

'What are thinking, Chrissie?' Sarah asked.

'That it's funny how it takes a death to bring us all together and to make this room come alive.'

'Hmm, we don't know for sure if Ricky Rake died in the fire and… it's not death that brings a room alive, Chrissie. It's people.'

Matt shifted his position in the armchair. 'How come Nick were there in the first place? I don't get it.'

Chrissie shook her head. She felt drained. All the evening's emotion and fear, along with the cold had taken their toll and she no longer had the energy to try and understand. 'I don't know, Matt.' She shook her head again. 'I hope he's all right. If he phones anyone it'll probably be you. Your number is in my contacts.'

'I could ring you an' ask 'im how 'e is.'

'Ring me?' Chrissie frowned and then got it. Her brain must be seizing up. But before she could get hung up about it another thought muscled in. 'What about Kat? Wasn't Kat supposed to be coming to the fireworks tonight with Nick?'

'Maybe they had a bust up?' Sarah suggested.

Matt shrugged. 'Don't suppose you've got somethin' to eat?'

'There's pizza in the freezer. It'll take twelve minutes in the oven. Is that OK?'

'Yeah, great.'

Chrissie padded out to the kitchen. She'd kept her thick socks on after kicking off her walking boots. If only she could feel as cheerful as the reds and orange colours of her woolly feet. She switched on the oven and before she knew what she was doing, her finger was between her lips and the plum varnished nail between her teeth. She was about to nibble and gnaw, to chew it back to the finger pulp. But the unfamiliar feel of the plum nail varnish stopped her in her tracks. It had been an expensive manicure. Slowly a deeper, more complex part of her brain recognised the nervous compulsion for what it was. No, I'm OK, she told herself but she knew the anxiety and the memories underlying it couldn't be so easily suppressed.

She rummaged in a kitchen cupboard for more drinks. All she found to offer them was the cooking sherry or a bottle of Limoncello, Italian liqueur still unopened after a holiday in Italy with Bill.

‘Do you want the good news or the bad news first?’ she called out.

‘Good,’ Matt replied.

‘The pizza’s on track.’

‘And the bad?’

‘We’re not so flush on the alcohol front. It’s either lemon liqueur or cooking sherry.’

‘Wicked!’

# CHAPTER 29

Nick sat in his hospital bed, an oxygen mask on his face, a cannula in one wrist and a bag of clear liquid dripping into a vein. Something was strapped to his finger and a monitor flashed and beeped on his bedside locker. He felt dreadful. He thought back to the chest X-ray. That had been easy, but the blood tests were a different story. The arterial sample had been agony.

'What are all the tests for? What's happening to me?' he'd asked a pretty nurse.

'You breathed in smoke and it can damage your lungs. So we're keeping an eye on you and checking how much oxygen is getting through your lungs and into your blood. The other tests are for things like carbon monoxide poisoning and making sure your liver and kidneys are working OK. Does that answer your questions?'

Nick wasn't sure it did. He wanted to know if he been affected, damaged by the smoke but she'd looked so pretty and her voice was kind, so he'd nodded anyway.

'Tell us if you get a headache.' She studied a chart. 'There's another litre of this to run through when that bag's finished. I'll be back to check on you soon,' and with a smile she'd gone.

Nick closed his eyes and rested his head back on the pillows. The air in his mask felt dry and cold in his nose. What had she said? Oh yes, it was oxygen.

All this fuss, he thought. At least he'd managed to hold his breath all the way along that corridor. But he'd taken a lungful when he gulped and gasped for air as he fell on the concrete outside the entrance. That's when the smoke got him.

His mind went back to Ricky. Had he really tried to shake Nick off as they ran together? Had he really wanted to leave him to die, overcome by heat and fumes in that inferno? The man was unhinged. Clearly he'd been drinking, but was he a killer? Nick didn't know. 'Why did I go back for my toolbox?' he groaned. Would Chrissie say it was irony that in the end he'd had to leave it behind in the inferno? It's going to be *me* being asked the questions next.'

Nick opened his eyes. Beads of sweat broke on his face. He felt his heart pounding, his breathing shallow and fast. The monitor by his bed alarmed. A nurse came running.

'Steady, now. Just breathe slow and easy; nice and slow. Don't panic.' She looked at the monitors as she spoke. 'Steady now. That's better.'

Nick recognised the signs: the sweating, the rapid breathing, a hollow in the pit of his stomach, his pulse drumming in his ears as if his head would explode. The panic attacks were back. Of course the police would want to interview him. They probably thought he'd started the fire. The idea nearly made him retch.

He needed to speak to someone who wouldn't bully or threaten. A policeman he could trust. At least he was safe while he was in hospital, but what about after he was discharged?

Sunday morning dawned in Ipswich Hospital with drug rounds, breakfast rounds and ward rounds. Nick had slept fitfully, disturbed by his monitors, his oxygen mask and his dreams, but the doctors seemed pleased when they examined him. They wanted more blood tests, more checks. He felt as if he was on a merry-go–round but at least an idea had surfaced from his troubled sleep. He had Chrissie's phone and he was pretty sure he'd find Clive's number amongst her contacts.

It only took him a moment to locate a mobile number listed under the letter C. He pressed the automatic dial and waited, pulse racing, hoping the DI would answer.

'Hi, Chrissie.' The voice sounded sleepy.

Nick's throat dried and his words came in a rush, 'Is that Clive Merry? Inspector Merry?'

'Who is this? Who's speaking?'

'It's Nick… Nick Cowley. Chrissie's friend.' He wondered if he'd phoned too early.

'Why are you phoning on her mobile? What's happened to Chrissie?'

'Nothing. Look, I need your help. Something… something terrible's happened. Not to Chrissie, she's OK, It's me. I'm in hospital, Ipswich. She gave me her phone to use. Mine went in the fire.'

'What? What are you talking about?'

Nick gulped. He didn't know where to begin or how to explain and he sensed Clive thought he was either rat-arsed or playing some prank. He started again. 'Did you know there was a fire at Ricky Rake's place in Hadleigh last night?'

'No, how could I? I was at home with my kids and I'm still off duty. It's Sunday morning.' He sounded very much awake.

Nick marshalled his thoughts and tried to keep his voice even. He spoke fast, his anxiety doubling and then tripling as he recounted the evening's events. 'I should've let him take the locket. They'll say I killed him. They'll say it's all my fault.' His breath came in rapid gasps. 'It's like it's all happening again. Like last time when they interrogated me. They'll say I started the fire. Please you've got to believe me.'

'Slow down, slow down, Nick. So what do you want?'

'Just to tell you what happened and what he said. I need to be interviewed by someone who won't try to twist what I say, or shout and threaten me, that's all. I think I can cope if it's you.'

Clive took a moment before replying, 'I've got to drop the kids off with their mum for lunch. I can be with you at about two o'clock. Is that OK? Now just calm down.'

'Thanks, Inspector. And sorry I've troubled you on your day off.'

Nick slipped the phone into his bedside locker. He shook his head. He didn't remember Chrissie mentioning anything about Clive having kids, but then she didn't talk about her personal life much. And that reminded him. 'I never phoned Kat! She'll think I stood her up last night.'

•••

Nick checked the time as he rested against his pillow. 14:20. He felt exhausted. Clive wore jeans and a sweatshirt, and Nick couldn't decide if he'd chosen his clothes with an eye to emphasising he was off-duty or to put Nick at ease. No one could have guessed he was a detective inspector interviewing a suspect, not from his manner or dress. He'd even smiled and made encouraging noises as Nick spent the last twenty minutes faltering through his account.

'So to sum up; he actually told you the locket belonged to Minnette Mann?' When Nick nodded, he continued, 'And he implied they'd been close? Like lovers?'

Nick nodded again.

'And he admitted shooting at you with the air rifle in Jim Mann's garden and then again with a rifle at Alderman's Point?'

'Yes, and he said it was because of me he had to finish Jim off quickly.'

'Well, let's hope the gun cupboard survived the fire. We've got some bullet casings we may be able to match with his rifle.'

'It wasn't a gun cupboard, it's a gun safe. Mr Rake had it installed inside the wooden cupboard, like camouflage. It's a thick metal thing. It might even be fire-proof. Kat, she's my girlfriend, says you can buy fire-proof ones.'

'Hmm, and you watched two men on the CCTV monitors trying to set light to the warehouse?'

'Yes. He said they were Rivetts.'

'And then they set light to the building you two were in? Ricky Rake's office?'

'We assumed it was them. There was a smell of petrol and then the lot went up in flames.'

'And he thought Jim Mann was in MI6?'

'Or MI5. That's what he implied, yes.'

Nick listened to his heartbeat thumping in his ears while Clive wrote in a note book.

'This is really a case of his word against yours unless the guns and locket have survived the fire, you do realise this don't you Nick? The CCTV footage will probably have gone up in smoke.'

His anxiety cranked up a gear. 'That's why I wanted to tell you first, and without any bullying.' Nick thought for a moment. 'It's his word against mine. So are you saying he's alive? Did he survive the fire? I thought he went back in for the locket. Please say he survived.'

Nick watched as Clive shook his head. 'I don't have all the details. After you contacted me I phoned to find out what'd happened. They found a body in the brick building. But remember they'll have to identify it first and after a fire it could take a while to be sure who it was.'

'Oh God,' Nick sighed and turned to look at something - anything to distract from the charred black image threatening to fill his mind. 'It's all crazy.'

'I know and you look pretty tired, Nick, so I guess I'll let you get some rest.' Clive stood up. 'Hey, isn't that Chrissie over there?' Clive smiled and waved.

Of course, visiting time, Nick thought as the blackened image faded and a feeling things might turn out OK permeated his consciousness. He grinned and waved his arm, the one with the drip in. 'And Matt!'

'Hi! Hi, Clive. And Nick, how are you?' Chrissie radiated obvious bonhomie. She turned to Clive. 'We've had one hell of a time finding him: We've checked Accident & Emergency, Acute Admissions and the Assessment Unit. Matt just remembered it began with an A. We've done most of the ground floor already. How did you know Nick was here?'

'How do you think? You gave your phone to him. That's how.' Clive smiled again.

Nick watched Chrissie blush. She assumes Clive tried to phone her and got me instead, he thought. Well, she'd find out the truth of it if she ever bothered to check calls made from her mobile. He grinned as he caught the glance from Clive.

‘So, how are you, Nick?’ she asked as she ignored Clive for a moment. She looked concerned as he told her about testing for carbon monoxide poisoning and checking his lung function. ‘Do you think they’ll let you out soon?’

‘Hope so. You OK Matt? You look kind of uncomfortable.’

‘Yes, Matt. You’ve been like this ever since we arrived. Like you’re out of your tree,’ Chrissie added.

‘Don’t like hospitals an’ the lemon stuff’s done me head in.’

‘Limoncello. The lemon stuff is Limoncello. An Italian liqueur. We all needed a drink after the fire and that’s all there was after we’d finished the wine,’ Chrissie explained.

‘You never said it were Italian, Chrissie. Might’ve tasted better if I’d known.’

Nick laughed and then he remembered. ‘Clive says it’s my word against Ricky Rake’s, you know, about the fire last night, Chrissie.’

‘That’s rubbish. Sorry, Clive but we were there. Matt, Sarah, who’s a friend of mine, and me. We stumbled on two Rivett boys kicking the hell out of Dan, that’s Ricky’s nephew, at the Aldham Common firework display. You know, in Hadleigh.’

‘Nick didn’t tell me about this.’

‘Well he didn’t know, Clive. He never got to the firework display. We definitely heard the Rivetts saying they were going to pay Ricky a visit as some kind of pay-back for Jonas Rivett. And that’s why Dan wanted to go to the storage unit to warn his Uncle. And then Sarah and I followed when we’d worked out where he’d gone.’

'That was bloody dangerous Chrissie. You must have been crazy to follow him.' Clive frowned. Nick thought he looked cross.

'No, he'd taken Matt and the scooter. I was really worried for Matt.' Chrissie paused. She seemed to grow more serious as she gazed at the floor. 'We smelt the petrol as soon as we arrived at Ricky's warehouse. Sarah phoned for the emergency services, which proves she was there and... well if Nick had poured petrol everywhere there'd be some evidence he'd carried cans of the stuff in his car. Why don't you check it? It's still parked somewhere near the warehouse. The ambulance brought him here, so it stands to reason his car's still there.' She glanced up at Clive. Nick recognised the defiance in her look.

Nick thought she'd finished, but Chrissie had something else to say. 'I think you should check if Dan or Ricky attended the A&E department in Bury St Edmunds on the night Jonas Rivett was burnt in that fire. I think you'll find that–'

'Ricky Rake got a burn on his arm,' Nick finished for her. 'He probably received treatment for it there.'

When Clive frowned again, Nick explained, 'I was just leaving A&E at the time. A hornet's sting on the ear! It'll be in their records.'

Nick watched as Clive ran a hand back from his forehead and through his short hair, as if it might clear his mind. Nick knew he'd been right to think Chrissie would have some answers. But there was something else still troubling him.

'I haven't been able to phone Kat yet. The number was on my mobile and she'll think I stood her up.'

'That's OK, Nick. We'll get a message to her through the gun shop, if nothing else. Don't worry.' Chrissie smiled and then turned to Clive. 'I'm so glad you're here. Thank you, Clive.'

Nick noticed a slight flush spread across Clive's face. His expression definitely softened as he looked at Chrissie.

'If you could make up your minds which of you is going to hold onto Chrissie's phone, it would be a help.'

'Here, Chrissie you take it,' Nick said as he reached for his bedside locker.

•••

Matt followed Chrissie out of the ward. He felt uncomfortable. It reminded him of when he'd broken his wrist. Hospitals were places to avoid. As far as he was concerned only pain and misery lurked here.

'Come on, Matt.' Chrissie strode ahead, Clive at her side.

Matt thought back to the evening before as he tried to keep up. He remembered giving Nick a hug and dragging him out of the smoke. He'd thought for one dreadful moment his friend was dead. The pain had been overwhelming, his sobs and tears flowing uncontrollably. 'Shoot,' Matt groaned, 'I hope Nick don't remember.'

*Beep-itty-beep*! *Beep-itty-beep beep*! His mobile burst into life. Now what could Tom want, he wondered as he read the caller ID.

'Hi,' Matt muttered, keeping his voice low.

'Hi, it's Tom. You aint called me for weeks. Heard you got mixed up in some trouble. You OK, kid?'

'Yeah, Tom. I'm OK.' Matt kept his answer short. It was usually safer that way with Tom and anyway, he didn't want Clive or Chrissie to know who he was speaking to.

‘Oh yeah, you sure? Heard there was a fire. Ricky Rake’s place. A little bird told me you was there.’

‘Yeah, I gave that bloke a lift. The one who came to the Academy. Remember?’

‘Course I remember, Matt. What I want to know is… what happened to Ricky Rake?’

‘Walked back into the flames. The firemen couldn’t stop ’im. It were horrible, Tom. Horrible.’ Matt’s voice cracked as he spoke. He didn’t want to be reminded. He wanted to forget. ‘Look Tom, I aint speakin’ now. Got to go. Call me. OK?’

‘One last thing, Matt. You’re sure about that? He walked back in? Kind of… topped himself?’

‘Yeah, Tom. Everyone saw.’ Matt ended the call. He felt sick. Limoncello and Tom; it was a bad combination.

# CHAPTER 30

Chrissie looked up at the cold November sky. There was no sun, just a complete canvas of pale grey. Snow could fall out of that, she thought and shivered. It had been two weeks since the fateful Saturday night in Hadleigh. At first she hadn't been able to banish the picture of the fire and the spectre of Ricky Rake as he disappeared into the smoke. But day by day the images had appeared less often, slowly fading so that now she could only summon them if she really tried, and for the moment her mind was on other things. The sky and Clive.

She made a decision. She'd phone Clive.

'Hi,' she said a few moments later as he answered her call. 'Look, they're forecasting snow. Do you think it might be more sensible if this evening we just stayed in Woolpit? We could eat at the White Hart. It would save on the driving and, well their food's OK. What d'you think?'

'I'd wondered about booking a table at the Italian restaurant, you know, near the Theatre Royal? But if there's snow forecast, well maybe it would be more sensible if…. Are you sure you don't want to go to Bury?'

'Well it would be nice, but not if it means shovelling snow in a high-vis jacket.'

She smiled as she listened to him laugh and then rang off after he'd confirmed he'd see her at eight o'clock and they'd eat at the White Hart.

No one could accuse her of being high maintenance, she thought as she slipped her mobile back in her handbag: a coffee in Costa, a curry in Bury and this evening the

White Hart in Woolpit. She supposed this counted as their third date and the thought made her feel a little edgy.

Several hours later she still felt nervous, although now her nervousness was tinged with excitement. Her front doorbell rang, the electric buzzer still sounding like the noise of a dying rattle snake. It always made her jump and her stomach seemed to flutter as she checked the time on her watch. Clive, she thought, he's dead on time. She wrenched the old door open and a gust of cold air swept through her narrow hallway.

'Hi! Come in, come in, Clive.' She smiled, thinking how attractive he looked and then left him to close the door and follow her through to the living room.

'It's bitter out there, probably too cold to snow.' He took off his Jack Wolfskin anorak as he spoke.

'Just chuck it down there if you like. Wine? I've a bottle of Chablis in the fridge.' She glanced around her living room. She was pleased with the effect. An old Gerry Rafferty CD played quietly in the background and the low energy light bulbs gave a soft light. As Sarah had said only a fortnight earlier, it was people who brought her home alive and this evening it felt alive.

'You've got it nice and warm in here. It's homely.'

She couldn't help laughing. 'Thanks, but I think you're mistaking small for homely, Clive.'

'Well, in estate agent speak, let's say bijou, and it's nice.'

She smiled and turned away to hide the flush threatening to spread across her face. 'The table's booked for eight-thirty,' she said over her shoulder as she headed for the kitchen. Her hands were shaky and she fumbled as she tried to open the bottle.

'Oh no!' she yelped as the cork broke off short. Should've put the cork-screw in further before pulling at it, she thought.

'What's the matter?'

'Nothing,' she lied as she fished for the cork fragments floating on the wine.

'Thanks,' he said as she handed him a glass. He seemed to hesitate and then sat on the sofa. He looked up at her. 'Are you going to sit down then?' He smiled, obviously amused as she stood, trying to decide where to sit.

He'd taken the initiative and it made her feel slightly silly. Her face felt hot as she sat on the sofa, not exactly next to him but at an angle so that she was almost facing him. 'Cheers!' She sipped her wine.

'Cheers,' he said and smiled again. 'Good choice, this wine. It's nice, Chrissie.'

She watched him for a moment. 'Thanks for being there for Nick. I don't know what you've managed to sort out but the anti-terrorist mob certainly rattled him last time, so thanks.'

'It was easy. The gun safe survived the fire. All the evidence backed up his account. So you see I didn't have to do much. There has been one surprise though.'

'Oh yes?'

'The DNA. We've got the result.'

'And? Come on Clive, tell me.' She started to laugh as he scooped a fragment of cork from his glass. 'Come on, stop messing about and tell me.' She tapped him playfully on the shoulder and with the unthinking contact, her awkwardness evaporated.

'You might have been expecting the answer, Chrissie but I certainly wasn't.'

'Expecting what answer? You still haven't told me who?'

'It's Minnette Mann. The bones and teeth on Alderman's Point. The DNA matches hair from her hair brushes.'

'Good God! Are you sure? Of course you're sure, silly question. So she's been buried up there all these years. I knew it. I've always had a feeling.' The implications of Clive's words slowly sank in.

'Ah, another one of your feelings.'

'Yes, but… so who killed her? Do we know how she died?'

'Not really. No clues on that. She could have been strangled or smothered or even stabbed. That's assuming the blade didn't mark any of her bones. The only murder weapon we have is a gun from Ricky Rake's gun safe. The bullet casing in the orchard where Jim Mann was shot has markings that match a rifle in Ricky Rake's gun safe.'

'So Ricky Rake shot Jim Mann?'

'Unfortunately we'll never be able to ask him. As you know, Ricky didn't survive walking back into the fire. That's official. The body found inside the office building was definitely his. It's been identified.'

'What a way to die. So we'll never know for sure if he pulled the trigger?'

'Precisely, but it's probably a safe bet.'

'And the locket?' Chrissie asked, suddenly remembering.

'It was in the gun safe as well. And it matches the locket Minnette wore in the photos we found amongst her things in the storage unit. I guess it belonged to her. We've shown it to the second Mrs Mann and she recognised it as the locket the unknown visitor wore when he spoke to her husband.'

'Probably Ricky Rake again.'

'He keeps cropping up, doesn't he, Chrissie.'

'So why did he shoot Jim Mann, d'you suppose?'

Chrissie watched Clive frown and shake his head, but when he didn't answer she said, 'Well I've got a theory. I think Minnette and Ricky were lovers. Either Jim found out or caught them on Alderman's Point. I think Jim killed her and then buried her up there. A kind of justice for her betrayal. Then he plays a long game, keeping all her possessions as if she'll come back; the heart broken husband. But of course she doesn't return.'

'That works for me so far,' Clive murmured.

'Then it all goes wrong. He marries wife number two. She gets Minnette's stuff put in storage and guess whose name crops up again?'

'Ricky Rake's. She chooses his storage firm.'

'Exactly! He's Minnette's ex-lover. Of course he finds the locket when he searches through her things. He knew Minnette well enough to guess she'd never have left it behind. He becomes suspicious; maybe he'd always been suspicious.' Chrissie paused to sip her wine and gather her thoughts before continuing, 'Jim had been vocal recently in blocking a phone mast application on Alderman's Point. That could be relevant too.'

'It could just be coincidence?'

'Possibly but I doubt it. If he'd buried her body up there then he certainly wouldn't have wanted any construction up there. Of course that must have made Ricky suspicious. He'll have put two and two together when he discovered the locket. He knew it was a special place for Minnette

- their special place and, more importantly a place Jim didn't want disturbed. So perhaps he went poking around and found bones. Maybe he went up there several times and we just happened to disturb him that last time. He'd have worked out Jim must have killed her: the bones, the location, the locket. The gun casing matches Ricky's gun and… we can guess the rest.'

They sat in silence for a moment. 'It's like a very sad love story, isn't it?' she murmured. 'I know Ricky was a killer, but somehow you feel he had more love in him than Jim.'

'Twisted love, more like. What a mess. Three bodies: Jim, Ricky and Minnette. We can't prosecute dead men, you know, Chrissie.'

'But the bones unlocked the whole thing, didn't they?'

'The last piece in the puzzle. Come on, let's go and eat. All this solving of my cases is making me hungry.' He stood up and smiled; a warm living smile.

Enough of dead bodies, she thought. 'You haven't told me what happened about the red diesel.'

'Oh yes, Operation Nancy. They've done pretty well. They found incriminating evidence in Ricky's storage facility along with an underground tank holding a couple of thousand litres of red diesel. And of course the Fens removal vans had red diesel in their fuel tanks.'

'Ricky would've been, what do they call it, well stitched up? What about the Rivett thugs and Dan?' she asked as she stood up.

'I understand the Operation Nancy boys have rounded them up.'

Chrissie grinned.

‘They’re still in custody. Operation Nancy will also investigate who started the other fire. The one that killed Jonas Nunseon Rivett.’

‘It seems Ricky had a finger in many pies. He must have realised everything was about to fall apart. But to walk back into a fire? It says a lot about the man.’ Chrissie shivered.

Outside the cold November air gusted and swirled. Chrissie drew her thick winter coat closer around her cream cashmere jumper, a figure hugging top she’d chosen more with an eye to warmth than the fine decorative beading along the neckline and one shoulder. ‘Damn, I forgot my gloves,’ she moaned as she pumped her hands together.

‘You’d forget your head if it wasn’t attached at the neck.’ Clive grasped her freezing fingers. ‘Here is that any better?’ he asked as he put his hand, still holding hers, into the warmth of his anorak pocket.

They walked in silence for a moment. ‘That’s nice,’ Chrissie murmured. ‘Thank you for the loan of your pocket.’

‘Well, you could borrow both, but then we’d have difficulty walking to the White Hart.’

Chrissie laughed and looked up at him. Clive bent and kissed her. A soft warmth on willing lips.

*The End.*

Printed in Great Britain
by Amazon